CRYSTAL heart

BOOK THREE OF THE PARADISE SERIES

IVANA L. TRUGLIO

JONQUIL
PRESS

First published in Australia in 2017
by Jonquil Press
ABN: 99871403756

Copyright © Ivana L. Truglio 2017
www.ivanaltruglio.com

The right of Ivana L. Truglio to be identified as
the moral rights author of this work has been
asserted by her in accordance with the
Copyright Amendment (Moral Rights) Act 2000 (Cth).

This book is copyright.
Apart from any fair dealing for the purposes of
private study, research, criticism or review, as
permitted under the Copyright Act, no part
may be reproduced by any process without
written permission.

National Library of Australia Cataloguing-in-Publication data:
Creator: Truglio, Ivana L., author.
Title: Crystal heart / Ivana L. Truglio
ISBN: 9780992565480 (paperback)
Series: Truglio, Ivana L. Paradise series ; book 3
Subjects: Fantasy fiction

Cover illustration by Les Petersen

Typeset in Minion Pro 10pt/12pt

For Pat,
Pér's glory is yours

ABOUT THE AUTHOR

Ivana lives in Sydney, Australia and works for a multinational publishing company. She devotes most, if not all, of her spare time to writing the Paradise Series.

At various times, she has studied aviation, archaeology and ancient history at university. She currently holds a private pilot licence and rides a motorbike.

She has also been known to play the flute, dance ballet and fence (although not all at the same time). During her studies, it was rumoured that she lived in the university library.

Ivana is married and has two young children who reap the benefits of having a mother with a wild imagination. She has been writing since she was a child and the characters in the Paradise Series have been living in her head for around 15 years.

ACKNOWLEDGEMENTS

My first thanks goes to my test reader, Patrick Harper, for always being there to listen to my ideas and help me work through the plot holes. I know *Crystal Heart* wouldn't have been the same book without you.

To my wonderful editor, Lydia Low, thank you for willingly giving up your time to help me perfect this book and make it a more enjoyable read for everyone, even if it drove both of us crazy sometimes!

To Kylie Abbenhues, my friend and biggest fan, thank you for all your help to nudge my books along. I can't tell you how much I appreciate your support in this adventure! It's always a joy to hear how my books are constantly being checked in and out of the library at OLR and passed around amongst friends.

To my husband, thanks for reading my books and having such amazingly good reactions to them. It's an added bonus that you don't look at my browser history and think any the worse of me for the research topics my books lead me to.

Lastly, to everyone who bought a copy of *Rilla* and *Illaria*, particularly those who shared with me certain characters or scenes that you liked, thank you so very much. Without you, I may not have continued writing the series so thank you a thousand times over for your enthusiasm!

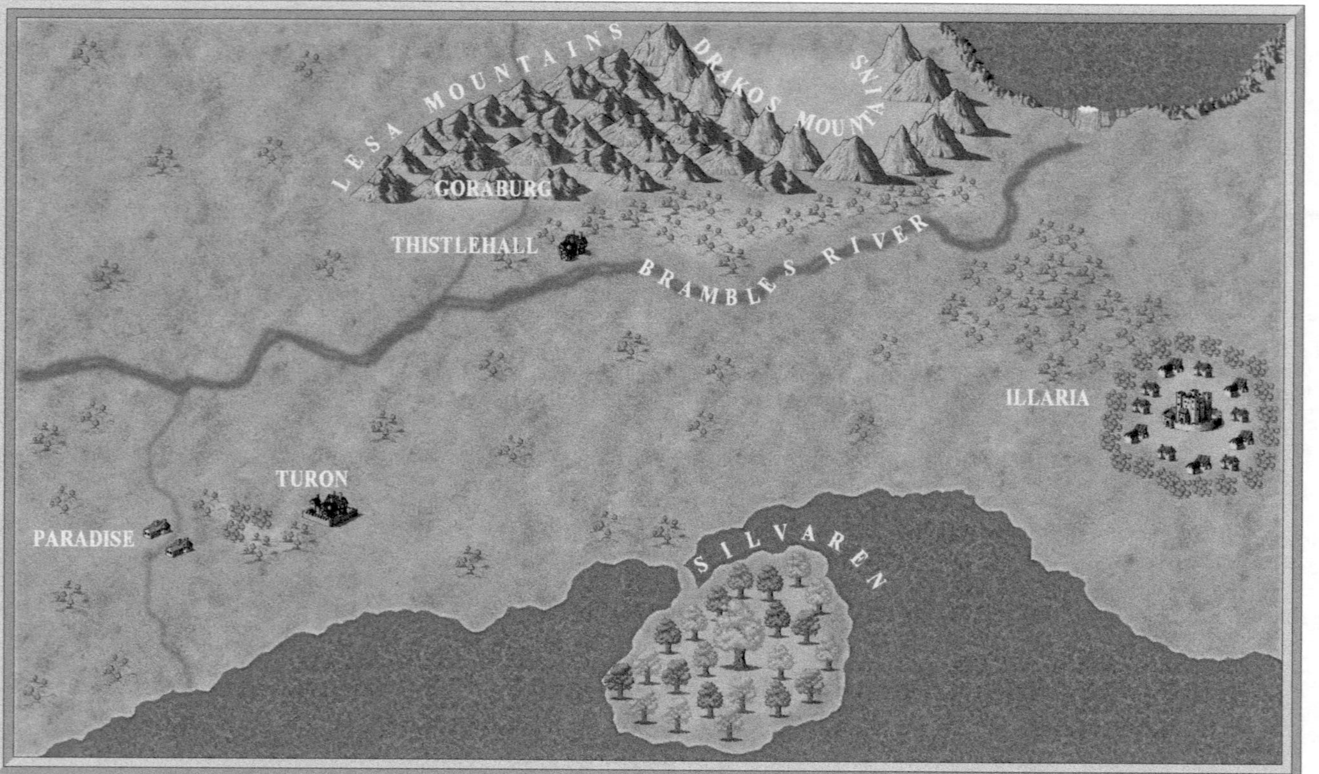

LESA MOUNTAINS
DRAKOS MOUNTAINS
GORABURG
THISTLEHALL
BRAMBLES RIVER
ILLARIA
TURON
PARADISE
SILVAREN

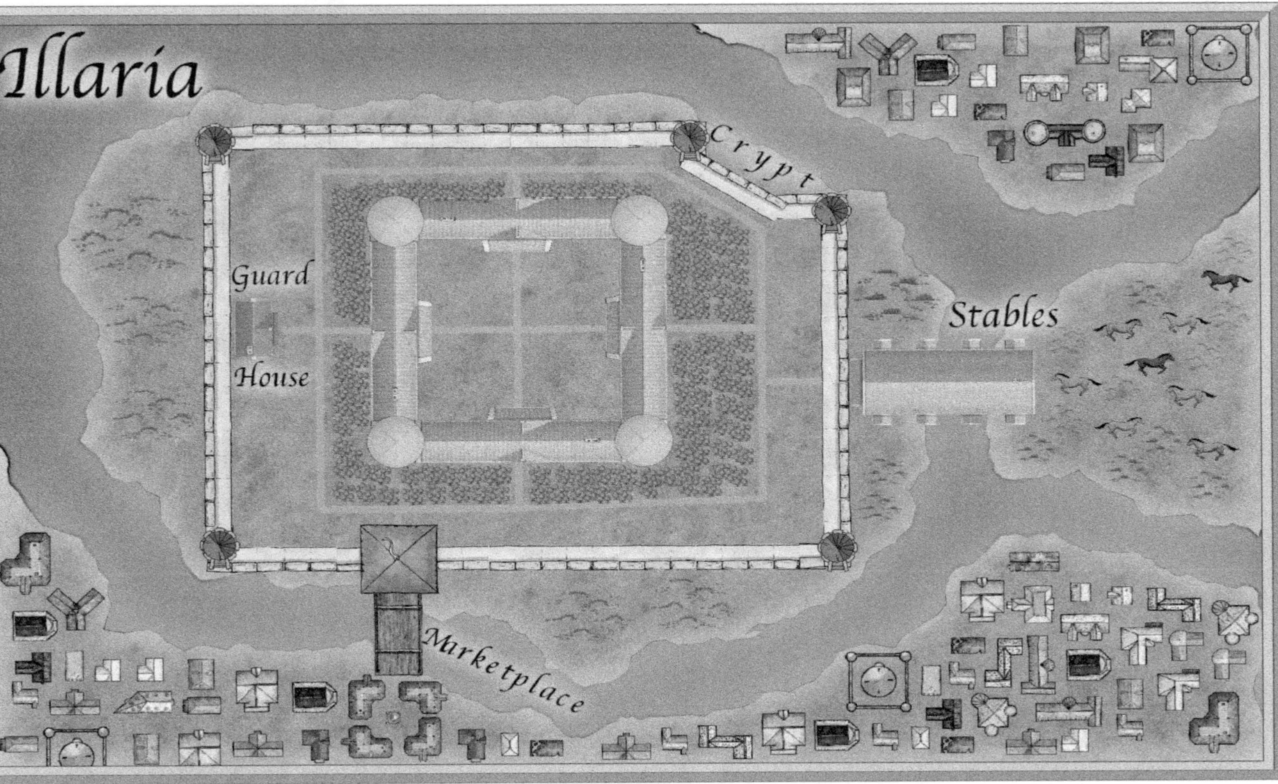

Illaria
Crypt
Guard
House
Stables
Marketplace

Chapter One – Reunion

Kora stopped and marvelled at the bustling marketplace. She closed her eyes and breathed in the crisp autumn air along with familiar scents she'd missed so much in her Paradise.

Cinnamon! She sighed, remembering instances she and Nyssa had pilfered cinnamon scrolls from the kitchens.

Looking around, she noticed merchants in the square already had their wares out, calling to passing lintep, urging them closer to try some delicacies or feel the soft, silky material held out for them. Beyond the square and across the cobbled bridge, stone walls loomed high enough to hide the beautiful sandstone castle which lay behind it. She laughed to herself as she noticed the unpatrolled section she had regularly used to sneak out of the castle and into town.

I'm home. She smiled, briefly, before the worry set in. *Father. Plyke.*

Kora had been lost in thought for so long that she was caught by surprise when Fleuris pulled on her lead at the sudden increase in noise, Kora's arm jerked forward. Kora weaved her way past lintep and stalls, barely noticing whether Eliséo and the karliki were keeping up with her.

Suddenly, a strong lintep caught her arm.

"Lady Kora?" he asked as she turned towards him. He beamed at her with tears in his eyes. "I knew it was you. You've returned. Lady Kora has returned to us at long last!"

Shocked by the skin contact, Kora threw up her mental wards, knowing that none of the merchants would consider hurting her. She looked closely at the man and grinned.

"Pér, I should have known you'd never make it into the castle with your unique songs!" she exclaimed as she drew the burly minstrel in for an embrace. "It's been too long."

"Too long indeed, my love," he whispered softly into her hair before pulling away from her. Other lintep started to gather around them, wondering if it really was Lady Kora returned from the Outworld.

Regretfully, Kora moved away from Pér with an indication in her eyes that she would find him later. With no way to hide her approach now, Kora found her companions in the growing crowd and led her mare to them. Lintep crushed in around them, making it dangerous to walk with the horse and the karliki in the same place. She ushered her companions forward, trying not to harm or lose them.

A path finally opened up between her and the bridge. Kora gazed up and waved to the guards atop the wall. She saw one instantly run to start ringing the bell to alert the castle of her return. Laughing with happiness, Kora wondered if she'd ever engendered so much affection from the people when she was still living here. She doubted it, but smiled nonetheless as townspeople tried to touch her skirts or arms as she passed them.

She hadn't walked half way across the bridge before she saw her father, running through the garden, straight towards the bridge. She doubted he understood why the bell was rung. That was confirmed when, on the bridge, he took in the sight and faltered in his tracks.

More nervous than she expected, Kora quickened her pace to break away from her companions. As she neared her father, he held out his arms to her. She dropped Fleuris' lead and broke into a run, tears streaming down her face. Kora flung herself into her father's outstretched arms, burying her face in his shoulder.

"I'm so sorry I left you," she cried softly. "I'm so sorry. I'm so, so sorry."

"My little girl. My Kora," her father choked out, hugging her so tightly she almost stopped breathing. "You never have to apologise to me. Everything will be fine now that you've come home."

It was as though no time had passed since they had last seen each other. She could only hope things would go as smoothly with Plyke.

Her father disentangled himself before she was ready to let him go. She drew back, knowing there was much to do even though she had just arrived.

"Father, you already know Eliséo," she said as she wiped the tears from her eyes and drew attention to her companions. She smiled gratefully to the elf, who had taken up Fleuris' lead. "This is Ilya Mikhailovich, son of Mikhail Alekseevich, heir to the clan leader. Beside him is Anya Nikolaevna, master stonemason. Behind is Kazimir Sergeyevich, Lord Mikhail's oldest friend and most trusted advisor. My friends, this is my father, Lord Aaron."

Lord Aaron bowed his head to each of the karliki. "We are honoured to have such esteemed karliki favour us with their presence. If there is anything you need during your stay, only ask and it will be provided."

"You are most gracious, Lord Aaron," replied Ilya with a bow. "We are grateful to be visiting magnificent Illaria."

Kora noticed the small smile between Ilya and Eliséo. She couldn't help but wonder how much he had schooled the karlik in diplomacy on their way here. Before she could ponder any longer, King Lukys and a dozen masters and mistresses came hurriedly onto the bridge. It suddenly occurred to Kora, the last time the bell rung had probably been when Lishe attacked Rilla and Shuut. It was no wonder that all the lintep within the castle reacted as though the bell signalled a threat.

"It's alright, Lukys," Aaron called. "Kora has returned. The bells are for my girl."

"Well, I'm glad she brought my horse back," Lukys replied. Kora returned his beaming smile and kissed her uncle on the cheek. "We'll talk soon. First, let's get you and your companions settled."

She nodded gratefully, realising she must smell worse than the stables. It was been days since she had left Silvaren and almost the entire time had been spent astride Fleuris.

"No doubt, Master Edric will be glad to see Fleuris," Kora said.

"Yes, however, he will have to wait until this afternoon," Aaron told her. "He's taken Plyke, Tika and another student out for the day. They probably won't return until late afternoon."

Kora felt butterflies in her stomach. She tried not to think of Plyke.

"I'm certain the stable hands will take care of Fleuris and we have much to discuss, not least of which is what to do with the crystal dragons sitting out amongst your farms. I told them to wait until we sent word for them. Perhaps the pasture attached to the stable can be cleared for them?"

"Indeed, that is a fine idea," Lukys replied. "I shall organise that immediately. Eliséo, your chambers are ready for you, as ever. Aaron, can I leave you to organise our karliki guests while I attend other matters?"

With a nod from his cousin, the king took Fleuris' lead from the elf's outstretched hand and led the gentle mare towards the stables.

Kora linked arms with her father and walked through the small crowd of masters and mistresses still on the bridge. She left Eliséo to escort the karliki behind them. As they walked towards the castle itself, Kora's breath stuck in her throat. She'd forgotten how beautiful it was with the carved figurines, stained glass windows and elaborate designs.

"Kora dear," her father brought her out of her musings, "I gave your room to Plyke when he arrived. I hope you don't mind, but I wasn't expecting you back at the time. Why don't you take Adina's old room? Just until we can rearrange things."

"Of course, father," she managed to reply, her throat constricting. *Poor little Adina!* She could still see her sister's bloody corpse laying motionless on the grass. "We don't need to move Plyke out of my room if he's settled in."

"Nonsense, we shall have you back in your room as soon as possible. I don't have to be patting your hand to know what horrors you're recalling."

Kora fought the urge to remove his hand from hers. It was one of the things she hated most about all lintep – their assumption that it was fine to pry into anyone's thoughts or feelings through skin contact. She had imposed her beliefs on Plyke as he grew up in the Paradise and now wondered whether he had finally understood why she was so firm on that point.

Kora parted ways with her father as he headed off to attend the karliki. He had given her the key to Adina's room. She closed the door. It was like stepping back in time. Nothing had been changed in those chambers. She walked through the common room to the bedchamber beyond and immediately saw the same forest green coverings over Adina's bed that were used when her baby sister was still alive.

Knowing what she would see, she opened the wardrobe to find Adina's little clothes in there. She had yet to commence her schooling before her cruel murdered. Memories of her sister, brothers and mother threatened to overwhelm her. She shut the wardrobe, breathing rapidly, leaning head on hands, fighting back both panic and tears. When she finally steadied, Kora proceeded to the bath chamber.

Less than an hour later, she emerged from Adina's room looking like Lady Kora once more. While she bathed, a maid had left her a new gown and undergarments. She carefully placed a thin book in the folds of her sash belt. It contained a map of the locations for each of the Paradises she'd found. She wasn't certain if she would have a chance to speak to her uncle about it, but the book was the one item she owned and rarely, if ever, let out of her sight.

Kora walked along the carpeted hall to her father's chambers and knocked. There was no reply. She continued to walk around to her uncle's chambers, but likewise, they were empty. Kora doubted everyone would have gathered in Eliséo's room, so she headed towards the Council Chambers, passing by the throne room just in case.

As she reached the Council Chambers, she heard muffled voices from within. She knocked once more and this time was rewarded with an instant reply. The door was opened a crack, until Aislen saw her. Princess Aislen smiled as she pulled Kora through the door and held her in a tight embrace.

"I've missed you," the princess told her quietly. "There aren't many lintep who think like you. Your presence has been sorely missed."

"I've missed you too, Aislen! I've so many things to tell you," Kora replied just as quietly, before pulling away from her cousin.

"Kora, come and join us," Lukys called out from the head of the long table. Already seated at it were the three karliki, Eliséo, her father and Guiscard. Her eyebrows narrowed as she noticed the absence of any masters or mistresses but she refrained from commenting on it. Instead, she took a seat between her father and the librarian. Both patted her on the arm, but she noticed that Guiscard was careful to only touch her sleeve. She gave him a thankful smile, which he immediately returned.

If only she could talk to him in private. He, along with Aislen, Braedan, Luisella and Pér, were the only ones who truly felt the same way she did about their powers and how they should be used. Lukys liked to think that he was the same as the six of them, but there were often times when his opinions didn't match theirs.

However, the one thing they all agreed on was the Paradises should be destroyed, though only Lukys and Guiscard really knew what she had been doing in the Outworld. It was possible Aislen, Braedan and Luisella had guessed, but she had been careful not to tell them anything in case they were blamed for her sudden departure. In fact, she hadn't told the librarian, but knew he had guessed what she was going to do before she did it. Pér would have insisted on following her if he'd but known. Hence she had left Illaria without mentioning anything to the aspiring minstrel. Her heart ached at the years they had spent apart.

"We were discussing the best way to bring in the dragons without wreaking havoc in the city," Lukys informed her. "I think we should send out our best communicators to use the lintep whistle in various parts of the city. It's probably the fastest way to send out word so that they know what to expect.

"If we organise that to happen now, we can bring the dragons in by this evening. That will also give the stablehands plenty of time to secure all the horses in their stalls."

Aislen rose to her feet and pulled the silver handle by the door of the Council Chambers twice before swiftly returning to her seat.

"Now, we can get down to other matters," Lukys continued. "I think everyone in this room is aware of the misadventure with Lishe's mind snares?"

Heads nodded around the table.

"Very well, then let's deal with that first. Eliséo, would you please explain why you brought three karliki, on dragon back, to Illaria?"

Eliséo slightly bowed his head towards the lintep king.

"In truth, King Lukys, I was on my way to Goraburg when I was contacted about the mind snares locked in a chest. Initially, we thought the crystal dragons might be the best hope to release those powers, however, it was pointed out to me that the dragons would not be able to reach the place where they are currently stored.

"I decided it best to ask the karliki for their assistance, as they had already proved capable of helping Shadow with a unique gift bestowed upon them by the crystal dragons. We assumed the same method might work on the other powers. If we are mistaken, perhaps the chest can somehow be brought out to the crystal dragons so they can help us themselves," Eliséo explained.

"What was this unique gift, may I enquire?" Kora asked, eyebrows raised.

She noticed the look that passed between the elf and the oldest karlik, Kazimir Sergeyevich, who nodded ever so slightly.

"How much do you know about the creation of the crystal dragons?" the elf asked.

"As much as most people, I suppose," Kora shrugged. "Two karliki carved them out of crystal and breathed life into them somehow."

At this flippant comment, the blonde karlik huffed and crossed her arms, glaring at a surprised Kora.

Eliséo cleared his throat. "Anya, why don't you explain it to her?"

Kora was taken aback at the gentle way that Eliséo spoke to the karlik. It was enough to soothe Anya. Kora found it difficult not to flinch as the karlik fixed her with a stony stare, her green eyes sparkling dangerously.

"Many years ago, when magic was still a part of every karlik, my ancestors, Sascha Vladimirovich and Nadya Grigorevna, carved the first pair of crystal dragons. Such was their love for their creations that they tried to bring the figures to life.

"They passed all of their magic into the two creatures. It was just enough to give them their own spark of life. Unfortunately, both Sascha and Nadya gave so much of their own life force to the dragons that they themselves did not survive.

"No karlik understands exactly how it happened but, over time, the dragons bred and grew until they became the massive beasts they are today.

"This next part is the most important of my story, so pay attention," Anya warned Kora icily. "By the time the first crystal dragons died, magic had already disappeared from the karliki. The next generation of crystal dragons gave the descendants of their creators the most wonderful gift – the crystal heart of Sascha's dragon.

"This gift held more power than we could hope for. It was the only way for karliki to have any protection against mind magic. Without powers of our own, we were left completely vulnerable to any who wished us harm. The crystal heart had the power to remove any foul magic used against the mind."

Stunned silence greeted Anya's story. None of the lintep had heard the entire story before, though at least some had heard of the crystal heart.

Lukys regained control of the meeting. "Very well, if the three of you agree, we will attempt the release this evening, once the dragons arrive, so they can help us if we need it."

"I agree, it would be best to do this deed under the cover of darkness," Ilya nodded thoughtfully. "The fewer people the better."

Beside her, Kora's father shuffled in his seat. "We'll need at least a few lintep there in case things go wrong. I would trust Master Aurelius in this matter. He and I have already had to deal with this danger."

"And Master Jorg?" Lukys asked.

Kora could have sworn she heard Eliséo bite back a retort at the mention of that particular master.

"Much as I appreciated his help on the day, it was Aurelius who proved to be the most useful in this matter," her father insisted.

Is father twisting the facts? Kora thought to herself.

"It's agreed, then," Ilya announced. "Kazimir, Anya and myself, Lord Aaron, Master Aurelius, Ambassador Eliséo and King Lukys."

"What about me?" Kora asked before she could stop herself.

Ilya gave her a curious look. "Forgive me, Lady Kora, but I meant what I said about the minimum amount of people," he insisted gently. "We three karliki need to be present for our task to be accomplished. Ambassador Eliséo has seen us in that capacity before and he is more familiar with the lintep than we are. Master Aurelius and Lord Aaron must be present in case we don't succeed and presumably King Lukys holds the key to where the chest is kept, not to mention the fact that he was present when the other lintep were involved with the task of removing the mind snares, so may be able to assist us.

"As much as you may want to be involved in this process, I do not believe it would be to our advantage at such a delicate time. I apologise if that seems a harsh decision, but you will note, I have also excluded your princess and librarian."

Before Kora could protest, Guiscard squeezed her arm gently, but firmly. There would be other battles to fight. Best not to start one over this.

A knock at the door interrupted their meeting. Aislen moved to open the door. The messenger she had sent for, arrived. Lukys quickly instructed the boy to summon Masters Graham and Aurelius to him after morning classes. That would include both the messages to be delivered to the inhabitants of Illaria, and of that evening's expedition. Once dispatched, Lukys turned his attention back to them.

"Kora, are you in a position to report on your assignment in the Outworld?"

All eyes turned to her. Kora's heart raced at the attention. She reached down to the sash belt between her corset and skirt and pulled out the thin book concealed there.

"This book contains all of my findings. I used the map Princess Ophélie drew in an attempt to find the Paradises she created," Kora began. She did not know how much information to divulge about Ophélie's creations. It was possible she was not even meant to mention the map. "I found eleven of the Paradises. From the map, it is unclear whether there were more, but I believe it is a possibility. Most of the Paradises are the same as the one Plyke and Rilla came from, a few are worse and fewer still actually resemble the Paradises Ophélie had in mind when she created them."

"How far is the nearest one?" Aislen asked. Kora was not at all surprised that Aislen wanted to move as quickly as possible to destroy the Paradises.

"Actually, not that far." She gave a half smile. "It would take only half a day's horse ride from the boundary, but if we were on the backs of dragons, it would take no more than an hour or two. How many people do you think the dragons can carry?" Kora turned to Eliséo. He considered the question for a few moments.

"Celtan and Pyrid are not the largest crystal dragons, but I believe they could easily carry at least three people each. Whether they would agree to do so is another matter," he warned them. "They are mainly here because Anya Nikolaevna obliged them to help us, however I had to tempt them further with mention of the prophecy. It is possible that they will refuse to help us without meeting Rilla."

"I will not allow those creatures to sink their claws into another member of my family!"

Kora flinched at her father's tone. The air around him became icy, as sparks of fire danced in his eyes.

"Calm yourself." Lukys placed a hand on his arm, forcing Aaron to calm down. "No one is suggesting we offer her up as bait. We will allow them to see her with a capable escort if, and only if, they insist. She will not be taken away from you."

"You may prevent the crystal dragons from taking her from you, however I think you'll have a difficult time convincing Rilla she isn't to come along to the nearest Paradise, if that was indeed your intention," Eliséo pointed out. "For that matter, I doubt any of the children I escorted here would want to miss the destruction of the first Paradise."

"They won't have a say in the matter," Lukys informed him curtly.

"I find it interesting that you think the child of the prophecy, and the other children who lived with her, should not be involved in fulfilling the prophecy," the elf commented. "You must realise that whether Rilla actually destroys any of the Paradises or not, she must somehow be connected to their destruction."

"How dare you presume to put my grandchildren in danger," Aaron spoke in a dangerously low voice. "I will be keeping them as far away from the crystal dragons and the Paradises as possible."

Kora looked at her father in shock. She knew the loss he felt – she felt it too. But this was going too far.

"Father, I know you have their best interests at heart, but I don't believe you will have a choice in this matter," she told him calmly. "These children, all four of them in fact, are quite headstrong. I've known them most of their lives.

"You weren't in our Paradise when they went against all expectations to choose the Outworlder for their mentor. You didn't see the way that Rilla quietly fought against the insane rule of her father. You don't know their determination. If they want to be a part of this endeavour, then nothing you can say or do will stop them."

Her father's injured expression shot arrows through her heart. If anyone was meant to stand by his side and support him, it should have been her. Yet here she was, going against everything he wanted for his family, just as she always seemed to do.

The bell tolled for the end of the morning lessons, dispelling the tension in the air. Lukys stood from his chair.

"Aurelius and Graham will be arriving soon. For those who wish to remain behind to talk with them, you may do so. For everyone else, I urge you to visit the dining hall before the students eat everything in sight."

Chapter Two – Plyke's reward

Plyke woke with a smile. Today was the day of his research reward. Well, it was Dorian's reward too, but he couldn't help think that his new friend would not appreciate their reward as much as he would. It was a day free from studies, to ride horses around the expanse of Illaria with the stablemaster, Edric, and a stablehand. He was hoping they would allow Tika to be the stablehand. They couldn't possibly be so cruel as to send another stablehand along, could they?

Excitement bubbled in his stomach – he refreshed himself and dressed in the travel clothes he had received in Silvaren. With a smile at the thought of freedom for a day, he ran along the carpeted hall and down the spiral stairway leading to the inner courtyard. Barely pausing to wonder if the cooks and scullery maids would be awake so early, he ran straight towards the castle kitchen.

The kitchen was bustling with activity. Scullery maids were peeling potatoes and chopping vegetables while the kitchen maids helped apprentice cooks prepare dishes for the morning meal. Plyke closed his eyes and breathed in the warm smell of freshly baked bread. A moment later, he was jostled aside by a grumpy girl carrying a heavy basket of apples.

"Mind where you're walking," she told him haughtily. "You shouldn't be in the kitchen. Food will be brought into the dining hall as soon as it's ready. You can have your fill then."

"I'm sorry." Plyke attempted to help her with the basket. "I'm going on a day trip and need to organise food for myself and three others. Can you help me?"

"You'll need to talk to Cook Palmyra," the girl told him, holding the basket of fruit even closer to herself, affronted by his offer of help. "And you should have organised that yesterday."

Plyke's good humour deflated. He hadn't realised it would be so difficult to organise the day's food.

"Then, could you point me towards Cook Palmyra?" he asked, releasing his hold on the basket. The feisty girl nodded towards a spindly old lady who was talking sternly to a robust man. Plyke thanked the girl and headed towards the pair. He patiently waited until their conversation ended and the man had moved away.

"Cook Palmyra?" he asked hesitantly. The cook looked him up and down, peering closely at his eyes.

"What can I do for you, mi young lord?" she asked. Plyke stared at her in surprise. She shrugged. "Anyone with your eyes must be related to Lord Aaron, you must be 'is son or 'is grandson. Seeing as 'is boys were killed years ago, that leaves 'is grandson. So, once you've closed your gapin' mouth, you can tell me what you wants, as we're quite busy in this 'ere kitchen afore meal times."

Plyke shut his mouth and gathered his thoughts. "I'm going on a day trip around Illaria with three others. I only realised this morning that we should bring food along."

"So you comes 'ere 'opin' for a packed lunch?" she asked with a laugh. "No wonder Taniya is so put out."

Plyke looked over to the girl with the basket of fruit whom he'd just spoken to. She scowled at him darkly.

"Taniya!" the cook called out to the girl. She barely waited for the young scullery maid to run over before issuing her orders. "I wants you to get this 'ere young man a fresh loaf o' bread, a small wheel o' cheese, 'alf dozen apples and a knife. Wrap 'em up in a cloth for 'im. 'E'll also be needin' four waterskins filled to the brim, but, if you shows 'im where they are, 'e can fill 'em 'imself while you go and gets everythin' else ready."

Plyke cringed as Taniya's scowl darkened. He hastily thanked the head cook and followed the scullery maid. Secretly, he was glad to be filling the waterskins himself, as he didn't quite trust the girl not to spit in them out of spite.

Plyke took the waterskins to the nearest tap. As he filled them, he looked around the kitchen. Back in his Paradise, he had been in the kitchen a few times, but that was tiny in comparison to this. The Paradise cooks had only needed to prepare food for a few score of people, not the hundreds who came to the castle each day. It was no wonder Taniya was angry with him for expecting to be able to take food while they were still preparing for the first meal of the day.

He waited by the sink as the scullery maid huffed and puffed all around the kitchen, gathering the items Cook Palmyra had listed for Plyke. He turned to find himself being watched by a pair of kitchen maids. When they noticed his attention, they blushed, whispered to each other and giggled behind their hands. A sharp reprimand from the robust man he had seen earlier immediately quietened the girls. They glanced his way once more, smiling, and then resumed their work.

"What was that about?" Plyke asked Taniya, as she returned with his wrapped lunch. The scullery maid looked over to the two girls and rolled her eyes.

"Those two go starry-eyed over every boy they see. Don't flatter yourself that they flush bright red only for *you*," she informed haughtily him before returning immediately to her work.

Plyke walked out of the kitchen wondering why any girl would go starry-eyed over him at all, especially without having spoken a single word to him. Perhaps they had heard Palmyra identify him as Lord Aaron's grandson. He shook the thought away. The kitchen was far too noisy for the girls to have overheard that from half way across the room.

Clearing his mind, he walked through the mist-covered gardens towards the stables. He knew Dorian wouldn't be there yet. It was far too early and Dorian lived out in the city, but Plyke didn't mind waiting in the stables. It was Tika he was really hoping to spend the day with. Perhaps if he could talk to Master Edric before plans were made, he could convince the stablemaster to let his Partner come along.

He'd barely set foot inside the stable when Tika ran headlong into him.

"I knew that head of yours would be good for something!" Tika almost shouted at him. "You won the day of horseriding and Master Edric has already agreed to let me be the stablehand for you and Dorian."

Plyke grinned at his Partner. "I was just on my way to ask him that myself. Guess I'm too late for that. Here, you may as well make yourself useful and put our lunch in one of the saddlebags."

He handed Tika the cloth-wrapped food and waterskins, following him further into the stables. Unlike his Partner, he'd never felt any sort of affection for horses but standing there, surrounded by the magnificent creatures King Lukys owned, he couldn't help but marvel at them. They were far superior to any of the horses back in their Paradise.

"They're true beauties, aren't they?" Edric asked him from inside one of the stalls. "Each and every one has a special place here. They are well looked after and want for nothing."

Plyke peered over the gate of the stall, allowing the horse to smell his hand. He was surprised to see the stablemaster sitting on a stool on one side of the stall, near the horse's feed.

"Shouldn't your stablehands be looking after the horses for you?" he asked before he could stop himself. As Tika glared at him, he felt his face burning up. "I simply meant that I thought you wouldn't want to get your hands dirty if you didn't have to."

Just stop talking, before you dig yourself into a deeper hole, he told himself as he saw Edric's surprised expression.

"Being the stablemaster doesn't mean I have any less respect for all the work that needs to be done in the stables," the well-muscled man told him. "I've worked in these stables since I was a boy, younger than Tika. I've done every possible job during that time. Being in charge of these horses doesn't mean that I don't pitch in when work needs to be done, or sit with horses that are ill or close to calving.

"It would make me a very poor stablemaster indeed if I let everyone else do the work for me so that I didn't know about the mood and health of each and every one of the horses in my care."

"I'm sorry," stammered Plyke. "I suppose we didn't have very good examples of master tradesmen of any sort in our Paradise. I mean, we might have, but we were never allowed to really watch any of them until after The Choosing and that's when we left…"

He suddenly fell silent, not knowing why he had offered up that nugget of information. In a panic, he looked at Edric's hands to make sure they weren't touching his skin. To his surprise, the stablemaster's hands were both occupied with the horse, brushing it down. He looked over to Tika for support.

"He has that effect on people." Tika laughed. "He knows we are all in such awe of him that we end up telling him our life story as an excuse for doing our chores out of order or feeding the horses a mere few minutes late."

Edric looked at Plyke with a spark of amusement in his eyes. "No harm done, young Plyke. Now, go along and find Dorian so that we can set out on our trip. No doubt Tika has already informed you that he's coming with us. We'll have the horses ready by the time you return."

Plyke began to walk out of the stables, but stopped and turned suddenly. "I don't know where Dorian lives. How will I find him?"

"Dorian is a city student," Edric replied without looking up. "Wait for him at the bridge and you'll see him soon enough. I doubt he'll have slept in today."

Plyke smiled to himself as he walked away. He'd been too excited to sleep much either. How was it that Edric seemed to know everyone so well, yet no one really knew anything about him?

He walked once more along the perfectly manicured garden paths, passing very few people on his way. The dining hall wouldn't be open yet and lessons wouldn't start for at least another hour. He marvelled at how quickly he'd gotten used to life in the castle. Even being apart from Tika wasn't as arduous as he'd initially anticipated. They still saw each other at least twice, if not more times, a day. Everything would be perfect in his life, if only Kora was with them.

Thinking of his mother always brought Plyke mixed emotions. Of course, he was angry with her for not telling him who he really was or teaching him more than the bare essentials, but most of all, not taking him to Illaria herself. Despite these, there was always the admiration he felt for the woman who had stayed in such an unforgiving Paradise to care for and protect her child from certain death. She had taught him the only skills she could to keep him as safe as possible. Master Aurelius himself had marvelled at the wall he had built at Kora's instruction. If he could wish for anything, it would be to have his mother here, watching him learn new and wonderful skills and helping him find a way to destroy the Paradises.

It was an idle hope, he knew. If Arishen's vision was anything to go by, Kora had fled from their Paradise weeks ago. Had she decided to come to Illaria, she would have been here by now. She knew the way. Plyke's only hope now was that she was at least safe, wherever she was.

He finally reached the bridge and shook all thoughts of his mother from his mind. There was little traffic in and out of the castle grounds at this hour of the morning, so it wasn't difficult to spot Dorian when he walked across with a spring in his step. The younger boy waved happily to Plyke. He returned the wave with a smile. Aside from the twins, who Plyke loved to pieces, Dorian was his favourite class mate.

He knew that Dorian had helped with both his and Rilla's healing tests and hadn't told the other students how Rilla worked with her powers. That alone was enough to ensure Plyke's friendship. However, it was his unabashed happiness to be friends with Lord Aaron's grandson and still treat him as he would anyone else that completely won Plyke over. He'd seen the way that Réne treated Rilla and he was not impressed with it. Dorian was nothing like that.

"Are you ready?" Dorian asked him as soon as they were within hearing distance.

"I've got us some food for the day," Plyke told him as they walked towards the stables together. "You should have seen how angry one of the scullery maids was with me over that."

"I can imagine," Dorian laughed. "My sister works in the castle as a kitchen maid. She used to come home almost every day with a complaint about some lord or master who decided he needed a meal for a party to be prepared within an hour."

Plyke laughed alongside him. "Well, I've learnt my lesson well enough now to never leave it until the last minute."

"Tell me one thing," Dorian said, trying to hide his smile. "Did you fill up our waterskins yourself?"

Plyke laughed and nodded.

By the time they reached the stables, Edric and Tika were waiting for them with four stunning horses, just as the stablemaster had promised. Plyke looked at the tall creatures with a twinge of nervousness. *What if I can't even mount one without falling over?*

"Now, you two city boys won't have ridden before, so we're going to take this day nice and slowly," Edric told them, as though reading Plyke's thoughts. Without realising what he was doing until it was already done, Plyke fortified the walls in his mind, even against the kind and gentle stablemaster. "Tika and I will help you up into your saddles and then your first lesson will begin."

Plyke watched as Edric mounted and dismounted his horse. It looked easy when the stablemaster did it, but Plyke was certain he wouldn't look anywhere near as graceful.

"Tika, you help Dorian. I'll help Plyke," Edric ordered his stablehand. Plyke nervously walked over to the horse Edric pointed out to him. It was a beautiful golden mare with a white mane and tail. His breath caught in his throat her beauty and the thought of being allowed to ride her.

"This lovely palomino is called Goldfire. She's a gentle girl – good for a beginner and very forgiving."

Edric took Plyke's hand and placed it on Goldfire's neck. Before he could protest about their skin contact, Edric removed his hand and Plyke felt his mind brush against Goldfire's. It was tamer than he'd expected, so gentle and full of life. Plyke closed his eyes and stood closer to the horse, leaning his forehead against her golden neck, breathing in her warmth and passion.

"Look at that, Tika, your Partner has just understood what you've known your entire life."

Plyke heard the words whispered behind him. At any other time, that statement might have affronted him, but standing here, so close to Goldfire, he knew Master Edric spoke the truth. Tika had known horses were like this from their youngest days. Plyke didn't know how he could have missed it for so long.

He finally stepped away from the mare, keeping his hand gently on her neck. "I think Goldfire and I will get along just fine."

Master Edric smiled broadly. "Right, now to get you up in that saddle. Hold the pommel with both hands. That's it. Now place your left foot in that stirrup and up we go."

As Plyke hopped, trying to get up into the saddle, Edric deftly took a hold of his right foot and heaved his leg up and over the saddle. Before Plyke knew it, he was sitting up high on Goldfire's back.

It felt amazing to be atop such a magnificent horse. He'd never been this high up before and yet, to his surprise, he found he wasn't at all afraid of falling. He looked over to Dorian and saw his look of amazement mirrored in his friend. They both broke into a grin as Edric and Tika mounted their horses.

"It's early in the morning, so we're going to be respectful to the townsfolk," Edric told them all firmly. "We'll walk through the city and out to the east as quickly and quietly as possible. Once we're out in the open grasslands, we'll see how the two of you go with your riding skills. That will determine how we spend the rest of the day."

Edric placed them in single file, with himself at the front and Tika at the back, to ensure neither Plyke nor Dorian fell too far behind.

The four of them rode slowly past the flower gardens, along the pathway from the stables to the main gate. As they neared the drawbridge, one of the guards looked down at them and waved to Edric. Plyke marvelled at the fact that the stablemaster was probably one of the most well known people in the entire castle, yet he would likely have never known him had it not been for Tika.

As they rode across the bridge, Plyke recalled the last time they were there – Rilla and Shuut being burned by Lishe and the mind snares on them. He closed his eyes against the vision and felt Goldfire start to fret. Tika immediately rode up to his side.

"Calm down, Plyke," he said gently. "Goldfire will pick up on your mood. Try not to think about the past. Just enjoy today, with me, riding horses around Illaria."

Plyke looked over at his Partner and forced a smile. How was it that Tika could understand everything that was going on in his mind without being a mind-reading lintep? Since they'd arrived in Illaria, it felt as though the widening rift between them had finally started to close.

Once Goldfire had settled down, Plyke took Tika's hand to lead him through the magical barrier before his Partner returned to the back of the line. Plyke then let Goldfire follow Dorian's horse as he took in their surroundings. He'd only been through the city the day they'd first arrived in Illaria. Even though he could see a portion of the city and surrounding countryside from his bedchamber, it wasn't in any sort of detail from that distance.

They passed a number of merchant stores and trade workshops along the way. He would have to remember to ask where Master Timothée's workshop and Master Reuben's house were on the way back, so that he and Tika could visit Arishen whenever they were both free.

The mist rose as they rode through the outskirts of town. The sleepy city had only just started to stir as they passed through it. Plyke savoured the earthy scent of grass as their horses trampled over the fine green blades. It had only been a few weeks since he'd travelled over grass every day, but already he'd forgotten how liberating it felt to be out in the open.

Once clear of the city, Edric called a halt. He instructed them on the finer details of how to trot, explaining they would get to the canter and gallop only after they had mastered this first gait. He sent Tika on his way, to demonstrate to them how it was done. Plyke watched his Partner with a glimmer of pride. Tika was already an accomplished rider. Plyke wondered if Edric had been letting him exercise some of the horses in the paddock attached to the stables. How else could he already be so good?

"Your turn, Dorian," Edric urged the younger boy along. "Just stand up and sit down in your stirrups as your horse trots along. You'll soon find your rhythm."

Plyke winced as Dorian bounced uncontrollably in his saddle all the way to Tika. It looked a very painful way to ride. He risked a sidelong look at Edric. The stablemaster cringed and shook his head.

"I'm guessing you weren't expecting us to be quite so bad as that," Plyke ventured. Edric tore his eyes away from Dorian.

"I haven't had to teach city children for quite some time," he admitted, scratching absently behind his ear. "But the principle is the same no matter who you are. I'll trot on over to them so you can watch once more. Then it's your turn."

Before Plyke could protest, Edric had already spurred his stallion ahead. Plyke watched as the toned man expertly rose and fell in time with his horse's movements. Before Plyke was ready, it was his turn. He gently placed a hand on Goldfire's neck and leaned in close to her ears.

"I'm new to this," he whispered to her. "Help me along as much as you can and I'll be sure to give you one of my apples."

A sudden rush of excitement ran through the palomino. Plyke took that as a sign and gently tapped his heels against her sides, urging her into a trot. Just as he'd watched Tika and Edric, Plyke tried his best to rise and fall in time with Goldfire's gait. Initially, he bounced all over the place, just as Dorian had, but by the time he reached the others, he started to find his rhythm.

"You'll be an expert in no time," Edric clapped him on the back as Plyke suppressed a smile. "Now, let's go for a longer trot across this field. If you can manage that, we might even try a canter later in the day."

The sun had moved well above the horizon by the time Plyke's stomach began to rumble. He turned around to see how far they'd come. He could still see the city, but the castle beyond that was a haze of sandstone. His legs and buttocks were already hurting from the morning's exercise.

Edric finally called a halt to their journey. Plyke and Dorian gratefully slid down from their saddles and fell awkwardly to the floor, their legs buckled beneath them. A good-natured laugh roared out from the stablemaster. Plyke bristled as he heard Tika join in.

"We're not so bad as all that," Dorian complained bitterly. The laughter slowly ceased, but the smiles remained.

"I've seen worse, but not in a long while," Edric admitted, trying desperately hard not to laugh. "Now, how about we give the horses a little rest and stretch our legs out?"

The three boys nodded. Plyke went to his saddlebag and pulled out four apples. He handed them to each of his riding companions, then fed one to Goldfire, who nuzzled up against him, before munching on his own one. It was only then that he noticed Edric's questioning look.

"I promised her an apple," Plyke said with a shrug. No need to tell them that it was his bargain with the horse to help him learn how to trot. He didn't even know if Goldfire had understood him, but Plyke could see he was having an easier time of it than Dorian.

They started walking, leading their horses beside them. Edric and Tika were out in front, Plyke and Dorian followed. Plyke could feel Dorian watching him.

"When did you promise her an apple?" he finally asked. "I didn't hear you back at the castle."

"Promise not to laugh?" Plyke replied hesitantly. Dorian nodded earnestly. "I promised her an apple if she helped me learn how to trot after I saw you bouncing all over your saddle."

"But…she's a horse," Dorian retorted. "How could she even understand you?"

"I don't know, but I seemed to have at got the gist of it a bit quicker than you and with no other reason for it. It might be worth a try, you know," Plyke insisted. "Just close your eyes, brush your mind against your horse's and talk to him. It might not do anything, but it can't hurt to try."

"Brush my mind against a *horse's*?" Dorian whispered incredulously. "Are you mad?"

Plyke tried to hide how hurt he was by the comment. He simply shrugged and looked ahead once more. They walked together in silence. Eventually, Dorian spoke to him again, in a calmer voice.

"Have you … have you ever tried that before?" he asked, hesitantly. "I mean, brushing your mind against a horse or another animal?"

Plyke shook his head. "I was taught not to use my power on anyone. It was too dangerous in the Paradise and Kora thinks we especially shouldn't use our powers on humans because they are defenceless against us.

"Since leaving the Paradise, there haven't really been many animals for me to do this with. But … I don't think I would have tried with any other animal. Goldfire, she seems to understand me."

"That's sort of what Rilla does, isn't it?" Dorian looked at him with his large, thoughtful eyes.

"I suppose so," Plyke answered warily. He knew he wasn't meant to talk about Rilla's way of working with her power. What he'd done with Goldfire seemed quite similar, but he didn't want to get either himself or Dorian into trouble. "You don't have to try it, but if you do, please don't tell our teachers or I'll never hear the end of it."

He wasn't sure what he hoped to achieve with that final comment, but when he saw Dorian reach his hand up to stroke his horse's neck, Plyke smiled quietly to himself.

Chapter Three – Crystal dragons in Illaria

In the distance, Tika heard the frenzied ringing of bells. He turned to his Partner, knowing Plyke would panic at the sound. To him, the bells could only signal one thing — Lishe returning to attack his cousins and this time he wasn't there to help them. Goldfire stepped backwards in agitation, almost right into Master Edric's horse.

Within a second, the stablemaster moved his hands so that one was on Goldfire, the other on Plyke's arm, trying to calm them both at the same time. Tika knew the skin contact would make Plyke completely lose control. Both he and Rilla had expressly forbidden their teachers, and their grandfather, from using touch to control their feelings.

"Don't touch me!" Plyke shouted at the stablemaster. "I have to get back to the castle."

Without a second thought, Tika turned his own horse around and trotted over to them. He deftly removed Master Edric's hand from Plyke's arm, and turned to his Partner and spoke as gently as possible.

"Plyke, calm down. The bells could mean anything. It's not necessarily Lishe," he tried to soothe his Partner as best he could. "And listen...they've stopped ringing so quickly. The day Lishe came, they rang until after the masters and mistresses chased her into the city. If they've already stopped now, it won't be for her."

Tika was so focused on Plyke that he didn't see the expression change on Master Edric's face until the older lintep burst into laughter.

"Is *that* what this is about?" Edric asked. "Plyke, the bells aren't just to signal danger. Most of the time, they're rung to signify the return of some important lord or mistress."

Dorian had finally managed to bring his horse around to the rest of them. "Yes, in my entire life, it's only ever been rung for celebrations. The only time it was ever rung for danger was that day with Lishe."

Tika smiled his thanks to Dorian. He could already see Plyke begin to calm down with their reassurance – without touch. All he had to do now was make sure Master Edric and Dorian didn't try to touch him again, without alerting them as to why. Rilla and Plyke had made it quite clear that they would be in trouble if word spread amongst the students.

"Well, I guess we should keep going then," Plyke forced a smile. Tika knew he was trying his best not to be overwhelmed by the situation. He found it difficult not to be overwhelmed himself. He tried to keep Plyke as calm as possible. Tika knew Plyke wouldn't admit it to anyone, but he had been so troubled since Lishe's attack. They'd heard snatches of whispers that Kora was quite powerful, possibly just as powerful as Nyssa, and Lishe would take her power as soon as look at her. Since Arishen's dream of Kora fleeing the Paradise, they'd had no indication of where she might be. He knew Plyke was worried that the same fate had befallen his mother, but they might never find out about it if that happened.

As they continued riding their horses and walking them, by turns, Tika noticed both Plyke and Dorian drastically improving with their riding skills. He wondered if they were touching minds with their horses. Master Edric had never mentioned whether that was possible or not but, if it was, Tika was certain Plyke would have figure it out by now.

It was mid-afternoon by the time Tika decided to chance the conversation. It was something he had been wondering the entire time he'd been working in the stables because the horses reacted so differently depending on which lintep was handling them.

"Master Edric, I know lintep can touch minds with other lintep and humans. I assume they can with elves, karliki and crystal dragons too, but can they touch minds with animals?"

The stablemaster looked at him with an odd expression. "Now, what would make you ask a question like that, young Tika?"

Shrugging, Tika tried to make light of his question. "I pride myself on how well I handle animals of all kinds, especially horses. I can't hide that I'm a little jealous of some of the other stablehands who seem to have earned the trust of the stable horses more than I have."

To his surprise, the stablemaster looked at him guilty and rubbed the back of his neck with a large hand. Before answering he glanced over at Dorian and Plyke, both of whom were now listening attentively to the conversation.

"Well, now, you have to understand, I spend all day with horses," the stablemaster sheepishly explained. "I have done since I was a young lad. Back then, there weren't many people who would befriend an orphaned lintep with parents of dubious nature."

"Wait, what does that mean?" Tika asked. "Parents of dubious nature?"

"Let's just say neither of them were very powerful and both were happy to help Princess Rilla in her fight to help humans," Master Edric replied. "In any case, King Lukys took me in and apprenticed me to the then stablemaster, Master Rhyse. None of the other stablehands would talk to me much, so I spent more time than anyone else with the horses.

"When I began lessons in the castle, no one wanted to practice their skills with me, so … well, I practiced a lot of my mind skills with the horses."

There was a moment of silence as his words sank in.

"How long did it take you to think of trying that?" Dorian asked, with a sidelong glance at Plyke. Tika caught the flicker of uncertainty in his Partner's eyes.

"It was a good few months after I started my training. I could tell the others must be practicing outside of our lessons. There was no other way they could be improving so much more quickly than me."

"How many of your stablehands do you suggest this practice to?" Tika asked, feeling more left out about not having powers than he ever had before.

"Any I feel it would benefit, and who I trust not to misuse their powers or tell others who would misuse it," he answered carefully. "That now includes the three of you, so if you decide to do anything like that, just treat the horses with respect."

Tika saw Plyke and Dorian exchange guilty glances. Apparently, so did Master Edric.

"Unbelievable," the stablemaster muttered under his breath. "Out with it. What have you done?"

"Don't blame Dorian," Plyke blurted out. He proceeded to explain everything to them.

Tika listened, in awe of his Partner. He'd known Plyke since before he could remember. In all that time, he knew there was something different about him, something special. It had taken years for him to realise that Plyke might not be quite human, and still years after that before it was proven. With all of that, he'd assumed that it was his lintep heritage that made him different.

It was becoming more and more apparent that it wasn't only that – it was Plyke himself. Possibly the way Kora tried to impart her own views and the way he'd had to hide his powers from Erton and everyone else in Paradise both played their part. He wondered if Rilla had ever thought of something similar, then remembered she'd already done more with a Fringa. She probably wouldn't even see the difference between that and using her powers with a horse.

Once Plyke had finished explaining and Dorian had elaborated on his own experiments throughout the day, Master Edric sighed heavily.

"I should have known something like this might happen. I'm entrusting you boys with an awfully dangerous and precious secret. King Lukys may suspect what has happened over the years but, without expressly asking me about it, we've never had to ask other lintep if they agree with the practice or not.

"Imagine what might happen if a cruel lintep, a farmer perhaps, found out about this and decided to force his beasts to work harder than they should. What would happen if a man caught his wife in the arms of another and decided to use an animal to deliver a swift death to one or both of them? How would you be able to prove his guilt?"

His words shocked all three of them. The mere thought of those horrible acts made him feel sick. It was clear why Edric did not make it public knowledge.

"I can see you all understand. Now I think it's time we head back," Edric told them, turning his horse towards the city.

They rode their horses in silence until Dorian pointed to something on the far side of the farm in front of them. Tika saw what looked like a small rocky hill, if it not been for the blue and reddish-orange colours.
"What *is* that?" Dorian asked.
"It can't be," Plyke shook his head in disbelief.
"It must be," Tika replied, equally disturbed by what they saw. "What else could it be?"
"What are you two talking about?" Dorian looked from one to the other.
Tika looked warily at Plyke. "They're crystal dragons. That sapphire one might be Celtan, but I've no idea who the other one is."
"What are they doing here?" Plyke asked no one in particular. "If Lord Aaron finds out about this, he'll fly into a rage."
The crystal dragons were directly on their way to the castle. It would take too long to go around them so, carefully, they kept going. As they continued, Tika noticed all three lintep bring their horses to a halt and listen to something he couldn't hear. Tika waited until they relaxed to find out what had happened.
"Was that the lintep whistle?" he asked. "What did they say?"
Plyke and Dorian turned to Master Edric. His face had turned stone cold.
"These two *beasts* are to be given leave to romp around *my* pastureland. How can they possibly think the stablehands can ensure the safety of my horses without me there?" Edric almost yelled in disbelief. "Follow me, lads!"
Tika instantly urged his mount forward. Edric led them right up to the two crystal dragons until they were mere metres from their snouts. Tika was right – the sapphire one was indeed Celtan. He would have recognised him anywhere.
The crystal dragons turned their attention to the four riders in front of them. Tika instantly wanted to flee. He knew the danger these beasts had posed to Rilla when they were in the Drakos Mountains. Was the danger any less real simply because they were now in Illaria?
"Are you here to tell us we can fly to the pasture now?" Celtan rumbled out as Tika and the others stopped in front of him. "We've been waiting here most of the day, since Lady Kora insisted we could not approach the castle until she had made arrangements for the horses to be secured first. Such a tedious way to spend the day."
"Lady Kora?" Plyke asked, almost in a whisper. Tika turned to see his Partner had turned pale. "Lady Kora has returned?"
"Did you not hear the bells this morning?" the sapphire dragon asked him. "No doubt to celebrate her arrival."

"Did she arrive alone?" Tika asked immediately, without giving Master Edric the chance to give the dragons a piece of his mind. "Did you bring her here?"

"So many questions from one so young," Celtan fixed him with a cold blue stare. "You weren't nearly so talkative when you were in the Drakos Mountains."

"You weren't nearly so comfortable when we were in the Drakos Mountains," Tika retorted hotly. "Or have you forgotten that you told a mother and daughter the other was dead to advance your own interpretation of the prophecy? You made them miss so many years of each other's life and now Nyssa is dead. Both of her daughters will never have the chance to truly know their mother because of you!"

"But I might get a chance to truly know mine," Plyke said by his side. "Forget the dragons. Let's go find Kora!"

"*I* cannot forget the dragons so easily as you," Master Edric announced angrily. "I am the castle stablemaster. My horses are to make way for the two of you. If you so much as look at them the wrong way or spook them on purpose, I will make your stay here a living hell."

"Good stablemaster," the fire opal dragon finally spoke, "we do not wish your horses any harm. It is for this very reason that we have not already flown to the castle. We know how skittish horses can be, as we have our own in the Drakos Mountains.

"If it pleases you, even if a messenger arrives at this very moment to bring us to the castle, we shall not leave this spot until we have given you more than enough time to secure the stables to your satisfaction."

"That … is very generous of you …" Master Edric faltered.

"Pyrid, at your service," the magnificent beast bowed his head to the stablemaster. "This is Celtan, the oldest crystal dragon currently in our flight, which makes him our most reluctant leader." As Celtan turned to glare at Pyrid, the fire opal rumbled a low laughter, not loud enough to worry the horses.

"As for your questions, young human, Lady Kora did not arrive in Illaria alone. We encountered her here last night while escorting Eliséo, Ilya Mikhailovich, Kazimir Sergeyevich and Anya Nikolaevna. We sheltered them until early this morning."

Tika smiled broadly, turning to Plyke. "Eliséo is back so soon! Race you back to the castle."

He barely waited for Plyke to turn Goldfire around before spurring his horse into a canter, headed straight for the city and the castle beyond it.

Chapter Four – Hesitation

Kora found herself in the common dining hall, talking with Aislen, Braedan and Luisella when Plyke arrived with Tika and another boy. It was later than she had expected him, but still she did not know what to say to him.

The boys headed towards the table with Rilla and Shuut. Kora had been introduced to her oldest niece earlier that day and, even though Eliséo himself had accompanied her to the castle removing the need for the gesture, Kora had still found a quiet moment to deliver Elessa's flowers to Rilla. She hoped that if she became friends with her nieces, things would not stay awkward with her son forever.

Even though Eliséo had his own duties to attend to while in Illaria, Kora marvelled at the way he managed to find time to spend with Rilla and her cousins. It came as little surprise to Kora when Tika rushed towards the elf and almost knocked him off his feet with a fierce embrace. She smiled to herself as Eliséo returned the embrace with a ruffle of the boy's hair and a quick cheerful word.

As she watched their reunion, Kora's eyes were continually drawn to her son. He hadn't noticed her yet.

Should I go to him? Will he greet me as warmly as Tika greeted Eliséo? Or will his anger be too great? Will he berate me in front of the entire dining hall?

All these thoughts rushed through Kora's mind before she finally locked eyes with Plyke. Her breath caught in her throat as her heart stopped momentarily. She looked away, terrified.

In an effort to cover her own discomfort, she hastily returned to the conversation between her cousins. She couldn't face her son. Not now. Not like this.

* * *

Plyke swallowed the lump in his throat as Kora turn away from him. Despite having followed Tika over to their usual table, he had been searching the hall for a glimpse of his mother.

He looked away, desperately trying to hide the hurt in his eyes.

As he neared the table where Tika sat excitedly telling everyone about the crystal dragons, Plyke felt a sudden heaviness. He should have been as excited as his Partner about the day of horse riding and the two crystal dragons, but he wasn't. Not anymore.

"I think the riding took its toll on me today," he mumbled to Tika. "I'm going up to bed. I'll see you tomorrow."

"What about …" Tika left the sentence unfinished as Plyke caught his eye. He saw his Partner look behind him to Kora and then back again. Without a word, they understood each other. "See you tomorrow morning then."

Plyke walked out of the room, away from Kora and all his questions. He didn't notice Rilla follow him until he was half way across the inner courtyard of the castle.

"What do you want?" he asked, as he turned to face her.

"I thought you might like to know why Eliséo is here, with the karliki and the crystal dragons," she answered. Plyke noticed her intentional omission of Kora.

"You can tell me on the way to our rooms. I'm tired," he replied as he continued towards the stairwell at the opposite end of the courtyard.

"Eliséo listened to our conversation from the other night," she told him in a soft voice – there were already enough people who knew about her bond with the elf. "They've brought the crystal heart here and they're going to try to make it work, tonight, after the crystal dragons are settled in the pasture. The karliki are going to try to release the power that was used for the mind snares. If they don't succeed, then the chest will be brought out to the dragons."

"Do you think it's the answer?" Plyke asked. "If it works, do you think that's how we destroy the Paradises?"

They had reached the winding stairwell now and even though he had whispered, his voice echoed off the stone stairs. Rilla put a finger to her lips and motioned him up. Plyke ascended the stairs in silence.

"Well? Is that what everyone thinks?" he asked her again when they were in his chambers. "Is this the way to destroy the Paradises?"

"I'm not sure." Rilla shook her head. "I think it will depend on a few things. First, we have to see if the crystal heart works at all to release the power when it isn't attached to anyone's mind."

"What do you mean?" Plyke asked, confused. "Why wouldn't it work?"

"Well, remember what the karliki told us? It was a gift to them, to give them a way to protect themselves against mind powers. What if it only works on minds?"

"I suppose that's a possibility." Plyke conceded. "We'll just have to wait and see what happens tonight."

Rilla tapped her teeth and looked at him with those big green eyes. He knew there was something else.

"They don't want us to go with them," she finally said.

"They won't have a choice," he protested. "We'll make them take us."

"Kora said they aren't even going to let *her* into the crypt when they try it."

Plyke froze at the sound of his mother's name. "You spoke to her?"

"She found us in the dining hall between lessons," Rilla replied, a little too casually. "I know you're not going to ask, so I'll tell you anyway – she didn't ask after you and Tika. I think she'd already been told that you were out for the day with Master Edric because she was complaining about having to wait until he returned before they could bring the dragons in."

Plyke shut out all thoughts of Kora. There was no point thinking about her now. She would only cloud his mind.

He suddenly smiled and looked up at Rilla. She raised an eyebrow at him.

"I know how we can get into the crypt without them noticing."

He explained his idea to Rilla. To her credit, she didn't instantly dismiss it. After thoroughly examining the plausibility of it, she agreed.

* * *

Kora watched from the corner of her eye as Plyke left the hall. She wanted to stand and go after him, when she noticed Rilla follow him. Would it make matters worse if she interrupted Plyke with his cousin? Kora was caught with indecision. It had been so much easier with her father.

"Let's go up to the library," Aislen jostled Kora out of her thoughts. "Guiscard agreed to meet us there tonight. We can have a look at your map and make a proper plan."

"What about Pér?" Kora asked. "Did anyone send word for him to meet us as well?"

"We thought you would have done so," Braedan told her. "It will be too late now if we send a messenger for him."

Kora nodded, annoyed with herself for not thinking to ask him earlier. If he couldn't come tonight, at least it would give her an excuse to go and visit him another time.

Kora entered the library with her cousins, expecting to see only Guiscard there. It surprised her that Shuut was already seated at a chair near the fireplace.

"What are you doing here?" she asked, in a harsher tone than she intended. The banwep didn't seem to notice.

"I've been talking with Guiscard about an odd occurrence with Lishe," Shuut replied, glancing over towards the librarian. "I have a feeling that she already knows the location of at least some of the Paradises."

"How can you be certain?" Aislen asked, taking the seat next to the banwep.

"I can't," Shuut shrugged. "All I can tell you is that she was trying to find Rilla. She said she'd been tracking us after we left the Paradise, but Rilla fooled her by using a false name – Karinya.

"How could she have found us in the first place if she hadn't been near that Paradise? Then follows the question, what reason did she have to be anywhere near that Paradise unless she knew it was there? There's nothing around that Paradise for miles in every direction. I only found myself there because the crystal dragons had told me how to reach it."

"How did the crystal dragons know where it was?" Braedan asked.

Shuut swallowed hard. "My mother told them after she left Rilla there."

Kora wanted to reach out, comfort her niece. *How could Nyssa abandon both her daughters?*

"If that's the case, then we may need to move faster than father realises," Aislen pointed out.

Kora's stomach clenched. They were already rushing more than was safe, but it still wasn't quickly enough. How were they ever going to be able to destroy the Paradises before Lishe got around to it, especially now that they were fairly certain she knew the location of at least one?

"Shuut, you told us at dinner that night we first met you, that Lishe attacked you twice herself and sent groups of men to attack you a number of times in your travels. Can you show us, on a map, where those attacks occurred?" Aislen asked her.

"If I have a map of the Outworld, yes."

Kora reluctantly pulled the thin book out of her sash belt. She gently opened it to the map of Paradises and stood back. She waited impatiently as Nyssa's daughter poured over the map.

"The first attack was around here," Shuut pointed to a spot on the map between Silvaren and the Bramble River. "Four men attacked us soon after we left the elves. The next time was from a distance. At the ferry crossing she sent her power out to us over … here." She pointed to another spot, much closer to the Bramble River. "That's when the mind snare was first placed on me."

"Neither of those places is very close to a Paradise," Kora pointed out, frustrated.

"I don't think we were attacked again after the mind snare, so the next attack was on the other side of the river again, when Rilla and Arishen were hit while the rest of us were on the other side," Shuut continued, pointing to the closest section of the Bramble River to the Drakos Mountains, on the opposite bank.

"Then she attacked me and Nyssa … over here," her voice faltered a little as she pointed to the forest between the Bramble River and Illaria.

Kora stood, frozen with shame. She hadn't forgotten her sister had died, but she only knew what Eliséo had told her – that Nyssa had been found and was brought back to Illaria. She hadn't even thought about the poor daughter who was tortured alongside Nyssa and then used as bait to get Rilla out of the castle.

"I'm sorry, Shuut," she said, placing a hand on the girl's shoulder. "I understand you had only just been reunited with your mother when …"

"Well, at least we can assume one thing," Shuut shrugged her hand away after a moment. "Lishe probably only knows the location of that one Paradise. What do we do next?"

Kora looked at the others gathered in the room. Everyone was looking to someone else for answers. She couldn't believe they were so close now and none of them had any ideas of what to do.

"If I might speak, I wish to know something more about the Paradises," Guiscard turned to Kora. "We've heard enough stories about the Paradise you lived in to glean an idea of what it was like there, but did you learn anything from the other Paradises you found? How long did you stay in each of them before moving on to find the next?"

"They're not very welcoming places unless you have a trade," Kora explained. "I only stayed in most of them a week before they realised I was not much use to the community.

"A few of them were just as hostile as Erton's Paradise, but most were more welcoming. The one thing they had in common was that magic was not allowed. In quite a few of them, people were hinting at a rise in suspicious deaths, but they couldn't give me any details for fear that they would be next."

"What about this one?" Luisella asked, pointing to the Paradise nearest to Illaria. "Was it one of the hostile ones with suspicious deaths?"

"Actually, yes," Kora replied. "I think the ones closest to Illaria were the most hostile, with others becoming more welcoming the further out I went. Erton's Paradise was probably different because he was a lintep himself and had brought a lintep daughter into the Paradise. Even if she never called him "father" when anyone could hear, we all knew their relationship."

"Once we destroy the Paradise, what will happen?" Luisella continued. "If the land in the Outworld is empty, I assume that means the village structures will become permanent. But what will happen to the people? We'll need to bring enough lintep to keep the peace in case the Paradise leader begins to attack the Paradisians who want to flee or the lintep who destroy the Paradise. If the leader is a lintep themselves, then we may be in for quite a battle."

"None of this was mentioned with father," Aislen said as she rubbed her eyes, trying to keep herself away. "Everyone is so focused on the destruction of the Paradises that no one is even thinking of the consequences if they cease to exist."

"I think there's another consequence you're forgetting about," Shuut spoke up. "I don't think any of the Paradises will have money. If people want to move away from the hostile ones, where will they go?"

"That's true," Kora admitted. "None of them used money to trade. They were all set up in exactly the same way, so that the community provided for the people living there. If they stayed, everyone had to give up all of their metal, including coins and weapons."

"Did they all keep the children away from their parents?" Shuut asked curiously. Kora shook her head.

"Only some. I don't think Ophélie set them up like that, but maybe too many children followed after their parents and so there were shortages in other areas of the Paradise. I can't imagine any other reasons for it."

"I can," Guiscard replied quietly. "If there were too many children and not enough workers, they could have initially devised an area for the children to be cared for while the parents were working. That could eventually have become warped into the system you saw in some of the Paradises, as a way to make sure the parents contributed to the community rather than just reap the benefits."

"That's awful," Luisella cried in horror. "If anyone tried to take my Umi and Ulf away, I would fight them tooth and nail."

"And perhaps that is how the hostile ones became hostile," Guiscard offered a suggestion. "If loving parents, such as yourselves, refused to give up their children, perhaps the Paradise leader threatened to kill the children if they didn't oblige. What would you have done then?"

Luisella didn't answer but looked up at Braedan, who stood close, arm wrapped around her shoulders. Her tears were enough of an answer for Kora. Luisella would have done exactly the same as she had – handed over her children to keep them alive.

Chapter Five – Deception

Rilla waited with Plyke, staring out his bedroom window, until they saw the crystal dragons approach the castle. She turned around and asked him the same question, one last time.

"Are you sure about this? If we get caught."

"I'm sure," Plyke replied firmly. "The prophecy mentions your name and a child from a Paradise. Whether or not you are one and the same, how can they presume to not involve us at every step of the way? I can understand not wanting Kora, Aislen and Guiscard there, but we've already seen the crystal heart at work. What more could come of us seeing it again?"

Rilla knew he was right, but she'd been avoiding the prophecy since she'd first heard it. Somehow, it seemed wrong to use it as an excuse to do something she shouldn't be doing.

Without giving herself a chance to protest again, she closed her mind off from Eliséo and Elessa, just to be safe. Rilla slowly pulled her power from her tower and wrapped herself and Plyke in a bubble, big enough so that they could walk freely within it.

With no more effort than blinking, Rilla enclosed her power around Plyke and with complete control over him, just like Lishe had done with Shuut and Nyssa. The thought made her shudder.

"What's wrong?" Plyke asked, with a note of concern.

"Nothing," Rilla brushed aside the images. "I just need you to tell me one more time that you're sure."

"Rilla, I trust you almost as much as I trust Tika," he held her by the shoulders and looked straight into her eyes. "I know you're not going to use your powers against me and this is the best way we can move around the castle and into the crypt unseen."

Rilla smiled shyly at him. She still wasn't used to having such good friends, or cousins for that matter. Nodding, she walked to the door with Plyke following. She opened a hole in her power for him to unlock the door.

He had only just locked it behind them and moved away from the door when Rilla noticed someone walking down the hall. Without hesitation, she put her hand over Plyke's mouth and pulled him to the window across the hall.

She watched as Kora approached them, looking behind to see if she was followed. When she reached Plyke's door, she stopped and stared, holding her hand up to knock. Rilla held her breath as Kora simply stood there. Long moments passed, and as it seemed Kora turned to leave, she stopped and finally knocked.

Rilla kept her hand firmly over Plyke's mouth. She didn't know if he wanted to go to Kora, but if he tried to, it would be disastrous. Rilla wished they had tested out if the bubble stopped others from hearing them. They would have to test it before the next time they tried something as dangerous as this.

Impatiently, she waited for Kora to leave. Only once the older lintep had disappeared into another room did Rilla remove her hand from her cousin's mouth. He shook his head at her. There was no doubt that Kora now thought Plyke was ignoring her as she had ignored him in the dining hall. He would have to deal with it later.

The cousins descended the stairs quickly, careful not to make too much noise. They walked across the inner courtyard and to the outer gardens just across from the crypt. Rilla waited until she saw King Lukys in view. He was leading a small party of people through the gardens, as though giving them a late night tour of the grounds.

Not wanting to let them get too far ahead, Rilla nudged Plyke into the garden. The pebbles crunched under their feet. They stopped immediately. Heart pounding, Rilla watched as she saw Ilya and Eliséo turn around. She cursed softly, then mumbled a few words under her breath to call up the shrouding mist around her and Plyke, calling back her own power at the same time.

Ilya turned back almost immediately, but Eliséo's attention lingered. Had he seen them?

"Does this mean no one will be able to hear us from outside?" Plyke whispered barely loud enough for her even with his face so close to hers.

"I'm fairly certain," she whispered back to him. "When I did it with King Lukys, I don't think he could hear or see me at all, not even the mist. And remember in the Outworld, it was meant to keep us hidden. It wouldn't have done a very good job if people could hear us. In any case, we'll find out if we keep walking on these pebbles."

Together, they took a tentative step over the pebbles. None of the party turned towards them. With a sigh of relief, they followed the others from a safe distance, across the gardens to the crypt. They crept slowly closer as King Lukys pulled out a key from his robes to unlock the massive door. This would be the most difficult part. How would they be able to pass him into the crypt before he closed the door?

Rilla waited until everyone but King Lukys had entered the crypt before grabbing Plyke's hand and running for the door. At that moment, Eliséo began walking back up the stairs to Lukys.

"Lukys, I know the karliki can see in the dark, but what about the rest of us?" the elf asked.

The question distracted Lukys momentarily, which was all Rilla and Plyke needed to slip past the two of them. Barely seconds after they were in, Lukys closed and locked the door. Lukys lit the nearest lantern along the wall. He, Aurelius or Aaron could light each lantern with their power as they passed.

At the bottom of the stairs, the crypt opened out before them in near darkness. Rilla gasped as she saw bitter oyster mushrooms glowing softly in blue patches over the damp walls. She hadn't noticed them that first time she'd entered the crypt. Nyssa's death had distracted her and the crypt was fully lit. As though her grandfather had read her thoughts, he quickly lit every lantern in the crypt, snuffing out the blue glow of the mushrooms.

"Where's the chest?" Ilya asked, looking around the crypt. Rilla looked everywhere other than at Nyssa's coffin. She did not need to be reminded of that day and the chain of events since, though she freely admitted that sneaking into the crypt tonight was not helping her to forget.

"We buried it over here," Master Aurelius pointed to a spot where the dirt looked freshly turned. "I hadn't thought of this, but how are we to get it out without letting the power escape and trap one of our minds?"

All eyes turned to Lord Aaron. Rilla was slowly realising that her grandfather really must have more skill and power than most lintep in Illaria. He wasn't a master, but many deferred to him as though he was elaborately tattooed.

"I suggest we three use our power to remove the dirt, then, as soon as we're near the chest, I'll burrow my power down and surround the chest to contain the two powers within." Lord Aaron barely needed a moment to decide on a course of action.

As one, the three lintep began their arduous task. Rilla watched on, feeling slightly guilty that she would be able to help them if only they weren't hiding.

"Don't even think about it," Plyke whispered, holding her back as she started to step forward. "They'll manage without you."

She nodded, but did not take her eyes off the three lintep in front of her.

* * *

Kora's heart sank as she realised Plyke was not going to open the door to her. She tried to push down the bitterness that welled up inside her, but it was no use. Much as she understood how angry he must be, she had hoped he would at least give her the chance to explain.

Blinking back tears, she walked down the hall to Adina's room. Her hand rested heavily on the handle before she stepped inside. Once again, she was flooded with memories of that horrible day. No matter what she had told her father, she could not sleep here – not even for one night. There was only one place she could think to go, a place where she had always felt safe, a place where she had always been welcome. She could only hope that was still the case after so many years – after what she had done.

As she stepped into the hall once more, Kora did what she had done so many times in her youth. She surrounded herself with part of her power, rendering her invisible to the casual eye. With a small smile at the memory, she disappeared out of Adina's room and travelled unseen down the spiral staircase.

Once in the outer gardens, Kora took care to walk on the grass, rather than the pebbles. She had once made the mistake of thinking she could not be heard through her power. Since that time, when her movements had startled the guards and sent them ringing the bells in the middle of the night to wake the entire castle and half the town, she had always remembered to walk where she could not be heard.

She still cringed at the memory of how angry her father, and every lintep within range of the bells, had been. Her punishment had been to help in the castle kitchens for an entire week. Cook Palmyra had been just as annoyed with the punishment as Kora herself. For days she had been a thorn in the cook's side, until she had finally learnt how to peel a potato without cutting her fingers and tell the difference between herbs. She wondered how many dishes she had ruined that week from ignorance.

Shaking the thoughts from her mind, Kora focused on the task ahead. She was as close to the tall sandstone walls as she could get without leaving the soft grass. Now it was time for the skill she had never mentioned to anyone, which she had discovered and become so adept at. Little by little, she sent out her power to create an invisible stairway to the top of the wall. The first time she'd attempted it, the stairway had taken almost half the night to create. Since then, it had become easier and she had become faster at it so that, even now, after all these years without practicing, it only took minutes before she was standing atop the castle wall, looking out upon the sleeping city.

She breathed in the chill night air and shivered. It was much colder than she had anticipated. Rubbing her arms, she created yet another stairway – this one on the other side of the wall, down to where the drawbridge now stood firmly shut. It was at least a thirty-foot stretch from the castle wall to the cobbled bridge, but such was Kora's power that she had no difficulty in spanning the distance. It had been one of the reasons her motive had not been uncovered that one night when they'd found her sneaking around the castle grounds. The thought had never occurred to any of them that she could create a small stairway, let alone a platform, which could span the moat to reach the bridge.

Once her feet touched the cobbles, she took off her shoes, drew her power more snuggly around her and ran. Her feet would freeze, but at least her footsteps would not be heard. If she were not turned away from her destination, there would soon be time enough to warm up.

Kora knew the way so well, she could have run there blindfolded. Every bump in the street, the smell of every shop she passed told her exactly where she was. It wasn't much further now.

In minutes, a breathless Kora stood at the blue wooden door. The paint was only slightly more faded than it had been years ago. Her heart was racing, as much from her exertion as the fear that she might not be welcome.

She knocked softly on the door as she put her shoes back on and withdrew her power from around her body. Within seconds, she heard the sound of footsteps approaching. She almost turned and fled.

Will this be worse than going back to Adina's room?

Kora stood frozen with indecision.

Suddenly, a wave of calm flooded over her. Kora didn't try to fight against it, but wondered whether he knew it was *her* panic that he could feel. Letting the calming wave flow over her, she closed her eyes, tears of relief streaming down her face. This would always be the one place where she would be safe, where her mind could be at peace even if it had no right.

"I almost thought you'd forgotten about me again," Pér said as he opened the door for her. "Come on in."

Kora stepped into the warmth, instantly sucking heat towards her from the fireplace, and looked around the room as Pér closed the door behind her once more. There had been very few changes in the years since her last visit. A replaced chair here, a mended cushion there, but essentially, it was the same room she had fled to so many times in her youth.

"I didn't know where else to go." She didn't dare look him in the eye. *What am I doing here?*

"Father has given my room to Plyke, who won't open the door to me, and I've been given Adina's room for the night. I ... just couldn't do it."

"So you came here, hoping that the boy you abandoned so many years ago would welcome you back into his home once more," Pér replied harshly.

The words slashed at her heart.

"You should have told me where you were going, Kora. You *knew* I would have followed you."

"I couldn't! I simply couldn't ask you to follow," Kora tried to explain, eyes downcast. "It wouldn't have been fair to ask that of you."

"That wasn't your decision to make," he lifted her chin gently, forcing her to look at him. "I *wanted* to follow you everywhere. I thought I'd made that perfectly clear. Wherever you went, that was where I belonged. Do you have any idea how long I spent searching the Outworld for you only to find you and have you disappear on me all over again?"

"I'm sorry!" She ached from the pain she'd caused him – the pain she knew she was *still* causing him. She should tell him, but she couldn't bring herself to.

"Then a few weeks ago, rumours start spreading around town that a group of children from a Paradise had arrived, one of them claiming to be your own son. *Your son.*" Pér's voice cracked, breaking Kora's heart. "I hoped you would follow soon afterwards, but then Nyssa's body ... and Lishe. Even more rumours started. Rumours about the seer's visions. Do you know he had one of you fleeing the Paradise? I began to lose hope of ever seeing you again.

"When you walked into the marketplace today, I scarcely believed my own eyes, but it really was you. My love. And now you've come home to me."

Kora fell into his open arms, tears of joy streaming down her face. Pér held her tightly.

"Promise you'll never leave me behind again," he pleaded.

"I promise," Kora instantly replied. "I promise." They stood together, drinking in each other's happiness and sorrow.

"Now, I want to hear what brought you back to Illaria, other than me, of course," Pér grinned, as he stepped back from Kora and drew her towards the old cushioned chaise near the fireplace where they had spent so many nights in their youth.

When she had returned from the Outworld with more than half of her family gone, Kora had not known where else to turn. Pér had always had the ability to soothe her nerves and calm her enough she could finally sleep. Of course, it was unseemly for a young lady to be seen about town with a would-be minstrel, and it would have been even more inappropriate for him as a guest in the castle. That left Kora no choice but to make rather regular late night visits into town.

She'd been blind to the fact that Pér adored her when they were younger. It was only during that time that they grew closer together. Kora had devised a legitimate way for them to spend time together during the day as well. Once she, Aislen, Braedan and Luisella had started to discuss humans and Paradises in the library of an afternoon, after their lessons, it had been simplicity itself to include Pér in their meetings. The five of them, often with Guiscard, had spent a good deal of time discussing how lintep should or shouldn't use their power, especially on humans.

Fondly remembering those days, Kora pulled the precious book from her sash belt, opened it up and told him everything she had discovered about Paradises and their plan to destroy them.

Chapter Six – Hidden power

It felt like hours later, but Rilla doubted it had been more than half an hour, when Lord Aaron finally knelt and bent his head down in concentration to wrap his power around the chest. Rilla nudged Plyke, who had started to nod off beside her. He rubbed his eyes as she pointed to their grandfather.

Once they had completely uncovered the chest, King Lukys and Master Aurelius stood to either side of Lord Aaron, supporting him as he rose to his feet. They slowly guided him back to allow room for the chest to be set down in front of him.

"Ilya, it's time now." Eliséo placed a hand on the young karlik's shoulder and pulled the crystal heart out of his pocket. Ilya held out his hand for the flower-shaped crystal and gently closed his fingers around it.

"What will happen if it doesn't work?" he asked, turning to Lord Aaron.

"In the best case, I manage to contain both powers in the chest again. In the worst case, each one latches onto someone and ensnares their minds," he replied, without a hint of worry. "If that happens, then the crystal heart should work anyway because it will then be the same as when you healed Shuut in Goraburg."

"Very well." The karlik sighed heavily, stepping closer to the chest. "There's only one way to find out."

Anya and Kazimir flanked Ilya. The three of them put their hands on the crystal heart and placed it on top of the chest. They spoke the words so softly that Rilla couldn't hear them. She doubted even Eliséo, with his superior elf hearing, could have heard them.

Almost immediately, the crystal heart dropped to the floor. Anya cried out in shock as Ilya and Kazimir fell heavily to the floor.

"What is it?" Eliséo asked urgently. "Anya, what happened?"

"The power attacked them!" she cried in a panic. "I can't save them alone. The crystal heart needs three karliki."

"Only karliki?" the elf asked as he knelt down before her. "Anushka, will it work if myself and one of the lintep say the words with you?"

She shook her head. "I don't know. We've never tried it before. I … I don't think Lord Mikhail would like it if I told you the words to say."

"I think he'd like it less if you let his heir and oldest friend rot away because you wouldn't tell me."

Rilla could see he was just as afraid of that happening as Anya.

"Before you make that decision, Anya, will you permit me to try and remove the snares from Ilya and Kazimir?" Lord Aaron asked the karlik gently. She looked up at him, tears in her eyes, and nodded. "Aurelius, will you help me? I'll work on Ilya, you take Kazimir. Once we remove the powers, we can place them back in the chest again."

"What about me?" Lukys asked. Rilla found it odd that even their king would defer to her grandfather when it came to something as important as this.

"I need to you keep your power at the ready ... in case something goes wrong." He turned to look at Lukys. Rilla could now see his ashen face. "If that happens, I trust I don't actually need to tell you what to do."

Lukys nodded and gripped Aaron's arm firmly before releasing him to his work.

"What are they talking about?" Plyke asked Rilla, softly.

"I think Lord Aaron has just told King Lukys to do exactly what we're doing. It's possible that the only way to keep the power from attaching to every mind it touches is to completely cover it with another power," Rilla replied, stunned that they would even contemplate doing what they'd warned her and Plyke again – what the two of them had tried earlier in the evening.

"I saw Lord Aaron take the mind snare off you by himself and then help with the one on Shuut. I don't think they're going to have to resort to that," Plyke told her confidently.

"Yes, but from what we were told about that day, it took hours and Master Jorg had been helping most of that time," Rilla pointed out.

Yet, as they watched, it seemed that Lord Aaron had already had some success. He was motioning King Lukys over.

"I'm going to place the power in that chest again. Can you contain it while I help Aurelius?" he asked, his voice slightly strained. Lukys nodded.

Rilla watched the king. His features became quite drawn as he began to work with Aaron. Beads of sweat formed on his brow as her grandfather turned his attention to Aurelius.

The old master had his eyes closed in concentration, slumped over, as though he might fall at any second. When Aaron approached him, Aurelius' shoulders relaxed as though an enormous weight had just been lifted from them. Together, they turned towards the chest and worked with Lukys to contain both powers back in the chest. Eventually, only Aaron remained focused on the chest. Lukys and Aurelius went to the two fallen karliki to awaken them.

"How did he do that?" Rilla asked Plyke. "You said it took them hours the first time he dealt with it. How could he do it so quickly this time?"

"I don't know. Maybe it took him so long the first time because he had to figure out how to do it and this time he already knew." Plyke suggested with a shrug as Ilya and Kazimir opened their eyes.

"What happened?" the old Karlik asked, looking around in confusion.

"The worst possible outcome," Lukys told him. "The crystal didn't work and the powers ensnared both you and Ilya. We've managed to contain them back in the chest. We now have no choice but to ask the crystal dragons for their assistance."

Ilya looked crestfallen. Rilla could understand how disappointed he must have felt to travel all this way only to be of no use. The younger karlik said nothing as he and Kazimir took hold of the chest to carry it out to the crystal dragons while Lord Aaron contained the power within it.

"How does he do that?" Plyke asked Rilla as they ascended the stairs.

"Do what?" she asked him, making sure not to fall too far behind the others. She didn't want to be locked in the crypt without anyone knowing where they were.

"How does he do the most difficult things which either require so much power or skill that no one else seems to be able to really attempt it? And he does it all without breaking a sweat! I mean – did you see how much King Lukys and Master Aurelius struggled until Lord Aaron came to their aid?"

"I don't know," Rilla replied, wondering the same thing herself. "What worries me is that you and I might have that kind of power and don't realise it."

"*You* might," Plyke conceded, "but I very much doubt I do. I can't even master most of the simplest tasks."

Rilla was shaking her head before he finished. "That's just a lack of skill, a lack of practice. Once you've had time to work with your power for a while, I'm certain that will change. I'm not talking about your skill level, though. I'm talking about how much power you have."

"What's the difference?" Plyke asked as they ran up the last few steps and out into the night air before Lukys closed the door on them.

"Do you remember when we were first attacked by Lishe herself?" Rilla asked. "When Eliséo asked you to cast out your senses to see if you could feel anything wrong around us?"

"How could I forget?" Plyke grimaced.

"Then you'll remember how far away you must have sent your power," Rilla pressed him. "You said you could hear the roar of water, but the ferry crossing must have been at least a mile away. I've heard a lot of lintep struggle with anything more than a few feet. That's why they've got bells for messengers. Not all lintep would be able to send messages to each other, even across the castle grounds."

"That can't be possible." Plyke shook his head, as they followed the others across the courtyard towards the stables. "Lishe reached you from the edge of the city, according to Shuut."

"Yes, and how many lintep's power do you think she's stolen to be able to do that?" Rilla asked him. "Why do you think she was confident enough to attack us so close to the castle? Because she knows that most lintep don't have anywhere near that much power."

"That puts us more at her mercy than I thought we were."

Plyke's reply disturbed Rilla. She'd been worried about that herself. If Lishe was so much more powerful than every other lintep in Illaria, possibly even more than their grandfather, what hope did they have of surviving the next time they met her?

Rilla drew closer to Plyke as they walked through the stables. She hadn't been through this part of the castle grounds before. It frightened her when one of the horses snickered as they passed by. Eliséo and Master Aurelius turned at the sound, but seeing nothing, continued on their way.

Plyke pushed his hand to the side of the mist bubble and tried to pat a horse's nose through it. The golden horse shook her white mane and nodded her head as though acknowledging him.

"Oh, Goldfire, I'm sorry I left you so quickly this afternoon," Plyke whispered to the horse. "I'll come back and see you tomorrow, I promise."

Rilla waited nervously as Plyke spoke quietly to the horse. She didn't want them to spend any more time in the stables than necessary. The others were already at the far end and she didn't want to lose them. Not to mention the fact that she knew Tika must be in here somewhere. If he woke up, there was no way Plyke was going to continue without him.

"Can we get Tika?" Plyke asked as though reading her mind. "I'm sure he'll want to come with us."

"No, Plyke," Rilla replied, exasperated. "We shouldn't be here ourselves, especially when it looks like the horses can still sense or hear us. I don't want to get Tika in any trouble. King Lukys might change his mind about humans in Illaria if that happens. Let's just hurry and follow the others before we miss what the crystal dragons do."

Plyke grudgingly agreed. They hurried through the stables and out into the pasture beyond it. Rilla stopped as soon as they were out in the open. There, before them, were two massive crystal dragons. One, she had never seen before, a sort of fiery orange colour. The other, one she would never forget – Celtan, the sapphire crystal dragon who had ruined three lives, just to manipulate a prophecy.

"Hurry Rilla." Plyke urged her forward. "We need to get closer otherwise we won't be able to hear what happens."

Reluctantly, Rilla quickened her pace. They stopped just behind Eliséo. Ilya and Kazimir had already placed the chest before Celtan and stepped back behind Lord Aaron, who was keeping his eyes firmly averted from the sapphire crystal dragon.

"Well met, Celtan, Pyrid," King Lukys addressed the crystal dragons stiffly. "The crystal heart did not work the way we anticipated, so we find ourselves in need your assistance."

"I find that rather … odd," Celtan rumbled. "The crystal heart should work to release any mind."

"The powers don't have any minds in their grasp," the king explained. "Perhaps that is why it didn't work."

"Anya Nikolaevna, would you tell me what words you used?" the sapphire beast turned his snout towards the blonde karlik. She drew herself up proudly, walked directly to the dragon and whispered in his ear. Celtan nodded thoughtfully as Anya retreated once more.

"Are they the only words you were taught?"

Kazimir looked confused. "We were under the impression those were the *only* words which would work with the crystal heart."

"I told you it was a good idea we came." Pyrid nudged Celtan with his snout. "Imagine how much trouble they would have been in without us."

"Pyrid, would you be quiet!" Celtan growled at the fire opal dragon, before turning his attention back to the karliki. "It appears the crystal dragons who gave you the heart did not anticipate that you would need to use it for anything other than versions of this mind snare we've heard so much about. In actual fact, the heart is capable of almost anything, as long as you know the words to use."

"Anything?" Eliséo asked in surprise. "How can that be possible?"

"The heart is the source of all our magic," Celtan patiently explained. "This heart is smaller than ours, so it doesn't have quite as much power as our hearts, but the more people, karlik or otherwise, who are touching it and saying the words, the more powerful it becomes. It draws on their power to work."

"But, karliki haven't had power of their own for generations," Anya pointed out. "How can it draw on any power of ours?"

"All creatures have *some* power," Celtan informed her. "Karliki don't have enough to be noticeable, just like humans. But have you ever noticed that there are human and karlik seers? How do you think that happens?"

Rilla gasped. It all suddenly made sense to her. The minimum amount of karliki needed for the crystal heart was three, because they didn't have much power, not because of the actual number. That meant a lintep, or an elf, alone could make it work and the spell would be that much more powerful because there was more power to draw on. If Lord Aaron used it, that would probably be as powerful as it could get.

"I have to tell them!" Rilla exclaimed. She was just about the say the words to dissipate the mist when Plyke grabbed her arms.

"Rilla, don't you dare! Aside from the trouble you would put us both in by exposing us now, just imagine how badly the dragons would want to manipulate you if they realise you have elf magic as well. It's not worth the risk." He forced her to look into his eyes. "Promise me you will wait until tomorrow, when it's safer, to ask your questions or tell them what you've figured out. Just don't do it now! *Please* keep us both safe."

Rilla was shocked by the fear in his eyes. She had been so focused on the problems and solutions she saw, that she forgot everything else – even their own safety. He let her arms go as she nodded. They turned their attention back to the others behind them.

"Would it not be safer for one of you to release the power in the chest?" Anya asked the crystal dragons, looking hesitantly at Ilya and Kazimir. It was clear she was still rattled by the powers attacking her friends.

Pyrid shifted on his haunches and turned towards Celtan. The sapphire dragon looked decidedly uncomfortable. Rilla and Plyke edged closer to hear what was happening.

"We can't," Celtan replied.

"What do you mean, you can't?" Anya prodded. "You each have a heart bigger than this one. Surely either of you could release these powers yourselves."

"Shall I?" Pyrid asked, as softly as a crystal dragon could. Celtan nodded in reply. "The fact of the matter is that we crystal dragons can't use our hearts the same way you can. When we were created, all of Sascha Vladimirovich and Nadya Grigorevna's magic flowed into our hearts. That is what brought us to life. All of the power in the hearts is needed to keep us alive.

"If we chose to use our heart's power for another purpose, we would only be able to perform that one task before dying. Many a crystal dragon has ceased to live in this way."

Eliséo whistled lowly at the revelation. "I understand it now," he said. "All of the manipulation of other races, particularly those with power, was because you could not use any power yourselves. To change anything, you were forced to rely on others. Tell me, did your ancestors give the karliki a crystal heart so that you could call on them for help whenever it suited you?"

Celtan growled. "Our hearts make us immune to such magical attacks. We have no need for *other races* to help us."

"So it's true, then," Eliséo carried on, heedless of the furious sapphire dragon before him. "You couldn't even use *this* crystal heart if you tried, could you? The power to fuel it would have to come from your own heart, which would end your life."

The sapphire dragon snarled at the elf. Rilla found herself moving forward to protect him, but Plyke's firm grip on her arm kept her by his side. Furious, she watched as the fire opal dragon placed a claw on Celtan's snout. The growling became a soft rumble, eventually ending in a huff.

"I suggest we allow the karliki to release the powers within that chest now, before Lord Aaron collapses from exhaustion. There will be plenty of time to discuss this matter further another day, should either of you wish to do so."

At Pyrid's suggestion, the three karliki stood over the chest, their hands touching the crystal heart lying above it. They whispered the new words Celtan had told them so softly that no one else could hear.

Nothing happened.

Ilya, Anya and Kazimir stepped back from the chest, looking at each other, then at Lord Aaron, who was now smiling.

"You did it," he told them with an audible sigh, his entire body relaxing. "The powers have been released. I think we should all return to the castle now for some much needed sleep. We can discuss this further on the morrow. I think we're well on the way to figuring out how to destroy the Paradises.

"Eliséo, would you honour me with your arm. I'm feeling quite weary all of a sudden."

Rilla and Plyke moved out of the way just before their grandfather walked into them. In a sudden panic that Eliséo, Master Aurelius or Lord Aaron would call on them in their rooms when they returned to the castle, Rilla took Plyke by the hand and ran.

* * *

Once they had passed through the stables, Eliséo spoke softly with Lord Aaron. "Would you allow me to escort the karliki to their chambers? I can see that this evening has taken a toll on you and I know my way around the castle well enough to help on this occasion."

"Eliséo, that is very kind of you," the old lintep smiled wearily, patting him on the shoulder. "I had thought to discuss the outcome with Kora tonight, but I think it may be best to leave all conversations until the morning. I am indeed quite fatigued."

Eliséo bowed his head slightly as he passed Lord Aaron over to Master Aurelius, then slowed until he was walking beside Ilya. The two of them fell into a comfortable silence with Anya and Kazimir behind them. By the time they reached the castle itself, the three lintep had already disappeared from sight. Eliséo escorted his three charges to their chambers.

He wanted to ask what their intention was now that they knew the true nature of the crystal heart. Whether they intended to stay, to help destroy the Paradises, whether they would leave the crystal heart in his care once more so that he could help the lintep, or whether they would take it back home with them, back to Goraburg where even now it was possible that Vladimir was seeking out ways to attack Mikhail.

Leave them be. Elessa's voice sounded in his mind. *They are probably wondering the same things themselves. It won't make the decision any easier for them if you push the matter.*

"I'll call on you in the morning," he spoke softly to Ilya, not to disturb the other residents on their floor. "Sleep well, my friend."

It looked as though Ilya was about to say something to him, but instead he nodded his head silently and closed the door. Eliséo stood transfixed for a moment, but with quite some effort, managed to pull himself away from his friend. His thoughts now strayed to Rilla and Plyke. He should really talk to them before the night was through.

He slowly climbed the stairs to the top level and walked across to Rilla's room. He was about to knock when he realised that she wouldn't be there and he would only succeed in waking Shadow and have to answer her barrage of questions. Instead, he walked back down the way he had come and stopped at the door closest to the stairwell – Plyke's chambers. He knocked softly on the door, not wanting to wake anyone else or alert the lords to his presence.

"Who is it?" came a quiet voice from the other side.

"Eliséo," he answered just as softly. He heard a muffled argument before the door was opened a fraction by Plyke.

"It's late, Eliséo. What do you want?" Plyke asked. Eliséo raised an eyebrow at the young lintep and simply glared at him. "I suppose you'd better come in then."

Eliséo followed the boy into his room. He wondered if Plyke knew this had once been Kora's own room. It would be better for him not to mention the fact, in case it made the boy more intractable.

"Whose idea was it?" he asked, not wanting to simply assume it had been Rilla's.

"Mine," Plyke replied. "It was entirely mine. Even how to follow you was my idea. Rilla had nothing to do with it."

Eliséo looked from one face to the other. He saw the flicker of annoyance in Rilla's eyes before she managed to make her face a blank mask once more. At least some part of what Plyke has said was untrue. All he had to do was figure out which part.

"I'm willing to believe it was your idea to let her encase you with her power, because we both know she would never have suggested that herself. Let me just say that if any of the lintep had noticed what you were doing, you would have been punished so harshly that you may have wished Lishe had caught you after all.

"As it turned out, only Ilya and myself heard you walk across the pebbles and only I noticed what happened after you realised we could hear you. I believe you have been told enough times of the danger that you place yourself and others in when you so blatantly use that type of magic."

"What else could we possibly have done?" Rilla asked, her voice barely masking her anger. "If I hadn't switched over, we could easily have been exposed and the lintep would have known exactly what we'd been doing in the first place. Which option would you have preferred?"

"I would have preferred if you'd both stayed in your rooms tonight like you were meant to," he told them calmly. "What if something had gone terribly wrong? Even more so than it did. What would you have done then? Lukys could have trapped you in the crypt without anyone knowing you were there. The powers could have attacked the two of you instead of Ilya and Kazimir and, because Elessa's mist was hiding you, we would have assumed the plan had succeeded and left the two of you to rot away in the crypt with the mind snare."

As he chided them, he saw a grudging shame creep over their faces.

"I see you finally understand the issues. The danger isn't over yet. I'm certain you have ideas or questions about what happened tonight. Tomorrow, you must pretend that you saw and heard nothing – that is if anyone comes to talk to you about it. They may wish, for whatever reasons, not to divulge the events of last night to the two of you. In that case, you are not to come forward yourselves. That will raise just as much suspicion as if they had caught you tonight."

"But we do have questions. And so many ideas!" Rilla burst out. "We need to talk to them. What if they didn't figure out what we did?"

"What *you* did," Plyke pointed out sullenly. "You figured something out and you still haven't told me what it is."

'I'm sorry, Plyke," she turned to her cousin to explain, but before she could, Eliséo grabbed her wrist firmly.

"Don't!" He warned her. "Don't tell him or he'll have just as much trouble as you tomorrow when he tries to hide what he knows or suspects from everyone. At some point, Kora will probably try to speak with you, Plyke. It would not do for you to accidentally tell her what you did tonight when she herself was expressly forbidden from going along and managed to comply with that order."

Plyke stayed strangely silent. Eliséo knew something must have gone wrong with their reunion if he was acting this way. Kora had been so worried about their meeting that she could barely think, but Plyke had been excited to see her no matter what. Eliséo knew this from the last time he had spoken with Plyke. What could possibly have made him change his mind? Unless …

"Have you not spoken to Kora yet?" Eliséo asked the young lintep. Plyke shook his head. "Why ever not? I thought you couldn't wait to see her again."

"It seems the feeling was not mutual," Plyke replied stiffly. Eliséo knew he would not get any more answers out of him tonight. It was not his place to express Kora's fears, so instead he steered the conversation away from her.

"Very well then, Rilla, back to your room immediately, and don't forget what I told you. Do not reveal your actions to anyone."

Without letting either of them reply, Eliséo opened Plyke's door and escorted Rilla to her chambers before returning to his own. It had been a long night and a long journey before that. He was more exhausted than he had been in weeks.

Chapter Seven – Decisions

Dawn came too soon. After talking into the early hours of the morning, Kora had fallen asleep on Pér's chaise, exhausted. He had woken her with a kiss as the sun tinged the city with its orange glow. He would join her in the castle later that day, for the council meeting, which was inevitable now that they had so much to organise.

With practiced ease, Kora disappeared from view as she left Pér's house and returned to the castle. Once she'd reached the stairwell leading to the royal chambers, she pulled her power back within her, making her visible once more.

She would have to speak to her father about swapping her chambers. Last night was proof that she could not sleep in Adina's chambers. Hopefully they would be able to rearrange the rooms today without causing Plyke too much grief. Surely he would not object to the change. He would barely have had time to settle properly into her chambers.

Once outside Adina's door, she froze. How could she possibly pretend to have slept there the night before when she couldn't bring herself to enter the room again? Kora turned and headed down the stairs once more. She considered going straight to the dining hall and avoiding Plyke until he was ready to see her. Half way down the stairs, she stopped. *She* was the one who hadn't been ready to see him, not the other way around.

Perhaps he had every right to shut me out last night, but he can't avoid me forever, especially if we're to work together to destroy the Paradises.

She turned and walked slowly back up the stairs. Just as she was stepping onto the carpet-lined hall, she saw the door to his room open. He walked out, completely unaware that she had come to find him, and almost walked straight into her.

"Sorry..." Plyke stopped as soon as he locked eyes on her. "Oh, it's you."

Kora bit back tears. "Good morning, Plyke. I was just on my way to see you."

He raised an eyebrow. "You walked past my room and then doubled back again. It's too early in the morning for you to have been somewhere else already, so this wasn't your initial intention."

Images of her late night expedition flickered in Kora's mind. She couldn't tell Plyke that she had spent the night at Pér's place.

"I … wasn't certain you wanted to see me," she replied hesitantly. "You didn't open your door last night."

From the pained look he gave her, she wondered what he was about to lie about. She had always been able to tell when he was lying.

"I must have been asleep. I didn't hear you." He offered up his poor excuse. She gazed at him a moment, wondering whether or not to press him on the matter. Deciding against it, she simply shrugged instead.

"It's no matter. One more day after so long won't kill us."

"It certainly didn't seem to bother you yesterday evening. You didn't even greet Tika and you know how much he adores you."

The rebuke hurt more than she wished to admit. How could he possibly have known the turmoil that was inside of her? If only she hadn't frozen.

"Plyke, you have to understand, I didn't know if you'd want to see me." She explained. "After everything that happened in the Paradise, everything you must have learnt afterwards … I simply didn't know."

"Kora, all you had to do was talk to me," he replied, tears in his eyes. "You're my *mother*! You gave up *years* of your life to keep me safe from the most dangerous man I've ever met. How could you think I didn't want to see you?"

Kora listened in stunned silence. She had expected him to be furious, both for not telling him who he was and for not training him. She was completely unprepared for his unconditional love.

Still shocked, she found herself in a strong embrace. As a smile crept to her face, she returned the embrace and clung to her son as though he was giving her life. She kept her thoughts and emotions to herself and noticed he did the same. Had he figured out what they did with skin contact in this place? Did their embrace mean that he trusted her enough not to do that to him? She had given him enough hints throughout his life for him to know certain things would be possible even if he would never stoop to it himself.

"Well, it's nice to see that you two have finally reconciled?"

Kora started at the voice behind Plyke. She looked up to see Rilla, smiling broadly. She returned the smile easily. Finally, she was home with her entire family around her – more than she had expected to find here.

"Good morning to you too, Rilla," she greeted her niece. "I see you couldn't sleep either."

"How could I sleep knowing what they were doing last night?" Rilla replied with a groan. "I can't wait to find out what happened."

The door to Rilla's room opened once more and Shuut walked out, rubbing her eyes sleepily. "Even if I didn't care what happened last night, there's no way that I would be able to get any more sleep with you three making so much noise. Let's just go to Lord Aaron's room and ask him."

Kora wasn't certain it was the best approach, but she was just as curious as the rest of them to find out. She led the way to her father's chambers and knocked loudly.

"Father, are you awake?" Kora called out to him, hoping she wouldn't wake Kynon. She heard the sound of footsteps from the other side of the door and stood back. Her father stared bleary eyed at the small group of lintep in the hall.

"I see." He nodded to himself. "There's no need to ask what the four of you want so early in the morning. Give me a moment to refresh myself and I'll take you to see Lukys."

He closed the door to them once more. Kora turned to her son and nieces with a glittering eye.

"That's something at a least," she mused. "If they'd had no success, he would have just told us so."

She missed the look that passed quickly between Rilla and Plyke, but Shuut must have noticed because she tried to pull the two younger lintep away to talk to them.

"What was that about?" she asked softly.

"Nothing," Rilla and Plyke replied simultaneously. It was enough to rouse Kora's suspicion, but as she'd only just reunited with them, she didn't want to push their relationship. Shuut had no such trouble.

"Is this another one of those things that you can't tell me or you'll get all three of us into more trouble?"

The young cousins nodded vigorously and kept tight lipped. Kora wondered what else they had figured out that they weren't allowed to tell her. It could be anything, given this was Illaria, but it was interesting to think that they'd only been here a few weeks and had already broken rules that other lintep probably didn't dare to dream of breaking.

Kora turned back as her father finally opened the door. She smiled at how resplendent he looked in his burgundy robes. He would have made a fine master had he ever chosen that path. When she was younger, she had rarely understood concepts her teachers had tried to explain during their lessons. She often remedied this be speaking with her father who had always been able to explain things in a way that made sense to her. The only lessons she hadn't asked his opinion on were those she did not think he would approve of her learning about.

Snapping out of her memories, she walked with the others around the carpeted hall until they reached the king's chambers. Her father knocked louder than necessary, but given how tired he looked, she assumed they'd both had quite a late night.

Just as he was about to knock again, Lukys opened the door and stared at the five of them. His eyes widened in shock before a look of resignation came over him.

"Come in then." He waved them in out of the hall. "Wait here a moment. I'll call Guiscard and Aislen. Aaron, call Aurelius and ask him to bring Eliséo and the karliki with him."

With that, he left them in his antechamber, which was larger than most of the other entire chambers on the level. Kora settled herself into one of the chaises scattered around the room. She smiled as Plyke joined her. They sat in a comfortable silence as Shuut paced the floor and Rilla sat apart from everyone else.

Kora found herself wondering about the young girl. She appeared to be quite close with her sister and cousin, even if a little more reserved with her affections. At least that was one thing Erton had completely failed in – isolating his daughter to the point of driving away anyone who could help her with the prophecy.

Lukys reentered the room in an ornate forest green robe. This made Kora sit up and take notice. Both her father and uncle were now dressed rather formally for the day. Something must have happened last night, which meant they would have to act in their official capacity as lord and king. Was this the thing that Rilla and Plyke knew something about?

"We'll await the others here, but I fear these rooms may prove too small for our purposes," he informed them. "We may need to remove ourselves to the council chambers once again."

"Do you not think it worthwhile calling the others who were involved in the previous discoveries?" her father asked her uncle. Lukys shook his head decisively. Kora wondered what the previous discoveries had been. They hadn't spoken about them the day before. There was so much she was missing or didn't understand.

"I think the fewer people who know about this, the better," Lukys answered. "We should decide how we wish to proceed before informing too many people. The karliki have a difficult decision to make, so it may come down to that."

Kora watched her father carefully. He didn't disagree with his cousin, but his eyes glazed over, thoughtfully. She could barely wait to hear what had happened. Taking the opportunity to distract him, she motioned her father over to where she and Plyke were seated.

"Father, I haven't had the opportunity to speak with Plyke about it yet, but do you think it can still be arranged for us to switch rooms? I ... don't think I can last another night."

"Of course, my dear." Her father patted her hand. "I will organise it at once."

As he went to ring the bell for a servant, Kora felt Plyke's questioning gaze on her.

"I didn't realise father had given you my old room." Kora tried to shrug the issue aside, but when Plyke's eyes remained fixed on hers, grudgingly, she elaborated. "He gave me ... someone else's room and I can't stay there."

"Was it your sister or brother's room?" Plyke asked her gently. She nodded, biting back tears. "You should have said something yesterday. I barely have any belongings. If the servants can't help us, we'll do it ourselves." Kora smiled at his kindness and drew him even closer to kiss his forehead.

The sun had changed to a bright yellow by the time a knock sounded at the door. Kora sat on the edge of her seat as Lukys opened it. Eliséo, Ilya, Kazimir, Anya, Master Aurelius, Guiscard and Aislen entered together. The karliki and the master all looked the worse for wear.

What did they do last night?

Muted greetings were exchanged amongst them while everyone took a seat in the antechamber.

"I'll assume everyone knows what was attempted last night, so I won't bore you with the details," Lukys said, to many nods. "Suffice to say that the release of the powers used for the mind snares was eventually successful, due to the assistance of the crystal dragons. I understand you will want more information than that to satisfy your curiosity, but I do believe that it will be safer to restrict the knowledge until we are certain about what we wish to do with it.

"The main decision will fall to the karliki. Will any of you stay to help us? Will you leave the crystal heart with us if you go? Or will you take the it and return to your home? We cannot possibly formulate a plan without this knowledge."

Kora was stunned. *Is it really as simple as that? Have they figured out how to destroy the Paradises with or without the help of the karliki and the crystal heart?*

Ilya looked at Anya and Kazimir, both of whom nodded to him before he stood. "We discussed this at great length last night. I believe we have come to a decision that will be agreeable to all.

"Though I would dearly love to remain and assist with the destruction of the first Paradise, my father requires my swift return. The situation with Vladimir does not afford me any flexibility in this matter. During this difficult time, Kazimir would also be of greater assistance to the karliki back in Goraburg than here in Illaria.

"Anya, however, has no pressing matters urging her return to our home. She will remain behind to assist you in any way possible with the crystal heart. She is the descendant of Sascha Vladimirovich and Nadya Grigorevna and we trust her judgement when it comes to such a precious gift.

"We agree, it is in the best interest of all races for the Paradises to be destroyed as swiftly as possible to keep such vast power out of the clutches of Lishe. Anya will choose whom to entrust with the power of the crystal heart. We must ask you to respect her authority in all things related to it, whether you agree with her decision or not. Do not forget that the crystal heart belongs to the karliki and we allow the use of it for this purpose alone."

Kora let everything sink in. The crystal heart seemed to be the key to everything. With only one karlik remaining in Illaria, that illusion of how it worked was shattered.

"I don't mean to pry too far into last night's proceedings, but your decision makes it sound as though three karliki are not needed to make the crystal heart work." Kora left the unasked question dangling in the air. The karlik did not answer, but looked at King Lukys instead.

"We discovered a number of things about the crystal heart last night," Lukys responded for Ilya. "One of them was why three karliki were needed to make it work. That discovery has led to new possibilities, none of which we shall discuss at present.

"Ilya, would you like me to organise for one of the crystal dragons to fly you back to Goraburg?"

Kazimir blanched at the notion, but Ilya grinned like a child. "That would be most welcome, if you would be so kind. I have not yet had my fill of adventure, not to mention it will mean a much swifter return than my father had anticipated."

"Very well. I will speak with them as soon as we have discussed our next step." Lukys nodded to himself. "Kora, we'll need to know the location of the nearest Paradise so that we can test our theory. If we are correct, then we may begin the process as soon as possible."

"We'll be coming along too then, won't we?"

All eyes turned to Rilla as she spoke. She had every right to question them. The prophecy did name her, after all, and if any of them had good reasons to want the Paradises destroyed, it would be the four children who Shuut had taken from their Paradise.

"That was not part of our plan, no," Lukys answered carefully. "We may only be able to make arrangements for a very few people to come with us. There are only so many of us who would fit on the remaining crystal dragon."

Kora caught Aislen's eye. Her cousin nodded her agreement to what they had decided before. Kora returned the nod and firmed her resolve.

"It's not more than half a day by horseback." Kora tried to hide her smile as she foiled the king's plan. "Surely, the few who ride on dragonback can afford to wait for those who follow?"

She was still irritated that, after sending her out on her mission, Lukys had left her out of the previous night's proceedings. There was no chance she, or any of the Paradisians or Shuut, were going to miss out on the destruction of the first Paradise. It would mean too much to them.

"We shall discuss this later in the day," Lukys said, barely masking his anger. "For now, I shall escort Ilya and Kazimir to the pasture to secure their flight home."

"If you have no objections, I should like to join you," Eliséo voiced his request. Kora looked over to the elf in surprise. She hadn't noticed how close he was with the karliki, especially Ilya, but seeing the look that passed between them, she wondered how she could have previously missed it.

"Yes, certainly. Let us go now so we still have the rest of the day to work on our plans," Lukys announced. Before he left, he turned to the three young lintep. "I know you won't want to, but you all need to attend your lessons this morning. We don't need to cause any extra commotion in the castle. The rest of us will meet with others who need to be involved in the planning. After your lessons, you will be able to find us in the council chambers."

Kora saw the doubt written on their faces. "I promise you, I will not let them leave for the first Paradise without you."

They smiled, but she only had eyes for Plyke. She had rarely seen such gratitude towards her freely shown on his face. She savoured it.

Chapter Eight – Preparations

Eliséo followed Ilya, Anya and Kazimir out of King Lukys' chamber. They had arrived in Illaria two nights ago, spent a single night in the castle, and already two of them were leaving. He couldn't deny that he had been hoping Ilya would be the one to stay behind, if only to spend more time with him, though he well understood the duty, which bound him to return home as swiftly as possible.

There had not been any word that Vladimir had infiltrated Goraburg, but every day they were away left Mikhail at extra risk. If only there was some way to ensure the capture of Vladimir and his devout followers.

Eliséo was consumed by these thoughts and barely noticed when they reached the karliki's rooms. He waited outside with Lukys while Ilya and Kazimir gathered their possessions. There were last minute things they would want to discuss privately with Anya. Much as he appreciated that, Eliséo wished he could have a single hour with Ilya for himself. It seemed they were to be denied that once again.

The karliki emerged from their chamber shortly afterwards. King Lukys led them towards the pasture. Eliséo kept pace with Ilya and noticed, with gratitude, that Anya and Kazimir lengthened their strides to give the old friends some privacy.

"I didn't want to go," Ilya told him suddenly. "They had to fight me into submission. I wanted to stay here with you – help destroy the Paradises. I still don't like the idea of being Mikhail's heir, but father needs me now more than ever. That's how they convinced me that I must go."

"I know," Eliséo replied, swallowing the lump in his throat.

"Anya didn't really want to stay. She wanted to be home for the birth of her brother's first child. I threatened that I would stay if she left. That's the only reason she agreed to it ... I really don't want to leave you again so soon."

"I know." Came the same reply, more difficult than the first.

"We'll see each other again, my friend. I'm sure it will be soon."

Eliséo didn't reply, but looked down to find tears in his friend's eyes to mirror his own. There was nothing more to be said. They both knew that Ilya's hope for them to meet again soon was just that – a hope. Neither of them could predict what path their lives would take. Neither of them were entirely free to do as they wished – one the heir of the karliki clan, the other the ambassador for the elves and a secret prince.

As they walked through the pasture, towards the crystal dragons, Eliséo felt the heaviness on his shoulders. Why was no part of his life really his own to do with as he wished? Being the ambassador afforded him some amount of freedom, but it was not nearly so much as he hoped.

"King Lukys." He turned to the lintep. "I would consider it a personal favour if you could convince Celtan to keep a vigilant lookout for Vladimir Mikhailovich once Ilya and Kazimir have returned to Goraburg. He poses a serious threat to Lord Mikhail and I do not wish to hear anything untoward has occurred which we are in a position to prevent."

"Certainly, if you would like me to," replied Lukys slowly. "Though, I don't understand why you can't ask them yourself."

"Pyrid might agree to it, but I don't think I'm in a position to request anything from Celtan for a while to come," Eliséo answered evasively.

As they drew closer to the crystal dragons, Celtan and Pyrid turned their snouts towards the company. Eliséo stood quietly as King Lukys made his requests of the dragons, both to escort Ilya and Kazimir home and to keep a lookout for Vladimir. To his surprise, Celtan readily agreed to these requests.

"I am quite keen to return to the Drakos Mountains," he rumbled, "but Pyrid insists that he wishes to stay and see this first destruction through. I will gladly escort Ilya and Kazimir back to Goraburg as I should very much like to discuss certain things with Mikhail.

"If Vladimir is as reckless and ambitious as I have been led to believe, then it would be best to keep all knowledge of the crystal heart as restricted as it has been in previous years. We crystal dragons are a formidable foe when full size, but the young ones ... we don't want them to be targeted by Vladimir in an attempt to harvest more hearts if he learns the true nature of them. That can only lead to more trouble for everyone."

"More crystal hearts," Ilya mused. "Would it be possible for just one more heart? So that we can always keep one in Goraburg while the other is travelling the Outworld."

Celtan growled lowly. "It's dangerous enough to have *one* crystal heart in the Outworld. I don't want to imagine the havoc another one would wreak."

"It was only a suggestion," Ilya replied defensively, hands in the air.

"You and your *suggestions*," Kazimir chided the younger karlik. "It's time we get home and tell Misha the news. I'm sure he will be interested in our discoveries."

Ilya nodded and turned to King Lukys. "We thank you for your hospitality and urge you to remember our words about Anya Nikolaevna. She has complete authority over the crystal heart in our absence.

"Anushka," he said, turning to the blonde karlik, "you will be sorely missed in Goraburg, but I believe it is the right decision for you to remain with the crystal heart. I trust your judgement, and so will my father. Do what you think is best in each situation."

As Ilya made his farewells, Eliséo stood silently, his face a blank mask. Kazimir came and shook him by the hand.

"Look after our Anushka, won't you," he said quietly, not wanting Anya to hear. Eliséo nodded, looking briefly towards the master stonemason. "If there ever comes a time when I can send Ilyusha back to you for a short while, I shall do so. I too have known the pains of a friendship outside my boundaries ... It makes for a difficult life."

Eliséo blinked at the old karlik in surprise. Kazimir's eyes were full of sadness as he turned towards the sapphire dragon. It had never occurred to Eliséo that any other karlik might have had an elf, or even a lintep or human as a close friend before.

As Kazimir was lifted up to the spikes on Celtan's back, Ilya walked over to Eliséo and drew him further away from Anya and Lukys. "Well, old friend, it's time. I can't thank you enough for helping me to convince Misha to let me come along. Try not to take too long destroying those Paradises. The sooner you finish, the sooner you can come to visit me in Goraburg again."

"Let's hope so, Ilyusha." Eliséo bent down and embraced his friend – each time more difficult than the last. After his fifty-year exile from Goraburg, he treasured every moment with Ilya, but they were gone too soon.

Wiping the tears from his eyes, Eliséo stood straight and tried to regain some semblance of composure, though he knew his feeling were blindingly obvious to everyone.

Ilya was lifted to the spikes on Celtan's back behind Kazimir. The two karliki settled into place, each holding the spike in front of them, Ilya looking much more comfortable than Kazimir.

Without warning, Celtan rose to all four legs, spread his sapphire wings and beat them against the ground. The force of wind rushing towards them almost knocked Eliséo, Lukys and Anya off their feet. Eliséo braced himself against the rest of the blast, his chest aching at the sight of Ilya flying away on the back of a crystal dragon.

* * *

When Celtan was just a sparkle in the sky, Lukys turned his attention to Pyrid. He liked the fire opal dragon, which he thought was strange, considering his general distaste for crystal dragons. Eliséo had once mentioned that the different coloured dragons had different effects on him, but Lukys had never felt them himself until now. He found it rather disconcerting not knowing whether he could trust himself around these creatures, however, it seemed he had no choice in the matter. If they were to destroy the Paradises, the dragons, or their hearts, might be the key.

"Pyrid, I fear we must trespass on your good humour a while longer," Lukys spoke to the remaining crystal dragon. "The nearest Paradise is quite close. However, there is a certain amount of planning to be done before we set out. I doubt we will depart today. The lintep of Illaria have been made aware of your presence, so should you wish to spread your wings, please feel free to do so."

"Planning is a nice word for negotiations." Pyrid laughed loudly. "I thank you for the offer, but I promised Master Edric I would not worry the horses any more than necessary. I fear that my coming and going would certainly break that promise."

Lukys bristled at the dragon's assumption that he was heading straight into negotiations. He nodded curtly to Pyrid and turned towards the castle, Eliséo and Anya following him closely. This was going to be a long and exhausting day.

Lukys entered the Council Chambers and stopped dead in his tracks. The room was bustling with activity and more people than he had expected to find. In addition to Aaron, Aurelius, Kora, Aislen and Guiscard, he found Braedan, Luisella and Pér.

"What is the meaning of this?" he demanded as he slammed the door shut and strode over to his seat at the head of the table. He was surprised when Kora walked calmly to his side.

"Uncle, I know you must have your own ideas of how we are to deal with the problem of the Paradises, but you can't take everything on your shoulders. The six of us had been regularly meeting to discuss this very problem even before I left to find the Paradises.

"Last night we had quite a discussion about many things you may not have had a chance to think about. I believe it will be in everyone's best interest if all of us, including the children and Shuut, are included in your plans."

Lukys struggled to keep his temper. Kora hadn't even been back at the castle for an entire day and was already wreaking havoc in his court. It didn't help matters that his own daughter was in league with her. At least Aislen had the good grace to avert her eyes, but he could tell she was anything but sorry for her actions.

"I see that I have little choice in the matter." He bit back a sharper retort. "If everyone will take their seats, we have much to discuss."

He waited until all were seated, Aaron by his right as usual, and Guiscard to his left. The others arranged themselves as they saw fit. He was unreasonably irritated by how close Kora sat to Pér. Lukys had never been overly fond of the lyrics Pér strung together in his songs. Even though the man himself was quite likeable, Lukys couldn't pretend that he was glad the man had chosen to live by his family's trade rather than pursue a life as a minstrel. Dragging himself away from such thoughts, he began the meeting.

"As I'm certain you are all aware by now, we have discovered a number of things about the Paradises since Kora's arrival. What some of you may not know is that Master Aurelius has recently made an interesting discovery. Due to that, we believe we may have the answer to how the Paradises were created."

A murmur rippled amongst those gathered. Lukys held his hand up for silence.

"Please do not ask me to divulge this information as we may not yet be entirely safe from Lishe and I don't want to give her the opportunity to torture the information out of anyone.

"What we need to discuss at the present moment is the location of the nearest Paradise and who will be going to that site in order to try to destroy it. I know that everyone in this room wishes to come, but I do not think that a wise idea."

"If you'll permit me, I believe that is because you haven't thought of all of the consequences of your actions," Kora blurted out before he could stop her.

"Kora, you may be my niece, but do not think that you can overrule me in my own castle." He warned her in a low voice.

"Father, in this one instance, I suggest you at least listen to her," Aislen spoke to him firmly. "We discussed a number of things last night and the end result means that the more of us present at the destruction of the Paradises, the better."

Lukys struggled in vain to keep his temper in check. He was furious that his daughter, his heir, sided with Kora on such an important matter. What made it worse was his certainty that she had a good reason for doing so. Aislen was not fickle by nature so, he knew she had come to the decision slowly and thoughtfully.

"For you, Aislen, I will hear Kora's suggestions." Lukys relented, with a sharp edge to his voice. "I do not make any promises to act on those suggestions, but I will listen to them."

"Thank you, father." Aislen said, then turned and nodded at Kora.

"Thank you, uncle." Kora smiled at him. He did not return that smile. "I know your main objective is to destroy the Paradises, and it sounds as though you have indeed found a way to do that. We're not disputing that fact or asking you to include us in that side of it.

"What we're thinking of is what happens *after* you destroy the boundaries. If the Paradise is a peaceful one, it may prosper as it always did, but it will not have any money to trade with any other village. We will need to help them sell their extra wares either here, in Illaria, or in other human villages to set them up on their way.

"If, instead, it's as dangerous a Paradise as the one I lived in, once you destroy the boundary, the Paradise leader and his or her followers may attack you or the other Paradisians, if they side with you. Are you happy to have that bloodshed on your hands because you don't take enough lintep to defend yourselves and the innocent Paradisians?

"Now think about the future of these people. Whether the boundaries are destroyed peacefully or not, what will happen after that? They will be seen as a weak community to Outworlders. There are no locks on their doors or windows. They have no weapons and no idea how to defend themselves. You will have been responsible for exposing them to these conditions by destroying the boundary, which gives them some measure of safety. Have you considered how to prepare them to rejoin the Outworld?"

Lukys listened to Kora grudgingly, but as she continued he became quite impressed with what she was saying. It irked him that she was correct. He hadn't thought of any of these matters – only about destroying each and every Paradise before Lishe could steal the power of the boundaries for herself. It was going to make the entire process slower than he had anticipated.

"You've identified a number of problems, Kora dear, but have you considered the solutions yourself or are you calling on us to consider them now?" Aaron asked his daughter. Lukys hid a smile. If he'd tried to say something similar, he would have been on the receiving end of quite a rebuttal, however, coming from her father, Kora softened a little.

"We've thought of a few ideas of how to work with each of these issues, but it will require more lintep than you have currently decided to involve. We will need a skilled healer or two, a number of guards, some master tradesmen and, most importantly of all, lintep who are not afraid of, or disgusted by, humans." Kora didn't hesitate one bit. It was clear she had had a well thought out plan. Lukys felt ashamed that these details had never crossed his mind.

"Might I make a suggestion," Pér spoke up. "If the first Paradise you destroy is the nearest to Illaria, then if any of the humans need to flee or relocate until they can defend themselves, we could always bring them within our borders, just on the outskirts of the farmlands."

"Pér, much as I don't want to dismiss your idea out of hand, I would have a riot on my hands if we did that," Lukys replied sternly.

"Your lintep will never change if you don't try something different," Kora pointed out. Lukys took a deep breath instead of yelling at her.

"I think you will find that we *are* trying something different, simply by helping the humans find a safe way out of their Paradises," Lukys told her pointedly. "That is change enough."

Kora was about to protest once again when Lukys noticed Aislen gently rest a hand on her arm and shake her head. At least his daughter had not completely lost her senses over this ordeal.

"We have a lot of work to do, then." Lukys began to sort through the list in his mind. "Guiscard, can you talk to Kayte? Ask her if she is happy to help and if she can think of any other healers who would be willing to join her. I understand Rilla has quite the gift for healing and asks for a chance to use her skills. If Kayte thinks it a wise idea, she can take the girl under her wing.

"Aaron, I'll need you to talk to some of the master craftsmen in town. If we can have a blacksmith or two, they can help with the locks. A carpenter or builder might be useful to have along as well.

"I'll talk to the guards myself. They may be reluctant, but they are loyal. That leaves Edric to you, Aislen. You should ask Pyrid how many people he can carry, so we know how many horses we'll need.

"Kora, we'll need the exact location from you and any other information you can recall about this particular Paradise. Eliséo, Anya, Pér, if you can work with Kora to see what else we need, that would be most appreciated.

"Aurelius, I need you to talk to whichever masters or mistresses you think might be willing to help us. Kora is right – we don't know how the humans will react and we may need all the help we can get."

With those final instructions, Lukys stood from his chair and dismissed everyone. As people began to file out of the council chambers, he noticed Aaron softly close the door behind them and turn back with a look of concern.

"I realise this has all happened rather suddenly, Lukys, but I think we should make sure to follow through with the plans we made about Lishe. We need to discover any knowledge that was lost to most of us, find out from Pér Kora what the three of them were taught, and teach whoever we think is capable of helping us."

Aaron's words were no surprise to him. Kora had arrived so soon after their meeting with the past and current council members, that they hadn't really had time to implement any of their decisions. There was also the matter of teaching students extra skills, if they asked and were deemed worthy, though he doubted they would need to worry about that for some time to come.

"You're absolutely right, Aaron," Lukys replied, rubbing his forehead with his long fingers. "How long do you think it will take for you to talk to the craftsmen in town? Will you have time to do both tasks before the day is out?"

"I might," Aaron answered uncertainly. "It would be better if you ask Kynon to help me. He is ... surprisingly willing lately. It may not be in our best interest to send him out into the town, but I think he would work well with the old council members to document rare or forgotten skills. He is keen to keep his family safe from Lishe."

Lukys raised his eyebrows at the suggestion. He rarely thought of Kynon as an asset when trying to run the city. His younger cousin's lack of enthusiasm for any sort of political life had always been a sore point between them. With Eliséo's comment about the crystal heart, weeks ago, Kynon had surprised them all with his reaction. Since then, he had certainly seemed to turn a new leaf. Perhaps this could be the best way for him to finally begin acting like part of the royal family.

Chapter Nine – Forced revelation

Rilla walked to her morning class with butterflies in her stomach. She'd promised Eliséo she would not say anything about the previous night. It would be a long wait before she would find out whether she was allowed to join the others to witness the destruction of the first Paradise.

She found Miette waiting for her outside Mistress Isis' classroom. With the confusion and activity brought about by Kora's return, Rilla had forgotten about the reward they had won from Mistress Isis. Now, more than ever, she wished no one had suggested they learn to shoot fire from their fingers. If Miette hadn't overheard that suggestion, she would never have asked to learn it. Rilla doubted Mistress Isis would have asked the council about it yet and, with everything else going on, she wondered if the council would care to debate the question.

Rilla ignored Réne's attempt to goad her as they took their seats. Instead, she turned her attention to Mistress Isis. This was a difficult class for her at the best of times. She needed to learn control in this class. How would she ever do that today?

"We will continue on from our last lesson, with different partners please." Mistress Isis called the class to attention. Rilla was grateful for different partners. She didn't fancy having to work with Réne again – not after what he'd said about her sister. He had not forgiven her for breaking his nose, even if Guiscard had healed it.

"As before, each pair needs one lantern and one glass of water," she instructed them. "First group, using a small amount of your own heat, light the lantern and recover your heat. Second group, transfer that heat to the water, leaving no flame behind. First group, transfer the heat from the water to one of your white stones. Second group, transfer it back to the lantern.

"Continue until the end of class. It does not need to be done quickly. It simply needs to be done with the minimum amount of heat lost between transfers. I will observe everyone. Please be careful, as this is a task that requires both skill and concentration."

Skill and concentration – it would have been the perfect combination for Rilla on any other day.

"Do you want to go first?" Miette asked softly. Rilla shook her head. The initial lighting of the flame was her worst skill. It was in trying to light a flame from the heat in the air, which had made her lantern explode when Mistress Isis tested her.

Without questioning her, Miette simply stared at the wick of the lantern. In a few moments, she'd created a flame and sat back with a smile of satisfaction. It was so infectious that Rilla couldn't help but return the smile before she set to work on her task of transferring heat from the flame to the glass of water.

She reached out her power and dipped part of it into the water. Extending the same tendril out, she let it touch the flame. Careful not to let any of the heat come back towards her, she slowly transferred it along the tendril from the flame to the water.

Once the steam appeared, Miette sat up with mild surprise. The quiet girl took a small white stone from her green velvet pouch and placed it on the table. Rilla waited until her new friend completed the task. When Miette sat back again, she watched Rilla's every move.

Rilla hoped Miette's reaction wouldn't be like Réne's when he had discovered her skill level. Tapping her teeth together for a moment, Rilla sat forward, closed her eyes and took a deep breath. This was the difficult part – lighting the flame from the stone. It should be just the right amount of heat, but anything could happen without care.

From the corner of her eye, she saw Mistress Isis idly walking around the room, heading towards them, seemingly by chance. Her teacher must have been able to sense at least some of the turmoil within Rilla.

She closed her eyes again and drew in deep, steadying breaths. As she opened her eyes, she sent out a tendril of power to the stone. Without thinking, she tried something different. She drew all of the heat from the stone and kept it safely at the tip of her tendril. Careful not to let any of that heat escape into her body, she directed the tendril to the lantern's wick and pushed it quickly out. The flame was initially a bit larger than it needed to be, but soon settled without any mishaps.

"How did you do that?" Miette asked in surprise. Mistress Isis came and placed a hand on the mousey haired girl's shoulder to quieten her.

"I took the heat from your stone and transferred it to the lantern," Rilla replied in confusion. "Isn't that what I was meant to do?"

"That's not what I meant," Miette said in a quieter voice. "I mean, how did you make the flame so bright to begin with? There can't have been enough heat for that. Did you use some of your own heat?"

Rilla shook her head.

Another skill I do differently!

She looked over to Mistress Isis for help. How could she explain everything to Miette when she didn't know what she was and was not meant to be able to do with her power?

"I think you will find that Rilla uses her power in a unique way, Miette," Mistress Isis explained. "You were taught by your parents when you were young and then by the masters and mistresses when your parents thought it was time. Rilla has not had that luxury and has adapted to being a lintep quite quickly. She works with her power in ways you cannot imagine."

"But ... there's only one way to light a flame," Miette pointed out. "How can she create a larger flame than was there in the first place without using any of her own heat?"

"Rilla, can you explain how that happened?" Mistress Isis turned to her. Rilla stared between them, caught with indecision. She'd been warned not to tell other students how she was doing things differently. Why was Mistress Isis asking her to do exactly that?

"Well, I suppose when I drew heat from the flame in the first place and transferred it to the water, I didn't take it all at once, so there was more heat in the water than in a single flame."

"How did she do that?" Miette looked up at Mistress Isis. "That kind of control ..."

"As I said, Miette, Rilla works with her power differently." Mistress Isis smiled down at her. "No doubt, you would have taken the heat of the flame all at once, snuffed it out, and transferred it immediately to the water. Rilla performed the task in a different way with rather interesting results, wouldn't you say?"

Rilla cringed as Réne sauntered up to them. "You always tell us not to experiment, Mistress Isis. Why is Rilla exempt?"

Mistress Isis looked up at him with fire in her eyes. "Réne, I've taught many of you since your beginner classes in the castle. I told you from that day not to experiment because you could hurt yourselves or others."

"We're not in beginner classes anymore," he pointed out coldly, "and you never lifted the rule for us. Not once."

Rilla held her breath at the fight she knew was about to occur because of her. She was so startled when it didn't immediately happen that she looked up to see Mistress Isis glancing at her apologetically. Rilla's stomach turned to ice.

"Rilla is exempt from that rule because she doesn't know how you were taught in the first place," Isis answered loudly enough for the class to hear. "Everything Rilla does with her power is an experiment for her because she only recently discovered she was a lintep.

"Now, you want to know why that should make a difference? Rilla, why don't you tell them why you will never experiment with anything dangerous ever again."

"What?" Rilla asked aghast. "No!"

"Are you afraid we'll discover you're a fraud and shouldn't be in this class?" Réne goaded her.

"That's the least of her concerns, Réne," Mistress Isis chided him. "Go on, Rilla. It's all very well me giving examples in class of what *could* happen but if they hear from you what actually *did* happen, then they might finally understand the restrictions placed on them."

Rilla's heartbeat quickened. All of her teachers, in fact every older lintep, had warned her against this. What was Mistress Isis doing?

"I almost died once," she started.

"I heard you almost died a number of times," a boy from the back of the class called out, snidely. Rilla recognised him as one of Réne's friends. Anger bubbled inside her chest.

"This time in particular was because I took so much heat out of myself that I almost froze to death. I only survived because Nyssa made it across the river in time to restore enough heat to my body that it didn't completely shut down. Before that, I only stopped draining myself of heat because one of my friends shook me out of the stupor I had fallen into from the shock of what I was doing.

"I burned four massive humans beyond recognition. They had no chance of surviving once I started shooting fire at them. After that, the forest started burning and we were trapped. We had to experiment again to find a way through the burning trees before Lishe could catch and kill us. We didn't know who was after us at the time, only that it was an extremely powerful lintep who would kill us as soon as look at us.

"It was the most terrifying time I had in the Outworld. The only reason we survived the ordeal was because I experimented and forced Nyssa to experiment. However, we wouldn't have been in so much trouble in the first place had I not experimented and burnt those men."

The entire class stared at her in shocked silence. Rilla knew rumours of what had happened to the Paradisians in the Outworld had spread like wildfire throughout the castle, but none in so much detail.

She looked over at Miette and saw a deathly pale face. Rilla hoped she would understand her fear of learning the skill. Surely, Miette would change her mind.

"But, if you hadn't experimented, you and your friend would have died, wouldn't you?" one of Réne's friends asked her, finally finding his voice.

"Yes. Probably," replied Rilla. "I would never have done it otherwise. We were two untrained teenagers against four mercenaries. Everyone else was too far away to help us. Arishen had a vision of what would happen. He told me and I did it."

"So, it's not that your experiment almost killed you – you had no choice. It wouldn't have been so bad if you'd known what you were doing in the first place," Miette pointed out. Rilla's heart sank as she realised that the girl had not changed her mind about their reward. "What I want to know is how you even knew what to do."

"I told you, Arishen had a vision of me shooting fire at them," Rilla repeated herself.

"Yes, but how did he explain it to you so that you understood what to do?" Miette persisted.

"He didn't. We'd seen Nyssa do something similar in the Drakos Mountains, but only for a moment. I figured it out from that." Rilla shrugged, not really knowing how to explain the way she worked with her power. She glanced over to Mistress Isis to see a satisfied smile as she looked around at the students. Rilla followed as her gaze settled on Réne. He looked just as shocked and horrified as most of the students.

"I hope this explains why Rilla is exempt from my rule of not experimenting," Mistress Isis said in a quiet voice. "If there is nothing else, then I suggest you all get back to your lessons and stop assuming you should be able to do everything that Rilla does or work the way she works."

Miette and the others took the hint and returned to their tasks without a word.

After class, Rilla wanted nothing more than to hide in her room but first, she headed towards the Council Chambers.

"I'm sorry, Rilla." She heard Mistress Isis behind her. Rilla stopped, but didn't turn. "I know I put you in a terrible position and you probably didn't want to relive the horror of that day, but they had to know or Réne and all of his friends would have held it over you for the rest of your time in Illaria."

"It didn't change Miette's mind," Rilla said as Isis moved up beside her. "She still wants to learn how to do it."

"I understand that you don't want to hear this, but that's not as bad an idea as you assume it is, Rilla. I *can* teach you how to do that safely, so that if you're ever in a similar position again, you can protect yourself."

She knew Mistress Isis, and Miette for that matter, were right about this, but it didn't stop her breaking into a sweat at the thought.

"Just think about it," the young mistress said as she walked towards the dining hall. Rilla stared in shock. Had Mistress Isis had already spoken to the Council of Masters about her and Miette? Had they been granted leave to learn the powerful and dangerous skill?

She tried to shake the thoughts from her mind as she rounded the corner to the Council of Masters. Not surprisingly, the door was locked. She knocked on it just as Plyke and Shuut came up behind her. There was no answer. Rilla panicked at the thought of being left behind until she saw Kora coming out of the stairwell by the council chambers.

"Where is everyone?" Rilla asked.

"There was quite a discussion this morning, after you left for your classes," Kora informed her. "Turns out that we weren't as prepared to destroy a Paradise as it pleased some people to think. We've each been given tasks before we go on our first journey. Uncle Lukys hasn't said when we'll leave, but I doubt we can go before tomorrow."

"What kind of preparations?" Shuut asked curiously. "Please tell me someone suggested they bring enough people to defend the innocent humans against people like Erton and every other fool in the Outworld with more weapons than sense."

At Kora's smirk, Rilla realised that was precisely one of the things King Lukys had underestimated. She shook her head in wonder that he thought his responsibility would be over once the boundary was destroyed.

"Actually, Rilla, you may want to find Mistress Kayte sometime today." Kora turned to her. "There was mention of you wanting to test out your healing abilities again, in a more controlled and safe environment. This may be your chance to do so. Guiscard was going to talk to her about it."

Rilla's anger over her class dissipated like mist. She ran down the hall, not stopping until she saw the door with the serpent around a stick.

Rilla knocked until she heard hurried footsteps. As the door opened, she glanced inside to make sure none of the other students were there and then barged her way in and shut the door.

"Please let me come with you!" she practically yelled at the teacher. Mistress Kayte looked at her in confusion.

"Rilla, whatever are you talking about? Come with me where?"

"Guiscard hasn't been to see you yet?" Rilla asked. "He's going to ask you to help with the destruction of the Paradises – to go along as a healer to make sure no one dies if there is a conflict. *Please* tell me that I can come too! He's going to suggest you do so to let me test my skills."

Rilla was talking so fast in her excitement that she almost didn't hear the gentler, less frantic knocking at the door. Mistress Kayte left Rilla standing there in agony and went to open the door once more.

The librarian peered around the opening and into the room, breaking into a smile when he spotted Rilla.

"Why am I not surprised to see you here?" he asked, trying to suppress a laugh. "How did you find out so quickly?"

Rilla, with renewed hope, returned the smile. "Kora told me."

"Guiscard, will you kindly tell me what is going on?" Mistress Kayte asked annoyed. "Should Rilla even be here for this?"

"Yes, of course, Kayte," Guiscard replied, placing a hand on the fire teacher's shoulder. "Why don't we take a seat so I can explain properly?"

Rilla followed them to one of the groups of chairs around the room. She was so anxious and excited that she could barely contain herself. Guiscard waited until she was settled before elaborating on her garbled message to Mistress Kayte.

"Now Kayte, you know that we are currently engaged in determining the best method to destroy the Paradises? Well, we think we've stumbled across something that might work," Guiscard told her.

"Already?" she asked, eyebrows raised.

"Well, it isn't a certainty," the librarian admitted, "but we do hold great hopes for the plan. We need a number of things to execute it properly. You, my dear, are one of those things.

"It has come to our attention that the destruction of the Paradises may not be an entirely peaceful process. In fact, we have been led to believe that it may cause significant bloodshed."

"So you want me to come along to heal whichever humans are too weak or stupid to defend themselves?"

Mistress Kayte's words stung Rilla. Until a few months ago, she'd thought she was human herself. Rhanya had been a human and would have needed the healer's help were he alive. Rilla bit her tongue at a sharp retort. She needed to keep a level head.

"It may not be just humans who are hurt, Kayte," Guiscard pointed out to her. "There will be a number of lintep in attendance and we don't know how appreciative the humans will be. From what we've learnt, it's entirely possible that many of the Paradise leaders are lintep themselves, who could cause even more damage than humans."

Mistress Kayte silently looked between Rilla and the librarian. Rilla didn't take her gaze off the healer. She knew she would be there for the destruction of the Paradise – Kora had already secured that for her – but to have a task such as this would be more than she had hoped for. She had wanted to help in the infirmary, but Mistress Kayte had refused for fear she would cause more injury than anything else.

"What about Rilla?" Mistress Kayte asked. "Whose suggestion was it that I take her under my wing for this little … adventure?"

"It was, in fact, the king's suggestion." Guiscard's admission shocked both Rilla and Mistress Kayte.

"King Lukys?" Mistress Kayte confirmed hesitantly. The old librarian nodded. "Well, who am I to refuse my liege? Rilla, you will stick by my side every step of the way. If you overstep, I will move you back to the beginner class until you can prove you know how to listen to your teachers. Is that clear?"

"Crystal clear," Rilla replied, still in shock.

Chapter Ten – Mistress Isis

Isis knew it had been a difficult lesson for Rilla. She'd put the girl in an unenviable position, but there had been no other way to drive her point home to her class. Even the gentle and quiet Miette needed to learn that lesson. However, she was aware of the fact that she had forced Rilla to do what she had explicitly been told not to do. It was the reason Isis was on her way to see King Lukys – that and her need to discuss the proposed rewards with him.

Rilla was understandably reluctant, but if she were to play any part in the destruction of the Paradises, she would need to be more prepared than the last time she entered the Outworld.

Even though most lintep knew she was the youngest mistress and extraordinarily skilled with heat and cold, they didn't understand just how powerful she was. She was one of the few lintep in Illaria who could send her power out across the entire island surrounding the castle, which is precisely what she did now to find King Lukys.

He was down in the outer courtyard, near the guardhouse. Isis quickly passed by the dining hall and picked up a freshly baked roll and a crisp green apple before heading going to find him. As she walked closer, she could see King Lukys deep in conversation with Nicodemo, the head guard. Not wanting to disturb them, she leaned back against the bright yellow sandstone wall and nibbled the roll.

It appeared to be a heated debate, as far as the guard was concerned. Isis knew the castle guards were all fiercely loyal to King Lukys, whatever they were talked about had to be controversial enough for Nicodemo to argue against it.

Eventually, Nicodemo nodded and grudgingly walked back into the guardhouse. Isis caught the king's eye as he turned away from the guard. She saw a mixture of relief and anguish, before he wiped his expression clean.

"Mistress Isis, what can I do for you?" he asked, as they headed back into the castle. "I'm on a busy schedule, but I have some little time to spare for you."

"I think we had better talk behind closed doors, my king," she replied gravely. King Lukys looked at her curiously, but did not press for answers. It still amazed her that the king would bother wanting to know anything about her and spared time for her whenever she requested it.

He led her to his personal chambers. She had rarely been invited there, but in the past few days it had become an increasingly common occurrence. As she stepped into the amazingly lavish antechamber, her breath caught in her throat, as it did every time. Isis had been raised on a farm in the outskirts of Illaria. Even though she now lived in the city and had her own classroom in the castle, neither had any fancy trappings.

King Lukys closed the door and gestured to one of the magnificent chaises. She sat, slightly flustered as the king sat beside her.

"Now, Isis, what has you so worried?"

"It's Rilla, actually, and Miette," Isis answered, half regretting the consequences for what she had forced Rilla to do.

"Rilla?" Lukys asked in surprise. "If anyone, I would have expected Kayte to complain about her."

"Kayte? Why?"

"I may have made a comment which left her little choice but to take Rilla under her wing when we destroy the first Paradise," Lukys answered with a wave of his hand. Isis' thoughts raced ahead of her.

"That makes what I'm going to say just a bit more urgent than I thought. You see, Rilla and Miette won the reward for their research topic and it has been suggested I teach them something I would not normally teach them." Isis cringed as a scowl appeared on King Lukys' face.

"What was the suggestion?"

"Have you heard everything Rilla did with her powers in the Outworld?" Isis didn't know how to continue.

"You're referring to her rather spectacular display of fire, are you not?" King Lukys asked her, sitting back with a sigh. "I knew this day would come. I thought we would have more time to work out how to deal with it. They've asked you to teach them how to do it properly, haven't they?"

"Actually, Miette asked. Rilla is reluctant."

"Smart girl," Lukys sighed. "There's nothing for it though. You're right. It's more urgent she learns how to do it properly now that she's going back into the Outworld. How long do you think it will take to teach her?"

Isis chose her words carefully. "It would probably take no more than a single lesson. She has already figured it out. Whether she realises it or not. I cannot predict how long she will take to master it, though I doubt it will be long."

"What about Miette? Should I be teaching her as well?"

"I see your dilemma." Lukys rubbed the stubble of his beard. "Rilla *is* exceptional. Surely her fellow students understand that. Would it be so bad to teach Miette a safer version of what you will teach Rilla?"

"Ah, that actually brings me to the other reason I needed to see you." Isis averted her eyes from his penetrating gaze. "I ... may have forced Rilla to tell my class why she is allowed to experiment in her lessons when the rest are not.

"I could tell that she tried to discreetly dissuade Miette, but it didn't work. Miette seems more determined than ever to learn it now."

Isis sat uncomfortably as Lukys kept his deep brown eyes trained on her. She fixed her eyes on her feet.

"I was under the impression that most of her teachers were asking Rilla *not* to tell their students of her experiences in the Outworld. I understood they did that so that other students would not be encouraged to experiment. Tell me, why is it you've done the opposite?" Lukys asked her curiously. Isis remained silent. "Isis, there's no condemnation. I just want to know why you decided to go against what her other teachers have decided. I understand there was some minor falling out between you and Kayte over how you tested Rilla for your class."

"Perhaps because I'm the youngest mistress, " Isis replied faintly, smarting at the fact that rumours had spread about that. "Perhaps I haven't learnt the art of teaching as the older masters and mistresses have in their experience."

Isis blushed as King Lukys lifted her chin with the tips of his fingers. "Isis, I don't believe that for a second and neither do you."

Isis finally looked the king in the eye. She expected to see some form of reprimand, but there was only kindness and curiosity. It prompted her to tell him the truth.

"I think most lintep in Illaria are scared of Rilla. Not just for the amount of power and skill she already possesses with such little training, but for the way she could completely change how lintep in Illaria use their powers.

"The same thing happened to me, though to a much lesser extent, when I was younger. I could have become a mistress much younger than I did, but the older council members were afraid of the skills I possessed. Many of them are still quite cruel to me when they can afford to be, perhaps because they are jealous or afraid.

"I don't want the same thing for Rilla. She's had enough to deal with in her life. She doesn't need the extra restrictions that everyone is placing on her powers.

"Did you know that it took less than a day for the girl to realise that a lintep can manipulate the way you feel just by touching you? Most of my students still don't know that and they've lived here all their lives. By the time they finally realise it, it's become a normal part of their life and they don't think to challenge it.

"Rilla's not like them. She refuses to let anyone touch her. That was probably the first time she got herself in trouble here. The other masters and mistresses don't want her telling the other students because it might influence the way they react to it. They might not let their teachers have any skin contact and that will change the way they conduct their lessons."

Isis knew she should stop before she said too much, but she couldn't help it now that she had started.

"Rilla's other teachers don't want her telling students anything, because they're afraid students might experiment. That's just naive! *Of course* the students experiment! They may not do it in their lessons, but I can guarantee you most of them experiment with each other, or alone, almost every evening.

"The reason I wanted Rilla to tell my students about her experiences in the Outworld was so that they realise *some* forms of experimenting are dangerous, but not all of them. That's why they all know that Rilla is exempt from that rule in my class. I allow her to experiment because that's how her power works and I think it unfair for any of the other masters or mistresses to punish her for it."

Isis finally bit her tongue. She'd done it now. She had spoken out against them – against the way they had taught for probably hundreds of years. Worst of all, she'd said it to her king, who had the power to strip her of her status as a mistress and banish her from Illaria. She blinked back the angry tears that threatened to fall, but kept staring at King Lukys.

The king sat silently in his chair, so silently that Isis wondered what punishment he would choose. Her mind ran to Rilla. Had she just hurt the girl's chances of having any sort of normal life here in Illaria? Surely her uncle wouldn't banish her for Isis' decision that morning.

"Isis, I have a task for you," Lukys finally spoke. "Something I think you will enjoy, should you choose to accept it. I warn you that it may make you even more unpopular among your peers, but I think you are the only one suited to the task. I want you to head the committee that decides which lintep should be allowed to learn extra skills."

Isis sat up in shock. "You want me to be *part* of that group?" she asked hesitantly.

"No, Isis," Lukys shook his head. "You heard me correctly. I want you to *lead* that group, to be in charge of it. Your word will be final on every matter. What do you think?"

"I think ... I think you expect too much of me," she lowered her eyes once more.

"Isis, of all the lintep in Illaria, I have watched your progress the closest," he informed her with a gentle voice. "I have seen all of your struggles. I noticed the cruelty of your fellow students. I knew how much more difficult they made your test to become a mistress. I still see how the other masters and mistresses treat you – those who are afraid or jealous of you. It's true, this position may make matters worse, however, they will also know that *I* have appointed you so they will not dare second guess you.

"I have the ultimate faith in you, Isis. Just as you have in Rilla. All I ask is that you try to have a little faith in yourself and give every student in Illaria a chance to shine."

As he was speaking, Isis lifted her eyes to meet his. How had she never discovered how closely he'd been watching her progress? How had he found out all of that about her? There must have been other lintep telling him. Other lintep who ...

"Master Aurelius is one of them," Lukys told her, before she'd voiced the question aloud. "Mistress Kayte is another. I asked them both to keep an eye on you and report everything back to me – both your triumphs and your low moments. I know almost everything that has happened to you since you first came to live in the castle as a student. It hasn't changed just because you moved into the city. I *still* keep a close eye on you."

"I ... had no idea," she whispered. "But, why?"

"Have you not guessed?" he asked her with a smile. "I think you are spectacular, with your powers and skills. It would have been so easy for you to become arrogant and proud. Instead, you became humble and, well, brilliant. You are one of my favourite lintep in Illaria.

"Aislen was just as keen to follow your progress as I was. In fact, on a number of occasions, she asked me to intervene on your behalf, but I knew you could handle yourself and it would only undermine your abilities.

"This position I offer you is the first time I can intervene without making it obvious. You deserve it more than any other master or mistress in Illaria. Please accept my offer."

Isis wiped the tears from her cheeks. She stared at King Lukys in wonder and almost blushed again at the thought that he knew so much about her.

"I'll accept it on one condition," she told him. "All the restrictions placed on Rilla need to be lifted. The poor girl is already under so much pressure to learn as much as she can and fit in. She gets in trouble over rules she doesn't know exist. She's had such a difficult life both in the Paradise and the Outworld. We don't need to add to that if we can to prevent it."

Lukys' smile broadened. "I knew you would do it. I cannot make the decision about Rilla immediately. Just as I couldn't save you from everything you experienced. I won't be able to save Rilla from everything, but I am making as many concessions as I can. After all, there must be at least a dozen lintep in Mistress Kayte's class who should have been chosen to help her in the Outworld, but I chose Rilla. That will have to be enough for now. Agreed?"

"Agreed!" Isis smiled and wiped the last of the tears from her eyes. "Now, what about Miette?"

"She can be your first case. I will ask for a few other volunteers for the committee and then, together, you shall decide what she should learn."

Isis readily agreed to his terms. She got to her feet, thanked him for his time and left his chambers. For a moment, she stood outside, leaning against his door, trying to take in everything that had just happened, then walked away with a smile to find Rilla.

Chapter Eleven – Dangerous questions

Rilla bounced with excitement – she was finally going to be a healer! She was going to help people in ways that Rhanya could only ever have dreamed.

Free for the afternoon, Rilla searched for something to occupy her so that she wouldn't think about the next day. The dining hall had almost emptied by the time she arrived. None of her friends or cousins were there. The bell had already tolled for the start of afternoon lessons.

For a moment, she considered going out into the town to find Arishen, but knew that he would be hard at work with Master Timothée and would not be impressed if she came to distract him.

Taking a small plate of food, Rilla sat by herself on one of the long wooden benches and resolved to ask Nicodemo for a weapons. No sooner had she finished eating than Mistress Isis walked into the dining hall, headed straight for her. Rilla couldn't think of anything she'd done since her morning lesson to make the ice and fire mistress seek her out so resolutely.

"Rilla, I understand you have a free afternoon. I wonder if I might steal your time?" Isis asked without giving any hints away. Rilla simply nodded and followed the mistress out of the dining hall, up the stairs to her classroom. They entered in silence. Mistress Isis locked the door behind them.

"I'm going to suggest something to you and I don't want you to respond until you've heard everything I have to say," Mistress Isis told her. Rilla remained silent, curious to hear what she would say. "King Lukys has asked me to teach you the very skill that Miette suggested you both learn. I have agreed to this under the condition that Miette is also considered for this extra skill.

"I'm not certain when Miette's case will be considered, but King Lukys has impressed upon me the fact that you will soon be venturing into the Outworld again, therefore we have decided your need is immediate. Will you allow me to teach you how to safely draw as much heat as you need to use fire to defend yourself?"

Rilla shied away in horror. She had spent the entire morning trying not to hurt herself with fire, make a lantern explode or let a flame burn out of control. Now she was being asked to perform an even more difficult task.

"Isn't this something we should leave until I'm in your advanced class?" she asked hopefully. "I mean if I was actually capable of something like this, you would have put me in that class to begin with, wouldn't you?"

Mistress Isis gently led her to a set of chairs with a table between them. "Rilla, I know how much this particular skill scares you. I'd actually be more concerned if you weren't as terrified of it as you are. However, the fact remains that you are a target in the Outworld. Any human could decide to attack you when you least expect it, as you've already experienced. Not to mention that if Lishe somehow finds out where you are, she won't hesitate to try to kill you on the spot.

"I don't think she would bother trying to steal you power, great as it is, a second time around if there are other lintep who can protect you. It would take too much time. Her best option would be to kill you out of hand. You need to be able to protect yourself from her. *Please* let me teach you one way to do that."

Rilla panicked at the idea that Lishe would find her again. It almost made her want to run to Kora and tell her that she didn't want to go – that she didn't want to leave Illaria until the rogue lintep had been found.

"I'm sorry to have mentioned her, Rilla," Isis said, reaching out a hand to pat her cloth-covered knee. "But you can't forget about her just because she was driven away once. A person like that won't stop until she has achieved her goal, which includes killing you to stop the prophecy so that she can take all of that power for herself."

"And you think you can teach me to defend myself against her?" Rilla asked, finally finding her voice. "Even when Arishen's vision of Nyssa showed that she tried to attack Lishe with fire, only to have it turned back against her."

Isis looked at her with something akin to pride. "You know better than anyone that you are nothing like your mother when it comes to your powers. That was almost certainly the first time that Nyssa had attempted to use fire like that.

"Lishe had already been torturing lintep for their power years before that day. That's why it's so important you let me teach you now. I can help you learn the skills you'll need and hone them, so that Lishe will have a fair fight on her hands should she face you again."

"You ... you promise you won't get angry with me?" Rilla asked her suddenly. "I mean, if I make a mistake or blow up another lantern."

Mistress Isis' smile surprised her. "Of course not, Rilla. That's all part of learning. You can make as many mistakes as you like. I won't let you hurt yourself and if you hurt me, then Mistress Kayte is just in the next room. Now, are you ready?"

Rilla nodded, hesitantly.

"Good." Mistress Isis smiled at her. "First, I need you to tell me how you managed to gather so much heat in your test that you made the lantern explode. I asked you to use heat from somewhere other than your own body. What did you use?"

"I tried to copy what King Lukys did," Rilla told her. "He got so angry with me once. It felt like the room got colder, even though there was fire in his eyes. All I could think was that he took the heat from the air itself and drew it into himself, so I tried to do that."

"Oh, well done Rilla!"

Rilla was taken aback by the praise.

"That was a very clever deduction indeed! I think King Lukys underestimated your abilities at the time, or he never would have done something like that. He now understands his error and is trying to help me give you more freedom and extra guidance where you need it most.

"Now, what I want you to do is practice that very skill this afternoon. It's important you get it right because if you take too much heat from the air, it will become too cold for anyone to breath. By the same token, if you release too much heat into the air surrounding you, you run the risk of burning your lungs when you take your next breath."

Rilla listened to her teacher in fascination. She had no idea that the fire and ice side of her powers could have so many facets to it.

"Can I take heat from different parts of the room, so I don't cool any one part of it down too much?" she asked, running the ideas through her head.

"You can indeed, but it requires slightly more skill than you currently have in this area and you may not be able to do it if you're distracted. So, just for now, I want you to simply practice gathering a ball of heat in front of you, from the air directly surrounding us and then releasing that heat back into the air without burning us. Do you think you can do that?"

Rilla shrugged. "I can try."

Mistress Isis sat back and folded her hands in her lap. Rilla knew her calm composure did not mean that she was relaxed, but it made her slightly more at ease.

She concentrated on the air around her. It was cooler than it had been when she first arrived in Illaria. Cooler even than when Shuut had arrived and Lishe attacked. There wasn't so much heat in the air anymore, but she concentrated on it nonetheless.

Closing her eyes, she pulled a few tendrils of power out of her wall and let them flow freely around herself and Mistress Isis. Without thinking about whether it was possible or not, she tried to gather heat from the entire length of each tendril. As soon as she realised it was working, she drew it all together into a ball of heat in front of her. When she felt the air she breathed in cool down significantly, she stopped gathering heat and slowly guided the heat in the ball back through her tendrils, spreading it out evenly among them, being very careful not to let any of that heat enter her body. Once she was satisfied that it was evenly spread among the tendrils, she slowly dispersed it back into the air until it was once more the same temperature it had been when she started.

When she opened her eyes again, it was to see a look of satisfaction on Mistress Isis' face.

"I told King Lukys it would only take you one lesson to understand the concept," her teacher said proudly. "Now let's see how quickly you can master it. I want you to keep doing the same thing in as many different ways as you can think of until you find the one that suits you best. After that, I will show you how to use that heat as a flame."

"Mistress Isis, I have a question." Rilla hesitated. "If Lishe attacks me, and never in any other circumstance, what would happen if I took all the heat out of the air immediately surrounding her, or if she leaves herself unprotected, her actual body?"

Isis' face turned serious. "You've just asked the question that probably made them restrict this knowledge in the first place, Rilla. You would kill her, if you did it quickly enough and she wasn't prepared for it, but ... even in that case, if she was going to kill you otherwise, just know that people will see you differently if you do that."

Rilla knew what she meant. She would be seen as a murderer – the same as her father was in the Paradise. The only difference would be that she would have been defending herself, rather than attacking someone unprovoked and unprotected.

"Don't you think they already see me like that?" she asked Mistress Isis, eyes downcast. "If they've heard any of the rumours, they'd know that all of us killed people in the Outworld. Do they not already see me as a murderer?"

"Oh, Rilla," Mistress Isis cried out and leaned forward to embrace her, making sure not to make skin contact. "No, my dear girl, they would not think that at all. What you did was an accident. It resulted in their deaths, but it was an accident." Mistress Isis pulled away from her. "The difference with Lishe, if you kill her like that with your power, would be that everyone would know you had planned to do it. This skill I'm teaching you requires a lot of practice and control. If you stripped heat from the air around her, or from the rogue herself, you would have to know exactly what you were doing. You may think it's necessary, but just try to remember there are other ways to incapacitate someone, even a lintep."

Rilla nodded her understanding and resumed her lesson for the afternoon, trying not to dwell on the reality of using her powers against Lishe. She didn't want to admit to herself that she would do almost anything necessary to stop the rogue lintep.

Chapter Twelve – Final preparations

Aaron trudged up the long stairwell to his cousin's chambers. As he knocked on the door, the sound of voices from behind it abruptly stopped. A moment later, Lukys ushered him in. Aislen was sitting on her favourite chair with a cup of tea warming her hands from the chilly night air. Aaron smiled wearily as he sat across from her, glad for the comfort of the luxurious chaise.

"Did you have any luck with the craftsmen?" Lukys eventually asked him, sounding as tired as Aaron felt.

"There are some few who are willing to help, however, they made a good point when they said their services would not be needed immediately," Aaron told Lukys, before turning his attention to Aislen. "Your group of revolutionists was right to think of them, but the Paradisians won't instantly need to sell their wares or protect their houses once we destroy the boundary. It will take time for word about the destruction to spread to any other human settlements.

"Aside from that, I understand from my grandchildren it is not likely they would have extra wares as they only produce what they need. So a handful of craftsmen are happy to help when they are actually needed."

Aislen nodded. "Thank you, Uncle. I doubt that many of the townspeople would have agreed to help humans at all if it weren't for your words of persuasion."

"I had quite a time convincing some of them." Aaron smiled ruefully. "But there were others, like Master Timothée, who know that humans are not to be feared or hated. It was mostly thanks to those good men that I managed to convince as many as I did. I fear Pér's suggestion to bring humans into Illaria, even temporarily, will certainly cause the riots Lukys fears."

"Yes, well, Pér was always more controversial than the rest of us," Aislen laughed. "He would have followed Kora into the Outworld on her mission had he but known she was going."

Aaron stiffened at her words and avoided Lukys' quick glance in his direction. Enough had been said about that deception. His little girl was back home and that was all that mattered.

"Did you speak with Edric and Pyrid?" Aaron asked Aislen, turning the conversation to safer ground. She nodded.

"Pyrid is ready to take flight at a moment's notice. He thinks he can safely carry four or five people at a time. Edric will keep all of his horses available for us, so that means, at most, another twenty people can travel. How many are we planning on, father?"

"Well, the three of us, no doubt," Lukys replied, scratching his chin. "Anya, Kora, Pér, Aurelius, Kayte, Rilla, Plyke, Shuut, Guiscard. I suppose that's the minimum."

"I think you will find that both Rilla and Plyke will hotly protest if you do not include Tika and Arishen in the company," Aaron pointed out to his cousin.

"Yes, I suppose you're right," Lukys agreed with a shake of his head. "Then any other masters or mistresses Aurelius has convinced to come with us, but I doubt that will be more than a handful.

"Nicodemo has offered up ten of his guards. That makes twenty-four, not including the masters and mistresses, so that may change depending on how many Aurelius managed to convince to help us. We'll have to leave it at that, unless we want Pyrid making multiple trips."

"Are we setting out in the morning then?" Aislen asked her father. He shook his head.

"It's too late now to get word to everyone who is needed. We wouldn't be ready until tomorrow afternoon, and by that time it would be dark before we reach the Paradise. It will be dangerous enough to do this as it is, I don't want to do it in fading sunlight. We can organise everything to leave the morning after.

"I don't want to delay any longer than that. If we succeed, the race will be on to destroy all of them before Lishe figures out how we did it. If not, we will still need to figure out how to destroy them."

"Has anyone thought to notify Cook Palmyra that we will need food for the journey?" Aislen asked. "That's quite a large company of people to feed for a day or two." Aaron and Lukys shook their heads. "Very well, I'll go and pay her a visit now to give her plenty of notice."

Aaron stayed seated as Lukys saw his daughter out. He had always gotten along well with her and knew she would make a fine queen when her time came, though he was disappointed she had never borne any children. It was too late for her now, and she would be forced to choose an heir from among her cousins. With the recent additions, that would now make quite a difficult choice for her when the time came.

"Are you ready for this?" Aaron asked Lukys as he returned to his seat.

"No," Lukys answered truthfully. "I had no intention of destroying the Paradises myself, nor of it happening so quickly after Kora's return. When I sent her out all those years ago, it was really just to have a clear record of where they were if we ever needed to know.

"I cannot help but think something will go wrong. There is no way Lishe can find out quickly enough to stop us, but if she is anywhere near Illaria, she will definitely notice Pyrid flying overhead with horses following him."

"Do you think we won't be able to stop her a second time?" Aaron asked him, feeling slightly insulted at the thought.

"Not at all," Lukys reassured him. "I fear what she will do when she realises what has happened. She's not one to take this lying down. I'm certain she will find some way to hamper our progress or distract us so that she can attack Rilla."

"It's an interesting topic. If it appears we can destroy the Paradises without her, why is Rilla named in the prophecy?" Aaron mused aloud. It was something that had been bothering him for some time now.

"I'm not sure," Lukys answered, holding his head in his hands. "Perhaps only *she* has enough power, using the crystal heart."

"She is certainly powerful," Aaron agreed, "but I doubt she has more power than I do. Besides, though he keeps it well in check, Plyke may well be more powerful than Rilla."

"If that's the case, I can't understand why she would be specifically named in the prophecy over anyone else in our family, particularly your side of it," Lukys answered, as much at a loss as Aaron. "Unfortunately, we can't change the fact that she *has* been named, so we will have to bring her along to each destruction, just in case, which means all of the Paradisians will be coming each time. Perhaps it's one of the four of them and not necessarily Rilla who is the key to the destruction.

"Whatever the reason, we can't change it now. Let's try to get some rest before morning. There is much to set in motion before we depart."

* * *

Aaron woke to the sound of bells tolling. He hadn't slept in this late for a long time. Rubbing the sleep from his eyes, he pulled the silver handle by his bed twice. There would be no food left in the dining hall at this hour and he would need enough to sustain him through the day.

Thinking of all he still had to do, Aaron decided to call on Kynon before his cousin decided to waste his day away. After quickly slipping into fresh robes, Aaron hastily walked the short distance to Kynon's chambers and knocked loudly. There was a shuffle from within before the broad shouldered lintep opened the door, his brown hair sticking out at all ends.

"You look terrible," he said as he motioned for Aaron to step inside.

"No worse than you," Aaron returned the compliment with a shake of his head. "I've just rung for food. Get dressed and come to my chambers. I have a task for you."

Without awaiting his reply, Aaron headed back to his own chambers and left the door ajar. The night before, Lukys had given him all the information from the Full Council of Masters and Mistresses. It was an important task he would be handing to Kynon. He hoped he had been right when he'd told Lukys that their cousin had changed for the better.

He was already seated at his large dining table, paper spread out before him in small piles, when Kynon joined him. Aaron looked up and hesitated for a brief moment before motioning his cousin to sit across from him.

"Lukys agreed with me when I suggested you were the person to help us with this. We're going to be quite occupied over the next few days, possibly even longer than that, and I don't want this task to go unattended during our absence."

"Absence?" Kynon raised an eyebrow.

Aaron frowned at his confusion until he remembered that Kynon had not been present at most of their meetings of late. Before he could answer, there was a knock at the door. Aaron went to let in the scullery maid who had brought his meal. When she noticed Kynon was there too, she handed a second tray to Aaron with a curtsey before leaving.

"What absence?" Kynon asked impatiently.

"A number of us are to travel into the Outworld for a short time," he explained. "While we're gone, I would appreciate it if you could follow up on our meeting with the Full Council of Masters and Mistresses."

Aaron began to eat, only noticing Kynon's silence when he finally looked up from his food to see brown eyes staring at him intently. Feeling slightly self-conscious, he put his cutlery down and returned the gaze.

"When were you planning on telling me about this journey to the Outworld?" Kynon finally asked him. Aaron was taken aback. It wasn't like his cousin to care about his comings and goings.

"I thought I just did," he pointed out levelly. "Though I'd barely call it a journey – more of a day trip."

"And you expect me to simply accept that without asking anything further?"

Making a rash decision, Aaron decided to tell Kynon *most* of the discoveries of the previous few days. He elaborated on everything other than Aurelius' discovery of how Paradises might have been created and what the crystal dragons had told them about the true nature of the crystal heart. Very few people knew that and Aaron agreed with Lukys that it was best to keep it that way.

"So you see, it may be a very short journey indeed," Aaron ended. He watched Kynon carefully, while making a show of sorting through the papers in front of him.

"How many lintep are going on this 'short journey'?"

"No more than twenty-five people," Aaron answered, taking another bite of his food.

"*People.* I see. That means not only lintep will be attending this event."

"Kynon, what exactly did you expect?" Aaron answered calmly. "Pyrid will need to fly some of us. Anya is in charge of the crystal heart and is taking that responsibility very seriously. She won't go anywhere with us unless Eliséo accompanies her. Then there's the matter of the children. Do you honestly believe that any of them would agree to be left behind when they're the reason we realised why the Paradises have to be destroyed? They who lived in one of those creations almost their entire lives? Not even Lukys could stop them from coming and believe me, he tried!"

"So I'm the only royal lintep staying behind while the rest of you go out to play saviours?"

"Kynon, be reasonable. You know that's not the case. Daegan, Marilisa, Braedan, Luisella and the twins won't be coming either. Besides, what I need you to do is of equal importance. I would be doing it myself, were my daughter and grandchildren not insisting on seeing the destruction themselves. With Lishe out there somewhere, I would never forgive myself if something happened to any of them that I could have prevented."

Finally taking a bite of his own food, Kynon asked "What's this task then?"

Aaron drew a silent sigh of relief as Kynon's mood shifted.

"I need you to go through these notes from the council meeting. Somewhere in here is the key to what other skills Lishe has that we are, as yet, unaware of. If you could meet with the old masters and mistresses, perhaps we can see how the young rogue could have construed the information in any way other than what was intended.

"We know she's been stealing power, controlling and torturing lintep and searching for Rilla in the hopes of killing her. The truth is that we don't know what else she's capable of. Has she tried the mind snare on other lintep, or was her first attempt on Shuut? Does she simply keep experimenting, or did her classroom lessons somehow teach her all of this? We need to find out as much information as possible to have any chance of actually defeating her rather than simply driving her away for a time."

"You're asking the impossible," Kynon told him bluntly. "If she was in classes with your daughters the entire time, Kora should know what she's capable of. I doubt you'll discover anything from the masters or mistresses that Kora couldn't tell you herself. It had to have been over twenty years ago. I doubt our teachers have such long memories for individual students."

Aaron nodded. "You may be right, but if we question them the right way, they might discover links themselves between what they taught the girls and what experiments could have come from those extra lessons.

"As for Kora, she seems reluctant to discuss her days with Lishe. I don't want to push her on that. She has enough to worry about for now."

Lukys woke with a throbbing head. There had been too many late nights since the Paradisians arrived in Illaria. He'd had so much to contend with since granting the humans leave to stay within their stronghold. His first public audience after that decision had been fraught with angry and concerned townspeople.

Timothée and Edric had taken on one of the humans each as an apprentice. Both lintep were well respected throughout Illaria and the thought of them both taking humans under their wing was too much for people to bear, considering it was difficult enough for young lintep to be apprenticed to such talented craftsmen.

Increasingly of late, he had begun to allow Aislen to take half of the petitioners for herself. There were too many of them for him to deal with alone and that was only going to get worse when they started interfering with the Paradises, especially if it meant either or both of them would be away from Illaria for extended periods of time.

That last thought made the decision for him. He sent a tendril out to Aislen's chambers, hoping she would still be there. He was immediately rewarded for his efforts with the gentle touch of her power. A few minutes later, she knocked at his door.

"What troubles you, father?" she asked him without preamble. He smiled at her. She always knew just how to read his moods.

"Do you remember our last public audience?" he asked her.

"It was certainly one of our most animated," she replied grimly.

"I fear things will only worsen," he told her. "I don't think we can afford to miss any audience days and, though the people may be disappointed not to see me, they will be placated to speak with you instead."

Aislen sighed and shook her head. "You wish me to stay behind when you go off to destroy the Paradises?"

"I'd much rather have you by my side when we go to the first Paradise, however we both have to do what is best for our people. It will not do to have both of us away at the same time."

Aislen was quiet for a time. Lukys hoped she agreed with him or he would have yet another argument on his hands. He was exhausted and fervently hoped this would not be another of those conversations.

"Father, have you thought what might happen when the Paradises are destroyed? Are you certain you'd rather be the one there? It might be better for our people if you stayed behind and I went in your place."

It took Lukys a moment to realise what she was saying. He moved to sit by her side, taking her shoulders in his hands.

"Aislen, there is no doubt in my mind that our people would be happy, and well looked after, if you were ruling them. In fact, if the worst were to happen, it would be better for it to happen to me than you – you are younger by far and would have many healthy years left to rule them. I'm certainly not yet in the twilight of my life, but I harbour no delusions about who should be left to rule between the two of us."

Aislen stared at him with her big grey eyes that were so like her mother's. He saw them glaze over. Lukys drew his daughter into a gentle embrace, dreading what he had to say next. He had been putting it off for years, but with the possible turmoil on their doorstep, he could afford to do so no longer.

"Aislen, my dear, I have one more thing to request from you. It is not something you need to decide immediately – in fact, I hope you take your time with this decision.

"I have never found fault with you for not starting your own family, but it does pose somewhat of a problem in terms of a clear line of succession. Should something happen to me in the Outworld, you will become queen – that is an undisputed fact. However, when the time comes for the next ruler, there is no clear choice. Some might say it should fall to Lord Aaron as he is my oldest cousin. Though many lintep may accept this without question, they would not accept his oldest daughter's child for their next monarch. Nyssa's daughter she may be, but Shuut will always be seen as a banwep by many lintep.

"I'm not suggesting you choose Kynon over Aaron, but you may have to think carefully about who you would like to rule after you and name them as your heir as soon as possible after your succession. If you do this, no one can later dispute it."

He searched his daughter's face for any sort of reaction but found none. She was keeping her thoughts tightly locked within her walls and her skin out of his reach.

"Whom would you have me choose, father?" she asked without a hint of emotion.

"That is not for me to decide, Aislen," he told her calmly. "If I could think of anyone better than yourself to follow me, I would have no hesitation in naming them as my heir for the good of our people. However, you know my views on the matter – you've been well trained and the people adore you. You are the natural next choice."

"Let us hope the day is far off when such a decision must be made," she answered, getting to her feet. "I will stay behind as you wish. It will give me time to consider everything."

Lukys watched his daughter leave without pressing her any further. It was cruel of him to make her think these things the day before he departed for the Outworld without her, but it was something that could not be put aside forever. He hated to think what would happen with Kynon, Daegan or Marilisa as eventual rulers, but he freely admitted to himself that it would take quite a bit of persuasion to convince the people that Shuut, Rilla, Kora or Plyke should lead them instead. Perhaps it would be best for her to name Braedan as her heir – at least that way, they were certain to have a level-headed monarch who had lived in Illaria all of his life. The people would readily accept him, even if the rest of his family argued that they were ahead of him in the normal line of succession.

He did not envy Aislen her task, but before too long he would need her to make a decision. With the destruction of the Paradises and Lishe still in the Outworld somewhere, anything was possible – even his own death.

Chapter Thirteen – Miette

Miette watched Lord Aaron's grandchildren descend the twisted stairwell together. She hadn't seen them in the dining hall that day, neither before nor after their morning lesson, which was unusual, as they had shared most meals together since Rilla had befriended her in the library. As royal lintep, they were well within their rights to dine in their own chambers for every meal, but they rarely did.

The cousins parted ways in the long sandstone hallway, each going to their own classroom. Miette waited quietly as Rilla wound her way towards Mistress Isis' room. They hadn't spoken since Rilla had revealed her stunning history with fire to their class the morning before. Miette knew the red headed girl had tried to dissuade her from her lesson choice, but it was simply too tempting a prospect to give up.

Growing up on a family farm, on the outskirts of Illaria, Miette had always stood in awe of the lintep who lived in the town or the castle. Though she knew it had nothing to do with their power, it often seemed as though the less powerful lintep lived on the outskirts of Illaria. On the farm, she was seen as an anomaly. Her family had been so proud of her power as she grew up. She had more than any of them. It quickly became apparent that she had more power than lintep on the neighbouring farms as well.

She had never been happier than the day her father had informed her that she would begin classes in the castle the following week. It hadn't dawned on her that city lintep would jeer at her for being a farm girl. She hadn't contemplated that lintep like Réne would be wary of her because she didn't come from a powerful family. All she had thought was that she was going to be taught by the best masters and mistresses in all of Illaria – and she couldn't wait!

It had been a rude shock to realise that most of the other lintep in her classes refused to speak with her because she was younger, more powerful or more skilful than them. There were a few lintep likewise boarding at the castle, but none of them had grown up as close to the boundary as she had. At least those ones spoke to her kindly, if they bothered to speak to her at all.

Early on, she'd accepted that was the way it would be until she finished her training, but all of that had changed when Rilla befriended her in the library just a few short days ago. Suddenly, she'd gone from relative obscurity to a friend of Lord Aaron's granddaughter.

She couldn't pretend that it didn't chafe when Rilla tried to convince her not to learn as much as she possibly could about fire. The Paradisian had explained her reasoning, but it made no difference to Miette. She was here, in the castle, to learn as much as she could and make her family proud – if that also meant learning to protect herself from anyone who might wish to harm her, even better.

Miette greeted Rilla with a nod, not knowing what to say after their last words. They stood together silently, waiting for Mistress Isis to appear. Miette noticed an older boy walking up to them. She'd seen him around the castle, but had never spoken to him before. He could not have been more than a few years her senior. She held her breath as the dark haired boy stopped in front of them.

"You've got all the luck," he said to Rilla a shake of his head. "Master Aurelius and Mistress Isis!"

Miette noticed Rilla's smile before the girl replied. "Well, I'm not sure how lucky I'll count myself tomorrow. It will be my first lesson in Mistress Kayte's advanced class. She's bound to make certain I know exactly how painful her lessons can be."

The boy whistled lowly. "To be placed straight into her advanced class, I've no doubt that she wants to be certain you know what you're doing. The test to get to the intermediate class was bad enough – I've no desire to try for the advanced class any time soon."

"Kalydron, run along to Mistress Vika's class," a voice behind the boy made him turn. Miette spied Mistress Isis opening classroom door. "Talking with two pretty girls is no reason to invoke her anger. You can speak with Miette and Rilla after class."

Kalydron, Miette thought to herself. *He's one of the lintep who won a prize for seers and prophecies. How does Rilla know him?*

"Of course, Mistress Isis," Kalydron replied with a grin before turning his hazel eyes back to Rilla. "See you after class then."

Miette turned to watch him walk away, missing the fact that her classmates had already entered Mistress Isis' room. Belatedly, she realised her lapse in concentration and ran to find a seat beside Rilla, only to notice that one of Réne's friends was already there. She looked around the classroom with a sinking feeling. The only free seat was the one beside Réne himself.

"Little Miette, come sit by me," Réne called out to her as though she were a child. Miette felt her face flush in anger and embarrassment.

"That's enough, Réne," Mistress Isis instantly silenced him. Miette was glad her teachers felt no animosity towards her, but sometimes their reprimands of Réne and his friends only made things worse for her. The young student inwardly sighed and took her place beside the bully.

"I'm setting a new task for this lesson. You will work with your partner to transfer heat back and forth between two lanterns," Mistress Isis informed them. "This may seem an easy task, however, I want you to do it in a particular way. The initial source of light will be from the fireplace."

Miette, along with all the other students, were startled by the sudden combustion of wood in the fireplace. It took her a moment to realise that Mistress Isis was talking again.

"You will each light a lantern from the fireplace then, working together, you will transfer that flame at the same time as each other, to your partner's lantern. I will demonstrate for you once and then you may begin."

Miette watched closely as Mistress Isis stood behind the large desk at the front of the class. The fire mistress lit both lanterns in front of her. Miette watched in amazement as the two small flames detached from the lanterns and travelled slowly through the air to the opposite lantern before alighting on the wick.

A gasp went through the class at the amazing display. Miette had never seen such a thing done before. From the sound of her classmates, neither had they. The mousey haired girl turned her attention towards Réne to notice her amazement mirrored in his eyes.

Well, she thought, *at least this is one lesson where he doesn't already know the skill before we begin.*

"I cannot stress this enough – you must work *with* your partner. If either of you tries to work independently of the other, we may end up with exploding lanterns. I'm only warning you once that you'll both be cleaning the mess should that occur.

"Also notice *how* I transferred the flames. I didn't draw the heat out and transfer it to a different source, as you've done in the past. I moved the flame itself. If this proves too difficult for you, you are free to do it the way you've been doing it so far."

Miette stood with the rest of the students to get a lantern. Réne had moved quickly to discuss the task with his friends, leaving Miette free to find Rilla.

"I don't know how I'm going to get through this lesson. I'm certain Réne will figure out this skill quicker than I will and hold it over my head all afternoon," she whispered to Rilla. The green-eyed girl looked at her intently.

"You're a smart girl, Miette. Just ignore him and focus on your own skills. Imagine how good it will feel if *you* figure it out first." Rilla winked at her conspiratorially before getting one of the last lanterns and returning to her seat.

Miette found herself smiling at the thought of being able to learn the skill faster than Réne. She took the last remaining lantern and walked slowly back to her seat, trying to figure out how to do it.

"Hurry up," Réne chided her as she returned to her seat. "Here in the castle, we move faster than on the farms. You should know that by now."

Miette ignored him as best she could. Jibes like this had quickly become Réne's normal way of talking to her. She'd been in the castle over a year now, but it still nettled her whenever she was made fun of for growing up on a farm.

She took her seat and placing the lantern on the low table between them, then concentrated on the flames in the fireplace. It was unusual for Mistress Isis to ask them to experiment in their class, but since Réne's outburst in their previous lesson, it wasn't wholly unexpected.

Somehow, she would get a flame to travel the short distance between her lantern and Réne's. Miette closed her eyes briefly, sending out a tendril of her power to the fireplace. She drew heat in the only way she knew how – pulling the heat into her tendril, but not bringing it back to her body. When she was certain she had just enough to light her lantern, she brought her tendril back and carefully pushed the heat onto the wick.

To her delight, she'd lit her lantern before Réne, which gave her a precious few moments to consider her next move before having to transfer the flames. She thought back to her lesson with Rilla, and remembered that it was possible to draw more heat out of the flame than was there to begin with, but that wasn't what she wanted to do. Mistress Isis had transferred the flame itself. How had she done that?

"Let's do the first transfer like we normally would," Miette suggested. "Just to get into the rhythm of it."

To her surprise, Réne simply nodded. There was no jibe, no snide comment. Silently, they both snuffed their flames and relit them in the opposite lantern. By some unspoken agreement, they continued to do this, giving them time to come up with any idea of how to transfer the flame itself. After they'd been working on their task for over ten minutes, Miette found herself completing the task without any effort whatsoever.

How did she do it? she asked herself over and over. She glanced over at Rilla to see she had already completed the task Mistress Isis had requested and couldn't help but feel a little envious of her. *No, not how did Mistress Isis do it. How can I do it?*

In that moment, she saw the answer clearly. She'd been trying to mimic her teacher's actions without knowing how it was done. Finally, she turned her mind to her own strengths. What was *she* capable of with fire? What did *she* think was possible?

With a small smile, she finally tried something new. Instead of drawing the heat into her tendril of power, Miette surrounded the flame with her power, careful not to snuff it out completely. She lifted the small orb of power from the wick of the lantern in front of her and fought to keep her concentration as the flame moved away from the wick. It flickered and floated just above the wick for a moment as she gazed at it in wonder.

Quickly noticing that Réne had already lit that lantern once more, she gently pushed her orb towards Réne's lantern and carefully positioned it so that the flame could touch the wick. It instantly took to the wick and steadied itself once more.

"I did it!" she exclaimed quietly, looking up to see the amazement on Réne's face.

"How did you do that?" he asked her without any trace of his usual superiority. Miette was torn with indecision. She was saved from making a choice by Mistress Isis' sudden appearance.

"Well done, Miette." Mistress Isis' brown eyes sparkled as she smiled. "Only a handful of you have managed it so far. I don't want anyone explaining how you did it. I understand all of you were keen to experiment and any explanations will prevent that from occurring."

Miette nodded, as did Rilla and another three students. To her surprise, neither Réne nor any of his friends complained about this latest restriction.

"Let's get back to it then," Réne said, as he snuffed his flame once more. Miette lifted her flame in an orb and repeated the task over and over the rest of the afternoon.

As soon as the bells chimed, students began returning their lanterns to the back of the classroom. Réne still hadn't worked out the skill, though a number of other students, including some of his friends had. Miette, not wanting to see how long his good humour would last, quickly returned her lantern and followed Rilla closely out of the room.

She noticed that Rilla was heading towards her chambers rather than the dining hall.

"Rilla, weren't you meant to meet Kalydron after class?" Miette asked, not wanting to miss the opportunity to be introduced to another lintep who might talk to her. To her relief, Rilla stopped and turned with a smile on her face.

"I'd almost forgotten. Come on, let's find him in the dining hall."

"Are you sure he won't mind me coming too?" Miette faltered. "I mean, I don't really know him."

"It won't be a problem," Rilla reassured her. "I only met him a few days ago myself. Let's hurry though – I promised Kora, Eliséo and Anya I'd dine with them tonight."

Miette nodded, trying to hide her disappointment. Rilla and her family had become a beacon in her castle life. Eating in the main dining hall had always been a lonely and, sometimes, unpleasant affair. Réne and his friends didn't often decide to taunt her there, but the occasions were often enough to make her wary. She always tried to sit near anyone who they avoided or, more rarely, respected in the hopes they would just ignore her.

Ever since the research day, Miette had finally begun to enjoy her life in the castle. Rilla looked back at her, a frown momentarily creased her brow.

"I'm sure Kalydron won't mind if you dine with him if you don't want to stay with Umi and Ulf. I don't think they were invited tonight. In fact, if they're there, you may not have a choice." Rilla ended with a laugh. Miette caught herself laughing along with the strange girl, half wondering if she'd somehow read her mind.

Rilla is too young and inexperienced to do anything of the sort, isn't she? Only the most gifted masters or mistresses can do that... Miette dismissed the thoughts running through her head. If Rilla could read her mind, she surely would have reacted to those thoughts.

It didn't take long to find Kalydron. He was waiting for them in the inner courtyard, near the entrance to the dining hall. With a bright smile, he waved them over to him.

"I thought you might have singed yourself in Mistress Isis' class," he teased Rilla as they approached.

"Not Rilla. She's the most skilled student in our class." Miette found herself answering before she could stop herself. Kalydron looked over at her thoughtfully with his hazel eyes.

"I've seen you around the castle quite a bit recently," Kalydron said.

"I think you've yet to be introduced," Rilla quickly stepped in. "Kalydron, this is Miette. She and I..."

"...won the prize for medicines and herbs," Kalydron finished her sentence. "Yes, I remember. Pleased to make your acquaintance, Miette."

He held out his hand to her. Miette froze in surprise. Most lintep in the castle didn't try to befriend her so quickly. It took a nudge from Rilla before she shook his hand.

"I was hoping you might keep Miette company for me," Rilla said, breaking the silence. "I forgot I'm to dine with Kora, Eliséo and Anya tonight."

"The elf and the karlik? Well, how can I compete with that? I suppose I'll have to content myself with asking the lovely Miette about your fiery exploits then," he joked. Miette noticed Rilla pale at his offhand comment.

"There's not all that much to tell," Miette deflected. "I'd much rather talk about what you discovered that won you the prize for seers and prophecies."

Miette caught Rilla's thankful look before she bade them farewell. Kalydron watched Lord Aaron's granddaughter until she disappeared into the stairwell leading up to her chambers.

"So, Miette, would you do me the honour of keeping me company in the dining hall?" Kalydron turned to Miette with a spark in his eyes. "I may yet find out all there is to know about her mysterious past with fire. There were rumours all through the castle yesterday and I'm certain you know the truth of the matter." Miette cringed at the thought, but followed him into the dining hall nonetheless.

Chapter Fourteen – Paradise

It was early morning when Rilla awoke. The bed beside was empty. Her sister was dressed and waiting for her in their antechamber, tending to her weapons. Rilla smiled to herself. Of course Shuut would want to take her weapons with her. She would feel completely defenceless without them in the Outworld.

Unlike herself and Plyke, Shuut still hadn't managed to use her power as everyone assumed she would be able to do now she had Nyssa's power. Rilla hadn't asked her, but it seemed as though Shuut kept Nyssa's power locked tightly within her wall and had not attempted to use it.

She could understand that, to a certain extent. It would feel quite strange indeed to have someone else's power inside her. Rilla doubted she would want to use it either, but she was in a different position to Shuut – she had a significant amount of power of her own. Besides, Nyssa had freely given that power to her – she shouldn't feel bad about using it. Rilla decided it was a topic best left unspoken.

"Get your weapons ready before we go." Shuut looked up at her as she entered the room. "Your lintep powers are all well and good, but sometimes a sword is all you need and I hear you've been having lessons from the castle guard."

Rilla laughed at the memory. "Yes, he underestimated me a little. Lord Aaron neglected to tell him I'd been trained by an elf weaponsmaster and a banwep."

"That *would* have been interesting," Shuut agreed, laughing.

Within a few minutes, Rilla and Shuut were ready to go. They headed down to the dining hall, hoping to meet some of the others there. The previous night, Kora had named a handful of people going on the expedition. The only thing she had promised was that all the Paradisians and Shuut would be going.

As the sisters walked down the stairs, they caught up with Plyke.

"I wonder if King Lukys understands the power he is unleashing with us," Plyke remarked. Rilla saw his eyes dart to their weapons and noticed the axe strapped to his back. "Tika will be in the dining hall. I'll be surprised if he hasn't eaten half the food by now. We should hurry if we want anything for ourselves."

Rilla walked at the back of their group as they hastened down the stairs. She kept an eye out for Miette, even though she knew it was too early for her to be up and about yet. She hadn't been allowed to tell her friends about their sudden journey. Privately, she wondered if that was such a good idea. They would certainly notice the absence of a number of lintep in and around the castle, even if they didn't hear the horses leaving the city or see the dragon fly overhead. How was that to be explained to people?

She entered the hall with Plyke and Shuut, and immediately spotted Tika, Kora, Eliséo and Anya at their usual table. Rilla took a single apple from the buffet table before she joined the others – the thought of the day ahead made her lose her appetite.

"Good morning, Rilla," Eliséo greeted her. It had been less than two weeks that he'd been away, but Rilla couldn't deny that she had sorely missed his company.

"Good morning," she returned softly, sitting close by his side. Even though she shied away from skin contact with most people, she almost craved it with the elf. "Have you discovered any more about what's happening today?"

"Not yet," he answered.

"No one seems to know very much," Rilla pointed out, taking a bite of her apple, "but looks like a few more people are coming with us."

Through the double wooden doors, Rilla watched as a number of lintep, including Master Aurelius, Guiscard, Mistress Isis, Mistress Kayte and Nicodemo, came to eat their fill. It was still too early in the day for them to be preparing for lessons and Rilla already knew that at least Master Aurelius and Mistress Kayte were coming with them.

She caught Mistress Isis' eye as she went to sit with her fellow teachers. They exchanged a smile, but nothing more. Rilla knew Eliséo had observed their short exchange, so she closed her eyes momentarily to send the memory of her private lesson to him. When she opened her eyes, the elf stared at her in wonder. He must not have expected her to learn those skills just yet. She found herself blushing at his unspoken praise until a commotion caused her to look towards the double doors once more.

King Lukys walked into the hall flanked by Lord Aaron and Princess Aislen. The cousins looked ready for battle. It was the first time Rilla had seen any of them dressed in anything other than the robes most lintep wore around the castle. Instead, they had close fitting leather pants and loose shirts with weapons strapped to their sides, though Rilla doubted they would have need of them, considering Lord Aaron's display of skill when Lishe had attacked.

"Why is Aislen dressed in her normal robes?" Rilla whispered to Eliséo. The elf shrugged.

Once the three lintep reached the table reserved for the royal family, they turned and faced those gathered. Lukys raised his hands for silence. The murmurs quickly died away.

"As you know, we travel to the Outworld today. Lady Kora has provided us with the location of the closest Paradise to Illaria. Pyrid will fly a select few, while the rest follow on horseback. This will give us a chance to scout the area before we begin our task.

"No doubt everyone will remember the trouble we've already had with Lishe. We will be doing everything in our power to guarantee everyone's safety today, including the residents of the Paradise itself.

"Princess Aislen will remain to watch over Illaria in my absence. Myself, Lord Aaron, Kora, Anya and Guiscard will ride with Pyrid. Once the rest of you have eaten, please make your way to the stables where Master Edric will have horses ready for you. Cook Palmyra has arranged for your saddlebags to be filled with waterskins and food enough for two days.

"We will leave once word has been sent that everyone is ready. Once we reach the Paradise. Pyrid will let us down and then guide the rest of you to us."

Rilla noticed the flicker of anger that passed over Aislen's face at the mention that she would stay behind and Kora was clearly surprised by the decision. Rilla saw her fight the urge to protest. Aislen was one of Kora's closest friends and, as Rilla had discovered the previous night, the key person involved in convincing King Lukys that he hadn't thought of everything about the destruction of the Paradises.

Within a half hour, everyone in the dining hall headed towards the stables. Rilla was pleased to see Arishen escorted into the castle courtyard by Timothée. Kora had promised none of the Paradisians would be left behind, but she couldn't help but breath a sigh of relief now that they were all together.

As Master Edric led the horses out of the stable, Rilla noticed the stable hands looking enviously at Tika as he stood with the company heading out of Illaria. A few of them came up to wish him luck in the Outworld. Rilla smiled that the lintep had embraced Tika so completely – it gave her hope that humans and lintep could exist side by side in the right circumstances.

It took another half hour for everyone to mount their horses and be shown what to do. Rilla had never ridden before, so she listened attentively as Master Edric gave them lessons in the basics of horse riding.

She glanced over at Plyke, who looked quite comfortable and familiar with his golden horse. She wondered if it was the same one he'd ridden for his reward. He and Tika were already walking their horses around the courtyard as if they'd ridden every day of their lives.

Once Master Edric had assured himself that everyone was ready to start riding, he led them to the castle gate and waved the guards to lower the wooden drawbridge.

Rilla looked around for Arishen and saw him riding at the back of the group. Not wanting him to be left behind the boundary again, she held her horse back until he had caught up with her. As they approached the magical barrier, she withdrew all her thoughts into her tower and held out her hand to him. She was surprised to see him hesitate before taking it.

Is he angry with me? She brushed the though aside as he smiled at her gratefully. Together, they walked their horses along the length of the cobblestone bridge, away from the brilliant sandstone castle.

She managed to pass through the marketplace without shuddering from the memory of Lishe. There was little chance the rogue lintep would dare attack her with all these lintep around her. With a twinge of apprehension, Rilla let go of Arishen's hand and looked him straight in his bright blue eyes.

"Will you tell me if you have any visions about Lishe today? Or … anything to do with our safety?" Rilla asked him hesitantly. "Even if you think its irrelevant, will you still tell me?"

"Of course, Rilla," the seer answered readily. "Master Reuben has been working with me of an evening to go through my dreams, helping me figure out a way to determine which are visions and which are simply dreams. In any case, most of my latest waking visions haven't sent me to sleep, so I should be able to help you like I did on the river bank …"

His words died away as he stared at her. Rilla felt the blood drain from her face. Although she'd spent an entire afternoon training with Mistress Isis, she didn't think she was ready to protect herself safely with that skill, even if Lishe did attack them.

"Don't worry, Rilla. There are enough lintep here to keep you safe today."

She smiled as he reconfirmed what she'd been telling herself all morning. Rilla leant forward to pat her horse on the neck in an effort to urge her to go faster. As soon as her hand touched the mare's neck, she felt a wave of power flow through her. She lifted her hand away as though she'd been burnt.

"What's wrong?" Arishen asked at her sudden movement. Rilla shook her head, but saw Plyke look back at the two of them with a look of concentration.

"I think I need to talk with Plyke," Rilla replied, spurring her horse into a faster walk. Plyke slowed his horse with a quick word to Tika who turned to Rilla for a moment before nodding at his Partner. Rilla was certain that something had happened on their horse ride the other day.

"What do you know that you're not telling me?" she asked as she caught up to him.

"The tables have turned." He smiled at her. "Isn't this exactly what happened to us with the lintep touch in the first place?"

Rilla simply raised an eyebrow at him. She watched as Plyke made sure they weren't within hearing distance of the other lintep before he elaborated.

"I rode Goldfire the other day, with Master Edric, Tika and Dorian. The first time I touched her, I could have sworn I felt her strength flowing in and around me. Not that I was taking any of it from her, just that she was showing me what she was capable of.

"I didn't think much of it until later in the day when we were learning to trot. I placed my hand on her neck and asked her to help me learn more easily than Dorian. I didn't know if she could even understand me or not, but I promised her an apple if she did it."

"So what happened?" Rilla asked, intrigued by his story.

Plyke grinned at her. "I ate fewer apples that day."

"Did you tell Master Edric?"

"Yes, but it isn't something he wants everyone to know. Most of the lintep in Illaria aren't as … unique in the use of their power as we are, so they probably wouldn't even feel that rush of strength when they touch their horses. It would be just like a human touching a horse and nothing more.

"He made me promise not to tell anyone this information lightly as it could be used against the horses and get Master Edric in a great deal of trouble."

"You have my word as well," Rilla reassured him. It was becoming irritating how different the two of them were to every other lintep.

Making sure that no other lintep were watching her, Rilla placed her hand on her horse's neck once more and took in everything about her. She was strong and graceful, with an energetic stride. Rilla leant down close to her ear, her long red plait falling into her mare's mane.

"Let's see how much fun we can have today. You teach me how to ride and I'll make sure to take as good care of you as Master Edric himself."

Just like Plyke, she had no idea if her horse could understand her, but the mare moved her head up and down as though nodding. Rilla patted her neck and urged her into a trot, trying to catch up to the others who had left her and Plyke behind.

Tika turned at their approach and smiled, knowingly. Rilla couldn't help but return his smile. Even though she saw Arishen's look of confusion from the corner of her eye, she didn't try to explain it to him. Thankfully, the seer didn't press her on the matter. It was uncharacteristic of him, but she was grateful for the change.

Over an hour later, they neared the boundary of Illaria. Pyrid had already flown overhead and out into the distance so they knew which direction to head. Rilla found herself looking for Eliséo's company. He was riding towards the head of the group, at the rear of the masters and mistresses. She wasn't certain if she should disturb him while he was deep in conversation with them, but she didn't want to miss out on his company any more than required.

None of them knew if this Paradise would be destroyed as King Lukys hoped, which meant she wasn't certain how long Eliséo would stay with them. She hadn't even asked if he intended to stay for the destruction of every Paradise, or just this first one. There were too many unknowns.

She knew that he also wanted to help Ilya and Lord Mikhail with their problems in Goraburg. Vladimir still hadn't been found and remained a constant threat to, even though Celtan had agreed to keep an eye out for the traitor.

Pushing aside her doubts, Rilla urged her speckled grey mare forward. Other riders moved their mounts aside for her and she soon found herself riding beside the elf. She noticed with mixed feelings that Mistress Isis was on his other side. Had her teacher discussed their last lesson with him?

"Are you prepared for the day?" Mistress Isis asked her, peering around Eliséo. "Excited to be under Mistress Kayte's wing?"

Rilla smiled. "Absolutely! Though I don't think she's very impressed King Lukys recommended me for the task."

"Oh, don't mind Kayte's abrupt manner. She really is quite impressed with you, whatever she may say."

Rilla caught Eliséo's eye. "Perhaps Mistress Kayte is simply wary of Rilla hurting herself accidentally," he said, turning to Mistress Isis. "I saw Rilla do so on a number of occasions in the Outworld – not through any fault of her own, but because she was tired and untrained."

"You're probably right," Mistress Isis conceded. "Then again, how is Rilla to learn unless she experiences more trying situations than those in a classroom? How are we to know what she will have trouble with if we don't see her in action?"

Rilla was becoming slightly uncomfortable with their conversation. Mistress Isis seemed to think exactly the same way as she did, but Rilla understood Eliséo's concerns. Memories of when she healed Master Ensil flashed before her eyes and she cringed.

"Hopefully, I won't have a reason to heal someone by myself if it's something I haven't done before," Rilla said quietly. They rode on in silence.

It was mid morning when they reached the boundary of Illaria. Rilla looked back to find Arishen and Tika. They were both still near Plyke. Rilla turned her horse around and rode back to the three of them.

"We're almost at the boundary now," she told them. "Let's make sure that neither of you get left behind. I'm sure Eliséo will get through fine, but if either of you are left here and Marilisa is on border duty, she won't be making any effort to get you back to us."

The boys nodded and rearranged themselves so that Plyke could hold Tika's hand, giving Rilla enough room to touch Arishen's arm. Even though she knew he couldn't read her mind like a lintep, she was aware that it would only take a single lapse in her concentration for her thoughts to pass to him. With that in mind, she withdrew as far into her wall as possible.

It suddenly occurred to her that Arishen and Tika, unless Plyke had told his Partner, were the only two of their original company who didn't know about her bond to Elessa. For either of them to find out on this trip could be potentially disastrous, especially if Lishe discovered that information.

Pushing all those thoughts from her mind, Rilla gently placed her hand on Arishen's arm and escorted him across the boundary. As soon as they were on the other side, she lifted her hand away and moved her horse further to the side.

They travelled through the dense forest for no more than an hour before reaching the grassy flat lands surrounding Illaria. Rilla hadn't travelled on flat, open lands since Lishe had attacked them before reaching the Bramble River for the first time. She looked around warily, suddenly very conscious that they were now in the Outworld and not as protected as they had been in Illaria. As she searched the area surrounding them for any sign of danger, she noticed they all were – Shuut, Plyke, Tika and Arishen. Even Eliséo appeared more on his guard, though Mistress Isis looked no more worried than when Rilla had spoken to her earlier that morning.

The longer they travelled, the uneasier Rilla became. With such a large party, if Lishe was anywhere in the area she wouldn't be able to help but notice them. Even if she didn't attack Rilla immediately, as soon as she realised what they were doing, she would either try to stop them or watch from a distance to see how they destroyed the Paradise.

Rilla knew that not everyone had been told how the Paradise was to be destroyed. There were only a few select people, fewer now that Ilya and Kazimir were gone – who knew how it was to be done and only Anya and Pyrid knew the words to say. Much as she had been angry with King Lukys for not including them in all the planning, she now understood that he was trying to keep everyone as safe as possible in this difficult circumstance.

They rode for another four hours, with Pyrid flying back over them a number of times to redirect them to the Paradise. By the time they reached it, King Lukys, Kora, Anya, Lord Aaron and Guiscard were settled in a circle on the grass, discussing something in a heated manner. Rilla hoped to overhear what they were saying but as the large party approached them, the four lintep and the karlik immediately grew silent.

"Have you scouted around the area?" Pér asked as he dismounted and stood rather close to Kora, who gave him a withering look.

"Of course we have," she replied curtly. "No sign of Lishe or anyone else for that matter. Pyrid flew us around the surrounding area before we landed. There aren't even any settlements in a ten mile radius around us."

"So let's begin," the tall lintep continued brashly.

"We were discussing that very thing," King Lukys told him in a voice that warned him not to speak any further. "Eliséo, might we speak with you in private?"

Rilla refused to be excluded from the conversation. She made a display of lying on the grass from fatigue and closed her eyes. As soon as her lids were shut, she contacted Elessa and begged her to listen in on the conversation.

You know he will be angry with me for this, Elessa chided her.

I'll deal with that later, Rilla replied insistently. *Please Elessa, I need to know what they're saying.*

"Eliséo, Anya is insisting that you are one of the people helping her with the crystal heart," Lukys told him in a stiff voice. "Clearly, that is not the best idea for reasons you know well enough. If she wants the minimum amount of people, it would be best to have two of our most powerful lintep helping her."

Anya glared at him. "King Lukys, you promised Ilya that you would bow to my decisions when it came to the crystal heart, yet here we are at the first crossroads and you have already begun to question my authority on the matter," the karlik told him stonily. "I *will* have Eliséo as one of my three. I would like to keep it at three to ensure a rumour spreads that we always need three to make it work."

"Very well," replied King Lukys through gritted teeth. "Who will you choose for the final person? Might I suggest Lord Aaron, as his power far surpasses every other lintep in Illaria."

"Rilla?"

At the sound of her name, Rilla irritably cut her connection with Elessa and opened her eyes. Arishen was staring down at her with a strange expression on his face. Her irritation instantly vanished. Rilla sat up quickly as the seer crouched down in front of her.

"You told me to tell you if I had any visions out here ..."

"Yes?" Rilla asked urgently.

"I had one, but I don't know if it means anything. It was Anya and the four of us, you, me, Tika and Plyke, with their hand over something, a shimmer in the air and then the vision ended."

"You're certain it was all of us?" she asked carefully. He nodded. Rilla tapped her teeth together thoughtfully. If she had to be involved in destroying the Paradises, it *would* be better to have her friends with her, even if none of them were mentioned in the prophecy.

"Rilla," Eliséo called out to her from their small circle. "Would you join us for a moment?"

She exchanged a confused glance with Arishen, but walked towards the circle of people nonetheless.

"Rilla, as you are named in the prophecy and you undoubtedly have a vast amount of power, Anya has decided to name you as the third person to assist us," Eliséo told her. Rilla glanced around the circle. Most of them seemed pleased. King Lukys was the only exception, but she well knew why that was.

"I'm ... not entirely certain that's a good idea," she replied slowly. "Arishen had a vision and I wasn't the only one in it. All of us were. I mean all of us from our Paradise."

"All of us?" Kora burst out. "Is he certain?"

"Not you, but the rest of us and I've never known him to be wrong when it comes to the people in his visions," Rilla replied, but Anya was already shaking her head.

"No, no. This is the same seer who has faceless visions, isn't he?" the karlik asked suspiciously. Rilla nodded, without offering any extra information. "No. I have made my decision. It will be you. If we're going to do this at all, it will be as the prophecy says. Besides, everyone knows how powerful you are."

"You realise, the prophecy doesn't actually say I will destroy the paradises, just that everyone will bow to a child of Paradise, which could be any of the four of us."

"It also says people will hail Rilla," Anya pointed out.

"Yes, but it doesn't say what for," Rilla persisted. "I could do any number of things to make people hail me. Mistress Kayte might have me heal a lot of Paradisians. I might best a Paradise leader who was overly cruel to the Paradisians."

"She makes a valid point, Anushka," Eliséo told the karlik gently. "Would it please you if Lord Aaron looked at the vision to ease your mind?"

Anya grudgingly agreed to Eliséo's suggestion and Rilla swiftly went to find Arishen.

"What? No!" came the emphatic reply from the seer once Rilla had explained the situation to him. "I don't want him to look at my vision. What if he doesn't believe it was anything more than a dream? What if it convinces them that all of us should help them and then they can't destroy the Paradise? I don't want the blame for that."

Rilla looked at him incredulously. What was the point of him telling her about the vision if he wasn't going to let her act on it?

"What if Master Reuben looks at your vision instead?" Rilla finally asked. Arishen visibly calmed at the idea. Rilla hadn't realised how comfortable the seer was with his new guardian.

"Go and find him then and bring him over to us," Rilla instructed him. She returned to the others and alerted them to the fact that Arishen preferred Master Reuben to look at his vision.

Rilla watched Anya closely. The karlik was about to object until she caught Eliséo's eye. She didn't know what passed between them, but it was enough to let Anya agree to the turn of events.

When Arishen and Master Reuben arrived, they joined the others sitting on the grass.

"I understand I'm to look at Arishen's vision. Is that correct?" Master Reuben asked. Rilla saw Eliséo place a calming arm on Anya's knee.

"Indeed," the karlik replied evenly. "He told Rilla of a vision that has her refusing to assist us with the destruction of the Paradise. We wish to know everything about this vision to understand her reluctance."

"Very well. Arishen, relax your mind and focus on your vision," the mind master instructed his pupil. Both of them closed their eyes. Everyone waited expectantly. Rilla tapped her teeth together in anticipation. A few minutes later, Master Reuben opened his eyes once more and tapped Arishen on the shoulder. "That will do, for now."

Rilla waited expectantly for Master Reuben to let her out of the prophecy. She was certain everyone else was hoping she was wrong, though she hadn't the faintest idea why.

"It is true, the boy had a vision," Master Reuben finally told them. "However, I do not believe it is of this exact time and place. It did feature Anya, Arishen, Rilla, Tika and Plyke, each with a hand covering a stone and whispering a few words together. The air around them shimmered and then the vision ended.

"However, the reason I think it must be another time or place is that the dragon standing by them was sapphire blue, not fire opal like Pyrid. I'm sorry, Rilla."

Rilla hadn't realised just how devastated she would be by that news. She looked over at Anya just in time to see a smile of satisfaction briefly cross her face.

"That settles it, then," the karlik announced. "Rilla, you will help us today. If there comes another time or place when Celtan, or some other sapphire crystal dragon, is here then I may relent and allow all of you a turn. Are we agreed?"

Rilla was trapped again. She wished for some way, any way, out of the situation. She wanted to just slip away from everything.

"Control yourself, Rilla." Lord Aaron nudged her gently. Rilla flushed bright red as she realised she had started to fade into the background. It had been weeks since that had happened without her direction.

"Sorry," she mumbled. "I'll help with the destruction of this Paradise if you insist."

Anya got to her feet, Eliséo standing with her. "That's settled, then. Come with me so that I can tell you both the words you need to know."

Rilla followed the karlik and the elf away from the small circle of people. As she passed King Lukys, she saw a look of annoyance flash across his features. *That* she could understand. It was the lintep who had this prophecy. It was *he* who had sent out Kora to find the Paradises. It was *he* who had organised everything to do with the destruction and, in the end – he was being left out of the most important decision because Anya controlled the crystal heart.

Once the three of them were a good distance away from the others, Anya stopped and turned to them both. Rilla and Eliséo knelt down at her direction. She did not want to be overheard. Rilla thought Eliséo might offer to create his mist for her, but that would only expose the amount of power he had to the lintep gathered there. Besides, they wouldn't be able to use the mist when actually saying the words at the Paradise boundary.

"The words to release any foul power from a mind is 'Let your mind be at peace. Let your mind fly free'. Now, Celtan has informed us that will only work on variations of the mind snare, which has been previously placed on yourself and your sister.

"The words to release power which has nothing to cling to but other power are these: 'Be not afraid to fly alone. Fly free to the skies'. This did indeed work once, on the powers that were used on you and Shuut after they were taken away from your minds, but I am dubious of their effect on a Paradise. However, we have no option but to try."

Rilla stood beside Eliséo and stared in disbelief as Anya walked back to King Lukys to alert him they were ready to try. Could it really be that simple? Would it work with just the three of them? Perhaps they would need more people to add power to the crystal heart, though she knew her own power was vast and Eliséo's was more than it should be. She had little time to ponder such things as Anya returned with King Lukys and the rest of his company.

The king turned to the rest of the people milling around with the horses and dragon, clapped his hands together loudly and then held them up to gain everyone's attention. Everyone stopped and turned to face King Lukys in silence.

"We are ready to begin," he announced. "I want everyone to be on their guard. We do not know what we will find in this Paradise. Kora noted that it was fairly peaceful, though not at all tolerant of magic, when she first found it, but that was almost twenty years ago. Many things could have changed in that time.

"I want my guards at the front. Any master or mistress who thinks they will be able to help in a skirmish should stand behind the guards. Healers please stay behind the others and keep the children with you.

"Pyrid, if you would stay behind our small gathering, that would be best. It will make it easier for you to take flight to help us, if that becomes necessary.

"Anya, Eliséo and Rilla will now attempt to destroy the Paradise boundary. Everyone be on your guard."

Everyone moved into their positions, with Pyrid curling his body in a crescent behind them. Kora, Lord Aaron and King Lukys joined the lintep just behind the castle guards. Rilla was mildly surprised to see Guiscard head over towards Tika, Arishen and Plyke. Perhaps he wasn't a very powerful lintep and had only come along for his knowledge.

She was jolted out of her thoughts by a light touch on her elbow. She instantly flinched away from the skin contact, even after she realised that it was only Eliséo.

"Are you ready?" he asked her gently, his grey eyes filled with uncertainty. Rilla nodded, certain that her own eyes displayed similar emotions. Together, they followed Anya to the Paradise boundary. Rilla placed her hand on it and was instantly flooded with memories of Rhanya, the isolation hut, the increased deaths, the times she had disappeared from view without realising what she was actually doing. She pulled her hand away as though she'd been burnt.

"What is it?" the elf asked her in concern.

"Nothing," she lied. "The sooner we're done with this, the better. I want nothing to do with any of the Paradises. I hoped the others would be able to help. I'm certain they would have jumped at the chance."

Anya glared at her angrily. "They are not the one I chose for this task. It may interest you to know that it was not only because you are named in the prophecy that I chose you alone. I know your power is greater than almost every other lintep. I have been told that Plyke's power may rival yours, but he has less control over his than you do of yours and the humans have none at all. If it turns out that your skills are required when we use the crystal heart, I would rather have you by my side. Do you understand, child?"

Rilla nodded mutely. Anya's explanation was the last thing she had expected. It hadn't occurred to her that she might actually need to use her power, rather than lend its strength to the spell of the crystal heart. She flushed red, as she understood how foolish it must have looked for her to refuse the honour so staunchly.

"I'm sorry, Anya," she apologised in a quiet voice. "It didn't realise…"

"I know, child," Anya replied, her voice softening. "However, sometimes it may be best for you to try looking at things from someone else's perspective before you worm your way out of a given duty. Now, let us put this behind us. Everyone is ready, so let us begin."

Eliséo pulled the crystal heart out of his pocket. Rilla noticed how he positioned himself so that none but the three of them could actually see it. Anya nodded to her and the two of them placed their hands on the crystal heart, around Eliséo's hand. Eliséo moved the crystal heart closer to the Paradise boundary until it was completely surrounded by the thick barrier. He glanced briefly at both of them and then counted down from three.

"Be not afraid to fly alone. Fly free to the skies," the three of them whispered. Rilla felt a sudden rush of power in and around her. She glanced up to see the look of surprise on Eliséo and Anya's faces. Within seconds, the Paradise boundary began to shimmer and shake around them. She felt, rather than saw, scores of powers detaching from each other and releasing themselves into the skies.

Behind the shimmering air, Rilla began to see a small village in the fields before them. It looked so similar to her own Paradise that she had to rub her eyes and look again to be certain. The differences were very slight, but enough to convince her she was standing before a different Paradise to her own. Erton was not going to come charging at them, demanding an explanation.

"It worked," Anya breathed out in wonder. Rilla looked over to see a tiny tear fall down the karlik's smiling face. "We did it!"

She couldn't help but smile along with the karlik. They really had done it. One fewer of these monstrosities now existed. She began to wonder how quickly they would be able to destroy the others, but before she could run away with those thoughts, she heard a cry in the distance.

"Invaders! Outworlders!"

The cry was instantly taken up around the small village. Rilla was horrified that the Paradisians thought they were invaders. They were only trying to help. She was rooted to the spot. Eliséo dragged her out of the way as the castle guards began their slow march forward.

What are they doing? she thought in a panic.

"Eliséo, you have to get them to stop!" Rilla yelled at him. "They will only scare the Paradisians."

"Only King Lukys can stop them now," he told her, holding her arm firmly as she tried to break away from him. "He won't listen to you, Rilla. Don't even try."

Not knowing how she did it, Rilla instinctively made the skin Eliséo was touching as hot as she possibly could without actually burning herself. He drew his hand back in pain for only a moment, which was just how long she needed to run away from him.

"King Lukys, please stop them!" Rilla cried out as she ran towards her uncle. "Lukys, stop your guards!"

"Get back to Eliséo, child," Lukys waved her aside as he marched forward behind his guards. "If these humans are intent on fighting us, they will not find us unprepared."

Rilla couldn't believe her ears. Were the lintep so blind that they couldn't understand why the Paradisians were prepared to fight them? Changing her tactic, she grabbed Kora's arm and dragged her back towards Shuut, Tika, Arishen and Plyke. She was surprised that the older lintep didn't resist, but when she looked up at Kora, she saw her terrified expression.

"These lintep don't understand what it's like to live in a Paradise – only we do. The only way we're going to get ahead of them is if we get the horses and ride for the village. Before we get there, dismount and approach with our hands held out so that can see we have no weapons. Agreed?"

"Agreed," they all replied. Each of them scattered to quickly find their horses, while Mistress Kayte and Guiscard looked on with curiosity. Rilla was glad she had brought Kora back with her. The older lintep was probably the only reason they weren't being stopped by every lintep around them right now.

Chapter Fifteen – Dangers of fire

Aaron watched as Kora, his three grandchildren and the human boys galloped past him. It had been a slow advance on the human settlement so as not to cause alarm. It hadn't worked. He'd heard the cries of alarm.

"Invaders! Outworlders!"

It was at that moment Rilla had disappeared from his view. To see her riding past him with all that was left of his family, straight into danger, terrified him.

"Lukys, what are they doing?" he asked his cousin as he started running. There was no chance he would catch up to them even if he went back for the horses. Lukys was only two steps behind him, as were all of the guards. "They're going to get themselves killed!"

"This is why I didn't want to bring them in the first place!" Lukys yelled as they continued running.

Aaron could hear the guards keeping pace behind them. He didn't know how many of the lintep were now in pursuit of the foolish children and his own daughter on horseback, but suffice to say if the Paradisians didn't think they were being invaded before, there would certainly be no doubt now. There was no way to avoid that. He had to catch up to his family before they were slaughtered like lambs.

* * *

Rilla rode past her grandfather without the slightest hesitation. She had to reach the Paradisians before the others or there would be no end of bloodshed. It was only when they were already half way to the farms that she risked a backwards glance. Their stupidity almost made her rein in her horse and return to make them stop, but she knew none of them would listen to her.

The entire host of lintep were now running towards the sleepy little village, like an invading horde. She turned back, cursed under her breath and hoped she hadn't made things worse.

As they neared the farms, she saw farmers with pitchforks and scythes standing in a defensive line – more Paradisians arrived behind them with whatever makeshift weapons they could find. Among them, she spied axes, kitchen knives and carpenter tools. They would have to be very careful here.

One hundred yards away from the Paradisians, she and the others reared in their horses and dismounted. They walked forward with their hands held out in submission. She hoped they had ridden fast enough to outdistance the lintep, but doubted it for she could already hear the sound of them approaching at a run.

"We mean you no harm," she called out to the Paradisians as the six of them slowly approached the farmers. "We've come to help you."

"We don't need any help from the likes of you, Outworlder! Clear off before we cut you down!" one of the Paradisians yelled out, holding his pitchfork threateningly.

"The boundary keeping you safe has been destroyed," she tried to explain as they slowly walked forward. "You'll need our protection until you can protect yourselves."

"Come one step further and you'll see how well we can protect ourselves!" the burly Paradisian yelled aggressively.

Rilla stopped walking and put her hands out to stop the others. They stood in a line before the terrified and angry Paradisians, still holding their hands out passively. Kora looked over at her questioningly.

"What now?" she whispered. "Father will be upon us any second."

"I don't know," Rilla admitted. "It was all I could think to do." Talking with Kora, Rilla didn't notice that Tika had started to move forward.

"I said not another step," the Paradisian warned him.

"I know you're afraid," he told them as gently as possible. "We would have been too, had twenty-five people and a crystal dragon suddenly appeared at the border of our Paradise. But, I promise we mean you no harm."

The man began to lower his pitchfork, but raised it as his eyes looked behind them. Rilla glanced over her shoulder to see the lintep right behind them. As she turned back to the Paradisians, one of them threw a knife at Tika. Instinctively, she cast out her power as a shield in front of him. The knife stopped in mid-air and fell harmlessly to the ground.

"Lintep! Attack!" yelled the leader of the pack.

Before she knew what was happening, every Paradisian was running forward, weapons held high.

"Stop!" she screamed out, to no avail.

Elessa, help me! she called out to her tree. Within seconds, she was mumbling words that called up a thick mist between the humans and the lintep. Both sides ran into a wall of solid air. She knew her eyes were glowing a bright green, but there was nothing else she could do.

What are you doing? Eliséo demanded of her.

The only thing I can think of, Rilla replied hastily. *Elessa wouldn't have helped me if she could think of anything else for me to do.*

Rilla, you've just shown everyone who knows we are bound together that I must be a royal elf. She felt his heart break as he spoke. It almost made her falter, but she had to go on now.

"Rilla, what is the meaning of this?" King Lukys asked as he stormed up to her. "Get rid of that mist this instant!"

"No," she replied steadily. "Not until you all stand down. This is going to turn into a bloodbath if you keep going the way you are."

"They're the ones who took up arms against us," Lukys growled angrily, pointing towards the Paradisians hidden behind the mist.

"Only because they saw you as invaders," Rilla reasoned with him. "Tika was calming them down before you came running up behind us. Now, *please* stand down."

"Lukys, I think we have no choice," Lord Aaron touched his arm gently. "Let us move back a few yards and put down our weapons. We are perfectly capable of protecting ourselves without them if need be."

"We will do as you request, Rilla, but there will be consequences for you back in Illaria. Do you understand me?" King Lukys' voice was cold as ice. She shivered at the thought of what her punishment would be, but nodded nonetheless. Rilla waited as the king ordered his people to lower their weapons and stand well back from the wall of mist.

"What now?" Shuut asked, under her breath. "Can you walk through this mist or do you need to just pull it down?"

"I don't think I can walk through it," Rilla told her in a quiet voice. "Can you get Arishen and Tika away from here? I don't think they'll be able to defend themselves if the Paradisians attack as soon as the wall comes down."

Shuut nodded and ushered the boys back over to where the rest of the lintep were standing. She waited until they were all as safe as possible before putting up a shield of her own power and dissipating the mist.

As soon as the mist had dispersed, she saw the Paradisians, makeshift weapons at the ready. They charged at her, weapons drawn. Rilla fought the urge to draw her own weapons as they neared her, petrified that her shield of power would not withstand their attack. She felt each blow as the Paradisians attacked her. It was all she could do to keep her power wrapped around her.

"Magic!" one of them yelled. "Keep at it lads, she can't last forever."

That was when Rilla saw Lord Aaron appear by her side. They began their futile attack on him as well. He stood his ground quietly and calmly. Eventually, he raised his hands. Rilla was amazed that the men stopped their attack.

"You may keep attacking my granddaughter and I, but I assure you, you will tire before our power fails us. Please put down your weapons and allow us to explain."

None of them put down their weapons, but at least they held them a little lower.

"What's going on?" asked the burly man – the one she identified as the leader.

"I am Lord Aaron of Illaria. I've come with humans, lintep, an elf, a karlik and a crystal dragon to free you from your Paradise."

"What do you mean 'free' us?" the human asked angrily. "We weren't prisoners in here. That boundary you just destroyed was the one thing keeping us safe from the Outworld."

Lord Aaron looked thoughtful. "I think King Lukys had better explain it to you, if you'll allow me to introduce you to him." The man held his pitchfork down and nodded. Lord Aaron turned towards King Lukys and motioned him forward.

"King Lukys, this is …"

"Brynt."

"Brynt," he continued. "Brynt, this is King Lukys of Illaria. King Lukys will be able to explain to you why we had to destroy your Paradise so suddenly."

Lukys nodded to Aaron and glared at Rilla before turning to Brynt.

"Brynt, we apologise for startling you today," King Lukys began. "It has come to our attention that there is a lintep in the Outworld who wishes to steal all of the power in the Paradise boundaries for herself. This would make her extraordinarily power and dangerous. In an attempt to stop her, we have to destroy all of the Paradise boundaries before she can do so."

"I see," Brynt replied slowly. "So, you've destroyed our protection from the Outworld and won't be restoring it?"

"I'm sorry. There is no other way. However, we are perfectly willing to offer you our services until you can protect yourselves and trade with other villages."

Rilla relaxed as the two men continued to speak. She'd managed to avert a bloodbath, albeit at the exposure of her bond with an elf's tree and the strength of that elf's power. She left them talking and quietly walked away. At the edge of the clearing, she saw Eliséo standing with Anya. Not knowing where else to go, she walked towards them. Eliséo bent down and said something to Anya. The karlik nodded and walked towards Rilla.

"Looks like you averted quite the battle," Anya told her as they crossed paths. Rilla smiled grimly as she continued on to the elf. Eliséo simply looked at her in silence as she approached him.

"I'm sorry," she apologised, yet again. "I couldn't think of anything else to do and they were about to attack us. You told me if I was ever in actual danger, not to think about the danger I would put you in but to protect myself no matter what."

"*You* weren't in danger, Rilla," he replied calmly. "Perhaps your friends were in danger, but you proved, quite satisfactorily, that you were never in any real danger yourself."

Eliséo, don't be so hard on her, Elessa chided him. *I couldn't think of how to avert the situation any better than she could. We did what we thought best in the situation.*

"We can only hope most of the lintep don't understand what just happened," he said with a shake of his head. "King Lukys will need to devise a new plan for the other Paradises, or we're going to have a world of trouble on our hands.

"There is nothing we can do about it now. Let's just get back to the others and see what they have decided. At least your actions averted the death of many humans."

Rilla couldn't help but feel downcast about the entire affair. If King Lukys had only listened to her in the first place, she wouldn't have had to act so rashly.

She followed Eliséo from a distance, her anger burning away inside her. In the distance, she saw Mistress Isis turn and run towards her, shouting at Mistress Kayte to follow her. Rilla couldn't understand why she felt so hot when the air around her was so cold – cold enough to hurt her nose as she breathed it in.

Before she could react, Mistress Isis had a hand clamped around her arm. Rilla tried to wrench herself free, becoming even angrier that Mistress Isis had dared touch her when she had promised not to.

"Kayte, help me," the fire mistress called out to the healer. "Her feelings are out of control."

Rilla found herself trapped between the two mistresses, both holding her arms so tightly it hurt. She tried to free herself from their grasp until she realised she wasn't burning up anymore. Rilla stopped struggling and let her teachers calm her down. She could feel Mistress Isis carefully release the heat back into the air until it became easily breathable once more. Eventually, they let go of her arms.

Mistress Kayte turned to Mistress Isis angrily. "*This* is what happens when you teach students things they shouldn't know."

"I didn't teach her to draw heat into herself, Kayte," Mistress Isis replied calmly. "I've been trying to teach her to handle heat with care. This happened because the poor girl was furious with the situation she'd been put in to save lives.

"She should never have been allowed to halt her training for this. I will ask King Lukys to let me take her back to the castle immediately to continue her lessons. Plyke should probably return too, but I trust Kora and Lord Aaron to keep him safe for a few days. Stay with her until I return."

Rilla said nothing as Mistress Isis left. She was still stunned. She hadn't tried to gather heat into herself. Who knew what would have happened if Mistress Isis hadn't noticed?

"How did she know?" she asked. Mistress Kayte turned to face her.

"Isis is one of the most powerful lintep in Illaria. She has probably been keeping a tendril around you since we left the castle. It's the only way she could have noticed in time because you were only taking the heat from the air directly around you. It was so cold that if we'd left you any longer, your airways would have frozen."

"I don't understand," Rilla furrowed her brow. "If I was drawing heat into myself, why wasn't the air warming up as I breathed it in?"

"That is something you'll have to discuss with Mistress Isis. I am adept at those skills, but I don't presume to be able to explain it to you better than she can."

Rilla and Mistress Kayte fell into silence as they waited for Mistress Isis to return. They did not have long to wait. The fire mistress soon joined them once more, her long red skirt swirling around her feet as she walked swiftly towards them, Guiscard followed in her wake.

"Rilla, you're coming with us. Kayte, you can join us if you like. King Lukys does not think you or Guiscard will be needed the rest of the day," Mistress Isis told them. "We'll be flying on Pyrid. He will return here after escorting us home."

"I've never flown on the back of a crystal dragon before," Mistress Kayte smiled mischievously. "I'll come back with you."

Rilla smiled despite the circumstances. Now that she wasn't in danger from the crystal dragons, she would be able to enjoy the flight and it seemed even Eliséo liked Pyrid more than most of the other crystal dragons they'd met.

As the four of them approached Pyrid, he lifted his fire opal snout and lazily turned towards them. "That was certainly an interesting way of handling the Paradisians," he rumbled. Rilla flushed bright red, but kept all of her feelings in check so as not to have another disaster.

"Pyrid, would you be so kind as to escort us back to Illaria?" Mistress Isis thankfully ignored the comment. "King Lukys assures me you won't be missed for the time it takes you to fly there and back again."

"I will do it under one condition," he replied slowly, looking over towards Rilla.

"What is it?" Mistress Isis asked.

"I want to see the girl shoot fire from her fingers, like her mother did so often in the Drakos Mountains."

Rilla blanched at the thought. She retreated back behind Mistress Isis and Mistress Kayte.

"Pyrid, she has not completed her training yet. You cannot request such a dangerous display of power from her," Mistress Isis told him firmly. Pyrid turned his snout away from them and settled his head back on the grass once more.

"Let's just take the horses," Rilla suggested. "You don't have to continue our lessons in the castle, do you? We can do it as we ride."

Mistress Isis was just about to protest when Rilla caught her eye.

"Yes, you're right. It will simply make you concentrate more on your tasks." Rilla hid her smile as she realised Mistress Isis had understood her plan.

"Now wait just a moment there," Pyrid called out to them as they turned to walk back to the horses. "You don't have to be like that. I'll settle for a smaller display of power, but I do like fire, being made of fire opal. Could you simply light a candle for me?"

Mistress Isis smiled and pulled a small candle out of her pocket. Rilla stared at her in surprise.

"I like to be prepared for anything." Mistress Isis shrugged. Rilla and Mistress Kayte couldn't help but laugh at her. Guiscard smiled knowingly.

When she'd wiped the tears from her eyes, Rilla took the candle from Mistress Isis. She pulled out a tendril of her power and led it to the wick of the candle. Carefully, she gathered heat along the length of the tendril and led it to the tip. Once she thought there was enough heat there for an impressive display, she pushed the heat quickly to the wick. The flame was almost the length of her face before it quickly died down to normal. She leant forward and blew out the candle before it melted any further.

"Satisfied?" she asked Pyrid with a grin. His eyes sparkled as he offered her a claw to climb up.

* * *

Lishe watched from the cover of a tree. Lukys, Aaron, Kora, Guiscard and a karlik had searched the area. She'd seen them pass her by time after time, none of them noticed her.

It hadn't been difficult to follow them. After all, how could anyone miss a fire opal crystal dragon flying through the sky? Especially when it kept flying back and forth over the same area. They'd led her straight to the open field.

She'd found a tree with low hanging branches, climbed to a height where she could see for miles around and settled down to wait. With all the powers she possessed, it wasn't difficult to blend into the background and stay hidden from sight.

It was well past midday when she saw the rest of the party arrive. Her mind reeled when she saw both the little brat and the banwep. How had they survived? It took all of her self-control to remain where she was and watch silently. Her lust for power made it difficult, when so many great powers were gathered before her, but whatever faults she may have had, stupidity was not one of them. It would be completely reckless of her to attempt to steal any power when there were so many skilled lintep able to protect the girls from her. Instead, she watched and waited.

From her tree, she could not hear any conversation, it was difficult enough for her to see anything in detail. A group of lintep, including the greying King Lukys himself and that smug little Kora, were animatedly discussing things with a karlik and an elf. Lishe didn't understand why either of them were there. She would have to keep a close eye on them. They must be there for a good reason. No karlik ever left Goraburg willingly. Nor did any elf walk far from their tree in Silvaren for anything other than dire need. No, the two of them were here by design and she would discover the meaning of it.

A sudden movement caught her eye. The prophecy child walked determinedly towards the group, leaving a tall blond boy behind her. Lishe recognised him as the human Rilla had travelled with from her Paradise. With only a few words to the small group, the brat went to find the boy once more, spoke animatedly with him, then returned to the group.

What is she up to? Lishe wondered. After her encounter with the girl in the marketplace, she was now wary of the young lintep. She couldn't have been in Illaria more than a few days when she'd managed to turn a fireball back toward Lishe. Now she had been there weeks. The things she could have learned in that time. *If only I had killed her before she'd reached Illaria!*

Lishe watched with interest as Rilla, the elf and the karlik walked to a seemingly random place in the field. King Lukys was bellowing orders to his people. As usual, they mindlessly rushed to do his bidding. She used to be one of his people, used to care so much about his family – the most powerful family in Illaria. She'd assumed that fact also meant the most skilled. That was until she started training with Nyssa.

How could a lintep so powerful neglect her studies to the point where she was no better than Lishe, who barely had any power at the time? Even Kora, who was a few years younger than them, managed to climb up to their level because she worked harder than any other lintep in the castle.

Putting her thoughts aside, Lishe watched as suddenly the air in front of her rippled to reveal a small settlement behind the large party. She fought to keep down her rage as she realised they had just destroyed a Paradise. All of that power – gone! How had they destroyed it? She hadn't seen them do anything. They had all just been waiting. Waiting for what? Could it possibly have been the prophecy child with the elf and the karlik? The latter weren't mentioned in the prophecy. What could it possibly have to do with them, and yet ...

Lishe continued to watch, silently seething, as a handful of people rode horses towards the Paradisians who were now coming towards the intruders brandishing whatever tools they had been working with as makeshift weapons. They halted once the riders had dismounted, but as soon as the lintep behind them started charging, the humans attacked.

Lishe blinked in confusion. The Paradise and all of its people had just disappeared from her view. What had happened? There was no way Rilla was powerful enough to recreate the Paradise on her own. So what had the girl just done? If only she was closer, perhaps she could see, but Rilla was a blur behind a mob of lintep.

The Paradise, and all the people within it, reappeared. Whatever had happened, it was clear that Rilla had certainly not recreated the Paradise. She'd made it temporarily disappear. How was that even possible? Lishe could make herself blend into the background, probably better than most lintep. It was possible she might even be able to make a few people disappear, with all her stolen power. But an entire Paradise – or at least as much of it as was visible – that was beyond her power.

Within minutes, there was a flurry of activity around the girl. Two mistresses were raced towards her and struggled with her. Lishe knew it was risky, but she sent out one long tendril, comprised of many powers, towards Rilla. What had happened to make the mistresses so afraid?

The girl was burning up, stealing heat from the air around her. It didn't look like she even knew what she was doing, or how. Lishe withdrew her power before she was detected. For all her fears about what the girl had learnt, it was clear that her control over her powers was not as good as it needed to be. Had it not been for the two mistresses, Rilla would have killed herself, saving Lishe the trouble.

Silently, her mind swirling with ideas, Lishe descended from the tree and walked away from the broken Paradise.

Chapter Sixteen – Lord Kynon

Kynon watched the riders leave in the early hours of the morning. He'd initially been furious with Aaron for keeping the expedition from him. It was only after he considered his behaviour from his cousin's point of view that he calmed down.

He could barely remember the early years when his mother, Princess Ophélie, had still been alive. Thinking of her passion for life, he found himself smiling. Even when he thought of her dedication to her sister, Princess Rilla, and her work with humans, he still felt a glimmer of pride to be her son. His thoughts became sour once his memories turned to the day she was killed by humans over a simple misunderstanding.

It was that one incident that had changed him forever. His father had tried to reason with him, to explain that not all humans were to be hated and feared, but Kynon wouldn't listen. The loss of his mother created a gaping hole in his life, which he filled with hatred for humans. It was against everything his mother would have wanted and his father tried numerous times to change his feelings on the matter to no avail.

It wasn't long after his mother was killed that his father died. They told him it was from a broken heart, but he'd never believed them – he was convinced that his father had also been killed by humans. From that time onward, King Edamo and his wife, Adeline, looked after Kynon as though he were their own son. However, nothing anyone said could convince him to contribute to running the kingdom or soften his views towards humans.

Often left to his own devices, he grew idle and bitter. Eventually he found happiness with Cynestra, but that too was short-lived. He knew people whispered behind his back. Some said there was no chance she could have died in childbirth like a common human. He knew there had been rumours that she had taken her own life. Perhaps the truth was that she refused to fight for her life and that had made all the difference.

Whatever the cause, his wife had died, leaving him behind with twin boys. Daegan and Braedan were the only joy in his life and he was determined to protect them at all costs. He taught them to hate humans from their earliest days. If the subject of Ophélie arose, he only ever spoke of her death by human hands, not the fact that she had spent years helping her sister in her cause to assimilate humans with lintep, nor that she had continued to help humans with the creation of Paradises once Rilla had been killed.

It had been quite a shock for him to learn that Nyssa had managed to soften Braedan's view towards humans. Aaron had raised his family with an extremely different view to humans. The cousins had never gotten along since the day Ophélie had been killed. Kynon blamed his mother's death on Princess Rilla's influence over her. That blame had extended to Aaron, even though he'd had nothing to do with the matter.

Since Nyssa's death at the hands of a lintep, Kynon had had time to rethink his old ideas. If his mother had wanted to help humans perhaps, somewhere, there was a reason for him to change his views towards them. He could see that the very existence of Lishe brought his whole world into danger. It was no longer only humans he had to fear. His children and grandchildren would not be safe anywhere, even in Illaria, as long as Lishe was alive.

With a sigh, he turned from the window and readied himself for his meeting with Princess Aislen and the five retired teachers who had taught Kora, Lishe and Nyssa. He knew Aislen could only afford to stay for a few minutes. Lukys had left such a long list of duties for her to fulfil in his absence, it was a wonder she had agreed to assist him at all. She had already helped him to draft a letter to the mistress and four masters the day before, ensuring their appearance this morning.

Kynon opened his door to find Aislen, hand raised, about to knock. She lowered her hand and smiled a greeting to him.

"Have you had a chance to consider what you'll do with the information you recover from this morning's meeting?" she asked him without preamble. When he shook his head, she continued. "I thought you might like to involve Braedan and Luisella in the process. Braedan shared as many classes with Nyssa as Luisella did with Kora. Though they weren't in the advanced classes the girls shared with Lishe, they may have shared some information, whether accidentally or intentionally, to some of the other students at their own level."

Kynon stared at her in astonishment. He'd never have thought to involve his son in this matter. "What about Daegan?" he asked automatically. They were twins after all and may have shared multiple classes with Nyssa.

"I had thought Daegan less sympathetic to our current cause, but if you think it would benefit us, by all means include him," Aislen answered cautiously. Kynon regarded her thoughtfully.

"I know what you're thinking," he huffed. "As much as I attempted to turn my sons against humans, neither of them ever fostered the resentment as much as I did. Braedan, quite clearly, was easily persuaded by Nyssa to soften his views towards humans. With Daegan, the change was more subtle, but have you never noticed how he reprimands Marilisa whenever her views tend to extreme disdain?"

Aislen nodded. "I *did* notice that. Most recently, the night Aaron invited us all to dine in his chambers. I hadn't realised what that meant. In that case, both of your sons could prove quite useful after our meeting. I'll leave the decision in your capable hands. Perhaps I can meet you once I've completed my duties for the day."

As she turned to walk away, he called out after her. "Aislen, thank you. I know I should have taken more of an interest in the kingdom after Edamo and Adeline took me under their wing. I just wanted to say I'm grateful to you for your help in this matter."

Aislen looked back at him with an odd expression on her face. "It's the least I could do, Kynon. I only hope that this meeting proves as useful as father and Aaron expect it to be."

A knock sounded at the door to the council chambers. Kynon glanced towards Aislen hesitantly. She nodded to him encouragingly. He took a deep breath and opened the door. The five retired teachers filed into the room, taking off their robes to reveal their blue tattooed arms, and sat themselves according to rank, as they were accustomed to do.

Kynon studied their tattoos as he walked back to his own seat. All five of them had three bands around their arm, showing they had become truly skilled with their powers.

Master Elwood had the ∞ symbol for balance, as well as, the encircled cross for practical powers. Kynon remembered the day when Master Aurelius took over from Master Elwood as the most senior master for practical powers. Aurelius had been Elwood's student for such a long time that it came as no surprise. He assumed the position uncontested.

Mistress Chandrelle had a serpent wrapped around a staff – the symbol for healing. It was a well-known fact that she and Kayte had been more rivals than friends, even with their age difference. They were both such strong willed and stubborn lintep, as skilled as each other in their specialised area of expertise.

Master Amyas had the triwave symbol for mind powers. Kynon found him a curiosity. Most of the mind masters he knew had a superior air about them. They were usually the ones who were the most vocal against humans, yet Amyas had never expressed such views. He idly wondered if Reuben had been one of Amyas' students – that would certainly explain how the human seer had come to live under Reuben's protection.

Master Flyndar had the flame symbol. Unlike Mistress Isis who was the youngest ever lintep to be awarded Mistress status, Flyndar developed his skill much later in life, however that did not stop him from becoming one of the most skilled Masters in Illaria.

Master Bastienne had only the ∞ symbol for balance – nothing else. Kynon had never had much to do with this master. He found himself staring at the symbol long after he should have averted his gaze.

"You've never seen the like before, Lord Kynon?" Master Bastienne asked him in a strong, smooth voice. Kynon looked up at the wizened master guiltily, shaking his head. "I'm not surprised. There aren't many lintep like me around Illaria. Back in my home town, it was more common."

"You're not from Illaria?" Aislen asked, suddenly sitting on the edge of her chair.

"No, my lady," replied the old master. "I was brought here by Princess Ophélie when she passed through my village, oh, many years ago now. She was entranced by the skills lintep in my village possessed and persuaded me to accompany her back to this stronghold."

"So it's true then," she breathed out. "Master Elwood mentioned there might be other lintep settlements, but my father was skeptical about the prospect. This opens up a multitude of opportunities."

Kynon smiled at her excitement over such a minor detail. Master Elwood looked suitably annoyed at the lack of credibility afforded to him. Before he could take umbrage at the remark, Kynon started the proceedings.

"I'd like to thank each and every one of you for giving your time to this project. All of you taught either Lishe, Kora or Nyssa, perhaps even all three, in advance classes. We need to go through the extra knowledge you taught them to see how Lishe could have interpreted those teachings to become what she is. The five of you were the only ones to write down any extra skills you taught the girls, so we're hoping you hold the answers we need to defeat Lishe."

"I don't recall teaching Lishe anything that I didn't also teach Nyssa," Master Flyndar declared. "Though any student worth their metal would easily realise how dangerous their fire powers could be both for themselves and others."

Aislen nodded. "We've already seen what she can do with fire, though she may be capable of even more than what she's shown us. Even Rilla, as untrained as she is, has shown that she knows how dangerous her fire powers can be."

Kynon looked at her questioningly, but Aislen only shook her head. He'd heard only snippets of information about Aaron's grandchildren. He cursed himself for not thinking to talk to any of them before they left on their expedition. He lived such a secluded a life that he didn't know anything about his nieces and nephew.

"What about the other side of your powers?" Bastienne turned to Flyndar. "Did you teach them the opposite side?"

"Yes, but no more than any other student," Flyndar answered slowly. "I suppose it's possible that any of them may have experimented outside of my classes and discovered more than the others."

"What more could they have discovered?" Kynon asked in confusion. He had been an adept student, but had never pushed the boundaries – never sought more information. Flyndar exchanged a looked with Bastienne, but remained silent. "Master Flyndar, I understand that you may not want to tell me in case the girls never understood this particular intricacy of your skill, but we need to be as prepared as possible for the next time we face Lishe. Even the tiniest bit of information could help to turn the tide."

When it became apparent that Flyndar was less than willing to reply, Bastienne stepped in once more. "It all comes down to balance, Lord Kynon. This is where I think you underestimate my symbol. I am a master of balancing my power. You see the flames and you think of fire, but what is the opposite of fire?"

"Water?" Kynon suggested, looking to Aislen for support. Her face drained of colour.

"The absence of heat," she whispered. "Is that even possible?"

All of a sudden, Kynon felt cold all over, just for a moment. He rubbed warmth back into his arms, even after the air had returned to its normal temperature.

"What did you just do?" he asked in amazement.

"I simply demonstrated Princess Aislen's theory," Flyndar replied quietly. "That was a small example. Imagine if the air was colder over a larger area. Think of the implications." Kynon felt faint. The fire master nodded. "*Now* you begin to understand. I never taught these things to the girls, but if they were clever and understood the balance of their powers, they could not help but realise the possibilities."

Kynon was silent for a moment, trying to take in the new information. He thought back over what he'd heard about Lishe. "I don't think that's something Lishe has experimented with any further. She used fire to attack both Nyssa and Rilla. But from the sounds of it, she had trouble getting through the forest that Rilla inadvertently set alight. Had she understood the balance of that skill, I assume she could have snuffed the fire. Am I correct in that theory, Master Flyndar?"

"Well done, Lord Kynon," Flyndar complimented him without a trace of sarcasm. "Had she truly understood the opposite of fire, she could have doused any fire, no matter how strongly it raged. There are any number of ways to do this, but she must not have been able to think of a single one."

"Neither did Nyssa," Aislen pointed out. "From what we've heard, Rilla was the one who forced her to experiment with her power to get their small company through the blazing forest. Rilla didn't understand anything about her power at the time, so it's a wonder she managed to do even that, but Nyssa should have had some ideas had she understood about the balance of fire."

"This is good!" exclaimed Bastienne, to everyone's surprise. "We have discovered one very powerful advantage over Lishe. I doubt we'll be able to use it against her more than once before she understands the possibilities herself, but at least we'll have that one time."

Kynon hastily wrote down their discovery on a blank piece of parchment. Even if they discovered nothing else, Aaron would be happy with this nugget of information. He looked up at Bastienne. The old master intrigued him. This whole concept of balance was one that he had never explored before.

"Master Bastienne, once we finish this meeting, I would be most obliged if you would keep me company a little while longer." Kynon didn't know why he suggested it, but something urged him to find out as much about Bastienne as he could.

"I would be honoured, Lord Kynon," Bastienne replied, inclining his head slightly.

"Well, *I* would like to finish this meeting as soon as possible so I can get back to my family," Mistress Chandrelle interrupted. "I never taught the girls anything dangerous about healing. They were all quite skilled in that area and I taught them more advanced and intricate ways of healing people, but I never implied that anything else was possible."

"So you gave them an unbalanced view of your power," Bastienne nodded to himself. "A wise move with Lishe perhaps, but I think it may have benefitted Nyssa to know the opposite of how to heal – it could have saved her life."

"Don't be so hasty to judge everyone, Bastienne," Chandrelle snapped. "Nyssa didn't get a chance to touch Lishe. She would never have been able to save herself with that particular skill, even if she did know about it."

Aislen quickly stepped in at that point. "Mistress Chandrelle, you did well not to teach these three girls, or any other students who were not to become masters or mistresses, about these skills. It is indeed a dangerous skill to be taught to immature and reckless students. I'm certain Master Bastienne would agree with me on that point, at least for lintep in Illaria. Things may be different in his home town, and I would very much like to hear about that another day, however, I find that my time is in much demand at the present moment.

"I beg your forgiveness, but I must attend the royal audience in my father's absence. I hope the rest of this meeting is as informative as the initial conversations. Kynon, I would be happy to discuss the implications of what you learn today as soon as practicable."

"Of course, Aislen," Kynon patted her arm affectionately. "I will alert you when we are done." He waited for her to close the door behind herself before turning back to the retried teachers before him. Trying not to give in to his desire to speak only with Bastienne, Kynon turned towards the others.

"Master Elwood, Master Amyas, I'm not certain which of you to ask, as it seems to be a combination of both, but do either of you know how Lishe came to start stealing power from other lintep? Or how she discovered how to place her mind snare on them?"

The two masters shared a glance before Master Amyas replied. "The three girls were quite talented. Kora and Lishe practiced so much that they quickly became the most skilled amongst my students. Nyssa, I think it has been discussed enough, was so powerful that she could manage most tasks without needing to hone her skills. Ironically, this left her the weakest of the three.

"There was one day when we combined our classes, to show students how similar the mind and practical powers can be when used a certain way. In this class, there was a child who refused to listen when we tried to teach him. He thought he knew best. We had placed him in advanced classes because he showed the necessary skill, but he hadn't grown up in the castle. His parents only resorted to send him for castle lessons when he became too unruly for them to teach themselves."

Amyas stopped and looked over at Elwood. The practical master nodded almost imperceptibly.

"No matter what threats we used, he wouldn't listen. Eventually, we told him that if he didn't do exactly as we said, we'd stop him from using his power. He clearly didn't believe us, so we were forced to carry out our punishment. I used my power to surround the boy, closing in around his entire body so he couldn't even move without my permission."

Elwood interrupted him there. "You have to understand that we did not expect any of the other children to realise what had happened. This particular child did not have enough power of his own to ever replicate Amyas' action. It is, however, possible that Lishe, Nyssa and Kora realised what had happened. They had already shown tremendous promise in both our classes by that point."

Kynon thought back again to the stories he'd heard of Rilla and Plyke. Apparently, Nyssa had threatened Rilla the same way, then forced her to help contain Plyke's power when it tried to flee.

"Nyssa made the same threat to Rilla, though never carried through with it. More importantly, though, she requested Rilla's help to contain Plyke's power, essentially showing Rilla how to do it herself. We are fortunate that Rilla is not the type of lintep to use it the same way Lishe appears to have used it."

Kynon noticed that Master Bastienne stayed uncharacteristically silent at this turn of events. Was it possible there was no opposite power to this?

"Bastienne, do you not have any insight on the matter?" Mistress Chandrelle asked sarcastically, likewise noticing his silence.

"Mind powers seem to be the only part of power where both sides are taught in Illaria – projecting and listening. I'm quite intrigued how all powers became so one sided, except this one," Bastienne replied, ignoring the sarcasm. "As for practical skills, there are always opposites, but they are different in every case. For example, if you lift something up, you must also be able to push it down.

"In this instance of containing another lintep's power, there isn't an opposite as such – I would say the only defence to this is to realise what is happening before the action is complete and push the other lintep's power away or, in the most extreme case, contain the attacking lintep's power if you are stronger. Has there been a clear indication of how Lishe was stealing powers and how she put a mind snare on any lintep?"

"I think you'd best speak to Lord Aaron about that," Kynon told the old master. "He managed to stop Lishe from stealing Nyssa's power from Shuut, but was unsuccessful in stopping her from placing a mind snare on his granddaughters. From what I understand, she only managed it by leaving behind power that she had stolen from other lintep, otherwise she would have had to leave behind part of her own power, if that is even possible."

"It's possible," Bastienne said quietly. Kynon was perplexed by his comment. It was the first time the master hadn't elaborated on anything.

Kynon noticed the others growing restless. "Thank you all for coming to this meeting. I'm certain we can now at least be better prepared the next time we face Lishe." He bade all, but Bastienne farewell.

Bastienne remained seated until the others had departed. Only then did he rise from his seat. "Lord Kynon, I think there's something you need to know. In truth, I should probably tell King Lukys, but Princess Aislen will have to do in his absence. Do you think I might join the two of you when she is free from her duties?"

Kynon nodded, hoping Aislen would be done sooner rather than later.

Chapter Seventeen – Paradise children

The Paradise was wholly unremarkable. If Plyke hadn't known any better, he may easily have mistaken it for an ordinary village. In the Outworld, he had only passed through Turon and Thistlehall. Those villages had more buildings clustered together than this Paradise, and Turon had a wall around it, but that was where the differences ended.

Plyke was certain those two towns must have had some sort of leader. In this Paradise, Brynt was the man everyone looked up to. He was their leader in everything but name. The farmer was understandably unimpressed by the destruction of the boundary. Plyke couldn't help shying away each time the tall, muscular man looked his way. He, Tika, Arishen and Kora had been the centre of his attention since learning the four of them had lived in a Paradise for so many years.

"You lived in one of these safe havens, why would you help him destroy them?" he'd asked of them. Plyke was incredulous. How could he even begin to explain to this man who saw nothing wrong with the way he lived?

"As I told you, Brynt," King Lukys had intervened, "*all* of the Paradises are to be destroyed to keep the power surrounding them from the clutches of a dangerous lintep. Yours is the first, but it certainly won't be the last."

Plyke left King Lukys and the pseudo leader to their discussion. As usual, Tika had picked up on Plyke's mood change and led him away from them. Together, they walked through the hauntingly familiar Paradise. The boundary had been destroyed along the farming area. To the north, was the funeral pyre. Along the rapidly flowing river, the windmill, fishing huts and a few trade houses could be seen. Walking across one of the wooden bridges, they soon came to buildings that exactly replicated the ones they had been accustomed to in their own Paradise – the eating hall, the children's hall, the healers' hut, all the other trade houses.

Many of the Paradisians had halted their work for the day to observe the unusual event. A few of them had headed towards the tavern, knowing they would not be punished for neglecting their work. Most walked past the Partners, back towards Brynt, King Lukys and the lintep, taking little notice of the two boys.

As they passed him, even without skin contact, Plyke couldn't help but feel everything from each of them – fear, anger, excitement, curiosity. This had only rarely happened before. He tried to shield himself from their feelings, but couldn't control his power enough to do so.

Suddenly, he stiffened. Somewhere nearby, someone was terrified. He searched the faces passing by, trying to discover who it was. Plyke looked at his Partner as Tika gripped his arm tightly.

"What is it?" Big hazel eyes stared up at him questioningly.

"I don't know." Plyke shook his head in frustration. "Someone is terrified, but I don't know who and I don't know where."

"Think. Where did we used to hide? Any of the four of us, well except Rilla anyhow."

Plyke shook his head uncomprehending. Tika smiled at him.

"With our Partners. You and I hid with each other, Arishen hid with Parthak. We didn't hide in corners, we hid in plain sight. Whoever it is will have done their best to look as normal as possible. If we walk around, do you think you can feel if we're getting closer to them?"

Plyke hesitated before nodding. It would certainly be difficult, but if his power was flowing around him anyway, he may as well attempt to put it to good use. Together, they continued walking around the Paradise, Plyke allowing his power to lead him.

Eventually, they reached the children's hall and the school. Lessons had been suspended for the day. Children were making the best of this rare opportunity to play. Plyke searched each face carefully, walking slowly amongst them until the sense of terror overwhelmed him. He looked down to see a young boy glance his way, then quickly look away. That look betrayed everything. This was the child. He was terrified the newcomers would spell his doom.

"Tika, I'd like to watch the games for a while," he said, making a great display of choosing the perfect spot to observe from.

Find Kora! he thought the message as hard as he could in Tika's direction, not knowing if it would get through. He hadn't tried to speak to Tika with his mind before. Plyke paled as Tika stumbled backwards, but quickly recovered as his Partner smiled and nodded. Perhaps he could already control his mind powers better than he thought.

Plyke surreptitiously watched the boy as he waited anxiously for Kora. His outward confidence belied the terror that lurked beneath his facade. One of the children had retrieved a cowhide ball and they kicked it back and forth between them. He took little notice of the game itself, except to notice how the children interacted with each other.

None of them, save that one boy, showed any fear of the newcomers, either on the surface or below. There was a small amount of curiosity, but not enough to tempt them away from their game. Plyke could not tell if the boy had noticed his interest in him. If he had, he was making a good show of ignoring him.

It was a good half hour later that Tika appeared, arm in arm with Kora, talking amiably. Plyke smiled at his Partner. No matter the situation, Tika had always been able to blend in and make himself at home. Tika had to have known that Plyke had found the child but from the look of Kora, he hadn't mentioned anything to her. Plyke had no idea how he'd managed to lure her away without explaining, but he was thankful.

Kora, can you hear me? Plyke sent a thought to his mother. She smiled at him and nodded imperceptibly. *I think one of these children may be a lintep – that or he has a great deal to hide.* He flicked his eyes towards the boy in question. Kora casually glanced in his direction as she sat beside Plyke.

I don't sense anything, Kora told him. *How can you be certain?*

My empathy skills are quite developed. He's terrified of something. Plyke answered her. *You know as well as anyone the only reasons to be so terrified in a Paradise is if you have a hint of magic or have helped someone who does. He doesn't seem to be afraid for anyone but himself.*

Plyke moved to accommodate Tika, who had sat on his other side.

"I remember this game from our Paradise, Plyke," Tika said a little too loudly, nudging him in the side. "Don't you?"

Instantly, the children halted the game and ran over to them.

"*You* lived in a Paradise?" a young girl, perhaps eight years old, asked with a lisp. Tika nodded and smiled at her. Plyke hid his surprise at how easily Tika got the children talk to him.

"Yes, but it wasn't as nice as this one. Our Paradise leader was a mean old man. We had to escape from him," Tika continued. "We weren't even allowed to know who our parents were."

"We know who our parents are." A dirt smudged face appeared at the girl's side. He stood a head taller than her.

"Oh, that's wonderful! Do you get to live with them?" Tika asked, with genuine excitement.

"Oh no," replied the girl. "Mother says it's easier for the grownups to do their work without worrying about us, so we live in the children's hall."

"I see. We lived in a children's hall too. The best part was, I got to stay near Plyke. He's my Partner you know," Tika whispered conspiratorially.

"I have a Partner too," the lisping girl whispered back and turned to point. "He's right over there. Abelin."

Plyke was gripped by a sudden wave of terror. It must have been a reaction from the boy at being singled out by the girl. Instinctively, Plyke grabbed at Tika's hand. His terror lessened almost immediately, replaced by a serene feeling. He squeezed his Partner's hand thankfully, amazed by what Tika was capable of without even being a lintep.

"How wonderful! I hoped people were still becoming Partners in other Paradises. You and Abelin have made my day," Tika smiled at the girl. "What's your name?"

"Lorella. What's yours?"

"Tika. This is my Partner, Plyke, and his mother, Kora."

Abelin strode towards them purposefully, taking a slightly protective stance beside Lorella. "You said you weren't allowed to know who your parents were."

Kora stepped into the conversation. "They weren't, but even though it was dangerous, I had to tell Plyke that he was a lintep because the man who ruled our Paradise abhorred magic. If he'd found out what either of us were, he would have had us killed. I had to teach Plyke to hide his powers away, to keep us both safe."

Lorella and the other children stared in wonder at Kora's explanation. Plyke, alone, noticed Abelin's odd reaction – burning curiosity. He decided to chance a topic that was probably best left alone for the time being.

"Have you ever seen magic before?"

The children shook their heads. Lorella quickly glanced at Abelin before joining them.

"Would you like to see some?" he asked with a mischievous smile. Their eyes couldn't get any wider in their small faces. He laughed and turned to Kora. "Would you?"

She looked about to protest, but something must have changed her mind. From her pocket, she withdrew a green velvet pouch and selected three stones. She placed them on the palm of her hand and looked at them intently. Within a few seconds, they were flying in a circle around the children, much to their delight.

"Can *you* show us some magic?" Abelin asked Plyke once Kora had retrieved her stones.

"I'm not very good at the practical side yet," he answered truthfully. "They're teaching me in Illaria. I can speak to your mind, if you'd let me."

Hesitantly, the boy nodded. Plyke smiled at him and gently pushed a thought towards him, hoping it wasn't too soon.

I'm lucky to have a Partner who protected me in our Paradise. Looks like you are too.

Abelin's brow furrowed as he stared at Plyke. Suddenly, Plyke felt something push against his wall. He let his defences down just enough to hear the boy's panicked thought.

Are you going to take me away from her?

Of course not! If you want to come to Illaria, to learn alongside other lintep, I'm sure King Lukys will let Lorella come too, Plyke replied confidently. He could instantly sense that Abelin didn't believe him. *They let Tika be a stableboy in the king's own stables. I see him every day. King Lukys is my uncle – I'm certain I could convince him if you'd like me to.*

"What will happen to us now that the boundary is gone?" Lorella suddenly asked, breaking the contact between Plyke and her Partner. "Will we stay here?"

"That's what King Lukys and Brynt are discussing at this very moment," Kora answered her with a reassuring smile. "We won't leave you defenceless, if that's what you're worried about. Why don't you keep playing your game? I'm sure your parents will come and find you later in the day to tell you what plans have been made."

Tika looked at Kora with a slight scowl before turning to the children and whispering conspiratorially, "Well, you *could* keep playing your game, but if you wanted to meet more lintep or, I don't know, a crystal dragon, a karlik or an elf, you could always follow us ..."

The children gasped and quickly followed as Kora led the way back to the edge of the Paradise. Plyke was content to follow slowly behind them with Tika at his side. The two of them walked in silence, a good pace behind the others. Once they were out of hearing distance, he noticed Abelin stop to make a show of taking his boots off and shaking out the tiny pebbles within. Lorella waited patiently for him and looked up with a smile as the older boys approached them.

"Do you like living in Illaria, Tika?" she asked him. "Do the others in the stables treat you well?"

Tika looked at her questioningly then turned to see the smile on Plyke's face.

"I couldn't think of a better place to live," he answered her then quickly added, "Well, that's not quite true, if we're considering Silvaren as well, but they don't have horses, so I'd still pick Illaria if I had the choice."

"Where is Silvaren?" the young girl asked as they started walking again.

"Silvaren? Oh, that's where the elves live," he answered nonchalantly. "We stayed there for a few nights, longer anyhow than we stayed with the karliki in Goraburg."

"True." Plyke joined in the fun as he saw the children's jaws drop. "But we stayed in Goraburg longer than we stayed in the Drakos Mountains. The crystal dragons flew us out of there almost as soon as we'd arrived."

"Elves!" exclaimed Lorella.

"Karliki!" gasped Abelin.

"You flew on a crystal dragon?" They asked in unison, staring at each other in excitement. Tika hugged them both to his sides and laughed alongside them.

"Imagine the wonders that are all in that big, scary Outworld, if you just have to courage to enter it."

Chapter Eighteen – Bastienne's revelation

It was late in the afternoon by the time Aislen managed to extricate herself from the royal audience. Once the farmers and townspeople realised Lukys would be away from Illaria for an indeterminate amount of time, they were desperate to have their disputes or requests settled in case future audiences were cancelled.

Aislen was weary by the end of it. Although she had insisted on a short break for all the petitioners to eat in the dining hall, she'd spent that time going through mundane matters with the chief steward, Mirco. Her father had organised his trip to the Outworld in such short order that he hadn't had time to organise things with Mirco.

The events of the day only served to reinforce her father's reminder that she would need to choose an heir from amongst her extended family. It was not a decision she relished. Before that day, she'd completely discounted Kynon and Daegan as candidates, however, talking to Kynon earlier that morning, she began to doubt herself. Kynon seemed to be changing rapidly and Daegan appeared not to be as narrow-minded as she had once believed, though there was little doubt in her mind that Marilisa was everything *she* appeared to be.

Aislen shook her head to clear her thoughts. All of the petitioners had finally departed for the day. A servant entered the throne room, remaining just inside the door, eyes lowered until she motioned for the young boy to approach. He did so with an air of wonder about him. Aislen smiled at his obvious awe of being so near to her – the princess of Illaria.

"Do you have a message for me?" she asked him kindly. He tried to stammer out a reply, but settled for handing her a small scroll before quickly turning on his heels and running out of the room.

Aislen studied the scroll for a moment – Kynon's seal. She opened it curiously. It was uncommonly thoughtful of him not to contact her with his mind when he knew she would be busy with petitioners all day. She wondered how long the poor servant had been waiting outside the throne room for all the petitioners to leave. Breaking the seal, Aislen unfurled the scroll and quickly read it.

Urgent matter.

Seek me out at your earliest convenience.

I will be either in the library or my own chambers.

Aislen ignited the scroll with but a thought, and carried the ashes away to the fireplace with her power. She pulled two long tendrils out from behind her wall and sent them out to find Kynon. It didn't take long to locate him.

Locking the throne room behind her, Aislen quickly walked down the long hallway to the library. The closed doors momentarily confused her until she realised that afternoon lessons had already finished and the assistant librarians, in Guiscard's absence, would have turned away all researchers by now.

She rapped lightly at the door, not wanting to attract the attention of teachers or students who might still be walking the halls. As the library door opened with a creak, Aislen turned her head at the sound of conversation coming from one of the twisted stairwells. Moments later, Mistress Isis, Guiscard, Mistress Kayte and Rilla ascended into the hall.

"Guiscard, what are you doing here?" Aislen asked in confusion. "I thought the four of you were with father." The librarian gave her an odd look as he noticed the door to his library opening further to reveal Kynon's face.

"I might ask you the same question, Princess Aislen," he replied, failing to hide his irritation. "I realise you are second only to your father in Illaria, but even *he* has always respected my role as librarian and never dared to step into my domain without my permission."

Aislen flushed, partly from anger but mostly from embarrassment. "My apologies, Master Guiscard. Lord Kynon sent me a most urgent request to meet him here. I judged it best to seek him out as soon as possible."

"Forgive me, Master Guiscard." Kynon's deep voice had a soothing quality to it. "Your assistants let me in earlier this afternoon and insisted I use the library for as long as I required it today. Your return is quite fortunate as I had questions for Princess Aislen that you and your companions might be better placed to answer, if you would oblige me?"

Aislen struggled to keep an impassive face as she saw Kynon's words charm the old librarian into a gentler mood.

"Very well," Guiscard grumbled then turned to Rilla. "Be a good lass and ring the bell for food. I'm famished after the day's excitement."

The young lintep instantly went to the silver handle hanging by the librarian's own desk and pulled down twice. As she shut the door behind everyone, Aislen watched Rilla carefully. The girl walked a little unsteadily on her feet. Taking a closer look at the two mistresses and the librarian, she noticed they all walked carefully.

"Might I enquire how you come to be back in Illaria so soon after your departure this morning?" she ventured. "I confess I had expected you to stay a little longer. Was the mission successful?"

Aislen was surprised when no one immediately answered her. She waited as they took note of who else was in the library and, noticing Master Bastienne, exchanged wary glances. Aislen knew something passed between them, for all eyes eventually settled on Mistress Isis.

The fire mistress nodded. "The mission was fundamentally successful, though future missions will need to be thought out with a little more care. Everyone else stayed behind to better complete the mission. We returned rather hastily, on dragon back, as it became apparent that Rilla's training was more important than our further involvement with the mission."

"Did anything unfortunate occur, Isis?" Aislen asked, suddenly fearful.

"Nothing that couldn't be handled," Isis deflected. "All is well, Lady Kora. King Lukys will simply need to make slight modified plans for the future – that is all." Aislen bit her tongue. She would be asking Isis for a full report once they were done in the library.

"Isis," Master Bastienne mused aloud. "Mistress Isis, the youngest to ever be on the council? Isis, the fire mistress?"

"My apologies," Aislen quickly stepped in once more. "Master Bastienne, you haven't been properly introduced. You must already know Guiscard, as every lintep in Illaria does. This is Mistress Kayte, the finest healer currently teaching in Illaria. Mistress Isis is indeed the youngest and the most skilful fire mistress in Illaria. Behind you is Rilla, daughter of Lady Nyssa."

Bastienne nodded his head to both Kayte and Rilla, but his eyes strayed back to Isis. "I've heard interesting things about you, Mistress Isis. It would be my ultimate pleasure to sit in on one of your classes, if you would permit me."

"I'm not at all certain that would be appropriate, Master Bastienne," Isis replied, flustered. "However, I would gladly discuss the finer details of our skills with you at another time."

Aislen watched the exchange with interest. Clearly, she and her father hadn't been the only ones to take a keen interest in Isis' magnificent skills. "Isis is indeed one of our finest mistresses, but that is not why we have gathered here. Kynon, what was so important it needed my urgent attention?"

Kynon gestured towards Bastienne. The old master nodded gravely and motioned for the others to sit.

"I have come to understand, now more than ever, that the art of balance is not being taught to its full potential in Illaria. This first surprised me when Princess Ophélie brought me here from my hometown of Statera. In Statera, all lintep were taught the opposite of each skill.

"During the course of this morning's meeting, the lack of this practice in Illaria has begun to distress me. It is of some importance to understand the balance of lintep powers. However, that is a minor point in comparison to what I must tell you." At this point, the balance master glanced over to Rilla. "I understand, young Rilla, that a mind snare was placed on you by Lishe?"

Aislen watched the girl closely. To her credit, Rilla barely flinched at the mention of her ordeal, but simply nodded.

"I have also been led to believe that Lishe used another lintep's power to ensnare your mind and yet another for your sister?" Rilla nodded once more. Bastienne sighed audibly. "At least Lishe does not appear to be aware of other possibilities there."

"*Other* possibilities?" Aislen asked, intrigued by his line of questioning. Bastienne finally sat on a nearby chair, avoiding her gaze for a moment.

"I wonder how many of you know how the Paradises were actually created?"

His question took Aislen completely by surprise. She had no more idea than any other lintep about the creation of the Paradises. A cough behind caused her to turn towards Guiscard.

"There are a small number of us who have at least an idea," the old librarian answered cautiously. "That is, we *think* we understand the concept, but we can't fathom how it was carried out."

Bastienne laughed mirthlessly. "You mean you don't *want* to fathom how it was carried out. You wouldn't dare consider it yourself, so you can't understand how Ophélie convinced hundreds of lintep from towns, such as my own, to carry out the task."

"What are the two of you talking about?" Aislen asked irritably.

"My apologies, Princess Aislen, but I wanted to be certain at least someone understood the concept or I doubt I would be believed," Bastienne answered in a heavy voice. "What Lishe does with her mind snare is similar in nature to how the Paradises were created. The main difference is that she does not give part of her own power to the snare, but another lintep's power.

"What Princess Ophélie proposed, and what was eventually carried out, was the splitting of a lintep's own power. She initially requested fifty lintep to aide her in creating the first Paradise. The amount of power required to create a shield around the land was so great that many of those lintep died in giving so much of their power and the rest were left as virtually powerless husks.

"Ophélie quickly learned from her mistake and by the time she approached the people of Statera, she asked for double the amount of volunteers. These lintep were still required to give part of their power for the creation of the Paradises, but none gave so much as to die or be rendered effectively powerless afterwards."

Stunned silence greeted his words. Aislen was shocked to her core. She could never imagine parting with even the tiniest fraction of her power, let alone the amount that would be required to help create a Paradise.

"Does anyone else know about this?" she asked, barely trusting herself to speak.

"It appears the lintep of Illaria may be the only ones who *don't* know about this," Bastienne replied carefully. "Should you go to any other lintep settlement, you might still find some of those lintep who gave their power to create the Paradises. It was never a secret what they were doing. Perhaps not all of them told others exactly how they did it, but at least a few, like my father, explained the entire process to their families.

"It could be that these weaker lintep were the very ones who Lishe began stealing power from – those without enough power to fend her off. In any case, either she doesn't know what she could do or she is too power hungry to even consider it."

Rilla was the first to recover. "How could she manage to do that without anyone else in the villages noticing?"

"If she began long ago enough, she could have found villages littered with these lintep. Who would think their deaths out of place if they had never fully recovered from their initial loss?" Bastienne replied sadly.

"When my father returned to us, we were devastated by his loss. He had been one of the most talented lintep in Statera, training me himself. When Ophélie returned him to us, she suggested I come to Illaria to complete my training. There was little choice but to agree. I'd become quite a promising student, but with my father unable to teach me further, there was no one left in Statera who could.

"It is not more than a week's travel by horseback. I have often returned to lend a hand with promising students, sometimes bringing them to Illaria with me, but each of them quickly return home when their training was complete. Slowly, Statera has recovered from its loss and there are, once again, capable teachers who ensure a well-rounded view of skills to their students."

Aislen listened to his story in amazement. Everything she had ever known about the Paradises paled in comparison to this. Bastienne held the key to almost everything they had been trying to figure out since Kora's return.

"Master Bastienne, there are two things I would know." Aislen finally found her voice. "Do you know of any way to take these powers away from Lishe and will she survive if we do that?"

Bastienne thought for a long moment. "I don't believe she would die from the loss of those powers. From the sounds of it, her body didn't suffer at all when parting from three stolen powers. However, her mind might not survive the loss of all of them.

"As for whether I know of any way to do it, I can't claim that I do. I can well imagine ways that it *could* be done, but I would not want to be the one testing my theories – especially not on a lintep like Lishe."

Aislen nodded. She was still trying to make sense of everything that had happened that day. With a sudden movement, she rose from her chair.

"It's been a long day for all of us. Master Bastienne, you are welcome to stay in the castle as long as you like. I fear we will have need of your knowledge sooner rather than later. Kynon, I trust you can find a suitable room for our guest?" Kynon nodded and showed the old master out into the hall.

"Your highness?" Aislen turned at the hesitation in the fire mistress' voice. "I, too, would like to stay the night if you don't mind. Rilla has had quite a ... trying day. As her grandfather won't be here, I would beg your permission to stay with her."

Aislen caught the flicker of anger and then relief in Rilla's eyes. She still hadn't found out what had happened that day, but it was too late to talk about it now.

"That is a good idea, Mistress Isis," Aislen conceded, "as I would like a complete account of on the mission at first light. Rilla, I don't want you missing any more of your lessons than you already have. Get to bed now."

"Food first, Rilla," Guiscard urged her. "It's been a long day and you will not recover by sleeping on an empty stomach."

Aislen left them to await their food in the library. Guiscard was right. It had been a long day and she had been given her much to think about.

Chapter Nineteen – Aislen

Aislen lay in her bed the next morning, head throbbing from lack of sleep. She'd spent the better part of the night tossing and turning, haunted by strange dreams. Eventually, she had given up the prospect of sleeping and turned her mind to the problems facing her.

Lishe had been taught, or accidentally understood the concept of, some fairly dangerous skills. The only good news was that she had not experimented much further than what she had initially understood from her teachers, with the exception of stealing power. Even with that, it appeared she was still uncertain about how to develop that skill or she would already have started stealing power from Paradises.

At least Lishe only knew the location of one Paradise. Aislen knew she would have to convince her father that the next Paradise to be destroyed was the very one that Shuut and Kora had discovered, even if it was further away than some of the others. That shouldn't be too difficult, as the former Paradisians were probably thinking along the same lines as her.

A grumbling in her stomach reminded Aislen that she had not eaten the night before. Aislen sat up, reached for the silver handle that hung by her bed and pulled it twice. As she waited for her food to arrive, she lit a fire in the bathroom and filled the bath with steaming hot water. When a servant knocked on the door with her food, she sent out a tendril to unlock and open her door. The first time she'd allowed a servant to enter like that, she'd scared the girl half to death. Since that time, word had spread around the kitchens and Aislen noticed, with some amusement, the look of disappointment whenever she opened the door by hand.

Once the servant, Taniya by the sounds she made, had placed the tray of food on the large wooden table and closed the door behind her, Aislen finally stepped out of her bath. She drew heat from the fireplace to dry herself before dressing in a pale green robe. It was going to be another long day.

Not wanting to disturb them prematurely, Aislen sent out a tendril of her power to see if Rilla or Mistress Isis were awake yet. To her surprise, she found them both up and talking animatedly with one another. Gently, she brushed a thought against Isis' mind and was instantly rewarded with a reply that they would swiftly join her. No more than a minute later, she heard the footsteps outside her door. Employing the same strategy as before, Aislen opened the door with a tendril of her power. Isis walked in directly, not at all surprised by the action. Rilla, however, stood in fascination before a smile spread across her face.

"Good morning, Princess Aislen," the young girl greeted her. "What an interesting way to open the door."

"Rilla, we're cousins. I think you can afford to simply call me Aislen," the princess laughed as she closed the door behind the lintep without raising a finger.

"I wish I had as much control over my powers as you do, Aislen," Rilla said quietly, as she took her seat. Aislen raised a quizzical eyebrow at her young cousin. As far as she had understood, Rilla was quite the skilled young student, which was causing her teachers no end of grief.

"Rilla, every lintep has a small lapse or two during their training," Mistress Isis was quick to try to soothe her. "It's only natural. I'm certain even Princess Aislen was not perfect as she progressed through her lessons."

Aislen gritted her teeth at the memory of her power flooding over the expanse of the castle, taking in all the joy and pain of the lintep within it. Unfortunately, *those* were the minor lapses. The major ones were where she had accidentally influenced half the castle with her own feelings.

"Mistress Isis is right, Rilla," Aislen was quick to agree. "Every lintep, no matter how skilled or powerful they are, does not complete their training without a lapse or two. Whatever happened, I'm sure it's happened before, with other lintep, and will more than likely happen again. What was it this time?"

"I still don't quite understand it," the green eyed girl finally answered. "I was angry and my blood felt like it was boiling, but the air I breathed in was ice cold. Mistress Kayte told me that I was taking the heat from the air directly around me and drawing it into myself. I don't really know how it all happened."

Aislen struggled to keep her face a blank mask as the young lintep confided in her. She looked over to Mistress Isis who grimaced at the description.

"You must have realised what was happening if you're still alive," Aislen tried to bolster her confidence. Rilla looked quickly over to the fire mistress before lowering her eyes. She remained silent on the matter.

"As she told you, Rilla doesn't quite understand the turn of events," Mistress Isis explained. "I realised what was happening and intervened to bring things to a satisfactory conclusion."

"What Mistress Isis means is that she and Mistress Kayte had to wrestle with me to calm me down and draw the heat out of my body." Rilla looked up with a spark of anger in her eyes. "I should not be putting anyone else in danger because of my own lack of experience. Maybe the other teachers are right that I shouldn't be experimenting. Somehow, I always seem to get myself in trouble."

Aislen was surprised when Isis began to laugh. "Oh Rilla," the fire mistress cried out, "how little you understand it. I tried to explain it to you in our last class lesson, but I think you may have been too angry with me to take it in. Everything you do is an experiment exactly because of your lack of experience.

"Were you like any other lintep who was taught to use their power at the same time as they learned to walk, it would be different. However, you didn't know what you were until a few months ago. Even a normal lesson would be an experiment for you. To stop experimenting is most definitely *not* the solution to your problems."

"I must agree with Mistress Isis, Rilla," Aislen chimed in. "You come from an extremely powerful family. For any lintep to grow up not knowing what they are is a tragedy, as I'm sure you understood when you met Ratchin, but for a lintep as powerful as you ... it was reckless of both your mother and your father to leave you in the dark, with absolutely no training. You have a lot to learn and a short amount of time to learn it. You may have reached Illaria in time to keep your power, but that alone will not guarantee your safety if you do not hone your skills."

The red haired girl looked at her thoughtfully before drawing in a deep breath and nodding. "I know," she replied simply. "I'll do my best to master as many skills as I can as quickly as I can."

Aislen wasn't certain that was the best way to word it, but they had already spent too much time on this. Lessons would begin soon and she needed more answers. "Now, I need one of you to tell me exactly what happened yesterday with the Paradise. I understand no one was injured, but it rather sounded like a pitched battle was almost fought."

For the next half hour, before the morning bell summoned them both to lessons, Mistress Isis and Rilla described everything that had happened in the Paradise. When they reached the part where the crisis was initially averted, Isis let Rilla explain. It was clear to Aislen that Isis was, as yet, unaware of Rilla's bond with Eliséo. The princess herself should have been unaware of it, but there had already been too many instances where the girl had panicked or been forced to use her bond here in the castle and Aislen could not help but notice. It was a skill she had always taken great pains to hide, understanding the discomfort it would cause most lintep to know.

Rilla was suitably vague in her description of how she had created a wall between the two parties to avert bloodshed. Neither Aislen nor Isis questioned her further on the matter.

"So, we need to find a way to destroy these Paradises without having to resort to extreme measures to avert bloodshed. Thank you both for your report. You have given me much to think about. Don't let me keep you any longer. I know the morning bell will toll soon and you will both be eager to get to your lessons."

With barely a thought, Aislen unlocked and opened her door for the two of them once more. The student and the mistress walked out, leaving the princess alone with too many thoughts.

* * *

Lishe headed away from the broken Paradise. She hated walking alone. It always made her thoughts churn. She tried to avoid that at all costs because they inevitably brought her back to her childhood. Sometimes, she wished she'd been a boarder at the castle, so that she could have missed all that happened within her household. It was no use trying to close her mind to the memories. Once they started, there was no stopping them until they had run their course. She knew that from years of experience.

Her mother was a very talented and skilful lintep. Unfortunately, she was not very powerful. That was where the problems started. When Lishe was honest with herself, she would sometimes admit that wasn't really where the problem started, but it was easier to think it was. If her mother had been more powerful, then it wouldn't have mattered when her father had tried to beat her – he never would have succeeded. Her mother knew the skill. Lishe knew that because her mother had been the one to teach her how to defend herself against the possibility of an attack by her father.

The dreaded attack had never come, so Lishe had never tested her own strength against her father. She had often hidden in cupboards or behind doors as her father beat her mother senseless. Each time, she had promised herself that she would never let herself get into the same situation. She would never let anyone have such power or control over her.

When she had started lessons in the castle and met Nyssa, she was so envious of the little lady's power. It was so vast that the royal lintep could perform so many tasks without ever honing her skills. It made Lishe crazy with rage that such a power was going to waste. If *she* had that amount of power, the things she would do! So she had trained side by side with Nyssa and eventually with Kora, until the three of them were the most advanced students in the castle.

It wasn't long after Kora left the castle that Lishe applied to become a mistress. She was certain to pass any test they gave her, so the blow was all the harder when it came. They allowed her to take the test, but she soon learned they never had any intention of allowing her to become a mistress. Lishe was outraged! How dare they deny her that right?

She had immediately left Illaria after that. What was the point of staying when they would only try to stifle her dreams? If they wouldn't give her the tattoos she deserved, she would give them to herself. She never managed to discover how they made the blue ink for their tattoos, so she had settled for black.

With the small amount of power she had, Lishe knew there was nothing she could do to help herself in life or protect herself in the Outworld. Her aim quickly became to increase her power. Masters Elwood and Amyas had once slipped up and revealed something they had probably intended to keep from students – it was possible to stop a lintep from using their power. It had taken her a good long while to figure out exactly how they had done that, but it was worth the time to discover it. Lishe had then travelled the Outworld, finding small communities of lintep where there were some very weak powers.

She would never forget her first time. The day she had found the weakest lintep in a tiny village and used her own power to completely encase the lintep's mind. Her power was too weak to encase his entire body, but his mind was just the right size. She closed her power around his mind and drew his power into herself, leaving an empty husk. It felt ... strange to have another lintep's power within her mind. The power was so weak that it could not struggle against her. It was easy to tame. After that, every time was easier and more rewarding. She could go after more powerful lintep – lintep who hadn't bothered honing their skills and learning how to defend themselves as she had. Lintep like Nyssa. Really, they deserved what she did to them. If they didn't have the skill to use their power, they shouldn't be allowed to keep it.

It was in one of these small lintep communities where she had first learnt more about the Paradises and how they were created. Everyone in Illaria knew of the Paradises and of the prophecy calling for their destruction, but no one seemed to understand the power that was sitting there, just waiting to be harnessed. She could have it all for herself. She could become the most powerful lintep alive. It was all at her fingertips if she could just figure out a way to steal it.

Chapter Twenty – Ivy Hedge

It took Lishe almost two days of walking, but she finally reached Hedgefall. The town had gotten its name from the wall surrounding it. Long ago, it had fallen into disrepair and never been fixed. Ivy now covered what was left of it.

Lishe knew this town mistrusted lintep. Nyssa had told her about the town when she'd returned from the Outworld with her father and sister. It was from this town that humans had followed her family, intent on killing as many of them as possible.

From what the distraught Nyssa had confided in her, had her mother, Graesyn, not been so foolish, only her brothers and youngest sister would have died. In her sudden grief at having lost both Adina and Fredryck, Graesyn had attempted to save her oldest son, Vaughn. Vaughn had tried to save Fredryck, but pushed himself too far for his own powers to save him. Graesyn made the same mistake because she couldn't stand idly by and watch her child die. It was a beautiful, yet utterly pointless, act.

But of all the lintep in that family, Lishe was most wary of Lord Aaron. It was rumoured that he could have been a master had he but sat the test. He was famed as the most powerful lintep in Illaria, but rarely showed his skills. Unlike his wife, he had a calculating mind and could do what needed to be done, no matter how difficult the task. He knew that he couldn't save Graesyn, but unlike his wife, he didn't try to save her anyway. It would have cost him his life and left his two remaining teenage daughters alone in the Outworld, too far from Illaria to safely find their way back again.

Much as he had interfered with her plans for more power, Lishe had to admit that she admired the strength of his resolve. If she could find any way to break that resolve, it would be in Hedgefall.

Making sure to cover her black tattoos, Lishe asked around for the inn with the best ale in the town and was directed to the Ivy Hedge. She walked through the town, listening to passing conversations in the marketplace, until she reached the famed inn.

The Ivy Hedge was a wooden, two storey building with the same ivy covering it that grew everywhere else in and around the town. At least in this building, it was kept under control – the windows were clear and clean. She opened the door and walked confidently into the room.

Lishe knew she was a beautiful woman and she used that fact to her advantage. Keeping the sleeve of her dress easily covering her tattoos, she untied her hair, letting the long black tresses fall down past her shoulders. Her piercing blue eyes took in everything at a glance.

The innkeeper behind the bar idly cleaned a cup as he kept a close eye on her. His wife could be heard ordering the kitchenmaids through the adjoining door to the kitchen. Three tables around the edge of the room hosted dice and card games. Lishe smiled at that sight – she should be able to get all she needed from those humans.

"One of your famous ales, my good innkeeper," she said, loudly enough for everyone to hear, "and a room for the night, if you please."

The innkeeper looked at her warily until she revealed enough coins to show she wasn't wasting his time. He poured her ale as she sat at the bar. It wasn't long before she received an offer to join a few of the men at their table. They rarely saw a woman travelling alone, unless she was a banwep. From the look of Lishe, it was clear to see she was anything but a banwep.

"It's so kind of you to let me join you on my first night in town." She batted her eyelids at the men coyly. "Would you allow me to join your game as well?"

"Have you ever played cards?" one of the men asked her.

She bit her lip, before shaking her head. "Not since I was a little girl. I can barely remember it at all."

The men looked at each other with greedy eyes. "Then let us remind you how to play. The loser buys a round of drinks for everyone."

Lishe fought to keep from laughing. They were so eager to fleece her. She purposely lost the first two rounds, making a good show of trying to learn the game. By the time she started to play properly, the men already had two extra ales in them. Their tongues were loose and Lishe was ready to pounce.

"Has anyone travelled to the east recently? I passed by a small town, two days ago. I was going to rest there, but it appeared as though the townsfolk were fighting off some invaders. I decided it would be best to keep my head down and walk on."

"Two days east?" a freckled man asked, rubbing the back of his neck. "There's nothing in that direction for a full week's ride."

"Really?" she asked innocently. "I'm certain there was something there."

A muscular blonde man looked at the freckled man then over to Lishe, not knowing whether to speak. Eventually, the ale within him made the decision. "I've heard there is a Paradise about two days east from here. Mind you, that's just a rumour."

"A Paradise!" Lishe gasped, dramatically. "It can't have been. I could see it with my own eyes."

"I'll bet it's those pesky lintep," the freckled man announced. "Those good for nothing creatures probably destroyed the barrier somehow."

"You're talking nonsense, Judd," the innkeeper's wife said as she brought over another round of ale. "Paradises can't be destroyed."

"What's *your* explanation then?" Judd asked bluntly. "A town was built two days from here, so quickly that none of us ever heard of it? Don't be daft, Wynnow. It must have been those meddling lintep."

"Even if it was the lintep destroying a Paradise, Judd," chimed in the blonde man, "there's nothing to be done about it."

"Nothing to be done about it!" Judd yelled. "We go down to this town and kill any of those lintep who were stupid enough to stay behind so they can't destroy any more. They're *our* safe havens from people like *them*. They can't just go around destroying them. They need to be stopped. Who's with me?"

By this time, the inn's other patrons had all crowded around their table. Lishe sat back and hid a smile as the humans organised to leave for this new town early the next morning.

"You'll show us the way," Judd instructed her.

Lishe nodded, playing the bewildered traveller. The evening's work had gone better than she had dared to hope. She took her leave of the men, asking Wynnow to show her to her room. She followed the innkeeper's wife up a narrow set of wooden stairs to the first landing. Her room was the first to the right, with the bath chamber across from her. Lishe requested a hot bath – it had been weeks since she'd had the luxury. She sank down into the steaming water, smiling at her success.

The next morning, Lishe dressed in her finest travel clothes. These humans appreciated a well groomed woman. It would not do to have them fawn over anyone else. She would not be able to use her powers on anyone, lest she alert them to the fact that she was herself, a lintep.

They were waiting for her when she descended into the taproom. She noticed, with a hint of irritation, that the blonde man was not as resolute about the situation as the other townsfolk. The freckled man, Judd, had managed to gather an impressive crowd on such short notice.

"We've horses enough for half of us. We'll share them as we go to save our strength. Who knows what these lintep will try to throw at us."

Within minutes, the group of humans led by Lishe were heading east towards the broken Paradise.

Chapter Twenty-One – Broken Paradise

Lukys wearily rubbed his eyes. It had been a long few days. He and Brynt, along with a number of other Paradisians and lintep, had been discussing the best way to go about assimilating the new Outworlders into their current situation. The main problem was money. There just wasn't any available. For the Paradisians to acquire some, they would need to sell all their excess wares, of which there were precious few, to nearby towns.

There was also the question of distribution. How would they live from now onwards? Would the kitchen still provide food for the entire town? Would the money be kept by Brynt and spent as needed for the good of everyone? Or would they now each need to earn their own living. If they earned their own livings, would they need to become more like other towns in the Outworld or could their idyllic lives continue?

"Brynt, I don't think we can resolve anything without talking to your people," Lukys finally told him.

"They're not *my* people," Brynt insisted.

Lukys looked at him in barely disguised annoyance. "Yes, much as you say that, they all look to you for answers. In my book, that makes you their leader more than anyone else. Whether you call yourself that, or not, doesn't make a difference – they will still look to you. So talk to them!"

He stood up and walked towards the door, he hesitated before he departed Brynt's hut. "I know you don't like lintep to use their powers on humans, but I should tell you that I can feel the fear in most of them. They need you to reassure them. Together, you can figure this out. They won't listen to anything I tell them – I'm not *their* king."

Lukys left the hut, squinting in the early morning light. They'd been talking most of the evening, as they had for the past three evenings. Exhausted, he headed towards the tavern, where they had erected makeshift beds for the "intruders". Kora was waiting for him when he arrived.

"We need to talk," she said as soon as he'd entered the tavern.

"Kora, not now. I'm tired and hungry." He attempted to wave her aside.

"I'll talk while you eat." She led him to a table, sat him down and fetched him a bowl of stew. His hunger won out over his desire to be left alone.

"You have until the time I finish this stew to talk. Then I'm sleeping," he told her firmly.

"Did you know there are lintep living here?" she asked him softly. "Children, certainly, but there must be adults as well."

Lukys feigned indifference as he continued to eat. "No."

"What are we going to do about it?"

"Nothing."

"We can't do nothing!" Kora exclaimed. "What if the children have no parents to teach them? What if their parents are barely capable of handling their own power, let alone their children's? We can't knowingly let them lose their powers or die."

"Kora, exactly what are you proposing?" Lukys asked, already knowing her answer.

"Bring them to Illaria, of course," she immediately replied.

"Of course," he replied sardonically. "We'll provide food, board and lessons for them for nothing in return. Kora, be reasonable. If we destroy all of the Paradises and you find a handful of lintep children in each one, do you expect them *all* to live in Illaria at my expense? No. You'll need to find another solution."

"Another solution?" she asked in surprise. "What other solution can there be? Do you think any master or mistress is going to volunteer to live in these Paradises to teach them? Even if they wanted to, we wouldn't have enough of them to spare."

"They don't need to be masters or mistresses," Lukys replied wearily. "As long as they have completed their training, any lintep could volunteer. I'll leave the details to you, Kora, dear. Now I've finished my meal and need to rest. I do not wish to be disturbed."

* * *

Kora closed the door of the tavern behind her angrily. Since she had returned to Illaria, she'd found herself and her ideas constantly flung to the side. Lukys hadn't exactly suggested that she go on her expedition to find all the Paradises, but he had certainly encouraged her when she'd raised the idea. With her return, she had hoped that her ideas would be listened to. It seemed as though at every turn, Lukys had more important things to worry about and wouldn't give her more than a few minutes of his time.

Without thinking about where she was heading, she found herself walking towards the cluster of trees that passed as a forest in all Paradises. Erton had been oblivious to the fact that she would often hide herself away there when she needed some space from his idiocy. Now, finding herself in a similar frame of mind, she automatically walked there.

She traipsed in far enough into the the forest to be lost from view and then sat behind a tree. As she always had before, she closed her eyes and put her hands down to the ground, letting her fingers feel their way through the dirt, submerging her mind in anything but what was troubling her.

"You too?" a soft voice reached out to her from another tree. She didn't have to look around to know it was Eliséo. Her only response was to nod. Eventually, she opened her eyes and looked at the elf.

He was sitting on the ground, the same as she was. His black hair had grown long and had an unkempt look to it. Clearly his travels hadn't allowed him any time to tend to it recently. His elven travel clothes, while well worn, still looked as new as the day they'd been made. Kora knew elves needed little sleep, but Eliséo looked weary beyond a lack of sleep. His dull grey eyes held no joy, which she found odd as he was often the one to lighten the mood.

"Lukys won't listen to any of my ideas. He never seems to have time for anything I have to say. I thought things would be different once I returned."

"What happened this time?"

"Plyke found a lintep child. I still don't understand how he did it, but from half way across the Paradise, he found one. It's something I will have to talk to him about later.

"What I thought was more important was to let Lukys know. It's only a child. Who knows how things work in this Paradise, but if it's even remotely like our Paradise, this child won't be taught properly, if at all. He'll be shunned, possibly exiled. Lukys doesn't seem to care.

"I told him I thought we should bring the boy to Illaria, but he flatly refused. He said there might be a handful of lintep in each of the Paradises we destroy and he can't afford to bring them all to Illaria. Any lintep is apparently free to do what they will, but he won't have any part of it."

The look on Eliséo's face confused her. He wore a strange smile, his eyes finally shining a little. "I think you may have misunderstood what your king told you."

"What do you mean?"

"He told you any lintep is free to do what they will, but did he not say anything about *you*?" Eliséo asked her.

"Well ... yes, he said 'I'll leave the details to you.'"

"Exactly," Eliséo's smile spread further. "Don't you realise he has placed this task on your shoulders? Consider it, Kora. He must have so many matters on his mind at the moment. You've discovered a new task and brought it to him, expecting him to solve it but, he simply doesn't have time to deal with it. He has entrusted you to do the right thing. What would *you* like to do?"

"Me?" Kora asked, a little shocked by his reply. "Well, I suppose I'd like these lintep to be able to learn the skills their parents probably can't teach them. They may not be so skilled as to die if their power leaves them, but it would be a true shame to see any of them lose their power if I could help."

"Can you think of any way, other than bringing them to Illaria, that you could help them?"

"I thought, perhaps, one or two masters or mistresses might be happy to help. But I know that isn't a permanent solution. There aren't enough of them in Illaria to spare. Uncle Lukys did say that it could be *any* lintep – it doesn't have to be one of our teachers."

"Do you not have any ideas?"

Kora was silent for a while, letting ideas flood her mind. With a smile, she settled on a possibility.

"I wonder if we could organise a school somewhere, not in Illaria, but somewhere in the Outworld. Then all the lintep children could come to us for as long as they need to."

"That still poses a problem," Eliséo pointed out. "You won't have the resources to look after these children. Even if you did, their parents, if they have any, won't be able to afford to part with any money – the Paradises don't have any as it is."

"Do you think it would be better if they don't live at the school? What if it's a school that travels around to each of the Paradises and spends a few weeks at each one. Would that work?"

"It is certainly a better option," Eliséo agreed. "It might be a little too long between lessons if there aren't any older lintep in the Paradise, but it is at least a start. Depending on how many lintep you can corral to your cause, you might be able to visit the Paradises more often if you split into teams. It does still leave the problem of potential exile, but at least it's a start."

Kora finally smiled. "True, but you know, it just might work. I know Pér would be happy to help. Surely he would know of others in Illaria who might agree to this. Perhaps one or two of the older, retired teachers might volunteer some of their time. Thank you, Eliséo! You always know how to make things seem possible." Kora's smile faded as she noticed his still sad expression. "There's something I don't understand. When I came here, you asked 'You too?' What did you mean by that?"

Eliséo regarded her silently for a few moments. She felt him appraising her. She almost thought he wasn't going to answer when he lent his head back against the tree.

"It's Rilla," he told her quietly. "I find myself constantly forgetting that she isn't an elf, but a lintep. She looks the same age as some of the elves I know in Silvaren. They are already over one hundred years old – still considered children by elves, but old enough to control their feelings and actions. Rilla is most certainly not the same as them. I would not want her to be the same as an elf, but I wish she could exercise a little discretion."

"Is this to do with the way that she prevented bloodshed?" Kora asked gently. Eliséo only nodded. "I doubt many, if any, lintep would be able to put the pieces together from that. It's true they would certainly know that she had done something particularly ... unusual, but that doesn't mean they will be able to guess the truth. Even knowing the truth, I don't know what she did. I can only assume it had to do with the bond because her eyes were blazing bright green, but there weren't many people close enough to her to realise that. Perhaps you are too quick to reprimand her."

"She would certainly agree with you there," Eliséo admitted. "I don't think you saw what happened afterwards."

Kora listened as Eliséo explained Rilla's loss of control, resulting in both Isis and Kayte having to save her.

"Well, that explains Pyrid's sudden departure once the Paradise was destroyed," Kora thought aloud. "She really does have more power than sense at times, doesn't she? Just like her mother."

"I wouldn't necessarily say that," Eliséo instantly replied. "She has more power than she knows what to do with, but her control is lacking because she never knew what she was. You forget that the child has only known what she is for less than a year. For more than fifteen years she used her powers without knowing it and has only had a few weeks of proper training.

"It is remarkable that she did not die on our journey here. She has already learnt so much, but there is so much more that she still has left to learn with very little time. Isis was wise to whisk her back to Illaria, back to her lessons. If Anya insists on Rilla's presence every time a Paradise is destroyed, her lessons will suffer."

Kora broached a subject she knew was already fraught with disagreements. "Does it have to be Rilla? There was some debate about father doing it, so couldn't it be any lintep really?"

"It could," Eliséo admitted, "however, our karlik friends are a cautious people. They know about the prophecy mentioning Rilla in connection with destroying the Paradises. Anya, as much as any karlik, is stubborn. She has it in her mind that Rilla is the best lintep for the task, for various reasons, and it will take quite a bit of effort to change her mind."

"What about Plyke and the boys?" Kora asked suddenly. "Arishen had a vision of him helping. Couldn't that be an alternative?"

"Would you want Plyke to miss as many lessons as Rilla?" Eliséo asked, shaking his head. "No, that solution will not do."

"Could I help?"

Eliséo looked at her for a moment before shrugging his shoulders. "You can make the suggestion to Anya. I doubt you will succeed, but you have every right to try. For myself, I must ask my queen for her orders. Now that the first Paradise has been destroyed, she may require my return to Goraburg to assist in the troublesome situation Lord Mikhail finds himself in. I doubt she will ask me to be present at every destruction unless Anya insists. Even if she does, it seems as though it will be a while until the next destruction. Lukys and Brynt need to organise many things which may impact every other Paradise."

Kora said nothing. Together they sat in silence, lost in their own thoughts.

Chapter Twenty-Two – Negotiations

Lishe sat atop her stead, at the head of the procession. There weren't as many humans from Hedgefall as she would have liked, but it was more than she thought the small village would be able to muster. Close to fifty people wouldn't be enough to cause much trouble, but it was a start. She needed to cause enough disruption to delay the destruction of the next Paradise until she had understood how they had managed it.

They were nearing the broken Paradise. She would need to use all of her self control not to attack the lintep with her powers. If she did that, it would only serve to distance her from the townspeople of Hedgefall and that would not do at all. No, she would have to keep herself well away from the action.

"Judd," she called out hesitantly to the man walking beside her. The freckled man immediately turned his attention to her. "I'm afraid of what might happen when we reach the little village. Do you think there might be … fighting?" Her voice fell to a whisper at the last.

"It might come to that," he shrugged nonchalantly, though she could feel the fear within him. "Don't you worry, miss. You stay hidden with the horses and we'll take care of everything."

She smiled her thanks to him, noticing the blonde man eyeing her suspiciously from behind. He might prove to be trouble. She would have to keep an eye on him.

It was past midday, four days after she had left the broken Paradise. They were now within sight of it. Lishe dismounted, along with the other riders. All the humans passed the reins of their horses to her. She bit down a sharp remark as she realised they expected her to actually look after the horses in their absence.

Judd left her with an assurance. "We're just going to see what is happening around here. I didn't doubt your words, but I *am* surprised to see a town here. It really must have been a Paradise that they destroyed."

"And there won't be any fighting unless absolutely necessary." The blonde man came up to them.

"Orlan, you just don't want to dirty your sword. Stop being such a stick in the mud," Judd rebuked him.

Lishe fought to keep her temper with Orlan. He could ruin all of her well laid plans with that attitude. There wouldn't be another chance to do this. All the other towns were too far away and too much time would have passed by the time she got there. If he stood in her way, she would make him pay.

* * *

Plyke and Tika were playing with some of the children when the alert was sounded. The intruder alert didn't have the same urgency as when their own party had entered the Paradise, but it was urgent enough that everyone headed for the farms. Plyke was torn between staying to protect the children and seeing what was happening. His curiosity won out. The children would be safe enough if the intruders were kept at bay.

"Tika, can you stay with the children while I see what's happening?" he asked his Partner softly. Tika nodded, his black hair falling around his eyes. "Thanks. I'll be back soon."

Plyke was off at a run. He didn't understand how there could already be intruders. From what they'd been told, there wasn't another town within two days' ride from here. For anyone to have raised an alert, they must have passed by the exact same day as the Paradise was destroyed in the first place.

The hair on the back of his neck tingled as his thoughts ran to Lishe. Surely, she would have acted when they were trying to destroy the Paradise, wouldn't she? Unless she hadn't realised what they were doing until it was too late.

As he ran towards the edge of the broken Paradise, Plyke searched for any of the lintep who might listen to him. Kayte, Isis and Guiscard hadn't returned with Rilla. King Lukys and Lord Aaron had been reluctant to tell him the details of what had occurred but he understood it had been bad enough for his cousin to instantly return to Illaria and her lessons.

He continued to scan the passing faces until he saw one he recognised. The lintep's grey hair shone in the sunlight, catching Plyke's attention. He ran over to Master Aurelius, motioning him to one side.

"What's the matter, young Plyke?" The old master asked in concern.

"I think Lishe is behind this intrusion," Plyke told him without preamble. "There aren't any settlements closer than two days' ride from here. Only if someone was watching the destruction could they have reached a town and returned in such a short time. Even if they were passing by at the time, no one other than Lishe would have any reason to come back with more people."

The practical master regarded him thoughtfully for a time before nodding. "Yes, I think you may be correct there. However, Rilla is out of harm's way for now so Lishe will have no reason to strike out. I'll tell the others to be on alert for her. If we can neutralise her without Rilla around, that would be the best outcome. If not …"

Plyke didn't need to hear what would happen if they didn't stop Lishe. He brought his own powers safely under control as he followed Master Aurelius to the edge of the broken Paradise. From a short distance away, he heard the master talking animatedly with King Lukys and Lord Aaron. They glanced over in his direction and nodded. With a few more words exchanged, Lord Aaron accompanied Master Aurelius back to Plyke.

"You're right to be suspicious, Plyke," his grandfather told him, placing a hand on his shoulder. "Master Aurelius is correct that we shouldn't be in any danger from Lishe without Rilla here, however, if we can stop her now, that would be best. My main concern is what she's doing with humans. I'll spread the word to the other lintep to be on their guard for anything underhanded."

Plyke smiled his thanks to Lord Aaron and watched as he moved about the lintep, quickly spreading the alert. Not knowing what else to do, Plyke went to see what the intruders wanted. There looked to be close to fifty of them – more than the original party which had travelled from Illaria.

Even though Pyrid had now returned from Illaria, the fire opal dragon had frequently left the broken Paradise to find food. He was not lying in his usual field, but the depression in the grass there was difficult to mistake for anything other than a creature as large as the crystal dragon.

The Paradise itself had little over a hundred residents. Together with the party from Illaria, they easily outnumbered the intruders. That fact didn't stop everyone being on edge. Even with his powers pulled close around him, Plyke couldn't help but feel the tension surrounding everyone. Brynt, though he still refused to be called their leader, was desperately trying to put on a brave face for his people.

A flaxen haired man walked up to the group, led by a freckled, brown haired man. Plyke moved as close to them as he could, in an attempt to overhear the conversation.

"What is your business here?" Brynt asked the spindly, brown haired man. His blunt manner took the man by surprise and his expression darkened.

"We live in Hedgefall, not fifty miles from here and none of us have ever heard tell of a town in this location, not until two days ago when a young lady asked us about it. We want to know how this town appeared out of thin air."

"How does this question require so many armed men to travel fifty miles to ask it?" Brynt eyed their company. "Or is there something else you're not telling me?"

"She told us there was a dragon, a karlik, an elf and probably lintep here," the man replied angrily. "We came to find out what's happening. We don't like their sort in Hedgefall and don't want them so close to our homes."

"If you have a problem with them, I suggest you leave." Brynt's icy voice travelled over the entire group of people. The freckled man, furious by that point, made to draw his sword. He was stopped by the large blonde man.

"Judd, this is not the time." He forced the freckled man, Judd, back towards the rest of the Hedgefall townspeople before turning to Brynt. "I apologise for our unannounced arrival. A number of people were concerned that our town might be in danger from the sudden appearance of your town and the presence of such unusual company. My name is Orlan."

Plyke instantly felt Brynt relax with the change of tide. "My name is Brynt and I speak for these people."

"Goodman Brynt." Orlan extended his hand to the Paradise spokesman. "Would you be so good as to enlighten us on the unusual situation here?"

Brynt studied the man. Clearly deciding that he was sincere, the farmer man shook Orlan's hand and proceeded to explain the events of the previous four days, pointedly ignoring the freckled man.

"So you can see how we are wary of any intruders at the moment, whether they're human or not," Brynt finished with a veiled warning.

Placing a restraining hand on Judd's chest, Orlan spoke again. "I think the people of Hedgefall would be honoured to help you in this situation. Perhaps we can come to some agreement to become trading partners.

"If you show us any excess wares you have, we can begin from there. It may take some time to begin trading properly, as it isn't an easy distance to be doing regularly, but I'm certain we can make it work. What say you Brynt?"

Plyke watched as the people of Hedgefall instantly relaxed their stance. A wave of calm passed over everyone. Brynt agreed to the proposal. He and his Paradisians led the townspeople of Hedgefall towards the Paradise buildings.

It took a few moments for Plyke to understand what had happened. He looked at the lintep scattered around the gathering of people, taking note of their particular skills. None of the mind masters were there, but that did not mean that others, such as Master Aurelius, were incapable of the feat he was certain had just happened.

The old master saw the look of concentration on his face and walked over to him. "What is it, young Plyke?"

"Was it you?" Plyke asked him.

"Alas, no," he replied with a melancholy smile. "I quite possibly have the skill for such a feat, but not the power. No, my guess would be your grandfather. He has a rather subtle touch. I'm surprised you noticed it at all."

"The humans certainly didn't notice it," Plyke pointed out. "I only noticed at the very end. A wave of calm washed over me, like when a lintep can change another's feelings using touch. I didn't know it was possible without touch."

Master Aurelius regarded him carefully before motioning him to follow. Plyke didn't know where he was being led, but he trusted the old master. He shadowed his footsteps until they came to a large cluster of trees, similar to the one in his old Paradise where the isolation hut had been located.

Only once they were completely hidden from view did Master Aurelius stop. He sat on a moss covered stone. Plyke followed his lead, curiosity growing by the second.

"What you just witnessed is a rare skill to possess. When I said I possibly have the skill for it, I may have misled you. What I meant was, I may have enough control over my power to do such a thing over a very short distance, but I would never have as subtle a touch as we felt just now.

"Most lintep can eventually learn how to subtly change another's feelings through touch and almost every lintep will learn to understand another's feelings again, through touch. How well they can do this in the first place will indicate whether or not they will ever have the skill to do it without touch."

Plyke paled. He thought back to that first day in the broken Paradise when he could feel the emotions of all the humans around him. Some had been stronger than others, but he had felt all of them as if he had placed his hand on each of their arms. It hadn't occurred to him, but since that day, he'd been able to feel the emotions of anyone he concentrated on, all without touch.

"I suppose that means Plyke will eventually have the same skill as my father then," Kora said as she stepped out from behind a tree with Eliséo. Plyke looked up in surprise. He'd been so absorbed in his own thoughts that he hadn't heard them approaching.

"Kora, you should know the boy is too young to be displaying such skills," Aurelius scoffed. Kora raised an eyebrow and turned to Plyke.

"Tell him what happened with Abelin," she told him. Plyke shook his head. He didn't want it to be true. He knew how much trouble Rilla was having because of the amount of power and skill she exhibited at such a young age – he didn't want to be like her.

"Who is Abelin?" Master Aurelius asked in confusion. When it became clear that Plyke wouldn't answer, the grey haired lintep turned to his mother instead. "Kora?"

Kora told Master Aurelius about the lintep child and how Plyke found him. Plyke would have found shock on Master Aurelius' face laughable had the situation not been about him.

"Did you talk to King Lukys about bringing Abelin and Lorella to Illaria?" Plyke asked, in an effort to deflect the close scrutiny under which he found himself.

"That may not to happen, Plyke. I have other ideas," she said. Plyke noticed Eliséo smile at her encouragingly. "However, that's not the matter in question at the moment. I want to know more about this different type of skill. Master Aurelius, I've never heard of someone being able to read or manipulate feelings without touch. I would have said it was impossible had I not known that Plyke can already read feelings without even being near a person. How is it achieved?"

"That's a tricky question, Kora," Master Aurelius replied before turning his attention back on Plyke. "When did this first occur, young Plyke?"

"Just a few days ago," Plyke answered reluctantly. "It was when Tika and I were walking through the Paradise just after it had been destroyed."

"I beg to differ, Plyke. That is not actually true," Eliséo interrupted with a lilting voice. "The first time it happened was when Shadow was struck down by Lishe's mindsnare."

"What! Is this true?" Master Aurelius asked incredulously. "Before your power peaked? That's amazing!"

Plyke recalled that day with mixed feelings. "Yes, I remember feeling something bad. I didn't know what it was at the time, just that something bad was happening. After that, Eliséo made me stretch out my senses to see if I could discover anything else. That was when I heard rushing water and more bad magic, though I couldn't tell what had happened."

"I don't understand," Aurelius stared at him in confusion. "What does that mean?"

"It means that Plyke could feel Lishe from over a mile away. She must have been sending out her combined power to reach us, so I'm not entirely certain if that's what Plyke initially felt. It may not have been the full distance when he felt the 'bad magic'. However, when I asked him to cast out his senses to see if he could discover anything else, Lishe would have withdrawn all of her power back around herself. She was at the Bramble River, at the ferry crossing. It was over a mile from where we were and Plyke felt her destroy the ferry."

"That's ... impossible," Master Aurelius stammered, as he placed his hands on the rock beneath him to steady himself. "That kind of power ... it's unheard of. His father must also be a powerful lintep for the boy to have such power. Do you know who he is?"

Kora nodded, but stayed silent. Plyke stared at her in shock. In all his years, he'd never asked her about his father. The only thing she had ever mentioned to him was that she was forced to stay in their Paradise because she had fallen pregnant with him. He'd always assumed his father was just a man she'd met in a town somewhere before finding their Paradise.

"You know who my father is and you've never told me?" he finally whispered. Kora looked at him with tears in her eyes. He could feel the fear coming off her in shattering waves. "Who is it?"

"I ... don't think I can tell you," she swallowed a lump in her throat.

"Kora, you've let me live my whole life without knowing who I was. *Please* don't keep this from me too," he begged her, reaching out to hold her hands. "Please!"

"Pér," she whispered. "It's Pér."

"But how can that be?" Master Aurelius asked, perplexed. "Pér didn't know where you went. None of us did."

"That's true," Kora agreed, "but Pér left Illaria to try to find me a little while after I disappeared. He found me in Turon. He spent a long time trying to convince me to either tell him what I was doing in the Outworld or to return with him to Illaria. I refused to do either, and left before he could convince me otherwise. He has no idea that you are his son, Plyke, though I'm certain he would be overjoyed to discover he is a father – after the initial shock wears off."

"Pér," Plyke mused aloud. "Isn't he a minstrel?" His question was met with a round of laughter.

"Pér would like to think himself a minstrel, but in reality he is a merchant."

Plyke smiled at the reply and the sudden laughter, but his mind soon wandered back to his father. "He's here, isn't he? He came with us and didn't return with Rilla to Illaria. Can I meet him properly?"

Kora stopped laughing, eyes wide.

"Please, Kora. I'd like to get to know my father and you said yourself he would be overjoyed to discover the truth."

"Better he finds out now from the two of you than later from someone else," Eliséo cautioned her. "Plyke, why don't you go to find Tika. I'm certain he won't want to miss this. Kora, surely you can find a way to convince Pér to accompany you back here to the trees."

Kora glared at him icily, but nodded all the same. She set off in the direction of the small arena, where Pér had set up a musical workshop. Plyke could barely contain his excitement as he watched her go. He smiled his thanks to Eliséo and ran off to find Tika.

Chapter Twenty-Three – Pér

Pér sat listening to his newest students. Their talent raw, but promising. He strummed his lute alongside them, the notes catching in the wind and travelling all around the crudely built arena. It had been years since he'd had the musical attention of so many people.

A movement at the edge of the arena caught his attention. Kora patiently waited for him to finish the tune he taught the Paradisians. She had that look in her eyes – the one that always made his heart stop. She had something important to tell him. It was the same look she'd had all those years ago, when she'd returned from the Outworld without her mother, brothers and little sister. The same look she had just before she left Illaria – though he didn't know why at the time. The same look she'd had when he'd finally found her in Turon, only to lose her again.

Signalling his students to continue practicing the tune, he held his lute gently and walked over to the most gorgeous lintep he'd ever laid eyes on. Kora stood waiting for him, her brown wavy hair blowing gently in the slight wind. He'd always loved the way she let it hang loose, with only a few strands tied back to keep the hair out of her light brown eyes.

He lent in close, brushing his lips against her cheek. "I know that look. What is it this time? You're not going to disappear on me again, are you? You know I'd never let you slip away another time, don't you?" His chest hurt with happiness as she smiled and shook her head.

"No, but I do have something important to tell you," she answered him with a gentle voice. "Do you think your students can part with you for a while?"

Pér regarded her closely. He certainly hadn't been mistaken. This was important. Without a second thought, he called out to his students to practice to their heart's content and he would listen to them again on the morrow. Turning back to Kora, he took her small hand in his large calloused ones.

"I'm all yours," he told her without reserve. She smiled at him in the way that always melted his heart. Squeezing his hand, she led him towards a small cluster of trees.

Pér followed her wordlessly. He knew Kora well. There was no point in pressing her to talk when she wasn't ready. His thoughts drifted back to their last days together in Illaria all those years ago. He'd known something had happened. She'd changed all of a sudden – become much more secretive and secluded. He should have known better than to take his eyes off her. If only he'd known where she was going, he would have followed her.

It had been a bitter tonic when he realised that she had left without saying goodbye. Bitter enough for him not to immediately chase her, but his anger with Kora could never last.

He eventually tracked her to Turon. She'd been so surprised to see him that, instead of being angry, she had run straight into his arms. They'd spent a blissful week together before he started to ask what she was doing in the Outworld and beg her to come back to Illaria with him. When she refused, he'd insisted on staying with her, travelling wherever she would go. That was the mistake he would come to regret for years afterwards. The very next morning, he woke to find her gone. After that, no matter where he travelled to ask after her, no one had seen or heard of her. Eventually, he'd given up hope of ever finding her again and returned to Illaria, heartbroken and alone.

"We're nearly there," Kora said, bringing him out of his reverie. "I hope you can forgive me ... again."

He creased his brow and enveloped her in an embrace. "I always forgive you, Kora. I don't have a choice." She looked up at him with her big brown eyes, making him wish he hadn't missed so many years of her life. "I'm ready for whatever it is you have to tell me."

Kora nodded, but he could feel the doubt swirling all around her. He'd always been able to feel everything she felt, even without touching her. She was special like that.

He followed her curiously deeper into the cluster of trees and was surprised to find a number of people waiting for them. Master Aurelius, the elf and two of the boys from the Paradise. He tried to hide the pain from his face. His heart ached as he realised Kora was finally going to introduce them. He withdrew all of his feelings carefully within his walls. He didn't want to frighten Kora away from whatever it was she was trying to tell him.

"Pér, I'd like to introduce you to my son, Plyke and his Partner, Tika," Kora said confidently, though he could still feel her uncertainty and fear. He swallowed his pride as he extended his hand to shake the boys' hands. It stung him, more than he cared to admit, that Kora had a child. He'd always hoped they would start a family together. It had never occurred to him she would start a family without him. For a moment, that sting distracted him from the excitement within the two boys, but only for a moment. He looked at them curiously, then back at Kora again.

"What is it you're not telling me, Kora? Why are these boys so excited?"

Kora bit her lip, a mixed feeling of excitement and fear cascading around her. "Well, they're excited to meet *you* in fact."

"Kora, don't tease the poor man so. Just tell him," Master Aurelius urged her. Pér looked from one face to another, utterly confused.

"Plyke is my son, but he's also yours."

Pér heard the words, but stood motionless. Plyke was *his* son! Kora hadn't started a family with anyone else. All of his bitterness, his sadness, his longing all fell away. With tears pricking eyes, he took his son in one arm, his love in the other and squeezed them until he was afraid they might break.

"My son," he choked out the words. "I have a son."

From the corner of his eye, he saw the elf lead Master Aurelius and Tika away, leaving him with his small family. *His* family. He couldn't believe it. Tears streamed unabashedly down his face as he alternately held out his son at arm's length and held him close, laughing and crying.

"You're not angry with me?" Kora eventually asked, as she disentangled herself from him.

"Angry?" he asked her bemused. "How could I possibly be angry with you when you've given me a son? It's all I ever wanted – to have a family with you. Now all that's left for me is to get to know him.

"Plyke, I want to know everything about you and everything about Kora that I missed in all the years you had her to yourself," he whispered conspiratorially. As Plyke smiled at him and nodded, tucking his hair behind his ears, Pér noticed the colour of his eyes for the first time. They were just like Lord Aaron's – one green, one brown. That one brown one was just the same shade as Kora's.

"Before you get carried away, just know that Master Aurelius will need to take Plyke away for testing at some point this afternoon," Kora warned him with a smile. "Otherwise, he's all yours. I'll leave you two to get to know each other."

"Oh no you don't," Pér pulled her close to him. "You're not going anywhere. I want my entire family around me. Let's sit here a while before I have to go back and share you with everyone else."

It was hours later when Pér finally relinquished his hold on Plyke. His son seemed quite shy at first, but it didn't take long for the two of them to talk each other's ears off, swapping stories of Kora and the years they'd missed knowing each other.

Eventually, Kora insisted that Plyke search out Master Aurelius. She still hadn't explained to Pér exactly why Plyke needed to be tested again, but he was in too good a mood to argue with her. He hugged Plyke farewell, promising to find him on the morrow and properly meet Tika, of whom he had heard so much about.

With an arm around Kora, he watched his son walk away through the trees. As he left, he felt Kora's heart ache.

"Kora, you have no need to worry. I'm really not angry with you," he attempted to reassure her.

"You can't possibly mean that, Pér." She looked at him solemnly. "I ran away from Illaria, albeit with Uncle Lukys' blessing, and didn't say goodbye. When you found me, I refused to let you help me or to come back with you and then left you once more. I kept your son from you for sixteen *years* and didn't introduce you as soon as I could. How ... how can you not be angry with me?"

He looked at her, drinking in her doubt and feeding her reassurance. "Kora, do you not understand by now that I love you, utterly and completely. It doesn't matter how many times you've left without saying goodbye. I may have been upset or hurt each time, but I knew there was something you weren't telling me – something important. Now I know what it was, I can understand why you did it. I would have followed you if you had allowed it. But all of that is in the past.

"I can find no fault in you keeping my son's existence from me. There could not possibly have been a way for you to get word to me from the Paradise you were stuck in. From the fear and uncertainty in you when you reached Illaria, I would not have expected you to even consider an introduction at the time. I don't know what convinced you at this point in time, but I am grateful that you told me. I don't think you realise how happy you've made me."

Without hesitating, he held her hands and opened himself up to Kora, flooding her with his feelings of happiness. She closed her eyes, smiling at the feeling. Pér's happiness only intensified as he watched the pain in her melt away to be replaced by her own sense of calm.

A short few minutes later, Kora opened her eyes, and withdrew her hands from his. Without a word, she got to her feet and waited for him to follow suit. Side by side, they walked back out of the trees, Pér's hand finding hers once more.

Chapter Twenty-Four – Deuterfoss

Lishe watched in frustration as somehow her champion, Judd, was pushed to the background in favour of Orlan. All of her work inciting the townsfolk of Hedgefall had been wasted. Instead of attacking the lintep, and possibly even the Paradisians, they were to become trading partners. How had this happened?

Once dusk settled in, Judd had come to tell her the news. It appeared as though the broken Paradise already had enough spare wares to begin trading. This was the worst possible situation she could have imagined.

Judd had apologised profusely to her. She'd made him feel so guilty for dragging her back to the broken Paradise for no reason. Their arrival had benefited the town, but that had not been her intention. She had not expected them to become trading partners. Lishe had made such a pitiful display of losing so much travelling time to show them where the Paradise was that he had quickly appeased her by offering her his very own steed.

She would have to try to incite other towns now – warn them of what had happened to one Paradise and that the lintep had plans for all the other ones too. It would be more work than she had intended, but if she could start some sort of rebellion, perhaps the humans would carry it on without her and delay the lintep.

No matter how much she played the memory over in her mind, she still couldn't understand how they had destroyed the Paradise, or what Rilla had done to prevent everyone from killing each other. They were two things that troubled her greatly. She had even less time now to figure out how to steal the power from the Paradises. Her main problem was that she only knew where one of them was located. It was the one where that meddling half caste had taken the children from.

Lishe wondered if it might serve her cause to find that Paradise again and warn them of the impending destruction of their home. She shook her head. That would have to wait. It was more important to delay the destruction of more Paradises until she'd had time to experiment with the one she knew the location of.

Lishe travelled north east, past Pebble Stream which branched off from the Bramble River and led straight to Illaria. The largest human city she knew of was Deuterfoss. Located in the little valley at the foot of the cascading waterfall which fed the Bramble River, it was sheltered on one side by sheer cliffs and on another by the raging river through which no ship could travel. The other two sides were enclosed by tall stone walls. It was a well fortified location. That was one thing about these humans – she couldn't fault them for, their tactical minds.

Humans in cities like this were more knowledgeable than those in small towns like Hedgefall. If she attempted to use her powers at all, they would most likely single her out as a lintep and attempt to kill her. Even though she felt confident of being able to protect herself, she didn't want the hassle of doing so. All of her plans would fail if she could not incite these humans enough to make them act on their own. She needed them to be the ringleaders of a rebellion against the lintep.

Perhaps at the right time, she could reveal that she was a lintep herself and help them infiltrate Illaria. That would be a risky move if they became suspicious of her. She locked away the thought against the time that she might be able to use it. For now, she would simply spread rumours in all the major taverns and marketplaces. With any luck, that would fuel the fire well enough that she might not need to take any action herself and could spend the time at the one Paradise she knew the location of to see if she could find a way to steal power from it.

It took her three days of riding before she could see Deuterfoss in the distance. The sight always took her breath away. It was a magnificent fortified city. Any invaders would pay dearly before gaining entry to that citadel. She slowed her horse and dismounted. There was no need for the horse to work up a lather now that they were so close. It would only arouse suspicion from the guards at the wall.

By the time she reached the gate, the sun had begun its descent into the western sky. Had she been delayed any longer, she would not have been permitted entry that day. That was another thing about human cities – they closed their gates at sundown and refused to open them again until dawn, even to weary travellers.

Pulling her cloak off her long black hair, Lishe walked up to the guards. One of them barred her way with his halberd.

"State your business," he commanded in a harsh voice.

"I'm travelling from Hedgefall. Some of my cousins there are looking for new trading partners and asked me to make enquiries for them," Lishe answered, knowing they couldn't possibly know all the residents of Hedgefall and wouldn't be able to tell if she was lying or not. The guard looked her up and down, taking in her travel clothes and horse. Eventually, he raised his halberd and let her pass.

"If I hear you've been making trouble, it's a trip to the dungeons for you lass."

Lishe nodded and quickly walked past him. As large as it was, she could well understand that. A riot in tight streets such as these could cause a lot of damage.

It didn't take her long to find the route to a small marketplace. A city this size was bound to have a number of smaller ones around the outskirts with a larger one in front of the main keep, wherever that was. She asked a handful of people where to find a decent inn. After a few recommendations, she settled on Hand's Hollow. It had provisions for her horse at reasonable prices.

Hand's Hollow was located not far from the main gate. A few winding streets later and she came to the wooden tavern. It stood two stories high with a stable yard beside it. She breathed in the aroma of freshly baked vegetables, drenched in butter, and smiled. It was one of the few things that made travelling around the Outworld worthwhile – the taverns, few and far between, that had a cook worth their salt.

She left her horse with the stablehand, a copper coin pressed into his hand to ensure he would take good care of the beast. She did not intend to leave this town in a hurry, but it was always good to have a horse at the ready, just in case.

Pushing the wooden door open, Lishe walked into a well lit taproom. A number of tables were set around a stage where minstrels took their turn in entertaining the patrons. At this time of the evening, there were already a few tables of men drinking away the day's problems. A few heads turned at her arrival, but most took no notice of her. Lishe found a small unoccupied table and sat with her back against the wall. It was difficult to break the habit learned from so many years in the Outworld. Had it not been for her rather feminine appearance, she might easily be mistaken for a banwep. That was not something she aspired to as it might not bode well for her self-imposed mission.

A serving lady came around with a well used dishcloth and wiped the table. "What's your poison?"

"A hearty meal and a barley wine to wash it down," Lishe replied easily. There was no use asking for anything specific. These sorts of taverns had one meal per night, like it or lump it. The barely wine might bring some attention from some of the other patrons, but she would have ordered one nonetheless.

As she waited for her meal to arrive, Lishe sat back, twirling a strand of her long black hair, and watched the minstrel on stage. He was a rather rotund man who could barely get his fingers onto the strings of his lute, but for all that, he was still a talented musician. He was singing was a lesser known song, but easily held the attention of the crowd.

Once he had finished, a young lady took the stage. She was encouraged with hoots and whistles from the young men watching her. The girl rolled her eyes and blew a kiss out to them before sitting down to sing a well known crowd pleaser. By the end of the song, half the tavern had joined in the chorus.

Lishe's meal arrived part way through the girl's second song. The crowd had settled down for this one. It was a sad ballad, sung with extraordinary skill. If Lishe hadn't known better, she would have sworn the girl was an elf or an extremely talented lintep. She managed to convey feeling with each pluck or strum of her strings. Subconsciously, she fortified the walls of her minds against any unexpected attacks.

As soon as the girl had finished her set, another minstrel took her place. Lishe had finished her food and was nursing her second barley wine. The tavern was becoming busier and noisier. Soon enough, there wouldn't be any free tables and someone would be forced to share with her. That was exactly what she was waiting for. There was no other way for her to easily start talking with any of the townsfolk. In a city as large as this, there were bound to be many pretty girls, so her charms alone would not guarantee the attention of any of the men.

Eventually, a group of apprentices approached her table shyly. "Mind if we join you?" one of them asked. "There aren't any other free chairs and this is our one night off."

"I'm not expecting anyone. I'm new in town." Lishe indicated for them to sit with a smile. "What trade are you in?" she asked them, all politeness.

"We're carpenters and Raleigh is a joiner," the same young man told her. "I'm Karsyk and this is Dassyn."

"That sounds like hard work," Lishe sighed. "Let me buy you a round of ale to end your day."

The boys grinned at each other and nodded. They gave their orders to the serving girl and started asking the usual questions asked to newcomers.

"Where have you come from?" Karsyk asked.

"From Hedgefall," Lishe answered truthfully. "Have you heard of it before?"

"I have an uncle who went to work there years ago," Raleigh replied. "But I've never been there myself."

"It's a pretty little town," she admitted. "I can see why anyone irritated with the rush of a city life would choose to move there."

"What's the news from Hedgefall?" Raleigh asked.

"They were talking about a new town they'd just discovered a few days back. It must have been a week ago by now."

"What do you mean 'discovered'? How can a town be discovered?" Dassyn asked curiously.

"That's what I wanted to know, so I travelled in the direction they mentioned, due east of Hedgefall, for two days before I found it. They were right. A new town was there when it hadn't been only a few days before."

"That doesn't make any sense," Dassyn pointed out, needlessly. "Did they tell you anything about it?"

"They didn't know much about it." Lishe shrugged. "It seems as though it was a Paradise but the barrier had been destroyed by a group of lintep." She purposely omitted the karlik, elf and crystal dragon. There was no need to scare the humans away from the broken Paradise. Besides, she didn't know if those three parties would be present at every destruction – the lintep certainly would be.

"A Paradise was destroyed?" Karsyk asked a little too loudly. That got the attention of a number of other patrons who all came over to hear the story. Lishe relayed the events exactly the way she wanted them to be known, making sure they weren't aware of the reasons behind *why* the lintep had destroyed the Paradise, but that they were intent on destroying every single one they could find.

"What does it have to do with them," Karsyk asked angrily. "The Paradises are *our* safe havens. The lintep have no right to be destroying them."

"Well, who's going to stop them?" Raleigh pointed out. "Even if we wanted to, what could we do about it? We can't get into their stronghold to stop them. We wouldn't be able to defend ourselves against their magic."

"I don't know," Lishe mused aloud. "I've heard that not many lintep are so very powerful. Maybe if there were enough humans, they would be able to attack before the lintep could do anything about it."

"Now, now, wait a moment." Dassyn held his hands out to calm the people. "You're talking about invading Illaria, the *actual* lintep stronghold, with no more proof than a story that they've destroyed one Paradise and want to destroy the rest. That will start a war that we haven't planned for. I don't think we should be rushing into this."

"I'm not suggesting you invade them." Lishe pouted innocently. "I'm only telling you what I've been told and what I saw with my own eyes as I passed by."

"Sorry, miss," Karsyk said quickly. "I'm sure that Dassyn didn't mean to offend you. We won't rush into anything, but you've certainly given us something to think about. We don't want the lintep destroying Paradises any more than the next town, but he's right, we'll need to investigate this new town ourselves before doing anything about it."

"Suit yourselves," Lishe replied airily. "I've had a long journey here. I'm off to bed." She found the innkeeper, organised a room for the next three nights and headed upstairs. There was no need to leave the city any time soon. If she expected these humans to do anything without her, she would need enough time to plant seeds of doubt in as many places as possible.

The next morning, Lishe woke with a start. She'd forgotten where she was. The comfortable bed was a commodity she was unaccustomed to. Stretching lazily, she thought back on the previous night's conversation. She'd certainly managed to let a lot of people know about the broken Paradise. Some, if not all, had been incited by the event. With any luck, that sentiment would spread like wildfire throughout the city. Lishe didn't have any delusions that Deuterfoss would initiate a battle with the lintep, but there just might be enough fools wanting to prove their bravery for some of them to travel down to the broken Paradise, if nothing else.

She broke her fast in the tavern before wandering around the town. Deuterfoss certainly had a lot of things to offer. She meandered through the winding streets, finding her way to each of the smaller marketplaces around the edges of the city. Lingering in each of them, she eavesdropped on a number of people talking about the broken Paradise in the ones nearest to Hand's Hollow. Further away from the tavern, news hadn't spread yet so she made it her business to ensure that it would. A few discreet questions here and there and people all over the smaller marketplaces were soon talking about the audacity of the lintep to think they had any right to destroy what were the only safe havens known for humans.

It was exhausting, but rewarding, work for her. She was careful not to change her story at all. If any of the townsfolk talked to people near Hand's Hollow, she didn't want to be caught out in a lie and chased from Deuterfoss. This was the most likely place for her to be able to start trouble for the lintep.

Two days later, her work was done. Enough people knew about the destruction of the Paradise to hopefully do something about it. There wasn't anything more she could do in this town. It was now more important to head towards the only Paradise she knew the location of.

Chapter Twenty-Five – Return

Eliséo cast his eye over the broken Paradise. After the initial palaver, it had turned out surprisingly well. Somehow, the humans in Hedgefall had found out about the destruction of the Paradise. The villagers had initially come to make trouble and ended as trading partners. It appeared to be a fine outcome for everyone involved. Everything else had been left to Brynt to tie up. The other residents of the broken Paradise had looked to him for leadership and, albeit reluctantly, he'd finally risen to the challenge.

A few of King Lukys' guards had volunteered to stay behind for a number of weeks, to ensure the new Outworlders were safe until they were able to defend themselves. A blacksmith would be sent for from Illaria to teach them how to forge their own weapons, after which time the guards would give instructions on their use. There was no more the lintep could do for these Paradisians.

Kora had carefully broached the subject of lintep within his village to Brynt. The man had been shocked to discover there was at least one they knew of living there, which meant there was a strong likelihood there would be more. She offered to bring them to Illaria for a week or two of lessons until she could put her more permanent plans into place. He'd agreed to that mercifully quickly.

Everything had gone along as smoothly as possible in the Paradise, aside from Rilla's sudden, and near disastrous, loss of control that first day. Ever since Rilla had been whisked away to Illaria to continue her lessons, Eliséo had kept a close eye on her. She seemed to blossom under Mistress Isis' tutelage. With Mistress Kayte, things were a little frosty, but the two of them were slowly getting used to working with one another. Due to the extended absence of a number of teachers, replacements had been brought in so that lessons could continue. Eliséo was mildly surprised that Kynon had finally begun to act like the lord he was.

With everything in order, Eliséo knew it was time for him to move on. Anya had expressed her wish to be present at the destruction of every Paradise. However, as the next one was not to be for a number of weeks, she had not too subtly indicated that she wished to return to Goraburg until such time as she was needed again. Pyrid had offered to escort her home and return her to Illaria when it was time.

After much discussion with Lukys, Eliséo had asked Pyrid to fly him back to Illaria before heading to Goraburg so that he could quickly travel to the karlik caves if Queen Liessa permitted it. It would be the easiest way for him to assist with the situation in Goraburg and still be present at the destruction of the Paradises.

His farewells with most of the lintep had been brief. Kora thanked him for helping her formulate ideas for her school. Lord Aaron and King Lukys shook his hand firmly with thanks for his efforts in bringing about this destruction. Plyke, Tika and Arishen hugged him fiercely. He would miss them.

Eliséo regretted the fact that he hadn't had a chance to see Rilla again. He hoped she would forgive him for not returning to Illaria.

"Are you ready?" asked Pyrid in a growl. A huge fire opal claw was gently placed on the grass for himself and Anya to climb on. As gently as a crystal dragon could, he lifted them to the spikes on his back where they settled themselves down and held on tightly. The fire opal wings beat strongly above the ground and they were suddenly propelled into the air, leaving the broken Paradise and all the people in it, far behind.

In a matter of hours, Pyrid had flown them the long distance between the broken Paradise and Silvaren, passing over the town of Hedgefall on their way. Eliséo idly wondered if any of the townsfolk had believed the story their people would have told of a crystal dragon in the broken Paradise. If there had been any doubts, they would now be dispelled.

Pyrid descended on the hill leading down towards Silvaren. With the island covered with enormous trees, there was no other place for the crystal dragon to land.

"Will you come with me?" he asked Anya as they descended from the back of the fire opal dragon. "You will be most welcome, I assure you."

Anya smiled at the thought. "It's not every karlik who gets to visit so much of the Outworld. I would be a fool to refuse such an offer. Pyrid, are you happy to wait for us?"

"I haven't had a decent meal in weeks," he grumbled. "You two visit with the queen. I'll hunt for fish."

"We should be able to get an audience with the queen fairly soon, however, I cannot promise that the matter will be quickly resolved. It is possible she will discuss the situation with her advisers and instruct me on the morrow."

"A new ruler is often indecisive to begin with," Pyrid rumbled. "I'm not in any hurry to return."

Eliséo bristled at the remark but knew the crystal dragon was correct. Queen Liessa was relatively insecure. It would take time and experience for her confidence to grow.

Without another word, Eliséo led Anya down the hill towards Silvaren and Elessa. He longed to see her again. They both knew it was to be a short visit, but such was the price of his freedom. Any other elf would never dare leave Silvaren, but they would have the comfort of always being near their tree.

Once they reached the narrow stretch of water dividing the islet of Silvaren from the mainland they sat side by side, watching and waiting for the tide to turn. Eliséo was lost in thought when Anya finally spoke to him.

"Do you think Vladimir has infiltrated Goraburg in our absence?"

Her question surprised him. Eliséo shook his head with a shrug.

"Celtan gave his word that he would keep an eye on things in our absence. Surely he would have sent word had anything untoward happened."

Anya nodded, but looked unconvinced.

"Do you not think Lord Mikhail would be able to defeat him should the traitor resurface?"

The karlik shrugged. "Lord Mikhail is not as young as he once was. Vladimir is cunning – he will find a way to regain control."

Eliséo remained silent. There was truth in Anya's words but he knew there was no point in speculating. She, and possibly he, would be in Goraburg soon enough and would be apprised of the situation. They could only hope that Lord Mikhail was still in command of the karliki.

"What do you make of Rilla?" Anya finally spoke again. "I find it strange that this prophecy names her. There seems to be no valid reason for it. We know there are more skilled lintep, if not all as powerful as she is. Why then is it so important for the girl to be involved?"

Eliséo pondered the question for a long while. Eventually, he gave his opinion. "It may be that it isn't being interpreted properly. It does mention Rilla, but it does not specifically say that she will be the one to destroy Paradises, as the girl herself keeps trying to point out to everyone. It simply states:

"*When a crystal heart beats in the body of another*
Their song will destroy that which was created
Every being will bow down to the child of Paradise
All will hail Rilla.

"The two won't necessarily be one and the same. What if the seer's vision is indeed accurate and the entire group of them destroys most of the Paradises?"

Once more, they lapsed into silence.

"If that's the case, then why is Rilla being hailed?" Anya asked the question that troubled them both.

"I don't know, Anushka," Eliséo answered quietly. "She can do some wondrous things with her power. Perhaps one of these feats will be witnessed by a mass of people. Whatever it is, it did not happen with the destruction of the first Paradise and we won't solve the riddle by sitting here."

"I think the sandbank is high enough now. Let us cross over into Silvaren and seek my queen's leave for me to accompany you back home."

They got to their feet and walked across the sandy pathway into the elven stronghold. Much as Eliséo wished to stay a while with his own tree before meeting Liessa, he lingered only a moment to pass his hand over her glossy black trunk before continuing on to Silva.

Once they arrived at the intertwined roots, Eliséo spied one of the younger elves, Raeslin, and charged her with running up to Queen Liessa to forewarn her of their presence. With Anya following him, it would take longer than usual for the long walk up to the throne room. Raeslin's warning should at least ensure they be admitted immediately.

Along the long, winding walk to the throne room, Eliséo told Anya about the history of Silva and how she came to be the largest tree in Silvaren, being made up of a number of trees over thousands of years. The karlik marvelled at the way the trees had shaped themselves into alcoves for rooms and sloping pathways instead of stairs. The glittering silver vines as doorways entranced her even more than the floating lights leading up the path.

As they approached the throne room, Eliséo saw a familiar figure.

"Good evening, Farrow."

The queen's personal messenger inclined his head towards the ambassador. "Good evening, Eliséo. The queen is expecting you and your companion." He pulled aside the silver vines, giving them easy access to the room beyond.

Eliséo entered first, with Anya close on his heels. The throne room held a small number of elves, including Queen Liessa, Lady Eléna and Ensil. He promptly introduced the karlik to the elves, then gave a brief report on the destruction of the first Paradise. His words were met with stunned silence.

"Everything went as well as possible," he assured them. "Now Anya Nikolaevna is to return to Goraburg until the lintep decide it is time to destroy another Paradise. With your leave, I wish to accompany her there to give the assistance I initially intended to give when I was previously there. Will my queen permit this?"

"I will consider your request, Ambassador Eliséo," Queen Liessa told him formally. "Is that all you wish to bring to our attention?"

"My lady, if I may speak?" Anya interrupted. A startled Liessa indicated that she should. "I think it quite beneficial to all involved to have at least one member of each race present at the destruction of the Paradises. It lends a feeling of unity. To that end, I would request that Ambassador Eliséo be allowed to attend each one of the remaining Paradises.

"Once the lintep decide upon a better strategy for averting conflict upon the destruction of each Paradise, I anticipate that the destructions will quickly follow one another. In that event, I would request that Eliséo remain in Goraburg to assist us with our current ... situation. This would be beneficial for both the karliki and the crystal dragons, who won't then need to travel all the way to Silvaren each time to collect him."

Anya's words were met with shocked silence. Eliséo, with all his training as Ambassador, had to stop himself from smiling at the effect this one karlik had on the elf queen's court. The few advisers present immediately began to whisper among themselves. Queen Liessa quickly moved to regain control.

"This is a delicate matter, Anya Nikolaevna. We will consider it with our advisers and alert you as to our decision on the morrow."

"Thank you, my lady," Anya inclined her head towards Liessa.

"Ambassador, show our guest to her room. We will call you later to discuss this matter," Liessa instructed Eliséo. He bowed and thanked her before showing Anya out of the throne room.

Eliséo waited until they were a number of levels down from the throne room before daring to talk. "That was an interesting way for you to voice your opinion, Anushka. You've barely known the queen a mere few minutes. What makes you think your strong words will sway her?"

"I've known all sorts of leaders in my life," Anya replied. "With all of them, one thing remains the same – they all respond to strength. Admittedly, not all of them respond *well* to strength, but your queen seems still unsure enough about herself that she may choose to agree with me so as not to anger the karliki."

Eliséo couldn't help but laugh at her answer. As much as Liessa wanted to be a good queen, it was still obvious to all around her that she had much to learn. He only hoped she learned it well before the truth about their family was revealed, which he felt certain was now only a matter a time away.

He led Anya to one of the guest rooms that the Paradisians had used during their visit. Without realising until it was too late, he led her straight to the room Rilla had occupied. He hesitated a moment before holding aside the vines for her.

"You will find clean water inside. Food will be brought to you shortly," he told her. "It's late now and most elves will have returned to their own trees for the evening. If it would please you, I will call on you tomorrow morning for a tour around Silvaren before Queen Liessa summons us."

He caught the odd look that Anya threw him, but turned away. She held out her hand and pulled his arm back.

"What was that moment of hesitation I saw?" she asked him softly. "I've known you long enough to know something is bothering you, Eliséo."

He sought out Elessa's counsel, knowing his eyes would glow bright silver as he did so.

I reprimand Rilla each time she reveals the truth of our bond to anyone, yet I find myself telling those closest to me as well. Should I tell Anya?

Elessa instantly replied, wrapping herself around his mind. *Eliséo, there is no fault in telling your friends. It may be helpful for Anya to know the truth. After all, she is to spend more time with the two of you than most other people in the Outworld. If you don't tell her, she may work it out of her own accord at some inopportune time. Would you rather that?*

No, he answered slowly, *nor do I want to tell so many people that Liessa or one of the other elves discovers the truth and tries to claim me as their king. Not only do I not want to be the king, but it may affect Rilla in some way that we have yet to consider. She may be forced to live in Silvaren to keep all three of us safe. Her freedom is not something I wish to sacrifice.*

"Eliséo?" Anya gently brought him out of his reverie. He looked at the karlik for a moment longer before shaking his head.

"I'm sorry, Anushka, but I will not speak of it here," he told her firmly. "Perhaps we will discuss this another time, when things aren't at such a ... delicate point."

Anya nodded sadly and disappeared behind the glittering vines. Eliséo let out a breath he hadn't realised he'd been holding and began the long walk back to his tree.

Elessa was standing tall and slightly apart from all the other trees, just as always. Her smooth black trunk shone in the moonlight. Eliséo looked up to see her branches were almost completely bare. After all, winter was almost upon them.

It made his heart ache that it had been such a long time since he'd seen her in full bloom. He wondered if he would be back in Silvaren by spring. Shaking his head, he reasoned it would almost certainly take longer than a mere few months for the rest of the Paradises to be destroyed and Vladimir to be completely vanquished.

You let your mind run away with you, Elessa chided him gently as he walked up the sloping pathway into his bedroom. *Liessa has not yet granted you leave to go back to Goraburg, nor attend the destruction of the remaining Paradises.*

Wearily, Eliséo climbed into the little alcove shaped into a bed and pulled the warm blankets over himself, making sure that the palm of his hand was flat against Elessa's smooth bark, in a place that had been stained silver by the amount of times he'd done that.

We both know she has no choice, he told his tree before he lapsed into a deep sleep.

Chapter Twenty-Six – Frozen

It was early morning when Eliséo awoke. Something was wrong. He opened his eyes to take in his surroundings, but found nothing unusual. Closing them once more, he felt for his link with Rilla and found her locked away in her tower.

Elessa, what's happening? He quickly asked his tree.

I don't know, she replied worriedly. *She's been like that for a few minutes now. I don't think she's been attacked, but her body feels ... wrong somehow.*

Rilla? Eliséo called out. There was no response. *Rilla!* He shouted as loudly as he could. A sudden shudder brought Rilla out of her tower and into a panic. With sudden realisation, Eliséo felt how cold her body had become.

Through Rilla's eyes he saw Mistress Isis lying on the bed beside her, fast asleep with no idea of the danger the girl she was meant to be protecting was in.

* * *

"Mistress Isis," Rilla whispered with near frozen lips. She tried to move her hand to shake the mistress awake but barely managed to move even her fingers. She was so very cold. She could feel panic welling up in her, but could do nothing to react. Her body was too cold for her to do anything.

Calm down.

Rilla heard a voice in her mind. It was a familiar voice, but she couldn't place it. It was so very familiar.

Focus on my voice.

Focus, Rilla thought to herself. *Yes, that's what I need to do. Why?*

Use your power. Draw heat into yourself from the air.

Rilla tried to understand who was talking to her, in her mind, but couldn't. *Use your power.* What did that mean? *Draw heat into yourself from the air.* How?

* * *

She's too cold, Eliséo told Elessa. *We need to do something. Her power can't instinctively work to save her if she's too cold to even understand that she is in danger. Can you do anything?*

There is something I haven't tried before, Elessa admitted, *but I don't know if it would work.*

I don't think you have a choice, Elessa. If Isis doesn't wake up to save her now, Rilla will die while we watch.

Rilla lay motionless and freezing on her bed. She couldn't feel the sheets or her clothes. Her body was so cold that it felt like snow. There were voices talking. Were they in her head? She couldn't tell.

She felt her hand try to move. She hadn't done that, had she? It seemed like a good idea. She needed someone to help her. Again, she felt her hand try to move. This time, she tried to help it. Over and over again, she and some unseen force tried to move her hand. Eventually, it started to inch closer to the sleeping figure on the bed beside her.

Finally, she touched the lady lying on the bed. The lady woke with a start. Rilla looked at her face in confusion. She knew her, didn't she? Who was she? A friend? A teacher?

Ever so slowly, Rilla felt her body warming up. She heard the lady talking to her but could not understand what she was saying. The presence of two other beings in her mind remained. She could feel them. But they were silent now. Had she really heard them before or had she imagined them?

With surprise, Rilla turned to find a fire blazing in the hearth of the next room. Somehow, the door had opened and a fire had been lit. She could feel the heat from here, warming her frozen body. Closing her eyes, Rilla savoured the heat.

"Open your eyes, dear," a gentle voice told her. Rilla unthinkingly obeyed. Kind brown eyes looked at her. Rilla smiled at that. "Keep looking at me. There's a good girl."

Rilla felt something on her hands. She looked down to find the lady's hands were holding hers tightly. One of the hands moved up to her chest. She looked at it curiously and smiled as she felt warmth radiating out from her chest to the rest of her body. Once more, she closed her eyes.

"Look at me, Rilla," the voice instructed her again, gently but firmly. Rilla opened her eyes and saw Mistress Isis in front of her. She sat up slowly and looked around her.

"What happened?" she asked her in confusion. She was surprised when Mistress Isis breathed a sigh of relief and hugged her. Rilla sat motionless, not knowing what to do. She pulled away and repeated herself. "Mistress Isis, what happened?"

"I don't know," her teacher replied truthfully. "I woke up to find you freezing. It's taken a nice roaring fire to get you back to a safe temperature. I don't think you recognised me there for a moment."

Rilla thought carefully before replying. "For a moment there, I didn't. I … heard voices in my mind. Was that you too?"

"No," Isis answered worriedly. "What kind of voices?"

"I don't know," Rilla replied. "Just voices. They tried to calm me down and use my power to draw heat into myself, but I couldn't think straight by then. I ... couldn't do it."

Suddenly, she was sobbing. Mistress Isis held her tightly and, for the first time, Rilla didn't pull away, she just cried. It felt like something had ripped inside of her. She couldn't stop the tears. Then the shaking started. Within seconds, she was convulsing. The contents of her stomach ended up on the bedsheets. Rilla stared at the mess, horrified, but still she could not stop sobbing and shaking.

She felt, more than noticed, Mistress Isis gently lead her away from the bed and into the bath chamber. As the warm water began to fill the bathtub, the young mistress helped her to undress. Shivering and shaking, Rilla stepped into the warm water. Sighing, she completely submerged herself.

Only when she felt her lungs burning for air did she lift her head above the water. Mistress Isis had taken her soiled clothes and was busy stripping the sheets off the bed. Rilla stayed in the warm water, watching as servants entered the room. One of them took away the sheets and clothes while another assisted the fire mistress to make the bed. New clothes were selected from her wardrobe and brought into the bathroom.

"I'm sorry," Rilla whispered, once the servants had left. Mistress Isis came over to the bath with a large towel. She held it up for Rilla and smiled.

"There's nothing to be sorry for, Rilla. You had an accident and I helped you. Don't you remember, that's exactly why I asked Princess Aislen if I could stay with you?"

Rilla thought back to the evening they'd arrived in Illaria on dragonback. That had been so many days ago now that she'd almost forgotten why it was that Isis slept in her room each night. Closing her eyes against the memory, Rilla stood up and wrapped herself in the towel.

"All lintep go through this to a certain extent," Isis reassured her. "We'll talk about it once you're dressed and ready to face the day. I'm sure you're starving after that ordeal. I've taken the liberty of requesting food be brought up to your room this morning. I'll wait for you in your antechamber."

Rilla stood in silence, holding her towel tightly around her, as Mistress Isis walked through into the antechamber and closed the door behind her. Not a moment after that, the voices in her head began again. This time, she smiled as she recognised them.

We were so worried about you, Elessa told her.

Indeed, you gave me quite a start when I awoke, Eliséo agreed. *We did everything we could to wake you.*

I noticed, Rilla told them. *Did you help me to move or was that my imagination?*

That was Elessa, Eliséo confirmed. *She had to try to move you so that Mistress Isis could be alerted to the situation. Are you feeling better now?*

Rilla nodded in her mind. *Better, but exhausted and ravenous. I don't know how I'm going to face my lessons today.*

Perhaps you can plead a day away from lessons, Elessa suggested.

No, Rilla and Eliséo said together.

She needs to keep using her powers, to learn everything about them so that things like this don't keep happening, Eliséo told their tree. *Keep safe, Rilla. I'm sure Mistress Isis will look after you.*

With a final embrace, Rilla felt them leave her mind. She was alone. Keeping as near to the fire as her body could handle, she dried and dressed herself. Reluctantly, she used a scoop of sand from a pot beside the fireplace to douse the flames. With a small shiver, she moved away from the smouldering logs and walked out towards the antechamber.

The small table was already laden with food. Rilla inhaled the savoury smell of freshly baked rolls, her mouth watering. Mistress Isis glanced over from the window where she was standing.

"Feeling better?" she asked. Rilla nodded and sat down to eat. Mistress Isis joined her after a moment. The food warmed Rilla from the inside, and banished the last remnants of cold from her body. They ate together in silence, Rilla kept her eyes on her food, knowing that the fire mistress watched her every move. When she had eaten her fill, Rilla sat back and finally met Mistress Isis' eyes.

"You said everyone goes through this, but I don't believe you," Rilla told her quietly. "I haven't heard stories of this happening to other lintep and Plyke certainly hasn't had this happen to him."

"I said 'to a certain extent', Rilla," Isis corrected her. "Not everyone goes through exactly the same thing, but everyone loses control at some point. That's what this was – a loss of control. You only think this hasn't happened to Plyke because you're not looking at all the possibilities. Plyke's strength does not lie in the practical side, but the mental. Can you not think of a single time when he lost control with his mind?"

Rilla didn't have to think back very far to remember Plyke's powers flooding out of him a number of times, especially when he tried to do something with his mind, like reading or projecting a thought.

"I can see you can indeed recall a time," the fire mistress said. "Now with you and Plyke, the loss of control creates disasters because you are both so powerful. With other lintep, the result isn't quite as dramatic. They might accidentally light a fire or project a thought a little louder than they intended, but all of these things would be just a bit more powerful than they intended and usually when they were trying to do it anyway.

"In your case, you didn't know you were a lintep growing up and your power is used to working without your express direction, to do what it thinks you want it to. That's the way it appears, whether that's what's actually happens or not."

Rilla listened to her explanation and tried to work through the jumbled mess in her head.

"Why would my power make me *that* cold?" Rilla asked, still not understanding. Mistress Isis smiled gently as she explained.

"Well, it's possible that you covered yourself up with too many blankets last night, after all it was quite a cool night. While you slept, your power may have instinctively tried to cool you down because you weren't taking the covers off yourself.

"Now this is where the loss of control comes into it – while it was cooling you down, it got out of control and instead of stopping when you were cool enough, it just kept going. If you hadn't managed to touch me to wake me, I fear you would have died this morning."

Mistress Isis kept her voice steady, but Rilla could feel the fear under the calm. That scared her more than her teacher's words.

"I didn't think my skills lay with fire and ice. I thought I was better with healing," Rilla pointed out softly.

"You have more skills than you realise, Rilla," Isis told her. "I would say your skills lean heavily towards the practical – *all* sorts of practical."

"Did anything like this happen to you, when you were younger I mean?" Rilla asked, hoping to find some comfort in the mistress' failure.

"Oh yes," she laughed loudly. "I didn't hurt myself, but I woke up to find my sheets singed a number of times. My parents were not impressed and soon after sent to me live in the castle until my powers were well and truly under control."

Rilla found herself smiling, despite her own recent loss of control. Mistress Isis began telling her about all the other lintep she knew who'd made a mess of things with their power. Admittedly, none of them were as life threatening as hers, but it was comforting to know that others had experienced their own troubles when their power peaked.

"Will you stay with me again tonight?" she finally asked the question that had been niggling at her all morning. "Until Shuut comes home. Will you stay with me?"

"Of course, Rilla," the fire mistress reassured her. "I will keep you safe. Have no fears about that. I shall discreetly let your teachers for today know that you may have a bit of trouble in your classes, but I believe you only lose control of your power when you're not thinking straight or when you're asleep. You should be fine in your lessons."

Rilla smiled her thanks as the bells for morning lessons tolled. Together, they descended the stairs to find the hall in front of the classrooms already teeming with students. They parted ways, Rilla watching as Mistress Isis went to find Master Aurelius' replacement.

Her first lesson of the day was the practical one with Kalydron. Rilla smiled instinctively as she thought of him. She, Miette and Kalydron were fast becoming the closest of friends. It was a strange feeling for her, as she'd never really had any friends growing up in their Paradise. Plyke, Tika and Arishen had only become her friends by default as they travelled through the Outworld together. Now, she couldn't imagine life without the boys and Shuut, but it was different with them – more of a forced friendship. Her relationship with Miette and Kalydron was completely the opposite. They just happened to be two students who she found that she got along with.

"Rilla!" Miette waved her over to the little alcove where she and Kalydron were waiting for her. She smiled and waved back as she weaved her way, slightly unsteadily, through the students to get to them.

"Ready for our first lesson?" Kalydron asked. He stopped and stared at her. "Are you feeling alright? You're pale as a sheet."

"I'm fine," Rilla brushed the question aside. It was all well and good Mistress Isis telling her about other lintep who had lost control of their power, but she hadn't mentioned Miette or Kalydron. Rilla didn't want them to think she was any less capable than they were in their lessons.

"If you say so." He shrugged but looked unconvinced. Rilla waved aside Miette's cocked eyebrow. Thankfully, she left the issue alone.

"I'll see you in the dining hall," Miette said as students began to file into their classrooms. Rilla and Kalydron nodded and headed towards their own room. Before they went in, he quickly pulled her aside.

"Mistress Emeline is going to give us our reward as soon as the seer returns from the Outworld again," he told her conspiratorially. "Do you know what he's doing out there?"

Rilla gave him a hard stare. He'd tried to ask her in a hundred different ways since she'd returned. It was no secret to anyone that she had returned on dragonback. Rumours had spread all throughout the castle about her absence from classes that day and her sudden reappearance. They all assumed it was the same reason a number of other lintep had disappeared.

It surprised Rilla that the truth hadn't been discovered yet. She wondered how the Illarians would take the news when it was finally revealed to them. This thought alone was enough to keep her tight-lipped about it.

"Kalydron?" She leaned in closely to him, her lips close to his ear making him blush brightly. "Mind your own business!" She fled into the classroom before he could question her further.

Chapter Twenty-Seven – Trapped

Eliséo descended from his bedroom to find Lady Eléna waiting in his common room. He stopped short, looking at her inquisitively. She watched him carefully as he struggled to keep a blank expression.

"You've had a rough morning?" she inquired. He nodded, knowing there was no way to hide the truth from her, but offered up no further information. "Very well. I thought you might like some company on the way back to Silva."

They linked arms and walked slowly across the forest floor. Leaves of all colours lined the dirt. All the trees of Silvaren lost their leaves in winter. It was the only time the forest looked sombre. They walked together for a long while before Eléna broke the silence.

"Liessa is starting to grow into her role," she spoke in a voice barely louder than a whisper. "Perhaps the danger will pass without ever coming to fruition."

He didn't want to doubt her words, but could not believe that things would go as smoothly as she hoped, especially not if more people discovered what Rilla was doing through their bond. It barely mattered that none of them were elves – the story was bound to travel if too many people found out.

"I hope you're right, my lady," he answered just as softly. "I value my freedom as much as the young lintep does hers. Neither of us wants to be tied down in Silvaren, as much as we may love it."

"I know," Eléna reassured him. "I've always known. That's one of the reasons I made you my ambassador all those long years ago. Liessa doesn't understand that need and so would keep you in Silvaren rather than constantly send you away. It was a difficult task to convince her to allow you to continue as both yourself and Anya Nikolaevna suggested, but hesitation gave way to reason with all of her advisers urging her towards that decision."

Eliséo creased his brow. "I had not realised it would be such a difficult decision to make. Surely, she could understand why it was important for me to assist the karliki and lintep?"

Eléna nodded and soothingly patted his hand. "She also recalls how marvellous it was to be able to speak with King Lukys without leaving Silvaren, all because you were here and Rilla was in Illaria. I wouldn't put it past her to ask Elessa to bind a karlik to herself so that she could speak with Mikhail Alekseevich at will. She would never let you out of Silvaren if that were to happen."

Eliséo missed a step. "Surely she wouldn't do that." When he saw the look on his mother's face, he paled. "I wouldn't let her. I would leave."

"You wouldn't," Eléna shook her head. "Much as you might be tempted, you wouldn't because then you would be branded a traitor and never allowed to enter Silvaren again. Even though Elessa would still stand, no one would dare kill her, you would never see her in reality again."

"Why are you telling me this?" Eliséo asked her, fighting the rising panic within him.

"So that you never make the mistake of agreeing to bind a karlik to your tree," she answered him softly. "They don't usually visit, but neither do lintep or humans and you still managed to let that happen with Rilla. Don't be tempted to allow Anya to touch Elessa. It may be wise for you to not even pass near her with the karlik for fear of what may happen."

They walked the rest of the way to Silva in silence, Eliséo's mind racing in a hundred different directions. How had his life suddenly become even more complicated than it already was?

Elessa tried to calm him. *They won't be able to tie you down. Although we don't like it, we know both of us can survive without you in Silvaren, just as easily as we can survive without Rilla nearby.*

True, but there is always a feeling of something missing when it I'm away for too long, Eliséo told her. *Don't you feel it too?*

Of course, she replied instantly, *but if it's a choice between that and you being trapped here for hundreds or thousands of years, we both know what you'd need to do. You cannot survive in Silvaren – not like that.*

Eliséo saw Eléna watching his glowing eyes, but he offered no explanation, nor did she ask for one. Soon enough, they approached the tangled mess of roots that supported Silva. Mother and son unlinked their arms to make the long climb up to the throne room.

They stopped on the way to collect Anya. Eléna raised her eyebrows when she realised the karlik had been given the same room as Rilla. It was clear to her where Eliséo's thoughts lay. She only hoped not too many other elves noticed. The more who knew about his bond, the more difficult it would be to continue to disguise how powerful he was.

Farrow showed the three of them into the throne room when they arrived. Eliséo was impressed that he now betrayed no sign of anger towards his queen for abdicating in favour of her daughter. Inside, Queen Liessa awaited them. Her advisers were absent. That was a bad sign. Even though Eléna had assured him he would be allowed to leave once more, the absence of any but the four of them in the room created disquiet inside of him.

"Ambassador, Anya Nikolaevna, we have thought long about your request. Our advisers have made it clear to us that we would be wise to allow Eliséo to leave Silvaren once more for the Outworld. I have agreed with them to a certain extent."

Eliséo felt his mother stiffen at his side. This was not part of the plan. His blood ran cold as he waited for the queen's decision.

"Anya Nikolaevna, Ambassador Eliséo shall indeed accompany you to Goraburg to assist in any way he is able with the situation surrounding the usurper, Vladimir Mikhailovich. However, once that task is complete, he will return to Silvaren once more.

"From your own report, I am certain that you will be able to continue destroying the Paradises without his assistance and I have other uses for him. He is not honour bound to Mikhail Alekseevich nor to King Lukys. Their wishes will not override mine in this matter. Considering they have not made any requests of their own, there will not be any cause for conflict."

Stunned silence met her words. Eliséo fought the urge to argue the matter. He knew that any word out of place could make his sister change her mind to allow him to leave Silvaren, even for this short time. Perhaps he could find some way to avoid her dictate once he had left.

He could sense that Anya was about to protest and quickly laid a hand on her shoulder. Now was not the time. The karlik looked up at him with a mixture of anger and disbelief, but made no attempt to speak. All three of them, Lady Eléna included, bowed their heads and left the room in silence. They dared not speak until they were well away from Silva.

Eléna quickly took the lead, walking towards their secret spot. There were few elves that knew of this hidden area in Silvaren and fewer still who ever travelled so far from the centre of the islet.

"What is she thinking?" Eliséo burst out. He could not contain his rage any longer.

"Calm yourself, Eliséo," Eléna chided him. "We may be far from Silva, but that does not mean you can't be overheard if someone has followed us."

"I'm sorry to say it, Lady Eléna, but I must agree with Eliséo. Has your queen lost her senses?" Anya's question made the former queen blanch.

"She is merely trying to stand on her own two feet." Eléna attempted to defend her daughter's actions. "If she constantly goes along with what her advisers tell her to do, they will soon begin to think that she is their puppet. She has little choice but to make a stand."

"My lady, this is the worst way for her to make a stand." Eliséo's voice was full of anger. "It cannot help for me to return to Silvaren once the situation in Goraburg is resolved."

"*If* the situation is resolved," Eléna said quietly, "then you will return as your queen commands."

That word "if" hung in the air. *If* held so many possibilities. How was Liessa to know that the situation in Goraburg was resolved unless Eliséo, or someone else from the Outworld, sent word to her? He could potentially help with the destruction of the Paradises, only returning to Silvaren at the end of that time, all the while pretending he was in Goraburg, helping Mikhail.

"That is a dangerous game to play," Eliséo said carefully.

"Is that danger worth it to you?" Eléna asked him. "How much do you value your freedom?"

Anya looked from one face to the other. "What are you two talking about?"

"Have you told her?" Eléna asked. Eliséo shook his head. "There was an incident here, months ago now, that has led Eliséo to become more valuable to Silvaren than he has ever been before in his capacity as ambassador. Queen Liessa intends to take full advantage of that. However, it would mean the loss of Eliséo's relative freedom. His presence in Silvaren would be required more often than not."

"I don't care about an incident that happened months ago," the karlik answered angrily. "All I care about is that your queen is trying to prevent a key person from attending the destruction of all the Paradises."

"Anushka, there is little we can do about it at present." Eliséo attempted to calm her, though the rage within him refused to die down. "Let us depart for Goraburg now. For all we know, the situation with Vladimir may last longer than we anticipate and all the Paradises will be destroyed in the meantime. That is all we can hope for now."

Much as he wanted to pass her by before he departed once more, Eliséo heeded his mother's warning about accidentally binding a karlik to his tree and stayed well away from Elessa. Anya walked silently beside him. The two of them were still stunned by Liessa's decision, but neither of them had the heart to talk about it any further. For now, all that mattered was that they return to Goraburg with all haste.

Pyrid was waiting for them at the top of the hill when they arrived. "To Goraburg?" he asked them. They only nodded in response. The fire opal dragon eyed them both closely, but eventually lowered a claw for them to climb into without asking questions. Once they were seated and holding on tightly, he beat his wings and rose swiftly into the air.

Chapter Twenty-Eight – Harsh realities

Lukys silently lamented the loss of Pyrid for his return journey to Illaria. Much as he prized his horses, he was not used to riding them for such an extended period of time. Beside him, Aaron and Kora rode comfortably, talking to each other. He was pleased his young niece had managed to find a solution to the problem of discovering lintep within the Paradise. Even the fact that she was temporarily bringing a young lintep and his human Partner to Illaria did not irritate him as much as it should have. He knew that she needed time to get her project up and running.

He looked back to see Pér talking animatedly with Tika and Plyke. It had been quite a shock to everyone to discover he was the father of Kora's son. He wondered if this meant Kora would ask Pér to live in the castle. Lukys sighed as he thought of the long hours he'd spent listening to Pér's *unsavoury* songs.

"Kora," he said suddenly, "if Plyke is so powerful, apparently even more so than yourself, then Pér..."

"Is quite powerful himself, uncle," Kora finished his sentence, smiling at his discomfort. "You always dismissed him out of hand because you didn't approve of his songs. It worked a charm at getting you to ignore him. Pér never wanted to be a master or be forced to use his powers in a way that best suited you, so he hid behind his music and he used his powers so well, with that very same music, that you didn't even notice."

"What do you mean?" Lukys asked in confusion. He saw the look exchanged between Kora and Aaron. "Aaron?"

"You know there are lintep who can use their mind powers without skin contact?"

"Of course," Lukys shrugged. "You're one of them, though admittedly I've never understood how you do it."

"Plyke is one of us," Aaron smiled. "The boy had no idea that what he was doing was, in any way, unusual. In fact, he didn't *try* to do it – it simply happened."

"What has this to do with Pér?" Lukys asked, barely hiding his annoyance.

"Well, Pér knew exactly what he was doing," Aaron laughed softly. "He'd spent enough time around me as he was growing up to realise what I was doing. It only took him a few months of practice, after his power peaked, to use his music the same way. He allows his power to flow out with his music, creating exactly the atmosphere or feelings that he would like to evoke.

"Once Kora and I realised how talented he was, he began to suspect that you might force him to become a master or serve you in some other way.

That was when his songs became less to your liking. He *made* you feel that way about him. To disdain him for no reason you could quite put your finger on. You think it's because of the type of song he sings, but I'll wager you never actually stopped long enough to listen to the lyrics to realise they aren't all that bad."

Lukys listened in stunned silence, occasionally staring back at the would-be minstrel. Aaron was right. Lukys couldn't recall the words of any of Pér's songs but it was the way he sang them that created his dislike of the man.

"Now you understand how Plyke can be so powerful." Kora smiled at him. "You might also reassure Pér that you won't use him as a pawn. Then he might favour you with one of his better tunes."

Lukys rode silently for a long while, even after he heard Kora and Aaron resume their conversation. There was so much for him to think about now. Aislen would have much to tell him upon his arrival. With any luck, Kynon would have some news to share. Then there was Rilla.

What was he to do with that girl? She constantly got herself into trouble, whether she tried to or not. Her latest act had nearly set the Paradisians in a battle against the lintep. She insisted that was exactly what she tried to avoid, however, he could not help but notice that was the opposite of what happened. Even Eliséo had shown his anger with the girl.

Lukys still had no idea how she'd done it, but the bond with the elf's tree had allowed her to put up a strong barrier between the two sides. It didn't appear as though most of the lintep had understood what she'd done. That was a small blessing. Even if Plyke was correct and Lishe had been watching the destruction, she would have little chance of understanding what had happened or that Rilla was bound to an elf's tree. Only those closest to her could have seen her blazing green eyes.

"Aaron," he called out, waiting for his cousin to finish his conversation with his daughter, "I think we need to do something about Rilla."

Aaron waved Kora back to her son and waited until she was out of earshot before speaking. "What do you propose to do, Lukys?" he asked, coolly. Lukys was surprised by his tone.

"She needs to learn respect and self control," Lukys insisted.

"She needs to learn to control her power, I'll grant you that," Aaron answered slowly.

"What she needs, is to swear allegiance and understand that she is never to disregard my orders," Lukys stated harshly.

"Lukys, this has nothing to do with her allegiance," Aaron shook his head. "This is about the fact that your actions, and mine no doubt, would have caused much bloodshed in the Paradise. Her actions put a stop to it and you don't like that she found a way around it.

"Now, I'm not suggesting you wanted blood to be spilt anymore than the rest of us, but you were certainly angry that *she* came up with a solution better than yours. It's up to you to figure out a way to avoid a pitched battle the next time we destroy a Paradise, without Rilla's interference."

"She still needs to learn control," Lukys answered in a huff, knowing that Aaron was correct in his assumptions.

"Isn't that exactly why Isis whisked her back to Illaria?" Aaron asked. "I just hope that they haven't had any trouble since they returned. I still remember what happened to me when I was her age."

Lukys grimaced. He remembered all too well the days Aaron's feelings had flooded through the castle, putting everyone in a sour or joyful mood the entire day, depending on his own mood.

He also recalled the day Isis' parents had come to the castle, requesting an audience with him. It had been quite a shock to him, hearing their stories of scorched bedsheets and their desperation to keep their daughter safe. He had instantly agreed to bring her into the castle and keep a close eye on her. He would never forget their gratitude to him and their pride when she became the youngest mistress ever in Illaria. Had her parents been less understanding, Isis could well have found herself derided instead of praised. She could have turned into another version of Lishe if they weren't careful with her.

"I can see your memories swirling around," Aaron told him gently. "Now ask yourself why you aren't being so lenient with Rilla as you were with the rest of us. Is it really because she doesn't respect your decisions or because she is determined to find a better way when you can't be bothered?"

"That's not entirely fair," Lukys attempted to protest.

"How long did you spend trying to predict the possible reactions of the humans before we destroyed their Paradise? You brought along all the guards, masters and mistresses you thought you might need to protect us. Your thoughts instantly ran towards strength of force.

"Let's be honest. Did you even consider there might be other ways? You should not take your anger with yourself out on my granddaughter – not when *she* was the one to avert the bloodshed you had almost guaranteed with your actions. Think of a better way before the next time Lukys. You might also think about apologising to a child who is still learning to control her powers and whom *you* sent into such a foul mood that she almost killed herself. If Isis hadn't been keeping an eye on her, I may have lost yet another member of my family."

Aaron turned his horse around and spurred it towards his daughter and grandson. Lukys stared after him in silence. Those words would haunt him. Much as he wanted to return to Illaria, he now dreaded what he would say to Rilla. If he were honest with himself, he would have to admit that he was more at fault in this than she was.

Chapter Twenty-Nine – Goraburg

It took them the better part of the day to reach the Drakos Mountains. Pyrid had decided to take them there first, reasoning that Celtan would be able to tell them if there had been any sightings of Vladimir in recent days.

As many times as Eliséo had visited the crystal dragons in their mountain home, he'd never arrived by dragonback before. The sight of all those huge beasts lying in the hidden valley amazed him as he gazed upon their many different colours sprawled across the ground.

He'd only ever had close dealings with Celtan, Pyrid, Loreli and Groldor before. Between them, that made up sapphire, fire opal and clear crystal. Before him were numerous other crystals – deep emeralds, light topaz, bright amethyst, blood red rubies and more. He knew each of those would evoke different feelings within him towards the great beasts. It was one reason he felt uncomfortable around the crystal dragons. He never knew if they were trying to manipulate him without his knowledge, though he hoped they knew better than that by now.

A few snouts lazily lifted to look at the new arrivals. Some of those roared a welcome to Pyrid, others returned to their slumber with little or no acknowledgment. Celtan alone walked over to them as they landed.

"What news Pyrid?" he growled, once Eliséo and Anya had descended from the fire opal dragon's back.

"One Paradise destroyed, many more to go," Pyrid answered easily. "This feisty little karlik has negotiated quite a nice bargain for herself. We are to escort her to the destruction of each Paradise. Lukys has requested one of us fly back and forth to Illaria every week to see when they are ready for the next destruction."

Celtan's laughter rumbled throughout the valley, causing no small number of beasts to grumble their displeasure at the noise. "The mighty crystal dragons have fallen indeed if lintep and karliki alike are ordering us around."

Anya suppressed a smile, but could not hide the concern beneath her mirth. "What news, Celtan? Has the traitor been found?"

"Sadly not, Anya," Celtan replied gravely. "Loreli and Groldor have been training up some of the younger clear crystal dragons in an effort to find him, but to no avail. Either he is far away from Goraburg, or or has kept well hidden.

"Perchance Mikhail Alekseevich has more news for you, but we've not seen or heard from the karliki since I escorted Ilya Mikhailovich and Kazimir Sergeyevich home a while back."

Eliséo attempted to ignore the growing feeling of dread in the pit of his stomach. It was not unusual for the karliki to keep to themselves, but with the newly forged relationship with the crystal dragons, he'd thought there might be more communication.

"Pyrid, can you take us to the field entrance now?" Eliséo asked urgently. "It will take us a good few hours to reach Mikhail."

Anya looked at him in growing concern. "Do you think something is amiss?"

"I don't know, Anushka," Eliséo replied, hurriedly climbing onto Pyrid's back. "The sooner we get to the centre of Goraburg, the better."

Anya was carefully lifted up to the spikes on Pyrid's back. As soon as they were settled, the fire opal dragon ascended into the sky again. Once up over the lip of the valley, he began a quick descent down to the mouth of the cave leading to the karlik tunnels.

"Thank you for everything, Pyrid," Eliséo said as his feet touched the ground. "Would you be willing to continue assisting with the destruction of the Paradises or shall we call on another when the time comes?"

The crystal dragon smiled, his deep red teeth glinting in the sunlight. "You won't get rid of me that easily. I've already discussed with Lukys that I will be the one returning to Illaria every week. All that is required now is a means for me to contact the karliki when the time comes."

"I will ask Lord Mikhail to post a sentry at this exit," Anya told him. "You need only scratch the floor here for the karlik to hear you. Will that be sufficient?"

Pyrid nodded and leapt back into the sky as Eliséo and Anya began their long journey to the heart of Goraburg. They entered the tunnels warily, Eliséo following close behind Anya, knowing how easily he could become lost in the outer tunnels.

Hours later, they descended into a cavern that should have been full of karliki hard at work. The silence in the garden cavern was eerie. Eliséo looked anxiously at Anya, seeing his concern mirrored in her eyes.

"Something is amiss here. This cavern is never completely empty," she whispered, knowing how sound echoed in the tunnels. Cursing the fact that he should be hiding his powers from everyone likely to interact with the elves, Eliséo quickly incanted the words to hide them both with the mist dome.

"We can talk freely in here, Anushka," he told her. "This mist will hide us. Let's get to the main caverns and see what the cause of this silence is."

Anya chose the fastest route to Mikhail and Ilya's own private caverns. By unspoken agreement, they began to run, as the silence extended throughout all of the tunnels and caverns they passed through.

Eventually, they came across a pair of karliki hurrying down a passage towards the audience chamber. Changing their course, Eliséo and Anya followed them at a distance, not wanting the mist bubble to bump into them should they suddenly slow. As they neared the audience chamber, they heard the murmur of subdued voices.

"My fellow karliki." The other karliki stopped talking as Ilya's voice carried across them. "It is with a heavy heart that I tell you my father, Lord Mikhail Alekseevich, did not survive the attack from two nights ago. The traitor, Vladimir Mikhailovich sent in one of his followers to do the deed that he could not bring himself to do. His life is now, without a doubt, forfeit to the first karlik who finds him. He is not to be spared for any reason.

"They seek to create chaos and confusion by murdering Lord Mikhail, but they will not succeed. My father named me as his successor. I will not allow Vladimir to ruin everything my father worked hard to create during his lifetime. Now, more than ever, I ask for your support and unity. Let us seek out the remaining rebels and deliver justice!"

A roar echoed off the cavern walls as every karlik in Goraburg cheered for their new leader. Eliséo smiled, despite the sorrow in his heart. He looked down to find Anya tightly gripping his arm, tears streaming down her cheeks. He knelt down to embrace her.

"Come, Anushka, Ilya is leaving the cavern." Eliséo led the mourning karlik through the tunnels, following his best friend to his private chambers. They quickly slipped in behind him, just before he closed the door.

With a single word, Eliséo dissipated the mist. Ilya was instantly on his guard, knife at the ready, but faltered when he saw them.

"Eliséo! Anushka! What are you doing here?" he cried out in disbelief.

Anya hurriedly explained the events, which had occurred after Ilya and Kazimir left Illaria, ending with their flight to the Drakos Mountains and their conversation with Celtan.

"Now we know we were right to fear the worst. I'm sorry, Ilyusha," Eliséo said softly. "We should have come back earlier."

Ilya shook his head sadly, leading his friends to the only chairs in his room.

"When we returned, over a week ago now, father still had not heard any word of Vladimir. We knew he must have been planning something.

"A few days ago, a number of karliki came forward to tell us they had spied one of Vladimir's followers in the lesser used tunnels. It was always a different karlik and always in a different location. There were too many leads for us to follow all of them, so we did all we could, sending out a few scouts and asking for extra guards.

"It was no use. I tried to convince father to stay in the most easily defensible chamber until the renegades were found. He insisted that if he did that, all karliki would soon think that he was afraid of Vladimir, and even if he weren't killed, they would stop following him.

"He was right, of course, but that did not make me agree with him. We fought long and hard over this, but in the end I had to accede to his wishes. It wasn't long before one of Vladimir's followers ambushed us. He struck quickly. Once father was injured, half the guards hunted down the karlik and killed him. Little good that did.

"The healers were brought in to see what they could do for father, but the damage was too great. They could only buy him a little time. He knew his time was running out, so he formally named me as his heir, with many witnesses. That was the end. His struggle ended only a few short hours ago."

The three of them sat in silence. Their grief was too raw to speak. Eliséo fondly remembered the earlier days in Goraburg, when Ilya and Vladimir were barely more than children and their mother still lived. Those had been happier times.

Eventually, his mind turned to the time Misha had caught him jesting with Ilya over who would win a sword fight between them. He tried to convince himself that if that incident had been avoided somehow, none of this would have come to pass.

It's not worth it, Rilla's voice sounded softly in his mind. *Do you know how many ways I thought of that I could have prevented Nyssa's death when we found out about it? It's a game you cannot win. No matter what else might have happened instead, some other small thing could have changed to still cause the death anyway.*

Eliséo did not reply, but held her in a tight embrace in his mind. He knew she would tell King Lukys about Lord Mikhail's death without his instruction. Perhaps Lord Mikhail could send a message to Queen Liessa about it. As soon as the thought crossed his mind, he panicked. If Liessa knew that Lord Mikhail was dead, his freedom would be instantly lost.

Rilla, I need you to do something for me, Eliséo suddenly spoke. *Tell Lukys what has happened, but advise him* not *to send a message to Queen Liessa. Things ... changed when I was last in Silvaren. I cannot allow her to force me to leave. Not now.*

Rilla readily agreed, though he could feel her curiosity. He broke contact with her and returned his attention to his surroundings.

"It must be such a comfort to still be able to talk with your tree with such a distance between you," Ilya said carefully.

"What are your plans?" Eliséo asked, immediately changing the subject. He knew Ilya suspected something. "Have you any idea where the rebel karliki are hiding or how many of them there are?"

"Unfortunately not," Ilya answered dejectedly. "We estimate there are at least another five or ten karliki still missing, but we don't know if any have perished in the Outworld. Vladimir doesn't seem to care how many lives he wastes in his attempt to gain command of Goraburg."

"Very well," Eliséo sighed. "How many karliki can be spared as scouts?"

"A handful at most," Ilya answered helplessly. "Father suspected it long ago, but is has become clearer in recent years – our population is dwindling. There are not enough young karliki to spare. If we commit too many as scouts and they don't return, we could jeopardise our future. The older karliki are battle hardened, but too old too send on mission like this. Our people are between a rock and a hard place. "

"We can work with that," Eliséo replied as he digested the bad news. "Give me two of your stealthiest karliki and we will leave this very night to see if we can at least find if there are any more of them within the tunnels.

"Anya, can you go now to ensure a guard is posted at the field entrance. Ask them to instruct Pyrid to immediately return to Illaria. Then I think we can spare you for the rest of the evening. Go find your brother and meet your new niece or nephew."

With a nod from Ilya, Anya quickly left the chamber to fulfil her task. Eliséo then turned to look at Ilya.

"I know that look, Eliséo," the karlik lord warned him. "That look always spells trouble for us. What new scheme have you thought up?"

"I think we need a lintep to help us," Eliséo answered thoughtfully. "Vladimir is avoiding all detection. I doubt I can find him, even if he hides in these very tunnels – not without the help of a team of elves. The way things stand with Queen Liessa, I do not believe she would send more elves to assist me.

"Our hope possibly lies with Plyke. I'll ask Rilla to find King Lukys and see if we can convince him to send aid."

"Very well," Ilya reluctantly agreed, "but after that, you're going to tell me exactly what happened in Silvaren to make you so afraid of your queen. The last I heard, she was so green that she second guessed every decision she made."

Eliséo grimaced. "Things have changed."

Chapter Thirty – Midnight awakening

Rilla woke and sat up rigidly, her eyes blazing green. The sudden movement brought Mistress Isis wide-awake. In the instant before her teacher locked eyes on her, Rilla shut her lids tight, keeping all trace of her bond hidden.

Mistress Isis is with me. What do you need? She snapped at Eliséo, making him understand she couldn't keep her eyes closed much longer.

Is Lukys back in Illaria? With Plyke?

Yes. They arrived late this afternoon.

I need to talk to Lukys. Now, Rilla!

Rilla was left hanging as Eliséo broke their contact. She opened her eyes to find the fire mistress staring at her anxiously.

"I'm fine, I promise. I just need to see King Lukys." Rilla tried to reassure her.

"Now?" Mistress Isis asked surprised. "Rilla, it's the middle of the night. You can't just barge into his room seeking an audience. It will have to wait until morning."

Rilla shook her head. "You don't understand. I need to see him *now*."

"I don't know how to explain this to you any other way, Rilla, but King Lukys is not entirely well disposed towards you at the moment. He will only turn you away."

Rilla closed her eyes for a moment, collecting her thoughts. Of course Lukys would be angry with her, but that didn't change the fact that she needed to talk to him.

"Let's wake Lord Aaron first then," Rilla said, giving Mistress Isis no time to argue. Quietly, the two of them tiptoed past a sleeping Shuut who had graciously agreed to allow Mistress Isis to remain with Rilla until they were certain her powers were under control. She had opted to sleep on a chaise in the antechamber.

Lighting a lantern just outside her room, Rilla led her teacher to her grandfather's chambers. She almost knocked on the door, but reasoned that she might wake more than just Lord Aaron if she did that. Tapping her teeth together, Rilla sent out a tendril of power. She disliked doing it this way, but grudgingly admitted there were some instances when it was acceptable to touch minds with another person, lintep or otherwise.

Within seconds, they could hear Lord Aaron fumbling on the other side of the heavy wooden door. He opened it and looked at the two of them with sleepy eyes, finally settling on her.

"Rilla, it's the middle of the night and I haven't slept in my own bed in over a week. What do you want?" he asked her tiredly.

Rilla almost told him, but caught herself just in time. Mistress Isis didn't know about her bond yet and she was desperately trying to keep it from as many people as possible. Instead, she spoke directly to her grandfather's mind, whispering in case her teacher overheard.

Eliséo needs to speak with King Lukys, she told him, before speaking aloud. "I need to see King Lukys and I don't think he'll agree to talk to me without you."

"I see," Lord Aaron patted her clothed shoulder. "Let me get my robe. I'll be with you in a moment." He left them waiting at the door.

Mistress Isis touched Rilla's arm gently. "What's going on?"

"I'm sorry, Mistress Isis, but I don't think I can tell you." Rilla shook her head. "I'm sure Lord Aaron will keep me safe until I return to bed. It might be better if you go back to sleep now. I don't want to be held responsible for making you tired tomorrow."

Mistress Isis raised her eyebrows at Rilla's audacity. "I think I'll come along if it's all the same to you."

Rilla was about to protest when Lord Aaron returned. He immediately read the situation.

"Isis dear, thank you for bringing Rilla to me instead of directly to Lukys. I'll escort her from here."

The young lintep could see that Mistress Isis was taken aback by her easy dismissal but the fire teacher knew better than to argue against one of the lords of Illaria. Rilla felt guilty. She wished there had been some way to keep Mistress Isis out of the entire affair. If only she hadn't woken the brown-eyed lintep when Eliséo had contacted her so suddenly.

Lord Aaron brought her out of her musing by taking her gently by the elbow and leading her away from her own chamber, past Lord Kynon's and around the corner to King Lukys' private chambers. He didn't speak to her along the way, for which she was grateful, though she itched to remove his hand from her skin. She didn't know what Eliséo wanted to talk to them about and was not keen to ask him when they were still out in the open.

When they reached the door to his private chamber, Rilla looked up at Lord Aaron, almost pleadingly. She'd already used her powers once that night in a way she didn't want to. He nodded and woke King Lukys himself. Rilla found herself standing slightly behind her grandfather as she heard shuffling footsteps behind the door.

The king poked his curly head out of the door. Seeing Lord Aaron and Rilla, he sighed and shook his head. "You'd better come in then," he said quietly. Rilla followed the two older lintep into the enormous antechamber and sat, rubbing her eyes and stifling a yawn.

"What's this all about, Aaron?" the old king asked his cousin.

"You'd better ask Rilla. It appears Eliséo asked her to find you," Lord Aaron replied, looking over to Rilla. Her shoulders sagged at the look in King Lukys' eyes. She wished she could just be nice and warm back in her bed. In her haste to get to Lord Aaron, she'd forgotten to put on her own robe. Rubbing her arms, she closed her eyes and contacted Eliséo.

I'm here, with King Lukys and Lord Aaron. What do you want? She asked the elf, trying to disguise her exhaustion.

I'm sorry, Rilla. This really is important. It will work best if we share everything. Hold their hands so that there is no need for you to relate what I say.

Rilla opened her eyes, locked the door to her tower, pulling in all stray thoughts, and reluctantly held out her hands for the old cousins to hold. She had been right – King Lukys was not as reluctant to see her with her grandfather in tow. Once they were both holding her hands, she allowed them to meet Eliséo.

Eliséo, this had better be important, King Lukys told him peevishly. *We've only just returned from the Outworld and I've a long day ahead of me tomorrow.*

It may be longer still once you hear what I have to say, Eliséo told him unapologetically. *Lord Mikhail Alekseevich is dead. He was killed by one of Vladimir Mikhailovich's supporters and Goraburg is in turmoil.*

Rilla felt both sets of hand tighten their grip on hers as the news was delivered.

The karliki are following Ilya Mikhailovich, however if Vladimir returns and proves to be the stronger brother, there may be more who would agree to follow him in favour of his brother.

This is grave news indeed, King Lukys said. His voice sounded strange in Rilla's mind. She found herself fighting not to push him out. That would only make things worse with how their relationship currently stood. *What are Ilya's plans?*

He intends to find Vladimir and all of his supporters. He would then see them executed, Eliséo spoke plainly. *I agree with this plan, but he cannot carry it out by himself. There has been some trouble in Goraburg resulting in too few young karliki to spare for this task.*

Ambassador, speak plainly. I am tired and cannot for the life of me see where you are trying to lead me, the lintep king implored him. *What is it you want of us? For there would be no other reason for you to contact us in the middle of the night.*

I'm sending a crystal dragon, most probably Pyrid, to Illaria. I would ask that Plyke accompany him back to Goraburg to assist with the search, Eliséo said, to the surprise of all the lintep.

Plyke? Lord Aaron asked in shock. *Whatever could you need Plyke for that another, trained lintep could not accomplish?*

Plyke has particular skills, Eliséo replied unhesitatingly. *During our travels together, he showed that he was capable of feeling where other lintep were, even if they were miles away. He showed a similar skill in the broken Paradise when he found the lintep child.*

Ah, that. Rilla felt Lord Aaron smile within her mind – a strange sensation indeed!

I think I understand what you are asking and I can assure you that Plyke is not trained enough to help you in this endeavour, Lord Aaron pointed out. *You want a lintep to use their skills to track down Vladimir and, if possible, all of his supporters so that they can't escape from you. Would I be correct in this assumption?*

Indeed, you would, Eliséo replied, slightly surprised.

Rilla was equally surprised as she had missed most events in the Paradise. All Plyke had told her upon his return is that Kora had told him who his father was. They'd spent a pleasant evening with Pér, but no one had thought to tell her how or why this fact had been revealed, in the broken Paradise of all places.

Plyke will not be able to help you, Eliséo, Lord Aaron repeated firmly. *Even if he could, I would not allow him to leave Illaria for such a dangerous mission when he isn't fully trained. I fear your choices are diminished. You could ask Pér, though I feel his skills are more for influencing than reading. I fear that leaves you with one choice – me.*

Rilla felt a hand grip hers so tightly it hurt.

I forbid it, King Lukys instantly replied. *Aaron, you are not to leave Illaria for Goraburg. It is too dangerous and we have enough troubles of our own.*

Rilla could feel Eliséo about to protest when her grandfather stepped in again.

Might I remind you how we destroyed the first Paradise? How we kept all of that power from Lishe? Lord Aaron demanded. *It wasn't through our own ingenuity, or solely with the assistance of the crystal dragons. It wasn't even the elves, though all of these races assisted in the end. It was the karliki! They had nothing to gain by helping us. Lishe would never have bothered herself with Goraburg, not in a hundred years. They helped us of their own free will so we should do everything possible to assist them in this tragic time of need.*

Aaron, this is neither the time nor the place to discuss such things, Lukys warned him to no avail.

This is absolutely the time and there is no other place, Aaron insisted. *Do not let it slip your mind that if you refuse to assist them, the karliki still hold the crystal heart and may choose not to assist you when the time comes to destroy the next Paradise.*

The cousins fell silent for a time. Rilla waited with baited breath to see what the king would decide. The fate of the karliki lay in the palm of his hands. Rilla's heart was beating so hard she was certain they could all feel it while linked with her.

It appears I have no choice, King Lukys finally acceded. *Send your dragon, Eliséo. Aaron will fly back to Goraburg and assist you in your search for Vladimir. However, let me make this perfectly clear, if my cousin is injured in any way, I will hold you personally responsible.*

Understood, Eliséo replied gravely. *Lord Aaron, Pyrid should arrive just after dawn. He will escort you to the only entrance to Goraburg that he can access. It is a long trek from there to the centre of the tunnels. I apologise, but I can think of no other way for you to easily enter the tunnels. I will have a karlik stationed there to escort you to Lord Ilya's private chambers.*

Rilla's mind was racing with possibilities. *I can think of a way.* Everyone stopped and listened to her. *It would be much faster for him to access the tunnels from where we entered with you, all those weeks ago. The only problem is to safely get him from the back of the crystal dragon down to the forest floor. I think I have a solution to that. Can you not create a sort of platform of air to carry him down?*

She felt Eliséo's shock at her suggestion, then Elessa's pride in her ingenuity.

Is that possible? Lord Aaron asked in amazement.

I ... I have never done it, Eliséo replied hesitantly. *It may be possible, but I would not be willing to risk your life on it. The other entrance is far safer.*

And hours further away, Rilla pointed out. *It took us well over half a day to reach that tunnel and only half an hour at most from the other entrance.*

Rilla, you do not know what you ask, Eliséo calmly tried to point out. *It is not so easy as you may imagine.*

Then surely Lord Aaron could do it with his own powers, Rilla insisted, turning her attention to her grandfather. *If your power is as great as everyone says, can you not use your power to get yourself down safely?*

She could feel him thinking, but he hid his thoughts well. Eventually, he spoke.

If Pyrid can hover in one spot, rather than fly around, it might be possible to use him as an anchor for my power, wrap a portion around my waist and let myself down gently. I confess, I have never tried such a manoeuvre, but it should be possible.

Rilla squeezed his hand gratefully. She knew how much Ilya meant to Eliséo. Keeping him alive was of the utmost importance to her. For Lord Aaron to assist in that goal was more than she could have ever hoped.

Very well then, we are all agreed, King Lukys said in defeat. *Eliséo will send Pyrid to Illaria. Aaron will fly to Goraburg and assist in finding the rebels as quickly as possible. Once all of this is done, I expect Aaron to be flown back to Illaria with all haste. There is much planning to be done for the destruction of the next Paradise and his assistance is invaluable in this.*

Agreed, Eliséo and Lord Aaron replied simultaneously.

With a quick farewell to, Eliséo broke the connection between himself and Rilla. She was left sitting between the two most powerful men in Illaria, each of them holding her hands tightly. Instinctively, she shook her hands to be free of their grasp. Her grandfather immediately let go. King Lukys held on tighter.

"Was any of this your doing?" the king asked, as he held her firmly.

"Of course not," she replied indignantly. "Eliséo woke me up and told me that he needed to speak to you. Mistress Isis reasoned you would refuse to see me, so I went to my grandfather first."

"If you hadn't done that, perhaps Aaron would not now be in harm's way," King Lukys replied icily. Rilla glared at him angrily, her body on fire with rage. Without meaning to, she made her skin so hot that Lukys was forced to let go.

"If you would talk to me more kindly, perhaps I wouldn't be forced to ask others to talk to you for me," she replied hotly. Too hotly, she realised. Where was Mistress Isis when she needed her? Another few minutes and she'd be in trouble again. The worst part was that she couldn't calm herself down. She was still so angry with King Lukys. He wasn't even bothering to apologise to her. She couldn't hear what he was saying, but the tone was not at all apologetic. He was yelling at her. Why was he yelling at her?

"Stop yelling at me!" she shouted. She was in so much pain. Her blood felt like a hot stream flowing through her veins. She fell to the floor, screaming and curled up tightly until, suddenly, she wasn't. Rilla lay still, breathing heavily, eyes closed tightly.

"Open your eyes, dear," Mistress Isis spoke gently beside her. Rilla opened her eyes to see the fire mistress lying beside her. Without moving, she looked around to see King Lukys' pale face, staring down at her. L0rd Aaron was beside him, smouldering with anger.

"This, *this* is what happens when you take out your anger on a child, Lukys," he spoke lowly, his voice betraying his anger. "Apologise to her this instant and stop forcing her to lose control because you are too stubborn to admit when you've made a mistake. If you cause yet another member of my family to die, I will *never* forgive you."

Rilla glanced in surprise at Mistress Isis who simply smiled as she held out a hand to help her to sit up. She was taken to a chaise, where the brown haired lintep gently sat her down. The entire time, Rilla noticed King Lukys' brown eyes on her, the colour slowly returning to his face.

"I'm sorry, Rilla," the king said in a soft voice. "I know you are always doing what you feel is the correct thing to do in each situation. It often differs to my ideas, but I suppose it's true to say that it's often a better idea. I should not be taking my anger with myself out on you. Will you forgive me?"

Rilla stared at him for a long while, thinking back on every time he'd made her boil over with rage and the few times she'd actually managed to contain that rage. She very much doubted the apology meant that King Lukys would stop getting angry with her.

"Will you stop yelling at me?" she asked him. He nodded. "Will you let me help you come up with a plan for the next Paradise?" she asked doubtfully. He began to shake his head and then caught the look in his cousin's eyes.

"Yes, Rilla," he finally agreed. "If you think you can help us devise a plan to avoid bloodshed without resorting to drastic measures, then I'll agree to that. At that point, it may be an idea to involve the other Paradisians, and your Aunt Kora. The five of you know best how these Paradises work. Any of you might be the key to the solution we seek."

"Shuut too?"

"Very well, Shuut as too," the king sighed.

Rilla suddenly smiled. "It's a deal." King Lukys held out his hand for her to shake. She looked at it hesitantly, but shook it without further retreating behind her power.

Rilla and Mistress Isis left the royal chambers, with the cousins still inside. They walked slowly down the carpeted hall towards Rilla's chamber. The young lintep was dreading the conversation they were to have. Things would be so much easier if she could just tell Mistress Isis. After all, Master Aurelius knew. What harm would it do to let Mistress Isis know as well? The fire mistress was the one protecting Rilla. It was getting to difficult to hide her bond with Elessa. She closed her eyes for the brief moment it took for her to have a short conversation with Eliséo and Elessa.

I think I need to tell Mistress Isis. There are too many times when she may discover it by accident, she pleaded with them.

That's exactly how I feel with Anya at the moment, Eliséo admitted. *I think we can't help but tell them. As you say, they will soon discover it for themselves and letting them know now will make things a significant deal clearer to the two of them. Tell her.*

Rilla opened her eyes once more to find she had almost walked into a wall. Mistress Isis looked back at her worriedly.

"Rilla, are you feeling well?" she asked. "Even aside from your loss of control, you've been acting a little ... strange this evening."

The young lintep smiled shyly at her teacher and protector. "I have something to tell you, Mistress Isis. I couldn't tell you before. Let's go to my room and I'll tell you everything."

Chapter Thirty-One – Favours

Aaron barely slept a wink the rest of the evening. Much as he had readily agreed to go to Goraburg, he had only done so because he refused to send Plyke in his stead. He did not know how long it would take for them to find all the rebel karliki, nor if Lord Ilya would require him to stay even if Lukys insisted he was ready to destroy the next Paradise. It was all such a mess.

For a lintep who hadn't left Illaria, or even really the castle, since his tragic trip to Silvaren, Aaron was becoming quite the traveller in recent days. As he dressed in the early dawn light, gathering a few personal items to take with him to Goraburg, he realised he hadn't had a chance to speak with Kynon about his meeting. It was such an important task.

Hoping his cousin would forgive the intrusion, he went to knock on Kynon's door. Kynon answered the door sleepily, although Aaron noticed, a lot less angrily than he had the previous times his slumber had been disturbed.

"Aaron, you've not even been back an entire day. Can you not wait another hour or two before you ask me?" Kynon half smiled at him.

"Sorry, Kynon, but I'll be travelling to Goraburg on dragonback this morning," Aaron explained. "Lord Mikhail has been assassinated and I'm to help find the rebel karliki responsible for the turmoil. I don't know how long I'll be away so I have two favours to ask you.

"The first is to tell me everything you learned while we were away. The second is ... more personal. Lukys will be quite busy for a time and I don't like to leave my family with no one to turn to. I'm certain we both know you won't be their first choice, but I would appreciate it if you could look out for them.

"Rilla and Plyke are at difficult stages of their power peaking. Although Plyke's loss of control rarely has a visible impact, Rilla's is getting quite out of hand. Mistress Isis has taken it upon herself to protect Rilla, but if she can't be there for any reason ..." Aaron trailed off.

"Of course, Aaron," Kynon readily agreed. "We may have had our differences in the past, but I'm coming to see that the way you've raised your family is much closer to how my own mother would have wanted me to raise mine. Have no fear. I'll do what I can for them in your absence.

"As for your first request, I think we were quite successful in learning a great deal about the Paradises. In fact, Master Bastienne has taught me so much that I can't possibly pass on all that knowledge to you in one short conversation.

"The one fact you might find interesting is that he isn't from Illaria. Did you know that? He comes from a small village nearby that I've never heard of before – Statera. In any case, the way they use their powers there is quite different from the way we are taught here in Illaria. I think it may prove useful for him to have a little talk with Rilla. He is used to dealing with powers which we find ... unusual in Illaria."

Aaron stared at his cousin in disbelief. This was the most amazing news. The fact that this discovery had led to a possible way to help Rilla with her current predicament was unfathomable. However, the part he found most uplifting about the entire scenario was Kynon's new attitude towards being a part of life in the castle.

"Kynon, I don't think you will ever understand what you've done for me this morning," Aaron replied, his voice thick with emotion. "Please, talk with Rilla when she wakes up. If Mistress Isis is there, she will be less inclined to brush you aside. Find a way for her to meet Master Bastienne even if she has lessons all day. The situation with her is getting more and more drastic by the day. If he can help her ... I don't know how I'll ever be able to repay you."

Kynon gripped his shoulder tightly for a moment. "Call it even for all the times I should have helped you and didn't, when your children went out of their way to help mine." Aaron nodded, holding his hand over Kynon's.

* * *

Rilla woke late the next morning. Shuut was standing over her bed, tapping her foot impatiently. Rilla looked up at her sister bleary eyed.
"What?"
"Don't use that tone with me," Shuut said irritably. "Your late night rampage with Mistress Isis left me with very little sleep. I won't let you make all three of us late for our morning classes. Get up, get dressed and eat."
Rilla heard Mistress Isis stir next to her. She looked down and was surprised to see their hands intertwined. After their talk the night before, Rilla had little left to hide from the fire mistress, but it still surprised her to notice that she hadn't objected to the skin contact.
"Right, I've got Master Reuben this morning," Rilla said as she carefully retrieved her hand. "Who are you with?"
"Mistress Kayte," Shuut replied with ease. "This lesson should be better than the first. Now I know she's going to ask us to cut each other, I won't try to attack anyone and she won't steal my strength away."

Rilla laughed mirthlessly. "That should be a change. At least you've got Plyke and the twins to work with. I don't know anyone in Reuben's class. Mind powers are not something I'm keen to work on with anyone, so we'll see how that goes."

There was a knock at the door. Shuut went to open it as Rilla and Mistress Isis dressed for the day. A few moments later, Shuut came back in. "Lord Kynon wants to talk to you. I told him you'll be late for your lessons, but he insisted."

Rilla glanced over at Mistress Isis. The fire mistress shrugged her shoulders. "I've no idea what he wants. I would suggest whatever he wants to talk to you about is important. He wouldn't make you late for your lessons for something frivolous."

"He said you could go with her," Shuut added. "He seemed to know you were here."

Mistress Isis nodded and Rilla followed the fire mistress out of her chambers, promising to meet Shuut and their cousins between their lessons. Together, they walked down the carpeted hall, past Kora's chambers, around the corner past Lord Aaron's chambers and across to Lord Kynon's chambers. Rilla hesitated a moment then knocked. She stood back a step as Lord Kynon immediately opened the door.

"Rilla, thank you for seeing me," Kynon said kindly. "Mistress Isis, you're most welcome as well. Please come in. This won't take too long."

The curious lintep followed the lord into his chambers. Sitting there was the old master they'd seen in the library the night they'd returned from the Outworld.

"I'm certain you remember Master Bastienne," Kynon reintroduced them, and then turned his attention to Rilla. "It has been brought to my attention that you are having some difficulties keeping your powers under control, particularly in Mistress Isis' area of expertise, which is why she shadows your every move."

"That's not *exactly* true," Rilla pointed out, slightly embarrassed to realise that her lack of control was more common knowledge than she'd thought. It surprised her to see Mistress Isis blushing – this couldn't possibly be more embarrassing for her than for Rilla.

"If you'll allow me to explain," Mistress Isis spoke in a very demure voice. "Rilla has been put in some ... stressful situations lately. They haven't so much caused her power, but more her feelings, to get out of control. Trust me, in the circumstances, it's amazing she hasn't lost control more often.

"There has only been one night when she lost control the same way many other lintep do, during their sleep. It happened to me so many times my parents sent me to the castle."

Master Bastienne signalled Lord Kynon, who was just about to speak. "Mistress Isis, no one is suggesting that you haven't taught the child well. Your skills are so impressive that your name is well known around Illaria. I know many parents send their children to the castle in the hopes they will learn from you.

"It was Lord Kynon's idea that I should spend some time with Rilla in Lord Aaron's absence. I am satisfied that you will keep her safe during the day. May I humbly suggest that you both spend an hour of your time with me this evening? I would like to learn everything about Rilla that I can and I'm quite keen to see exactly why your name is praised in every corner of this fine stronghold."

Rilla glanced over to Mistress Isis to notice her blushing ever brighter. It finally dawned on her that the fire mistress was flattered, not embarrassed. Smiling, she nodded to Master Bastienne.

"I have prior engagements for this evening's meal, but I can certainly spend an hour with you straight after my last lesson. Where can we find you?" Rilla asked enthusiastically. It would be nice to speak to someone other than her own teachers about her power. She found it oddly comforting that her grandfather had gone out of his way to arrange this for her before leaving for Goraburg. It had been a long time since any of her older family members had cared about her in that way. Nyssa possibly had, to begin with, but then she'd abandoned her in a Paradise with her father, who then refused to acknowledge her as his daughter. She shook her head once more at the insanity of it all.

"Meet me in the library tonight," Master Bastienne told her.

Rilla nodded. "I have to go to my lessons now. Master Reuben will be expecting me."

"Do you need me to come with you?" Mistress Isis asked her, clearly hoping the answer would be no. Rilla smiled and shook her head.

"I'm sure Master Bastienne would rather your company right now," she called out as she left the room.

Chapter Thirty-Two – Adjustments

Rilla ran down the stairs as quickly as she could. The halls were already empty of students. She hurriedly walked down the hall of classrooms, looking for Master Reuben's room. It was the same as Master Aurelius' room, with the tri-wave symbol. It didn't take her long to find it.

She knocked on the door, opening it just enough to peek in. The room was full of students all sitting in groups of four. She looked around curiously. Even though Rilla had had a few private lessons with Master Reuben, he had only given her leave to join his advanced class upon his return to Illaria the night before. It certainly didn't look like any of her other lessons, where they worked only in pairs.

"Welcome, Rilla," Master Reuben called out to her from one of the groups towards the front of the class. "Come in, come in. We weren't certain if you were joining us this morning, so we started without you. Now that you're here, you can take my place."

He offered her the seat and walked slowly towards a large cushioned chair at the front of the class. Rilla walked hesitantly to the vacant seat and sat with a group of students she'd never met before – two boys and a girl.

"We're sending out thoughts to multiple people," a sandy haired boy told her. "We pick whoever we want out of the group and then try to send the thought to those ones, leaving out one person."

"It's to teach us better control of our powers," the hazel eyed girl explained. "We all know how to send a thought to one person, or to everyone within our power's reach, but this is more specific. Master Reuben only started us on this task last lesson, so you won't be too far behind."

Rilla creased her brow. It wasn't what she was expecting from the class. She found herself smiling at the thought that everyone had to figure out what to do on their own.

"I'm Taddeo," said the sandy haired boy. "This is Odille and Zefiro. I'll start. We can't say who we're sending the thoughts to, otherwise they'll know to listen for it and might accidentally read our minds instead. Just sit back and wait."

Blue.

Rilla instantly heard the colour spoken into her mind. It was quick, non-intrusive and quiet. She smiled at the simplicity of it. The best part was that Taddeo was in and out of her mind so quickly that she didn't feel the need to push him out.

"Did you hear it?" he asked after a moment. She and Odille nodded.

"Blue," they said simultaneously.

"Odille, your turn," Taddeo told the girl. Rilla waited, but heard nothing. A few moments later, Taddeo and Zefiro called out the colour they'd heard Odille tell them.

"Zefiro, your turn," Taddeo instructed. It was clear he was the leader of the group, whether chosen by the others or by himself Rilla couldn't tell.

White.

Rilla was caught off guard. She had been thinking about Taddeo and wasn't expecting Zefiro to talk to her. She struggled not to push Zefiro out of her mind. The quiet boy lingered just a little too long in her mind. Rilla reasoned that though they were in the advanced class, they were clearly not all at the same skill level.

"White," she said through clenched teeth, along with Taddeo.

"Are you okay Rilla?" Taddeo asked her with a note of concern. She nodded, brushing off her thoughts. "Well then, it's your turn. Just choose two of us and send your message."

Rilla chose Taddeo and Zefiro. As easily as though she were talking to them, she passed a thought along to them.

Green.

For a second, both Taddeo and Zefiro held their heads and cried out and then the moment was over. Rilla looked at them in shock. Rilla saw Taddeo signal Master Reuben, who rose gracefully from his chair and walked over to them.

"We may need a little help here, Master Reuben," Taddeo told him. "Rilla can hear our thoughts perfectly and we can hear hers. *Loud* and clear."

"I see," Master Reuben said thoughtfully. *Rilla, have you used your mind powers to communicate with anyone since your loss of control in the Outworld?*

Rilla shook her head, not trusting herself to speak directly to his mind.

In that case, you may need to project in a whisper, he suggested. *Your power is quite magnificent, but I fear only a very little of it is needed for this task now. Taddeo and Odille appear to have heard your thought as a shout. Try with me now, so that you can change your tactic with them.*

Not wanting to hurt Master Reuben, Rilla sent out a quiet thought towards him. *Is this too loud?* The grimace on his face showed her that it was. Rilla proceeded to send out a whisper of a thought. *What about this?*

That's better, he told her quietly. *You have more power than you realise, Rilla. Don't let it scare you, but make sure you don't scare others either. This group will be good for you.*

"She's ready to try again," Master Reuben told the rest of her group. "Disregard her last word. There will be a new one momentarily."

They nodded at him and then looked warily at her. Rilla smiled half-heartedly at them. This was going to be a long lesson.

* * *

The bell tolled for the end of morning lessons. Plyke ran out of mistress Kayte's class with Shuut and the twins. He couldn't wait to introduce them to Pér. His father had returned to his home in the city once they'd returned from Illaria, only resurfacing later that evening to meet Rilla and Shuut. When the twins had found out about him, they'd badgered Plyke until he smilingly revealed that the minstrel was to join them in the dining hall between lessons.

The four of them raced down the stairs to the dining hall, startling all other lintep along their path in their haste to meet Pér. Plyke spotted him first and called out a greeting to him. His father was sitting beside Tika, happily chatting away with the small human, much to Tika's delight. Plyke smiled at the sight as he quickly closed the distance between them. He couldn't imagine anything better than his Partner getting along so well with both his mother and his father. The happiness almost burst his heart.

"Good day to you, my son," Pér said as he wrapped his arms around the boy in an exaggerated embrace, which Plyke returned. "And who have we here? I know these two scallywags by reputation alone! Umi and Ulf, I'd wager."

The twins smiled and laughed, protesting their reputation. Pér tousled their hair and invited them all to join him and Tika. The six of them sat together, talking happily with Umi and Ulf asking their usual invasive questions of the latest addition to their family.

They were so busy talking, they barely noticed when Rilla joined them. Plyke would not have noticed her at all for her silence. The only reason he did notice was that his newfound skill of feeling things without skin contact was getting a little out of control. He knew he would need to talk to Lord Aaron about it, but then, perhaps Pér could help him.

Rilla's feelings were a complete contrast to her sister and cousins. Plyke attempted to talk to her without raising anyone's suspicions.

What happened? He asked her gently. Rilla looked up at him, tears pricking her eyes and shook her head. *Rilla, you can always talk to me. What is it?*

The faintest whisper of a reply came from her. *My power is too strong. I hurt two of my classmates because I thought too loudly at them. I have to whisper now. It didn't used to be this bad.*

I know how you feel, he told her comfortingly. *You weren't in the broken Paradise to see it happen for the first time, but my powers are going out of control too. I could feel your sadness as you walked in the room. I don't know how not to feel things anymore, even without touching.*

Thanks Plyke, she said with a small smile. *I guess we're both learning. Maybe you can come with me to see Master Bastienne this evening. Looks like we both may need his help.*

Who is Master Bastienne? Plyke asked in confusion. *Did he start while the rest of us were still in the Outworld?*

No, he's an old master from a town in the Outworld. They learn to use their powers a little differently there and Lord Aaron thinks he may be able to help us both.

"Rilla, do you know where Lord Aaron is?"

Plyke was pulled out of his conversation with his cousin by Pér's loud voice. He looked around the dining hall and then realised he hadn't seen their grandfather all day. Plyke glanced over to Rilla to find her tapping her teeth together.

"He ... had to leave early in the morning," Rilla answered evasively. Plyke creased his brow at her. She shook her head almost imperceptibly at him. *Later*, she told him. He nodded and diverted Pér's attention back to the twins.

"Umi and Ulf have heard tell of your skills as a minstrel, Pér," Plyke said with a grin. "I'm sure we'd all be more than happy to have you play for us. When can we hear you?"

Pér laughed long and loud, causing almost every lintep in the dining hall to look his way. "If it's a performance you want, then a performance you shall have. I'll speak with King Lukys during your afternoon lessons. Either he'll allow me to sing in these halls once more or you can come and listen to me in the marketplace tonight."

Plyke cheered as excitedly as the twins and a number of other lintep. Pér's unusual songs were famous throughout Illaria, even if they hadn't been heard in years.

"Until tonight then," Plyke said happily as the bells tolled for their afternoon classes. "We need to go now. I have something to do just after class, but I'll find you after that."

Plyke and Rilla ran up the stairs to the classrooms and arrived before any of the other students. They sat together on a sandstone ledge as they waited for their teachers.

"Where is grandfather?" Plyke asked her in a whisper. He listened in shock and wonder as Rilla related the events of the previous night.

"So, he flew away early this morning on dragonback," Plyke mused aloud. "Do you know when he'll be back?"

"No one does," Rilla shrugged. "I suppose he'll stay there for as long as it takes to find all the rebel karliki. Eliséo wanted you to go, but Lord Aaron refused. He's ... quite protective of us."

Plyke was startled by her remark. "Why would Eliséo have wanted *me* to go?"

"He knows you're capable of feeling things a long way out. Eliséo and I didn't know that Lord Aaron can do the same and more. From what I hear, Eliséo wasn't around when Lord Aaron calmed the townsfolk from Hedgefall, so neither of us knew about his skills."

"I see," Plyke replied quietly. He looked Rilla in the eye and told her something he'd been wanting to for a while. "Rilla, you seem to find it strange that grandfather is protective of us. Don't you feel like his grandchild yet? You still call him Lord Aaron rather than grandfather. It almost seems as though you feel a great debt towards him any time he does something that any grandfather, or even a mother or father would do."

Once again, he saw her blink tears away. "I've never really had family like you, Plyke. I had Rhanya and I loved him dearly but as much as I wished he could have been, he wasn't my grandfather. My father and my mother, well, you knew them both as well as I did," she shrugged helplessly. "How was I ever to know what a family was really like? I suppose I could call Lord Aaron, grandfather and Kora, Aunt Kora instead, but would it really make any difference to any of them?"

Plyke laughed softly and hugged his cousin as other students began to file into the halls. He whispered into her ear, "It would mean more to them than you can possibly imagine. Even the King would probably appreciate being called Uncle Lukys."

* * *

Rilla drew back from Plyke, thoughtfully. *Grandfather, Aunt Kora, Uncle Lukys,* there were so many family members that she was yet to acknowledge as such. She wondered if King Lukys would soften further towards her if she called him 'uncle'. Rilla smiled at the thought and caught Plyke grinning back at her.

They parted ways and headed towards their classrooms. Rilla inwardly groaned as she saw Réne outside Master Aurelius' room. The practical lesson should have been one of her favourites, but with the arrogant boy in her class, it was difficult to enjoy herself. She didn't have Miette as an ally, but her newfound friendship with Kalydron made these lessons bearable.

"Hello Rilla," Kalydron's now familiar voice said from behind her. She turned to find him quickly closing the gap between them. "Are you pledged to work with Réne the Arrogant today or will my partnership do well enough for you?"

Rilla smiled and elbowed the tall boy in the ribs. "I suppose I can make do with you today," she replied in an offhand manner before they both burst into laughter.

"Master Aurelius!" Kalydron suddenly shouted. "You're back!"

The old master smiled and nodded. "Yes, I returned late last night. I hope my replacement hasn't made you all lazy in the past few lessons."

His students protested that they'd been worked relentlessly and were glad to have him back. Smiling, Master Aurelius unlocked the door for his students and waved them all in. He stopped Rilla for a moment before she entered.

"I've heard that you've had a little boost in your powers recently," he whispered to her. "Work with Kalydron today. He will easily forgive any excessive force you may use."

Rilla blushed as she nodded. Mistress Isis must have been busily running around, alerting all the newly returned masters and mistresses about her recent bouts of losing control of her powers. No doubt she had been discreet about it and not gone into more detail than necessary, but Rilla couldn't help but feel embarrassed all the same.

Master Aurelius laid a hand on her bare forearm. Rilla almost flinched away until she realised that his hand was quite a bit cooler than her skin. He calmed and cooled her down all at the same time. She sighed heavily, biting back tears, as he removed his hand.

"Thank you," she said. "I never thought I'd be grateful for skin contact."

He smiled and patted her shoulder. "Into class now, and remember your fellow students probably won't notice a difference other than Kalydron and you can quickly readjust the amount of force you use. We'll continue with passing stones today. That should be good for you and I'm certain everyone can use the practise after an absence from my lessons."

Rilla nodded gratefully and went to sit across from Kalydron as Master Aurelius went to his desk at the front of the class.

"Stones out, everyone," he called out loudly. He waited until students silently awaited his next instruction. "Start with one stone and add in as many as you can handle. This is not a race or a competition. I want to assure myself that none of you have forgotten this skill in my absence."

Rilla and Kalydron emptied the stones from their pouches onto the table in front of them. The last time they'd performed this task, they had only used the two stones Master Aurelius had prescribed them and had ended up chatting towards the end of the lesson because the task had become second nature. They were both confident of being able to pass more than two stones at a time this lesson.

They each picked up a stone and moved it towards their partner. Rilla cringed as her stone shot past a surprised Kalydron and hit the wall behind him, bouncing off to hit him in the head.

"Well, that's one way to show your displeasure with me," he joked as he bent down to pick up the stone, all the while rubbing the back of his head. "Or are you just trying to show off how powerful you are? I submit!" he said as he put up both hands in mock defeat. Rilla kicked him under the table, taking back her stone from his outstretched hand.

"I'll be a lady one day and then you *will* have to submit to me," she responded haughtily before they both broke into grins. "Alright, let's start again, maybe just with one stone to start."

Kalydron nodded and waited expectantly. This time, Rilla used the tiniest bit of her power, the smallest tendril she could form, to pick up the stone. She carefully guided it over to the patiently waiting lintep and dropped it lightly when she reached his power.

Shaking her head at the difficulty she might now have in all of her lessons, Rilla withdrew almost all of her power, leaving behind that one small tendril to catch and transport the pebble back and forth with Kalydron. It took her longer than she anticipated before she was comfortable with the amount of force she now needed to perform the task.

"Shall we add another one?" Kalydron cocked his eyebrow at her. Rilla hesitated, but nodded.

They spent the rest of the afternoon, under Master Aurelius' watchful eye, adding more and more stones to their circle. Rilla was pleased to note that she finally had her practical powers under control again. Secretly, she wondered how much more powerful she was now and if that was to be her new limit or if her power would continue to increase as she underwent training.

"Will I see you in the dining hall tonight?" Kalydron asked as he got up to leave with the rest of the students.

Rilla nodded. "Yes, perhaps a little later than usual. I need to ... have another quick lesson right now. Find Miette and I'll meet you both before we go to the performance. I wouldn't want to miss Pér's songs for anything." Kalydron looked at her inquisitively for a moment, then shrugged and waved her farewell.

Rilla caught Master Aurelius' eye as Kalydron and the other students began to leave the room. He settled back down into his comfortable chair to wait for her. Once all the students had left, Rilla quietly closed the door behind them and turned to face her practical teacher.

"I can't stay for long – I've got to meet Master Bastienne in a moment. I just wanted to ask, is there any way to test how powerful I am now, as compared to when I arrived in Illaria? Do you know if this sudden increase will be the only one? Does it happen to every lintep?"

Master Aurelius smiled at the torrent of questions and motioned to a chair. Rilla sat down, waiting for his reply.

"Rilla, you and your entire family are a wonder to the rest of us. Most lintep do have a few surges of power during the year that their power peaks. As for how many times it occurs, it's different for each lintep.

"Some have their initial peak and there it ends. Others have one or two small surges, nothing really of significance. The most powerful lintep, like yourself and Plyke will possibly have a number of surges, where your power increases dramatically and you lose control all over again.

"As Mistress Isis may have mentioned, she is one of the most powerful lintep in Illaria. She, herself, had three powerful surges during the year her power peaked. Since her skills lie strongly in the field of fire and ice, she burnt a number of sheets both in her own home and then here in the palace.

"Some of her teachers were known to keep a bucket of water in their classrooms in case she accidentally caught anything alight and couldn't control the flames," he smiled at the memory. "Of course, it never came to that, but people are frightened of anyone more powerful than they are."

Rilla looked at him with some surprise. Mistress Isis had told her of burning the sheets in her parents' home, but not the ones in the castle. Had she even known about the buckets of water?

"What about testing how powerful I've actually become?" she finally asked. "Is there any way to do that?"

"All in good time, Rilla," Master Aurelius said, getting up from his chair. "When we have all the time we could want, I will show you a few ways to test your strength. Until then, go to Master Bastienne. Perhaps he can help you."

Reluctantly, Rilla left Master Aurelius' room. Her irritation instantly disappeared as she saw Plyke waiting for her with a broad grin.

"Let's find Master Bastienne," he said optimistically. Rilla couldn't help but be infected by his enthusiasm.

Together they ran to the library. Knowing it was well past the hour that most students would be in the library, Rilla and Plyke knocked on the closed door to be admitted. They weren't left waiting long. The elaborately carved wooden doors swung open soundlessly.

"Rilla, I see you've brought company," Master Bastienne said with some surprise.

"This is my cousin, Plyke. He could possibly use your help as well," Rilla explained, as they walked into the library. She looked around to find Mistress Isis, but only saw Guiscard instead. "Will Mistress Isis be joining us?"

"Actually, no," Master Bastienne closed the doors and came to sit with the three of them. "Mistress Isis and I had a lengthy talk this morning. She's ... a little bit tired at the moment, so I gave her the evening off."

Rilla froze for a moment, the implications sinking in. "You mean she's exhausted from trying to keep me safe, don't you?"

"Rilla, what Master Bastienne is rather tactlessly telling you is that keeping your power under control requires more time and energy than one lintep alone can provide." Guiscard came to sit next to her, patting her arm over her sleeve. "Mistress Isis should really have shared the task with Mistress Kayte when it was only the two of them in Illaria. Now that the others have returned, we judge it best that the task be shared between whichever lintep you trust most. I'm sure you can understand, there is no point asking someone like Mistress Vika to help."

Rilla calmed down as she listened to the librarian. She always found it pleasant to be in his company. A sudden thought struck her. "Would *you* be one of the lintep to help me?" she asked the librarian.

"I'm not a master, Rilla," he told her gently. "There is little I could do to help you should things get out of hand."

"What about Kora?" Plyke suggested. "You've known her since you were three years old and she's one of the most powerful lintep in Illaria."

Rilla nodded. "Kora and Mistress Isis then."

"Yes, that's a good start, Rilla, but you'll need more than that," Master Bastienne pointed out to her. Rilla sat glumly and thought about all the lintep in Illaria who were both skilled and powerful enough to help her and that she could trust to save her.

"Perhaps Master Aurelius as well," Rilla said doubtfully. "Though I'm not certain he'll agree. I can't think of anyone else. Lord Aaron isn't here and I don't really know that many lintep yet."

"Do you trust me?" Master Bastienne asked her bluntly. Rilla hesitated in the face of such openness.

"I ... don't really know you yet," she pointed out as tactfully as she could, glancing over at Plyke, silently begging him for help.

"What about Luisella, you know, Umi and Ulf's mother? Or Lord Braedan?" Plyke suggested. "Kora is quite good friends with them. Even Pér might be able to help."

Rilla shook her head, feeling suddenly out of control of the situation. "I don't really know any of them. I ... can't do this." Without meaning to,

Rilla burst into tears. Hot salt water trickled down her face, burning her skin. Understanding that it was happening again, she looked up at Master Bastienne for help. He simply sat there, calmly watching as she began to burn up.

"Rilla, calm down," Plyke's voice was a distant murmur in the roaring of her boiling blood. She knew she needed to listen to him, but she didn't know how. Master Bastienne and Guiscard didn't know about her bond, so she couldn't find refuge there – not for long anyway. She closed her eyes tightly.

Help me! She screamed at Eliséo and Elessa. Instantly, they were both there, wrapping her mind in a calming embrace. They soothed her with meaningless words. She breathed a long sigh of relief as she felt her body start to cool.

Thank you! She said before she broke contact with them and opened her dull green eyes to find Master Bastienne staring at her intently.

"Whatever it was you just did, it worked," he told her confidently. "I don't know what it was, but at least it's a start. I'm sorry we had to push you, but I needed to see exactly how it all starts and if there's any way you know of to stop it before it's too late for you to react.

"It's good to know that there is. Now we can work from there. The first thing you need to learn is control of your emotions. That probably goes for both of you, so Plyke, you can join in these exercises."

Rilla was shocked to realise that Master Bastienne had purposely tried to make her lose control. It was bad enough when it happened accidentally, but for someone to force her into that situation when she was around people who either couldn't help her or she didn't trust was simply cruel. Before she could let her thoughts run away with her, she focused on the old master's words.

"Control of your emotions is much more difficult than control of your powers," he told them. "It requires more discipline and very few can achieve it with any success when they first begin. That is why it will be important for both of you to perform these simple rituals daily, even hourly if you can."

He closed his eyes as he sat before them. Rilla exchanged skeptical glances with Plyke and Guiscard before looking back at the old lintep. He wasn't moving. His breath was coming in long, deep breaths. When he opened his eyes, there was a look of serenity.

"What did you do?" Rilla asked him curiously. She knew he wasn't bound to an elf's tree and there was no other comfort she could think of that could be found in the mind.

"I breathed deeply and focused on the feel of the wooden chair under my fingers," he said smiling at her.

"That doesn't make any sense," Plyke pointed out. "How can *that* help us control our emotions?"

"Try it," he told them. "You too, Guiscard."

The startled librarian glanced skeptically at the old master, but closed his eyes nonetheless. Rilla shrugged at Plyke and closed her eyes as well. She breathed deeply and tried to feel what her fingers were touching. It was soft, smooth and almost cool under her hand. She tried to focus on it but her thoughts kept drifting away to her lessons, her dinner engagements, Pér's performance, Mistress Isis and all the other lintep who would need to help her. Her breathing became ragged again.

"Rilla, breathe in, breathe out," Master Bastienne guided her. "Concentrate on your breath alone. In and out."

She did as she was told. As she focused on her breathing, she noticed it become steadier, with deeper breaths. Surprisingly, it made her feel calmer. She opened her eyes to find the master smiling at her.

"And *that* is how you control your emotions," he told her with a hint of pride in his voice. "It's really very simple, but takes quite a bit of practice to make it work every time you need it."

Rilla looked over to see Plyke and Guiscard opening their eyes. Both of them looked more relaxed than they had before. It was surprising how well it worked.

"I think that's enough for tonight," Master Bastienne told them. "Rilla, you really will need to think of a few more people you can trust. I may not be one of them, but Mistress Isis and Kora cannot possible do it indefinitely between the two of them. I'll speak with Master Aurelius tonight, but it would be ... quite unseemly for him to sleep in your chambers."

Rilla blushed at the thought. "I'll talk with Kora tonight. Maybe we can think of something," Rilla told him. "Thank you for your help."

"Yes, thank you Master Bastienne," Plyke echoed her sentiments as they waved farewell to the two older lintep. Once outside the library, without needing to speak, they both ran towards the dining hall to find out where Pér was performing.

Chapter Thirty-Three – Heartstrings

Throughout the course of the day, Kora heard a number of lintep talking about the performance Pér had promised to some of the younger lintep. Word had spread like wildfire. Though it appeared he hadn't sung publicly in years, his songs were still well known throughout Illaria. She smiled to think that because of his intentional deception of King Lukys, her uncle had never understood how truly talented Pér was as a musician.

The performance that evening would take place in the marketplace just outside the castle. A small, raised platform had been erected on the side of the square years ago. It had become a place for new minstrels to try their hand at a few songs before the true artists came out for the evening.

She wound her way through the outer gardens of the palace, thinking of all the times she'd walked these same paths with Pér. She was so lost in thought that she barely noticed when Tika came running up to her.

"Kora!" he yelled at her. "Wait for me!"

She turned to find her favourite human running towards her. He nearly bowled her over with a fierce embrace. She smiled, returning his embrace.

"Let me guess. You don't know where Plyke is and you need help to cross the drawbridge to hear Pér's performance?" she asked him innocently. Tika smiled and nodded. "Alright then, come along. I'm sure we'll find them eventually."

Kora and Tika walked arm in arm as other lintep hurried around them, just as eager to get to the marketplace. Pér's fame had certainly not died. As they crossed the cobbled bridge, the crowd became thicker. Once people noticed it was Lady Kora trying to move past them, a pathway immediately opened up in front of them. She smiled and nodded towards those who moved out of her way, gently closing Tika's gaping mouth with her fingertips. She knew it must be so strange for the child who had known her all his life as a seamstress to see people treating her as royalty.

"Kora, wait for us!" Rilla and Plyke called out to her, two other students following close behind them. She slowed her pace with Tika to allow them catch up to her before continuing on to the marketplace. She found herself desperate to hear which song Pér would grace them with, or if there would be multiple songs.

Kora walked along with her family and their friends towards the sound of music and laughter. Once they had reached the market square, Rilla and the two students walked off to find their own place in the crowd. Kora was happy for her niece. In the Paradise, she'd never really had anyone other than Rhanya to talk to. Even Kora herself had been distant towards the poor girl for fear of Erton's wrath.

She noticed Tika kept a firm hold of her arm as Umi, Ulf and Shuut met them. She thought it sweet that he was so possessive of her. He must have always suspected that she was Plyke's mother. She'd become a sort of replacement for his own mother after Erton's men had taken care of her.

Kora listened as Pér played a string of popular songs on his lute. They always brought a smile to her face. She settled down for his real performance and watched as the crowed grew suddenly quiet. For a moment, she was confused until she realised Pér was quieting the people with his music and his power combined. She caught his gaze and raised an eyebrow at him. He only winked at her before beginning his next, slower tune.

"This is a new song," Pér told the expectant crowd as he strummed a few notes on his lute. "You can think of it as my one and only ballad."

The crowed murmured in anticipation. Pér had never before sung a ballad. Kora thought to herself that whatever he ended up calling it, this song would always be known by the people as "Pér's ballad". The murmurs died down as he strummed out the chords. With the first lines, Kora smiled as she realised he was singing about her.

Oh once, there was a young lass
with smiling, big brown eyes.
She walked through the market square
with flowers in her hair.

All at once, I felt my heart was gone.
It belonged to me no more.
I had given it to that gentle lass.
It was hers forever more.

We spent a pleasant year or two
round the castle and the town.
Then suddenly she was there no more.
My heart had gone and left me cold.

I followed where my heart did lead,
until I found that lass again.
We spent a pleasant night or two,
then my heart left me for dead.

The months and then the years did pass.
She returned to me once more.
My heart is home and with my son.
I shall never cry again.

* * *

The entire time he sang, Pér kept his eyes firmly fixed on Kora's, pulling at her heartstings. At first, they had been the smiling eyes he had fallen in love with. Slowly, they had filled with tears. By the end, she was holding their son and his Partner close to her on either side, heaving uneven sobs.

Pér opened his arms wide as Tika, Umi and Ulf pushed Kora and Plyke towards him. The crows erupted into a loud, resounding cheer as the three of them embraced.

"One more song," Pér announced, as he kissed Kora and released his family back into the crowd. "This one is for those of us who think it's high time for a change."

He caught Kora's warning look as he strummed his first few bars. *These* were the sorts of songs that had kept him out of King Lukys' good graces, and therefore far from his attention.

We are humans! We are brave!
We travel the Outworld warily

The Outworld is ours to share.
Let's stop the fighting!
We'll face our fears!
There are friends out there for us to find.

We are karliki! We're tough as gems!
We lost our magic in Goraburg.

The Outworld is ours to share.
Let's stop the fighting!
We'll face our fears!
There are friends out there for us to find.

We are elves! We are ancient folk.
We are bound to trees in Silvaren.

The Outworld is ours to share.
Let's stop the fighting!
We'll face our fears!
There are friends out there for us to find.

We are lintep! We are powerful!
We stay trapped inside Illaria
It's now time for us to roam!

The Outworld is ours to share.
Let's stop the fighting!
We'll face our fears!
There are friends out there for us to find.

Carefully, he used his powers to inspire their imagination, to lessen their fears and pique their curiosity. By the last chorus, almost every person in the market square was singing along. Pér played the chorus twice at the end, to firmly plant it in their minds.

* * *

Rilla watched Pér's performance with Kalydron and Miette. After the first song, she saw Arishen arrive in the market square with a few other young men. She assumed they were fellow apprentices. They struggled to find a place in the crowded square. With a wave, Rilla beckoned him over to where she and her friends had created a small space for themselves. Arishen edged his way towards her with one of the apprentices, a lintep just a head shorter than the tall human, with scruffy hair and a mischievous glint in his eye. Rilla wondered how much trouble the two of them found together.

When they finally reached her, Rilla introduced Arishen to her two new friends. Arishen introduced the other apprentice as Narseo. The five of them settled down to watch the rest of the performance. Pér had just started to strum a few slow bars. They listened as he sang about Kora. Rilla found herself fighting back tears as she watched both Kora's reaction to the song and Pér's careful eye on her.

"How can he forgive her after the way she treated him?" Narseo asked in disgust. Rilla glared at him angrily, but said nothing. She was surprised when Arishen spoke up for Kora.

"You don't know her side of the story." The blonde seer had lost his usual air of arrogance in the face of the performance.

"Oh and I suppose you do?" Narseo baited him. "You're just a fool in love, Arishen. That's why you think he should forgive her."

Rilla sat up in surprise at this comment. She watched as Arishen's well-known stormy look came upon him.

"Shut your mouth, Narseo," he said in a dangerously low voice. The scruffy lintep puffed out his chest at the demand.

"No. Everyone knows about it, so why should I?"

Everyone knows about it? Rilla thought to herself. *If everyone knows about it, why don't I?*

"Narseo, perhaps you should leave it be." Kalydron tried, unsuccessfully, to diffuse the situation.

"Maybe you should mind your own business," Narseo retorted.

"Maybe you should leave before I make you," Arishen almost yelled at him. Rilla could see the situation getting out of hand. She had to do something fast. The only reason Arishen was even allowed in Illaria was because of her and Plyke.

"Arishen, it's getting late and we've all had such a long day of lessons, but my friends were anxious to talk to the seer who saved my life in the Outworld." She was lying through her teeth, but hoped he couldn't tell or didn't care. "Would you accompany us back to the castle to tell them about it before the night is over?"

Rilla smiled sweetly as her words had the desired effect. Narseo's mouth hung wide open in shock. Arishen instantly calmed down and agreed.

I'm sorry to make you miss the last song, she sent a quick message to Kalydron and Miette, both of whom instantly reassured her it was fine. Together, the four of them got up and made their way back to the cobble bridge with some difficulty. Pér had started a rabble rousing song, which Rilla was certain King Lukys would disapprove of.

Once they were finally free of the throng of lintep, Rilla briefly took Arishen by the hand to lead him through the invisible barrier into the castle grounds. Lanterns had been lit all throughout the gardens. She walked over to one of the benches and sat there, not knowing where else she could possibly take her friends at that time of night.

"We've heard so much about you," Miette told Arishen as they sat down. "It must be amazing to have the skills you possess. I would give almost anything to have visions of the future."

Arishen laughed mirthlessly. "Trust me. It isn't often a blessing, as I'm sure Rilla will have told you."

"Well, I actually only told them about the one vision, where you saw fire come out of my fingers to burn the men," Rilla admitted. "I didn't really know if you'd want me to tell them about all the other ones."

"*All* the other ones?" Miette asked in surprise. "How many other visions have you had?"

Rilla smiled at Miette's enthusiasm. This was the sort of lintep she would like Arishen to become friends with – one who didn't care that he was a human, but was interested in his skills for what they were. She sat back with Kalydron, listening silently to the back and forth conversation between Miette and a baffled Arishen.

Eventually, the cheers for Pér's performance ended and lintep started drifting back into the castle grounds in small groups. Rilla kept an eye out for her family. She couldn't see Kora anywhere, but the rest of them quickly walked over once they spotted her. Even Luisella and Lord Braedan had made it out to hear Pér's music.

"Arishen, isn't it getting a little late for you to be in the castle?" Luisella asked the seer in a motherly tone. "I think Master Reuben will soon be worried if we don't escort you home. Come along, young man."

Rilla couldn't help but smile at the way Luisella had effectively wrapped up all conversation for the evening without giving anyone a chance to argue. She said a quick farewell to the seer and watched as he was taken away by the twins' mother.

"He's amazing!" Miette exclaimed once Arishen was out of earshot. "All those visions he has, the times he helped everyone in the Outworld, the way he can change the future by telling you what he sees. It's all just ..."

"Amazing?" everyone asked as they burst into laughter. Miette blushed brightly in the moonlight.

"Well, it is," she huffed, crossing her arms. "I'm off to bed now and you all should be too if you want to stay awake in your lessons tomorrow."

Rilla stiffened suddenly. She'd forgotten to talk to Kora about that night. She didn't know where Mistress Isis was and she hadn't had time to ask anyone else to look out for her that night.

Breathe! Plyke's voice sounded in her mind. Rilla instantly took his advice and calmed herself down before things got out of hand yet again.

I'll stay with you until we find someone, he reassured her. Rilla smiled her thanks to him as everyone else walked their separate ways.

Chapter Thirty-Four – The Duke of Deuterfoss

Leif, the Duke of Deuterfoss, sat in his study, coat wrapped closely around his broad shoulders, pondering the night ahead of him. Long ago, he'd formed the habit of going out into town, once a week, to hear the local gossip. It was all well and good his advisers telling him what they thought the populace was concerned about, but he preferred to hear it for himself. However, as the weather grew colder, he questioned whether it was strictly necessary to go on these trips. Perhaps he could convince one of the barons to go in his stead.

A knock at the door sounded just before Talise entered the room. All thoughts of staying in for the night fled Leif's mind. He would never trust the barons with such a charming young lady. Talise was not the prettiest lady at court, but she had many other qualities to recommend her. Leif remembered the first time he had laid eyes on her. It had been five years ago, at the midsummer festival. With flowers threaded through her long brown hair, it was clear that she was fresh from the farms – city girls never deigned to wear anything other than a thin circlet of flowers placed lightly upon their heads. For any other farm girl, it would have been just the beginning of the jeering, but for Talise, it was nothing. Her wit and charm soon had the other girls dancing alongside her rather than laughing at her. Leif grinned at the memory.

"What are you smiling at?" Talise asked with amusement.

Leif shook his head, closing the book he had been attempting to study. "Nothing important. Shall we go?" He stood and held out his arm for her. She took it with confidence and led him out of the room.

It had quickly become a routine for her to join him on these outings. Once a week, they would spend the evening in one of the taverns around the city. There were enough taverns that, if they continued to cycle through them in order, they would not become familiar to any of the other patrons. Tonight, they were bound for Hand's Hollow.

They entered the tavern, jovially talking with one another over nothing consequential. Leif scanned the taproom and nodded towards an empty table in the corner nearest the stage. In a well practised move, Talise wandered over to the table, purposely winding her way past a number of eligible young men, as Leif ordered two ales from the bar. He preferred to drink the heavier barely wine, but for these outings, it was important for both of them to keep a clear head.

A few minutes later, he headed towards the table where Talise had already accumulated a number of admirers. He was always grateful for her company on these expeditions. It was so much easier to get the townsfolk to open up when Talise was there to be impressed by them.

"Oh, Shaughn!" she called out as he approached, using the false names they had prearranged. "Listen to this. You won't believe the story I've been told! Go on, Karsyk, tell him."

Leif saw the young man's face colour at her attention. He knew all too well how she could affect any man around her.

"Well then, Karsyk, what have you told the lovely Shaelea that I won't believe?"

As he sat down to hear the gossip, Leif signalled a barmaid for three more drinks for their new companions. Karsyk was well into his story by the time the ales arrived.

"She said it was a broken Paradise, two days due east of Hedgefall. Apparently, a group of lintep destroyed it. She said they were planning on destroying all of them."

"Yes, but she didn't talk to the lintep herself," another of the young men pointed out. "She was told that by the townsfolk of Hedgefall."

"Raleigh, you're suspicious of everyone," Karsyk elbowed him roughly. "Why would anyone lie about that?"

"She was suggesting we attack the lintep, Karsyk," the oldest of them replied. "Why should we trust someone who wants us to attack a race with so much power?"

Talise dramatically covered her mouth with her fingertips as she gasped. "Attack the lintep!"

"That's what it sounded like she was suggesting." The third man shrugged his shoulders. "I don't like that idea."

Leif struggled to remain impassive as he listened to the rumours.

"It sounds dangerous." Talise chewed a strand of her hair nervously. "You wouldn't really do that, would you?"

"No," Raleigh reassured her. "Dassyn's right. We don't like that idea, but can't say it's the same for everyone. I heard tell there's some tradesmen got together to ride down and see for themselves what happened."

"To attack the lintep?" Leif asked lightly, trying to hide his disbelief that anyone could be so stupid.

Dassyn shrugged. "Who knows what men like that will do once they get there?"

"They were going to *invade* Illaria?" Talise asked, suddenly gripping Dassyn's arm, making the poor lad blush furiously and lose his tongue.

"No one knows exactly where Illaria is," Raleigh explained to her, as though she were a simpleton. "They were going to find the broken Paradise. That lady said a number of lintep stayed behind after it was destroyed."

"That's quite a tall tale," Leif's scepticism coated his voice. "I can't believe a bunch of tradesmen would be taken in by such a ruse."

"It's not a ruse!" Karsyk replied hotly. "I've heard the same news all over town the past few days. How could everyone know about it if it weren't true?"

"Oh Karsyk, don't mind Shaughn," Talise said, drawing his attention away from the duke, shooting Leif a warning look. "He never believes anything unless he's seen it for himself."

"Well then, he can join the group riding out for the broken Paradise," Karsyk replied, somewhat mollified. "Then he can see it with his own eyes."

"I've a mind to do just that," Leif replied, crossing his arms defensively and ignoring the admonishing look Talise gave him. "Just tell me where and when to meet them."

"Tomorrow morning," Karsyk told him. "When the fortress bells are rung for the start of the trading day, a group are due to meet outside the gate to join the others in the broken Paradise. I'll be there myself to see if you've got the nerve to show up."

"I'll be there," Leif said, standing up. "Shaelea, I think it's about time we head off."

Talise hid the flash of anger from her eyes, but not quickly enough for him to miss it.

"Thank you for a most interesting evening, lads." The young lady blew them a kiss as she followed Leif out of the tavern. She kept her hand on his arm only until they were out of sight of Hand's Hollow.

"How could you allow a boy, an actual child, to goad you to do such a stupid thing?" She turned to Leif and glared at him furiously.

"I did not *allow* him to do anything," Leif answered her calmly, continuing to walk towards the keep. "If you hadn't been trying to pacify the boy, you might have noticed I orchestrated everything to find out exactly when the group of idiots are leaving the city so that I can join them and stop them from doing anything too rash."

"What?" Talise called out from half way down the lane. "You can't seriously be thinking of joining them. I won't allow it. Your barons won't allow it."

Leif turned to see the cold winter wind whisk long brown hair around her shivering body and regretted what he knew he had to say. She had become all too comfortable with him in the few years since she had arrived from her family's farmstead.

"Talise, let me make this perfectly clear. I am the Duke of Deuterfoss. I do not answer to you, or any of my barons. And though your father's wealthy farmstead is important to ensure my people are well fed, it does not give you the right to make demands of me nor dictate my actions. I do not need your permission to run this duchy as I see fit.

"I will be going with this group of tradesmen to the broken Paradise, if for no other reason than the simple fact that it lies within my duchy and its people are now my people too. If more Paradises are to be destroyed, as your dear Karsyk so clearly believes, it is quite possible that a number of them may lie within Deuterfoss lands. I would know sooner rather than later if that is to be the case and if there is any way to prevent, or plan for, their destruction."

He turned away and headed back towards the castle, not expecting any sort of reply from the farm girl. It surprised him when she caught up to him and took his arm once more.

"May I accompany you, Duke Leif, to see this broken Paradise?"

There was no apology, no act of contrition – simply a request.

"Your father would have me hanged, drawn and quartered if anything happened to you," he replied, not daring to look her in the eyes.

"So make sure nothing does," she replied, likewise avoiding his eyes.

They walked back to the keep in silence, a hundred thoughts running through Leif's head. Much as he had claimed he did not need his barons' permission to do anything, they were not likely to be pleased that he was leaving on this mission at such short notice.

Leif had spent most of the previous evening with his steward, Barchiel, taking care of anything that would likely come up during his absence. He had slept a few short hours before waking to pack the few belongings he would need to take with him. Now, as he stood in front of his barons, he was assaulted with a barrage of questions, objections and demands. He had told them the news of the broken Paradise and his plans to visit it. Rather predictably, they were not at all happy about the news.

"Gentlemen, this conversation is over. If I am not at the city gates by the first bell, they will leave without me. Four of my guards will be accompanying us to the broken Paradise. We will bring a falcon with us to relay any important message back to you, but I expect to be back within a few short weeks. Barchiel has been apprised of all matters of importance to do with the duchy. You will defer to his judgement."

Without giving them a chance to object further, he draped his coat around his shoulders and walked out of his study. Talise and the four guards were awaiting him at the stables, already astride their horses. The falconer was standing discontentedly nearby with his finest falcon hooded upon his arm. Leif walked directly to the unsettled man.

"Brock, I know that look. Tell me the problem quickly as I'm running short of time."

"Of this entire company, I only trust the care of my falcons to you and I am not inclined to think that you will have time to spare. My apprentice is coming along well and can handle the remaining falcons in my absence. I would accompany you on this journey, if I may."

Leif had barely considered what he would do with the bird himself and found himself relieved with the suggestion. "Saddle up, Brock. You're coming with us."

The duke and the falconer quickly mounted their horses and the seven of them rode out to the gates of Deuterfoss. They approached just as the bells were ringing to signal the start of the trading day. A group of around twenty men were saddled and waiting, Karsyk, Dassyn and Raleigh among them.

"Duke Leif!" one of the other men bellowed out in surprised. "What brings you here?"

"Duke Leif?" Karsyk asked in surprise. Raleigh laughed and slapped Karsyk on the back.

"I knew there was something familiar about you last night," the joiner told him. "I just couldn't place my finger on it."

"Chrislan, I was informed of this expedition by the young Karsyk and thought I might come along to verify the story for myself. Raleigh, Dassyn," Leif greeted them with a nod. "I did not expect to see the two of you here."

"Well, we couldn't let Karsyk come alone. Who would keep him out of trouble otherwise?" Dassyn smiled at the look of bewilderment on his fellow carpenter's face.

"Duke Leif," Karsyk finally found his voice, "I apologise if I offended you last night. You too, Shaelea."

"Actually, it's Talise," the confident young lady informed him with a smile. "No offence taken, Karsyk. Now, why don't we set out before the day is done?"

"A fine plan indeed," Leif agreed. "Chrislan, if you will."

Leif could easily have taken control of the travellers himself, but knew Chrislan was a reasonable man who would have thought out this journey down to the last detail. He had known the blacksmith since his youth. Leif's father had taken great pains to make sure he knew the most valuable tradesmen in his city from the time he could walk. It would be easier to sit back and observe.

"Very well then." Chrislan accepted the compliment. "Let's be off then."

Leif motioned two of his guards to the front, the other two to the back of the company and settled in comfortably beside Talise for the long journey. She looked over to him and smiled that same smile that always warmed his heart. He returned the smile rather more cautiously than he usually did. What was he getting himself into with this girl? How had she managed to convince him to bring her along on such a potentially dangerous journey?

Chapter Thirty-Five – Discoveries

Aaron set out early in the morning on horseback, with the stablemaster himself, to meet the fire opal dragon who had flown most of the night and almost collapsed in the farmlands surrounding Illaria. It was the quickest way to reach Pyrid.

As he approached the dragon, Aaron noticed early signs of fatigue. Lazy as they generally appeared, Pyrid moved more languidly than usual. Aaron dismounted and handed his reins to Edric. He bade the stablemaster farewell before approaching the crystal dragon.

"How long did it take you to fly here, Pyrid?" Aaron asked curiously.

"I've no idea," the dragon replied tiredly. "I set out just after sundown."

"Well, I've no doubt Lord Ilya can wait half a day more for me. We can fly a few hours this morning, but you'll need to rest at some point. I don't want you collapsing out of the sky and leading us both to our death."

"We mighty crystal dragons never give in to fatigue," Pyrid grumbled.

"Well, we lintep do," Aaron insisted. "As long as we are back in the Lesa Mountains by sunrise tomorrow, I think that will do. Besides, I could use the break to practise my skills."

"Did I miss something?" Pyrid asked in confusion. "Am I not taking you to the entrance to Goraburg?"

"Yes, but not the one you're thinking of. *This* is where we need to go," Aaron told him as he projected the vision he'd stolen from Eliséo's mind of the closest entrance to the main caverns of Goraburg.

"How exactly do you think I'm going to land there?"

"Can you hover in one place?" Aaron asked. Pyrid nodded. "That's why I need to practice my skills. I am hoping to transport myself down into the mountains from up in the air."

"In that case, I shall rest a while before we reach the Bramble River to give you time to determine if what you propose is even possible."

Aaron wasted no more time, but climbed up on Pyrid's back and settled down between the spikes on his back. With a sudden beating of his fire opal wings, Pyrid rose into the air and turned towards the Lesa Mountains.

Aaron flew across the Outworld on the back of a crystal dragon. It was the second time in his life he had done so, and both times within weeks of each other. He closed his eyes and revelled in the feel of the wind in his face. *This* is what freedom truly was!

He caught himself in that thought and wondered if that was how the crystal dragons had ensnared both his daughter and his granddaughter for so many years. It was not something he wanted to dwell on. If he did, he would find himself refusing to deal with the crystal dragons and therefore not able to help Lord Ilya with the troubles in Goraburg.

Focussing on the task at hand, Aaron noticed they were nearing the Bramble River. Soon it would be time to try Rilla's suggestion of how to reach the closest entrance to the heart of the tunnels. He cleared his mind of all other thoughts and fervently hoped it would work.

Pyrid gently glided down towards a section of the riverbank that had been burnt to ashes. Sudden realisation descended upon Aaron. This must have been the place where Rilla had first shot flames from her fingers at the mercenaries Lishe had set on her.

Can we not land somewhere else? He projected the thought to Pyrid, keeping a tendril of his power within the dragon's mind to hear the response.

We could, but the ash will help revive me. Pyrid answered. *Ash is to a fire opal dragon as water is to a sapphire dragon. I'll need all the strength I can get to hover in one place for as long as it will take you to find a way down.*

Much as he wanted to get away from the place that had put his granddaughter in such great danger, Aaron acknowledged Pyrid's need to rest there.

The fire opal dragon barely landed before closing his eyes in exhaustion. Aaron was glad he had noticed how tired the massive beast was before they had left Illaria. It would do no one any good to drive a crystal dragon to his death through their own need for haste. He was certain Eliséo would expect him to arrive by sunset, but the elf would simply have to wait until sunrise instead.

Aaron used the time to mull over ways to descend from the back of an airborne dragon down to the ground. He thought of, and discarded, a number of ideas before settling on one. From the ground, he would need to create it in the opposite direction, but to practise that would be better than nothing. Within an hour, Aaron had perfected the skill. With any luck, it would work the other way around.

The sun had already set by the time Pyrid roused himself. Aaron, lightly sleeping against the crystal dragon's side, instantly awoke. He wasted no time in climbing up between the spikes on Pyrid's back. Within minutes, they were airborne once more.

Pyrid flew over the mountains a few times before he spied the tree they were looking for. Eliséo's memory of the single snow gum, in amongst all the darker trees and its exact location was clear in their minds. Pyrid made a careful sweep of the area, so as to ensure there was no possible way for him to land, then began the arduous task of hovering as close to the tree line as possible while Aaron worked his way down to the ground.

Building on his experiments earlier that day, Aaron let out a thick tendril of his power. He wrapped it closely around Pyrid's neck and then around his own waist. It was to be his safety net in case his plan didn't work.

With the rest of his power, Aaron painstakingly fashioned a set of stairs leading from the hovering dragon down to the ground. For most other lintep, this task would be impossible for the sheer amount of power needed to create such a structure. For Aaron, it was possible, but something he had never tried before that afternoon. It took him less time than he expected before it was complete.

Well Pyrid, now we see if a lintep can walk on air, he told the massive beast with his mind. He felt a nudge of encouragement from the fire opal dragon as he hesitantly placed a foot on the highest step.

To his surprise, he didn't fall straight through to the treacherous trees waiting below. Carefully, with his arms spread wide to balance himself, Aaron walked down the stairs made entirely of his own power. Had anyone been looking on, they would have thought he really was walking on air.

The wind from Pyrid's wings threatened to topple him from the stairs a number of times. Aaron's heart thumped loudly in his ears as he tried to remain as calm as possible. He'd thought at this stage in his life he would be done with experimenting but, thanks to Rilla, he found himself trying the most dangerous experiments he'd ever thought possible.

Finally, he reached the ground. It surprised him so much that he had to feel the forest floor with his own two hands to make sure he wasn't still somehow on his stairs. He smiled as his hands came away covered with dirt and leaves. With little more effort than blinking, Aaron withdrew the stairs and untied his power from around Pyrid's neck.

It seems a lintep can *walk on air.* He pushed the thought gently to the dragon. *I don't know how long I'll be in the tunnels, so if you would be so kind as to continue flying back and forth between Illaria and Goraburg every week, that would probably be best. If we have need of you, we will send a message to the Drakos Mountains with a trusted karlik. Farewell Pyrid. Many thanks for your help and make sure you rest!*

The crystal dragon belched out a stream of fire to match his opal body, before flying away towards the Drakos Mountains. Aaron found himself suddenly alone, in the heart of the Lesa Mountains where he had never set foot in his life. Hoping that Eliséo's instruction would prove to be correct, Aaron walked over to the white snow gum, searched for a metal handle and twisted it. He sat down on the roots of the tree to await the appearance of his guide.

When the ground opened up in front of him, Aaron was surprised to see none other than Anya Nikolaevna herself.

"Anya, my dear girl," he cried out happily. "I hadn't dared imagine they would send me such a wonderful companion to escort me into the tunnels."

Anya blushed at his words, trying to hide a smile. "Lower your voice, old man. They thought it best considering only a handful of karliki can vouch for your appearance."

"No matter the reason, I'm glad to see you alive and well," the old lintep told her in a softer voice. "I was quite sorry to learn of Lord Mikhail Alekseevich's death. I will do whatever is within my power to assist in rooting out the rebels."

"Your kind words bring me much hope, Lord Aaron," Anya told him with a sigh. "Come, I will take you directly to Lord Ilya and Eliséo. They await your arrival in anticipation. We expected you last night. What took you so long?"

"Pyrid was exhausted by the time he reached Illaria,"Aaron explained as he followed Anya down into the tunnels of Goraburg. "I made him rest before we arrived as the method of my arrival would have been even more perilous had he suddenly plummeted with fatigue."

Anya nodded her understanding as she indicated towards the lanterns on the side of the narrow stairwell carved into the mountain. Aaron took one and quickly lit it before the ground closed above him and he was lost to darkness. It felt strange to walk into a place that reminded him so much of the crypt within the castle grounds, where most of his family was buried.

The tired lintep shook his head and cleared away those morbid thoughts. Now was not the time to dwell on the past. He was here to help, in the most unusual of ways, to find Vladimir and his followers.

Anya led him for what felt like hours down the stone stairs. In the tunnels, he lost all sense of time. He knew, from Rilla's description, that it was in reality less than an hour. When they finally reached a number of small caverns, he expected her to stop, but she simply walked on as though they didn't exist. Clearly, she was taking him directly to Ilya and Eliséo, without giving him a chance to rest before they arrived. As his breath became more laboured, the karlik turn towards him.

"It's not much further," she told him quietly. "It will be safer if we do not stop to rest." He simply nodded and continued to follow after her, taking in the surroundings as they went.

* * *

Arishen had barely begun on his tasks for the day when the vision came. He stopped his work, and stared wide-eyed into the distance.

Lord Aaron was walking in the tunnels of Goraburg with Anya. A karlik was following them, unseen and unheard, knife held at the ready.

"Arishen, what's the matter?" Timothée shook his shoulder. Arishen looked up at him in horror. He didn't know how Lord Aaron could be in the tunnels of Goraburg so soon after they'd returned from the Outworld, but if he was, he was in grave danger and there wasn't anything he could do about it.

"I need to see King Lukys," Arishen told his master urgently. "I think Lord Aaron may be in danger."

Arishen knew Master Timothée had been told that he was a seer and hoped he wouldn't doubt the vision. With a sigh of relief, he heard the master carpenter shouting out orders to his journeymen and apprentices before hurrying Arishen out of the workshop.

Together, they ran through the streets of Illaria, towards the castle. As they drew close to the cobbled bridge, he held tightly to the carpenter's hand to avoid being left behind the magical barrier. Once they were in the castle grounds, Arishen saw Kalydron, one of Rilla's friends he'd met the night before, and called out to him.

"Kalydron, we're going to King Lukys. Find Rilla. Tell her to meet us there. Now!"

Not knowing if the lintep would listen to him, Arishen continued to run with Master Timothée towards the king's audience chamber. It was their best chance to find him at this time of day.

Together, they barged into the audience chamber only to find it empty. Arishen looked hopelessly at Master Timothée who had an intense look of concentration on his face.

"He's in his chambers. Run, Arishen!"

Arishen ran to the nearest twisting stairwell and raced up to the top level, leaving the carpenter to follow after. He sprinted across the carpeted hall to the King's chambers and pounded on the door. King Lukys opened the door and stared down at him angrily.

"Young Arishen, you are lucky to be in Illaria as it is. Mind you don't give me reason to throw you out."

"Lord Aaron's life is in danger!" Arishen yelled at him while catching his breath. "In Goraburg. A karlik is going to kill him."

The king's expression instantly changed. Surprisingly, he asked Arishen's permission to see the vision before plunging into his mind. It was a gentler touch than he had expected, though Arishen could feel his urgency as the lintep searched for the vision. Arishen remembered his training with Master Reuben, closed his eyes and brought the vision to mind, reliving it exactly. Within seconds, the king's power had withdrawn from his mind.

"I'm sorry I doubted you, Arishen," he told the boy in an unusually soft voice. "We need to get Rilla."

"She's on her way," Master Timothée told them as he rounded the corner. "Arishen told one of her friends to find her when we entered the castle grounds."

Rilla flew from the stairwell and almost straight into Arishen. She quickly stopped herself short, took one look at the situation and apologised to Arishen before jumping into his mind. He instantly brought the vision to the front of his mind again, not wanting her to see anything else.

Within seconds, she had left his mind. He stared at her in shock as her eyes burned bright green, just like an elf's. He glanced over at Master Timothée who was equally shocked. King Lukys was the only one of them not surprised by this action. Arishen thought through the recent events. He had asked Kalydron to find Rilla only because he thought King Lukys might doubt his word. King Lukys had called for Rilla with the expectation that she could help. He seemed to know that Rilla would do exactly whatever it was she was doing at this moment.

If Arishen didn't know better, he'd have thought that Rilla was somehow talking to an elf. An elf that was in Goraburg right now and could help Lord Aaron. The only elf it could be was Eliséo, but how was Rilla talking to him?

"Thank you, Arishen," Rilla told him once her eyes were a normal shade of green. "You've possibly saved my grandfather's life. How can I ever repay you?"

Arishen continued to stare at her in shock. Understanding dawned on Rilla. Her eyes glowed briefly again and then she looked at King Lukys. With a nod, the king opened his door for them all to enter. Master Timothée fidgeted outside for a moment before following them in.

Rilla waited until the door behind them had closed. "Arishen, I'm sorry not to have told you before, but there was the greatest need to keep this knowledge secret. It looks like I can't keep it secret any longer, most especially not from you at this time. Please forgive me for not telling you earlier."

She leant close and whispered into his ear, so that Master Timothée could not hear. What she told him shocked him to the core. Suddenly, so many things clicked into place in his mind. Everything that had happened with Rilla's power on their flight to Goraburg, through the tunnels and across the river all started to make sense. Rilla had been using elf magic as well as lintep magic since they'd left Silvaren.

"How is that even possible?" he asked as she drew away from his bright red face.

"It's just never been done before," Rilla shrugged. "I suppose that made everyone assume it wasn't possible without ever trying it. Never mind that now. If you have any other vision of Lord Aaron, Goraburg, anything around that, come and find me instantly. Any little thing can make a difference now."

Arishen nodded, still overwhelmed by the knowledge she had entrusted him with. He was startled when Master Timothée spoke.

"Would it help if he is absent from the workshop for the next few days?" the carpenter asked in a hesitant voice. "Only, if he has another vision, I don't know if I can keep running all the way to the castle."

King Lukys could not contain his laughter. Shaking his head, he reassured the carpenter. "No need, Master Timothée. I'll make arrangements so that Arishen can continue his work with you, but his vision can be quickly projected to the castle. I think Master Reuben will be happy to find volunteers for the task.

"Arishen, I owe you an apology. I should never have assumed the worst before stopping to consider what would bring you so urgently to my door. You've quite possibly saved my cousin's life and for that, I owe you everything. If you ever have a need to call on me, know that you will have my full attention and an open ear."

Arishen suddenly broke into a grin. "Pér will never believe it – a human with the ear of a lintep king!"

Arishen and Rilla laughed at the pained look on the king's face.

"Yes, well, be off with you now and ... thank you," King Lukys said as he waved them away. "Rilla, I'll expect to hear how this situation resolves itself."

Rilla nodded and joined Arishen as he and Master Timothée headed towards one of the sets of twisted stairs leading down to the inner courtyard.

Chapter Thirty-Six – Rescue

Eliséo's eyes blazed silver, as he sat rigidly with Ilya staring at him. Almost before his contact with Rilla was broken, he grabbed the karlik's wrist and half dragged him along as he ran down the tunnels. Lord Aaron was in trouble, Ilya couldn't run fast enough and Eliséo didn't know the tunnels well enough to find the rebel karlik alone.

Throwing caution to the wind, Eliséo used both his own magic and his bond with Elessa to call up a solid platform of air for himself and Ilya to travel along more swiftly. As they stood on the invisible platform, it swiftly floated down the tunnels, even faster than if Eliséo had been running by himself.

"What's happening?" Ilya asked him, deathly pale.

"Lord Aaron is here. Anya is bringing him to us, but there is a karlik somewhere nearby intent on murder. I've started us in the right direction, but you're going to have to lead us the rest of the way. You're the only one who knows which tunnels Anya will use. I'll call up another mist so no karliki can see or hear us. If we pass them by, they'll feel a rush of wind at the most."

To his relief, Ilya didn't ask for any extra information. He simply directed them until they were in the same tunnel as Anya and Aaron. The tunnel stretched into the distance, but the silhouette of a lintep and karlik walking side by side was unmistakable.

Eliséo's eyes were as sharp as any elf's, but as much as he scanned the tunnel for a hidden karlik, he could not see one. Not knowing what to do next, he dissipated the platform of air they had been travelling on, but kept the mist bubble. If the two of them suddenly appeared, they would frighten away the rebel karlik, which was the last thing they wanted to do. There was no way to get word to Lord Aaron without also alerting the hidden karlik.

"Keep your eyes open," he told Ilya. "If we see the rebel before the others, I will dissipate the mist and we can catch him. If they see him first, all the better."

"What if the attack comes before any of us realise it?" Ilya asked him sourly. Eliséo didn't answer. They both knew either Lord Aaron or Anya could be injured as badly as Mikhail had been. Side by side, they walked down the tunnel, towards the lintep lord and the karlik stonemason.

As they neared the odd pair, Eliséo saw a glint of steel behind them. With lightning quick reflexes, he dissipated the mist and leapt behind Lord Aaron to attack the rebel karlik. Seconds before his sword sliced through the karlik's neck, he heard a shout behind him.

"Don't kill him!" Lord Aaron yelled. Eliséo reacted instinctively and pulled back on his attack just enough not to kill the rebel. His blade rested firmly on the skin above the karlik's woollen shirt. The captive attempted to use the sudden halt in attack to his advantage, but Eliséo kicked away his blade before any damage could be done.

"What am I waiting for?" he asked through clenched teeth. "All rebel karliki have been sentenced to death."

"I'm certain they have," Lord Aaron replied calmly, "but this one is bound to know the identity of at least some of the others. It will be the easiest way for me to find them. So, if you will indulge me, I would like to bring this karlik back with us for ... a certain type of interrogation."

Eliséo motioned to the karlik with his sword. When the karlik steadfastly refused to move, he looked to Ilya for some rope – anything to tie up the karlik and force him along without any chance of escape.

"No need," Lord Aaron told them once he'd understood the problem. Before their very eyes, the astonished karlik rose to his feet and hovered just above the floor. "That should do nicely. Now, perhaps we can move out of these tunnels. I'd not appreciate being here during another ambush."

As they headed back towards Ilya's chambers, Eliséo noticed Anya glancing over in his direction a number of times before turning away. Eventually, she asked the question that had been bothering her – the question Eliséo knew would now force him to tell her about Rilla's bond with Elessa.

"How did you know to find us?"

Eliséo exchanged glances with Ilya. The karlik lord indicated they were almost at his private chambers. Nodding, Eliséo waited until they were all safely inside before answering.

"Anushka, there is something I've kept hidden from most people for a number of months now," he told her as Lord Aaron took the rebel karlik off to a corner of the cavern. "You already know there was an incident in Silvaren, when the Paradisians passed through. What you don't know is that my impulsive tree decided to bind Rilla to herself without thought for the consequences. This has had some unintended and, admittedly, some good side effects. One of them is that we can talk to each other over any distance as though we were standing side by side.

"The reason we knew you were being followed by a rebel karlik was because the human seer, Arishen, had a vision and immediately alerted King Lukys. Rilla was shown the vision. She passed it on to me and we came to find you with all due haste."

He watched Anya for any sort of reaction. "She lied to me," Anya replied crossly after a moment's silence. "I knew she had, but I didn't press her for the truth. Back when I was first leading you out of the tunnels and we were attacked, I saw her eyes glow bright green and she tried to dismiss it as the reflection of firelight. I should have suspected something then, but I didn't even know it was possible."

"No one did," Eliséo replied once he was over the shock of her statement. "Elessa has ever been a stubborn old tree. She will do whatever she pleases whether I agree or not. This was one of those times. It has never been done before, either because it was assumed impossible or other elves realised the difficulties involved in having a bond with another race."

"Eliséo?" Lord Aaron called out to him from across the small cavern. "A moment of your time, if you please."

Eliséo left a thoughtful Anya and crossed over to the lintep who was effortlessly keeping the rebel karlik in check. Even though Lord Aaron's power was renowned, it never ceased to amaze him when he saw the magnificence of the power first hand.

"I'd appreciate it if you could tell Rilla that I'm safely arrived. I'm certain Lukys won't rest until he hears the news," the old lintep told him, then added with a smile, "I must say, this idea of being able to communicate with my family from hundreds of miles away is astonishing."

Eliséo cursed himself for not thinking to instantly alert Rilla to her grandfather's safety. He quickly touched minds with her to relay the message, even going so far as to give her a brief glimpse of her grandfather to ease her mind. He smiled at the comfort it brought her. She was finally becoming attached to her family.

"It is done," he said aloud. "Rilla has already sent a message to King Lukys with the news. Apparently, your cousin has organised for one of Master Reuben's apprentices to shadow Arishen in case he should have another vision. Now, have you learnt anything from this rebel?"

"Indeed, I have!" exclaimed the old lintep with some excitement. "There are at least another four karliki along the tunnels, leading back to the entrance through which I arrived. It appears they knew Anya waited for someone to arrive and covered every possible route back to Lord Ilya's chamber to ensure assistance would be obstructed."

"Does he know if they will still be there?" Ilya asked, as he and Anya walked over to them. "Can we go and find them now?"

Lord Aaron's eyes unfocused for a brief moment, then he nodded. "They will still be there for another few hours. It was not expected that any assistance could possibly arrive as quickly as I did.

"A word of caution, if I may. These karliki will be on high alert for any suspicious movements. If any of them hear anything unusual, they will instantly run to alert the others in hiding."

Eliséo saw Ilya eyeing him carefully at those words. He knew he should have been more careful with the use of his powers, but it was becoming too restrictive not to use them.

"Eliséo, my friend, I need your help now more than ever," the new karlik lord told him. "There are a handful of karliki whom I would trust with this particular task, but if Anya or I go to find them now, it could easily alert the rebels. I need you to swiftly and quietly find Grigori Nikolayevich, Ermolai Nikitovich, Rufina Desinovna and Demyan Igorevich."

"I know what you ask, Ilyusha," Eliséo sighed. "I will find them and bring them to the locations. However, this is not something I can do alone. I will need Aaron to project the location of the rebels to each of your followers so they can direct us through the tunnels. I can find my way to the main cavern from here, if your four followers are there."

"Lord Ilya, would you permit me to see into your mind for the briefest of moments? I would ask you to think of these four karliki we are to search for. There is a way I can locate them if I know for whom I search."

Eliséo was startled by this comment. He'd never heard of a lintep performing such a feat. Aaron noticed his look and explained.

"It is not so very difficult if you've been trained well. Each person has their own unique mind markers. When Ilya thinks of them, these will show themselves clearly to me. I will then send out tendrils of my power to locate them. We can then follow those tendrils to each karlik."

Eliséo struggled to maintain a calm visage. "I've never heard of such power in a lintep, Lord Aaron. Is it a common skill to possess?"

"I doubt more than a handful, if that, are aware of it in Illaria," the lintep replied, "though I have a feeling that will change with my grandchildren roaming around the castle. It's not likely they've discovered it yet, but I don't think it will take them very long after they begin their mind lessons to realise it."

Ilya interrupted them with a cough. "We should make a start. I don't know how long it will take you to find my followers and then the rebels after them. What will you do when you find them?"

"I think it best that we bring them all back here. I will read all their minds to glean any extra information. Then you can do with them what you will," Lord Aaron replied. With a glance at the captive to one side of the cavern, he made a sudden decision. "I no longer require that one. He has given me all the information he can. He knows not the location of the rebels outside the tunnels."

Eliséo exchanged glances with Ilya before drawing his sword. He gave the rebel a quick and clean death. It was more than he deserved. Wiping his blade on a piece of cloth, he turned to await Lord Aaron.

As they travelled silently and unseen down the tunnels of Goraburg, following the first of four tendrils Lord Aaron had sent out to find Ilya's most loyal supports, Eliséo awaited the inevitable question.

"Are all elves capable of manipulating air the way you do or only royal elves?"

He inwardly sighed at his forced use of his rarer talents. "All elves are capable of, as you call it, *manipulating* all four elements. However, the degree to which they can do that varies depending on the amount of power they wield."

"Does the queen command anywhere near this amount of power?"

Eliséo shook his head.

"Even with the fabled crown?"

Again, he shook his head. Liessa's lack of power had been quite a surprise to all of the elves. Queen Eléna was fairly powerful without the crown. Everyone had expected her daughter to be likewise. It was one of the main reasons that it had been vital to keep Eliséo's identity secret. Every elf in Silvaren would rather have him as their king, than a queen who could not protect them under any circumstance.

It almost would have been better for Elena to have had more children than for this awkward situation to have occurred. Then the most powerful, or in fact *any* of the more powerful children, could have become their monarch rather than an elf that barely had more power than any common elf.

"We're nearing Grigori," Aaron told him, bringing him back to the present moment. "What is your plan?"

"First, let's find all of Ilya's followers and then take them to the rebels," Eliséo decided. "If we move quickly enough, word won't spread from one hiding rebel to another of their discovery and they can all be led back to Ilya's chambers by his followers."

"Can't we just bring them all back this way?" Aaron motioned to the air platform beneath them and mist surrounding them.

Eliséo shook his head. "I've never transported so many people at one time before. In fact, before today I have never used this platform with another person. It was a risk I took with Ilya to reach you in time. I do not know if it would carry so many of us. The best thing we can do is take one loyal follower to each of the rebels, help subdue them and move on to the next while they are being led to Ilya's chambers."

Thankfully, Lord Aaron did not object any further. Eliséo did not want to test his limits under such dangerous circumstances.

Before long, they came to the cavern where Grigori and a number of other karliki were talking in low voices. Eliséo dissipated his mist and platform around a bend in the tunnel leading to the cavern so as not to surprise the karliki. Leaving the lintep lord in the shadows, he walked into the cavern and motioned Grigori over to him. The karlik made his excuses and quickly joined him.

"Ambassador Eliséo, I did not expect to see you here," Grigori spoke softly, conscious that his voice could travel quite far in the tunnels.

"Grigori, Lord Ilya needs your help. You must come with me now," Eliséo told Anya's brother. He suddenly recalled something Anya had told him. "Congratulations on the birth of your daughter."

Grigori couldn't help but smile, even under the strange circumstances. Without hesitation, the young karlik followed Eliséo down the tunnel to where Lord Aaron awaited them. A few words whispered under Eliséo's breath recreated the mist bubble around them. Grigori asked no questions as he was suddenly lifted off the ground with a platform of solid air and whisked down another tunnel.

It took less time than Eliséo had anticipated gathering the others. Ermolai and Demyan were tending to the luminescent gardens. Eliséo could never get used to those gardens, no matter how many times he saw them. Rufina was concentrating in her workshop on a particularly fine work of art. Anya would be proud of her apprentice. Aside from Rufina, the workshop was empty. Eliséo took the opportunity to explain the situation to the four of them and discuss his plan for how they were to bring the rebels back to Ilya's chambers.

"They will not come willingly," Ermolai pointed out. "Even at knifepoint, they will struggle to get away and warn the others."

Eliséo looked over to Aaron. It had been his idea to bring them all back to Ilya's chambers alive. The lintep shook his head to the assumed question. Eliséo nodded his understanding.

"Rufina, do you have four lengths of rope?" he asked the stonemason. She rummaged around in the workshop and came up with three lengths of rope.

"Fear not," she told them fiercely. "I will not need a rope for the karlik I capture." Eliséo smiled grimly at her tenacity.

When they were all ready, he once more created the platform of air and the mist bubble around them. Looking to Lord Aaron for guidance, he manoeuvred the platform down the tunnels of Goraburg in search of rebel karliki.

Chapter Thirty-Seven – Warring emotions

Timothée listened from behind the children. He'd become accustomed to the human seer and his mannerisms. Had he not known any better, he would have mistaken the boy walking in front of him for a different person. He was more self conscious, talking in harsh, short sentences, almost as though he were afraid of saying too much or, quite possibly, the wrong thing.

The bell tolled to signal the beginning of morning lessons while they were walking down the twisting stairs. Timothée had heard the girl say that she would bring one of Master Reuben's most skilled students to the workshop after her class with Master Graham. Arishen had farewelled her hurriedly before returning to his master.

"I'm proud of you, young Arishen," Timothée told him as they walked back towards the city surrounding the castle. "You didn't think twice before trying to find a way to save Lord Aaron. Most humans would not have bothered to save a lintep, whether he was a lord or not."

The seer looked up at him quizzically. "I didn't think of it like that," he replied in a quiet sort of confusion. "It didn't matter if he was a lintep, or a human, elf or karlik come to think of it. He needed help and I couldn't stand by to watch him die if I could do something to prevent it. Rilla would never have forgiven me for that again."

The last sentence was so soft that Timothée thought he may have misheard it. "What do you mean 'again'?" he asked gently. The boy looked up at him with haunted blue eyes.

"I ... watched a lot of people die in our Paradise. They were murdered, but no one spoke of it like that," Arishen answered, lost in thought. "One of them was Rilla's best friend. I suppose you could say he was like a grandfather to her. He was the only one in our Paradise who ever really spoke to her. I watched him die in my dreams and said nothing."

Timothée was at a loss for how to help. He put his arm around the boy's shoulders and exuded warmth into him. "You said you saw it in your dreams. That means there was nothing you could have done by the time you woke."

To his surprise, the boy shrugged his arm away irritably. "That's true," he admitted, "but if I'd spoken up about any of the previous ones, Rhanya's death might have been prevented." There was nothing Timothée could reply. It was a harsh truth made only slightly less unforgivable by the fact that they both knew he would have been one of those murdered had he said a word to anyone.

Later that afternoon, Rilla walked into the carpenter's workshop with a lintep in tow. Master Timothée looked up and watched as she walked around the display area, admiring some of his handiwork. She stopped in front of a bird in flight, staring at it for a long while.

Timothée held his tools still as he saw Arishen watching her attentively. Any time she moved, the young boy quickly looked straight back at his work. Eventually, the young red haired lintep walked over to the seer and asked him the price of the bird.

"I think that one is two gold pieces," he stammered and then looked over to Timothée for confirmation.

"That particular one is five gold pieces," the master carpenter corrected him. The girl looked crestfallen at the steep price. Shaking her head, she motioned the older lintep over to the seer.

"Arishen, this is Tommaso. You remember, we met him when we first reached Illaria. Master Reuben trusts his skills for this particular task. Though he will not be able to project your visions as far as the palace itself, his whistle will carry quite far and as he runs towards the castle, either I or another lintep will reach out to see the vision. If it is another lintep, they will project it to me as quickly as possible. It's the best we can do for now."

Timothée watched as the seer thanked the young lady. She inclined her head towards him then walked out of the workshop. Arishen stared after her until she was out of sight. Timothée realised this girl must have been the one to knock some sense into the young seer the night before, at Pér's performance. From what he'd heard from Narseo, if she hadn't, the boy would have done something rash and Timothée may have had to revoke his status as apprentice.

The carpenter walked over to the scrap pile of wood where there were pieces not quite big enough for most of the artworks they created in his workshop. He found one piece that was just right for what he intended and brought it over to his workstation, claiming it for his own. Once he finished the cabinet he was currently working on, he would create something special, not commissioned.

* * *

As they neared the first rebel, Eliséo slowed his platform, not wanting a rush of air to alert the hidden karlik of their presence. Grigori had claimed the first rebel as his. The others had not tried to challenge him when they saw the fire in his eyes. Any one of these rebels would have tried to kill Grigori's own sister had she passed by them. He would make sure they never got the chance to try.

Eliséo stopped just behind the hidden karlik and soundlessly dissipated the mist bubble. Grigori stealthily stepped down to the tunnel, drew his dagger and smashed the hilt into the back of the rebel's head with such force that the now limp body fell heavily to the floor. Taking care to tie the knots properly, Grigori firmly secured the karlik's hands behind his back.

"That was pointless," Rufina pointed out. "Now you will have to wait for him to regain consciousness."

Grigori shook his head. "No, he does not deserve the privilege of walking. I shall drag him behind me. There is no need for him to live out his remaining minutes in comfort. You go ahead to find the others. I'll meet you back at Lord Ilya's chambers."

Eliséo watched as warring emotions flickered over Lord Aaron's face. The lintep had never spent any time with the karliki – not until Ilya, Kazimir and Anya had travelled to Illaria. It was clear he was uncomfortable with the amount of force Lord Ilya's loyal supporters were happy to use on these rebels, even though he knew they would soon be put to death.

"Move quickly, Grisha," Eliséo warned the karlik. "We don't need more eyes seeing this than necessary. We do not yet know if there are other rebels in these tunnels than the ones Lord Aaron has discovered. It would not do to alert them that we are out to destroy them."

With a whispered word, Eliséo called up the mist and once again they were encased in a bubble of invisibility. He looked to the lintep for direction and headed towards the next rebel, motioning for Ermolai to prepare himself.

Travelling on air, it did not take them long to locate the next karlik. He was perched on a ledge where none could approach him without his knowledge. It was a smart move, considering his task.

Ermolai looked up at the karlik with a scowl. "Have no doubt that I will capture him, but it may be noisy and bloody."

"Not if I can help it," Lord Aaron told him. "Eliséo if you would?"

Eliséo had seen enough of the lintep's powers to understand. He held a finger to his lips warning the karliki into silence before dissipating the mist. Within seconds, the rebel had been lifted off his perch and was travelling towards them, mouth wide open as though he was screaming without a sound.

Rufina handed a stunned Ermolai a length of rope, which he deftly tied around the karlik, binding his arms to his side. As this rebel was likely to make more noise than Grigori's unconscious one, Ermolai tore off a section of his sleeve to gag the captive.

"I'm ready," Ermolai told the lintep, warily. "Whatever you're doing, you can stop now."

Lord Aaron released the rebel from his hold. The captive's eyes were wide with terror. Through the gag, they could hear strangled cries as he struggled against the ropes that held him fast. Ermolai tugged roughly on the rope, his knife held at the ready.

"I'll meet you back at Lord Ilya's chambers. This one will not give you any trouble by the time we get there," Ermolai said maliciously.

Eliséo wasted no time in creating the mist bubble once more. There were only two more rebels to find and little time left to find them. Following the directions of Lord Aaron, yet again, Eliséo transported them through even more winding tunnels to the next hidden rebel.

"Where is he?" Demyan asked as Eliséo slowed them down. "I can't see him anywhere."

"Well, to begin with, you're looking for a she," Lord Aaron pointed out with a hint of amusement. "She should be just around this next bend or so I gathered from our first captive."

"Demyan's right," Eliséo agreed when they rounded the corner. "I can't see her anywhere."

"A moment please," the lintep closed his eyes as he spoke. A minute or two later, he finally reopened his eyes. "She was to escape to the surface if Anya didn't pass this way. She must have grown weary of waiting."

"How do you know that?" Demyan asked skeptically.

"If you must know, I sent out my power to Ermolai, and then found his captive's mind. There, I heard what each of them was told. All of them were to head to the entrance closest to the river, then one of them as not all knew the way, would lead them to their hideout if we didn't pass by them after a period of time," the lintep told them. "By my reckoning, this one left sooner than she should have. Which way to the surface?"

With Demyan and Rufina guiding them, Eliséo sped them through the tunnels on his air platform. As they neared the steep stairs leading up to the surface, they hit something. All four of them fell forward into the mist bubble with the sudden impact. Eliséo quickly dissipated the mist and drew his sword.

A knife was plunged into his side before he'd noticed the rebel behind him. With a loud cry, Eliséo turned, knife still embedded, and swept his sword in a controlled arch to sever the karlik's fighting arm. The rebel screamed out in pain.

"Enough!" Lord Aaron cried out. The rebel's cry was cut short by the invisible gag he put around her mouth. "Eliséo, I said I wanted them alive."

"I didn't kill her," he grimaced as he pulled the dagger out of his side. "I simply made certain she would not have the opportunity to strike again."

In amazement, he watched as blood stopped dripping from the karlik's arm. Lord Aaron had ripped a part of the skin from her severed arm and fused it to the remaining stump. Off to one side of the tunnel, Demyan retched from the sight.

"What about the elf?" Rufina asked with a raised eyebrow. "Surely you don't want him to bleed out before we get back to our own karlik healers."

"I'm inclined to let him wait for his own healing powers to work for him," the lintep said in annoyance. "You should not have harmed her so badly. Now her mind may be so focused on pain and fear that I mightn't be able to get anything sensible from her."

"Forgive me, Lord Aaron," Eliséo said as calmly as he could. "Had I not been trained to protect myself from any attack, I may have permitted this karlik to wound me without retribution."

"Enough bickering," Rufina scolded them once Demyan had returned, looking a shade greener than usual. "Lintep, heal the elf. Demyan, tie up this rebel and take her away. We've little time left to find the last one."

The shaken karlik ran to do as he'd been ordered. Within minutes, the last length of rope had been used to restrain an already wounded karlik. As she was still likely to scream out in pain or warning, he followed Ermolai's example and tore a section of his sleeve away to gag the rebel.

Eliséo barely waited for his own wound to be healed before recreating the platform and mist bubble. "Where to?" he asked Lord Aaron.

"I fear the sound of this commotion may have travelled down to the last rebel. He was not stationed too far away. We'll have to keep our eyes open for his retreat. Try not to fly straight into him," he admonished Eliséo once more as he pointed down another tunnel.

Eliséo bit back a sharp retort as he conveyed them down the indicated tunnel towards the last karlik.

You were right to defend yourself, Elessa soothed him. *The lintep is just as anxious as you to find all the rebels. You know he simply fears the last will now have forewarning. Besides, at least you didn't kill her. She will still be of use to him.*

As usual, Elessa's presence calmed him. He used that calm to focus his thoughts. With a sharper eye, he looked down the tunnel for any sign of a retreating karlik.

The sound of fleeing footsteps alerted him before he saw anything. With lightning speed, he released the platform and squeezed the mist bubble against the wall of the tunnel as close as possible.

Moments later, the karlik came into view. With a nod from Rufina, Eliséo dissipated the mist. She jumped out into the approaching karlik's way, knife at the ready. Before the rebel could react, a fist had collided with his nose.

Blood spurted out as he fell to the floor in surprise. The rebel made to pull out his own knife, but Rufina kicked him in the arm with her heavy boots.

"Rufina, enough!" Lord Aaron warned her. "I thought I made myself clear when I said they weren't to be harmed."

"This?" she asked, pointing innocently to the floored karlik. "This one isn't harmed. He's simply doing some strengthening exercises."

"I dare say he's had enough *strengthening*," the lintep replied sourly. "Eliséo, can we bring this one with us? We have no more rope and I find myself doubting whether this karlik would arrive in any fit condition for questioning."

Eliséo nodded. It was no more than he had already transported. "Rufina, which way back?" They travelled through the tunnels of Goraburg as quickly as Eliséo dared take them. It was doubtful Demyan would have reached Ilya's chambers by the time they arrived, but Grigori and Ermolai shouldn't be too far behind if they weren't there already.

Chapter Thirty-Eight – Decisions

It had been well over a week since Miette had made a decision for her reward. Isis had not forgotten. King Lukys had given her the important task of heading the committee that would decide which lintep were allowed to learn which skills. She had made it known to all masters and mistresses, current and retired, that she was looking for volunteers to sit on the committee. To her surprise, there had been quite a number of volunteers, and not only from current teachers.

This morning was to be their first meeting. She had advised King Lukys of the meeting and he had assured her that he would be present for the first few minutes, to make certain everyone understood that her decision was the final word on every matter. Isis was certain that announcement would cause an uproar, but Lukys had pointed out that they would have little choice in the matter if he gave her that power.

She was sitting in the council room, in her usual chair, when Lukys entered. With a relieved smile, she stood to greet him.

"Isis, you can't sit there," he told her bluntly. "In this matter, your tattoos are of no importance. You will sit here."

She gasped in horror as he pointed to the head of the table. "I couldn't possibly! Do you know what the others will think to see me sitting there?"

"I understand *exactly* what it will mean for them to see you sitting there," he reassured her calmly. "Or would you rather take my seat?"

Isis looked between the two chairs, shaking her head. She sat at the head of the table, just before the other masters and mistresses began to arrive. As usual, they took off their robes as they entered the room but halted when they saw Isis' tattoos were covered and she sat at the head of the table.

"Welcome," King Lukys said when the last of them had entered. "Please take a seat. Anywhere will do."

Isis cringed as she saw the looks on the faces of the gathered teachers. Most of them were seething with anger that such a young, and from their point of view, inexperienced mistress was apparently to reside over them.

"As you may recall, in our meeting some weeks ago, we agreed that there would be a committee set up to review the requests of student lintep to learn extra or more advanced and dangerous skills. I have asked Mistress Isis to head this committee as I believe she will be fair and just in her dealings with all lintep."

"If you have so much faith in her, I wonder that you requested an entire committee be formed," Mistress Vika said snidely. "Would it not have been more prudent to have your little pet make all the decisions herself?"

"Mistress Vika, do not forget your place," King Lukys warned her. "You are not the only teacher of your arts in Illaria and I'm certain you would not be missed for long should you decide to make an early retirement."

Isis hid a smirk as Mistress Vika fell silent and pale.

"As I was saying, Mistress Isis will head this committee at my request. I have appointed her because I know she will listen to everyone's opinion on each matter and make a sensible decision based on those views. Should there ever come a time when any of you are dissatisfied with one of her decisions, you may approach me. However, please understand that my time is quite limited and I won't take it lightly should you waste that time."

Isis waited until King Lukys had left the room and closed the door firmly behind him. With a serene smile, she turned to her fellow masters and mistresses, who had now seated themselves haphazardly around her. She'd already thought through what she would say.

"I'm not certain if any students have already come forward to other masters or mistresses, but I have been approached by one student so far. She did not know this committee would be formed at the time she requested the extra knowledge."

She was slightly surprised when Kayte raised her hand. The healing mistress was one of her closest friends in the castle and would normally have mentioned something like this to her. Everyone else around the table shook their heads. At least that would make this initial meeting easier than she had expected, although she was still curious as to who had asked Kayte to learn extra skills.

"Very well, then the first student we will discuss is Miette."

"The farm girl?" Vika asked with a sneer. "What could she possibly want to learn that needs discussing here?"

Isis narrowed her eyes. If the students hadn't formed their opinions themselves, she now knew at least part of why Miette was so derided for growing up on a farm rather than in the city.

"Miette, along with Rilla, won the research prize from me. She has requested to learn how to shoot fire from her fingers."

Shocked silence greeted her announcement. The only teacher who looked even remotely amused by the circumstance was Master Bastienne. She watched as he looked around at the other teachers. Isis looked to him for support.

"Do you know if the girl possesses the required amount of power to master this skill?" he asked her, purposely avoiding the gaze of the others gathered in the room.

"She does indeed," Isis answered. "I also believe that her gentle nature would prevent her from abusing this skill should she be allowed to learn it."

"Absolutely not!" Vika cried out. "No student should be taught that skill."

As calmly as she could, Isis tried to explain the situation to Vika. "King Lukys is quite adamant that knowledge is no longer to be restricted to lintep who have passed their test to become masters or mistresses.

"We are not here to discuss which skills should be taught, but rather which students we trust with that knowledge. Miette already knows such a skill is possible, as does her entire class, because Rilla was forced to tell them how she almost killed herself with her fire powers."

During the discussion, Vika began to back down. Her harsh features visibly relaxed as she listened to Isis' explanation.

"You say she has a gentle nature," Bastienne spoke up again. "I do not know the girl myself. Does anyone disagree with Isis on this matter?"

Isis smiled as every lintep, including Vika, shook their head. "Then it's agreed. I can teach Miette that skill as the reward for her research project. Now, Kayte, why don't you tell us about the lintep who asked you to teach her extra skills?"

Her friend looked slightly uncomfortable with the situation and Isis was beginning to regret the fact that they hadn't spoken about this beforehand.

"I'm certain, by now, that you have all had the opportunity to either meet Shuut or to hear of her. Lord Aaron's oldest grandchild is a banwep who has Nyssa's power safely locked away inside of her. She is refusing to use her mother's power. Instead she attempts to learn all the skills a full lintep would use with her half caste powers.

"The first time I met Shuut was in her first healing lesson. I didn't warn her that I would cut her to explain how the healing process worked. She reacted to protect herself and I found myself with the knife at my throat. I had no choice but to drain her strength away or she would have tried to kill me.

"Unfortunately, in doing that I showed the entire class the skill. I think most of them are still too young to understand exactly what I did. Umi understood what had happened, but she couldn't understand well enough to reverse it when given the opportunity.

"In any case, Shuut felt what I had done and asked for a full explanation and requested that I teach her that very same skill."

"You can't put that skill in the hands of a banwep!" a young, fiery master protested. "Just imagine how she would use that, either here or in the Outworld. We cannot allow that."

"Master Nasthen, I do not believe Mistress Kayte was finished," Isis swiftly intervened. Looking back towards her friend, she nodded. "I'm certain Shuut gave you a reason for wanting to learn that skill. Why don't you tell us now?"

"Shuut has already been at Lishe's mercy. Twice, she has had the mind snare placed on her. She needs a way to protect herself, and her sister, against any further attacks. Had she seen other dangerous skills, I've no doubt she would have asked to learn them as well, but for now this is the one she has chosen. I'm inclined to teach her as she isn't the type of person to use it on a helpless human or undeserving lintep."

"But she *is* the type of person to use it on another lintep. By the very nature of the skill, that is what she is telling you she will do," Master Nasthen protested yet again. "That skill should not be taught. Imagine what would happen if lintep went around using it whenever they felt like it."

"Master Nasthen, you are being unreasonable," Kayte told him. "I, myself, was forced to use it to protect myself. It's the very same reason Shuut wants to learn it. What right do we have to tell her that we refuse to teach her how to protect herself and her sister if she is faces Lishe again?"

"Does anyone else have an objection or comment to Shuut being taught this skill?" Isis asked the rest of the teachers gathered there. Mistress Vika raised her hand.

"I haven't had many lessons with the girl, but from what I've seen, she has learnt to use her power in a very ... interesting way. Do we know if she would even be capable of learning this skill?"

"Interestingly enough," Kayte replied, "this is one area where I doubt it matters how much power you have. It's more how well you can learn the skill that counts."

"I say we let her try," Master Jorg spoke up. Every lintep who knew him well stared at him in shock. "I admit, I would never have been the first to want to teach a banwep or a half caste extra skills, but I saw what this mind snare did to that poor girl and to have it placed on her twice and survive ... well, all I can say is that she's made of tougher metal than most lintep I've met. She deserves every chance we can give her to survive another attack from Lishe. I don't think I could live with myself if she were attacked again and we hadn't tried to arm her with any skills which she might use to protect herself."

"Well put, Master Jorg," Isis said quietly. "If there are no other objections, I believe we will be granting Mistress Kayte the right to teach Shuut this skill. I should mention that Rilla has already accidentally learnt this skill, though I'm not certain she realises it, and because she used it on Plyke, there is a good chance that he also realises how it works.

"It might be prudent to teach all three of them this skill as they will all be targets for Lishe, if she realises that Plyke is also Lord Aaron's grandson. Does anyone object to this?"

She watched Kayte's face carefully. Had she not known the healing mistress so well, she might have missed the flicker of anger that crossed her features, however, Kayte shook her head along with everyone else in the room.

"Very well, then. I adjourn this first meeting. I shall advise King Lukys of the decisions made here. Kayte, you can now teach Shuut, Rilla and Plyke at your leisure. I will teach Miette her skill within the next few days.

"Please spread the word amongst the rest of the teachers that if any of their students ask to learn extra skills, or if the teachers would like to make that suggestion to certain students, we can easily meet to discuss these matters. It may be best to do so in the evenings, so that we don't need to wait for everyone to be free from their lessons. Thank you for your time today."

Isis sat in her chair, at the head of the table, until the room was almost empty. Only Kayte and Bastienne remained. She refused to feel guilty for what she had suggested. If Rilla and Plyke were to stay alive, they needed to be taught all the skills they could possibly handle learning.

"That girl has enough trouble as it is keeping herself safe with the skills she already practices, Isis. Why would you force me to teach her this as well?"

"*That girl*, is much more capable than you imagine, Kayte," Isis retorted hotly. "Don't forget, I had trouble keeping my powers under control at her age too."

"She's not you, Isis," Kayte shook her head angrily. "You burned sheets – not other people or yourself."

"I was never attacked the way she was," Isis lowered her voice. "How would you have survived what she went through? At the first sign of danger, you stole Shuut's strength. She hadn't actually harmed you yet – imagine what you would have done if she had."

"This isn't about me and it isn't about you," Kayte reminded her. "This is about three young lintep who are still learning how to use their powers. They're already a danger to themselves and everyone around them and you want me to teach them more dangerous skills."

"If I might interrupt," Master Bastienne stepped forward. "Mistress Kayte, I do believe you have the best interest of everyone involved at heart. However, I think fear of what could happen is clouding your judgement. If these children are taught properly, there is nothing to fear. We have already established that none of them would use these skills unless given no other choice. What is left to us, then, is to teach them and teach them well."

"What good will teaching them do when Rilla, and to a lesser degree, Plyke, loses control of her power to such an extent that she almost kills herself?"

"Ah yes, you make a good point," he nodded and winked at Isis. "I have already begun teaching both of them to control their power in a ... slightly different way to that which they had previously been taught. I believe Rilla is already safer than she was a few days ago. You may have noticed the difference in Isis as well. She seems better rested, does she not?"

Isis found herself being closely scrutinised by Kayte. It made her slightly uncomfortable.

"You're not sleeping in her room anymore?" Kayte asked in surprise. They both knew whose room she was talking about.

"I'm taking it in turns with Kora," Isis revealed. "It seems Rilla doesn't trust enough people to share the load with many. Rilla has managed to keep her temper under control for a number of days now, mostly thanks to Master Bastienne. She is coming along quite well. However, she is joining Lukys and a few others for a meeting in a little while. I don't quite trust her newly acquired skills enough to not be present there for it seems as though her uncle brings out the worst in her temper."

Bidding them farewell, Isis left Kayte and Bastienne behind as she hurried up to King Lukys' chambers. She wanted to tell the king about their decisions before the next meeting began.

Chapter Thirty-Nine – Unexpected gift

Timothée waited until his apprentices and journeymen had left for the evening. He uncovered the bird he'd been working on for the past two days, between his other works. It was a smaller version of the one Rilla had admired in his window. He opened his box of paints. It wasn't often he decorated his art, but this bird seemed to call for it.

Timothée mixed a bright purple from his small stores of red and blue. He coloured the wings and body of the bird with the mixture and used black for the beak, eyes and feet. It looked like no bird he'd ever seen before, but the result made him smile – it was just what he had hoped to create.

Gently using his power, Timothée created an orb of heat around the bird to dry the paint quickly, but without cracking it. Within minutes, it was dry. He placed the bird on the table, took off his apron and washed his hands thoroughly. Not wanting to lose another moment, he quickly found a clean cloth, wrapped the bird safely in it and walked out of his workshop, locking the door behind him.

Aside from his tumultuous visit the morning before, it had been a long time since Timothée had last approached the castle himself. Any orders from its inhabitants were generally delivered by his apprentices or journeymen. Timothée only personally delivered particularly special orders – those he was especially proud of or wanted to make sure would not be damaged while being transported.

The afternoon bells tolled as he reached the cobbled bridge. He waved at the guards as he crossed. Though not a regular visitor, he was well known nonetheless. Hoping he wouldn't be too late to catch the girl, he headed towards the dining hall.

"Master Timothée?" a rough old voice called to him from across the gardens. Timothée turned to see the librarian walking towards him.

"Guiscard, it's been an age since I last saw you." He shook the librarian's hand vigorously.

"Indeed it has! What brings you to the castle?" the librarian asked him curiously.

"I was hoping to see that red headed lass, Rilla," he replied, feeling his cheeks colour. He was glad for the dimming sunlight. He very rarely made gifts for people. The fewer people who knew about it, the better.

"Her afternoon lessons are finished. She'll be up in her room by now." Guiscard state. Timothée looked up at the castle and grimaced. How was he ever to find her in all of those rooms?

As though the librarian read his mind, he ventured a suggestion. "I could take you to see her if the matter is urgent."

"No, not urgent at all," Timothée assured him. "I simply wanted to give her something and couldn't take time out of my work day to come earlier. I can come back another day."

"Nonsense!" the librarian exclaimed. "I'll take you to her now."

Before he could protest, Guiscard led Timothée into the castle, up one of the winding stairwells all the way to the top floor. Thankful as he was that Guiscard at least set a more leisurely pace than he'd been forced to use the day before, the master carpenter still found himself out of breath by the time they reached the carpeted hall. The librarian pretended not to notice and surreptitiously gave him time to catch his breath by pointing out the beauty of the stonemasonry around the windowed hall.

"This is Rilla's room," the librarian said once they'd walked a way down the hall. "I'll leave you here."

"Wait," Timothée called out as Guiscard turned to leave. "She won't remember me. I can't simply knock on her door."

Guiscard turned back, surprised. Timothée offered no further information. He stood back as Guiscard knocked lightly on the door. It was opened a moment later by an older girl with short, brown hair.

"Shuut, my dear, where is your sister?"

Timothée marvelled at the librarian's ease when talking to anyone, whether it be royalty or common tradesmen such as himself.

"Rilla, Guiscard is here to see you," Shuut called out as she walked back into the chambers, barely glancing at Timothée. A few moments later, Rilla came to the door, opening it wider. Timothée stood back, waiting for the librarian to introduce him.

"Rilla, you have a guest." Guiscard stood aside and motioned Timothée forward. "You may remember Arishen was apprenticed to Master Timothée?"

"Of course I remember." Rilla smiled broadly as her green eyes came to rest on him. "We're all ever so grateful that you took Arishen on as an apprentice! Not to mention your help in bringing him to the castle yesterday."

"I'll leave you two now. Rilla, I'll see you tomorrow." The librarian nodded a quick farewell to the pair before heading back down the carpeted hall.

"Master Timothée, will you come in?" Rilla asked him politely.

"I thank you, but no," Timothée replied awkwardly. "I have something for you."

He pulled the small cloth package from his pocket and held it out to her. Rilla looked at him curiously, unwrapped the cloth and gasped. She held the small purple and black bird up and looked at it from every angle.

"It's perfect!" she exclaimed with a grin. "Just like the fringa! How much will it cost me? I'm certain Lord Aaron will reimburse you for it."

"It costs common sense, but you've already paid for it," Timothée told her. The girl looked at him in confusion. "I know it was you who talked sense into Arishen the other evening, with Narseo. It would have cost him more than this bird if you hadn't done so."

"I don't think he listened to me more than anyone else that night," the girl replied, uncomfortably. "He rarely listens to anything I have to say."

Timothée couldn't help but chuckle, laughing even harder when her expression became one of confusion.

"What's so funny?" she asked. He knew he'd insulted her, but couldn't help himself.

"You have no idea?"

"No idea about what?" she retorted, hands on hips, colour rising in her cheeks.

"That he's head over heels for you," he explained. By the shock on her face, he knew he'd have to elaborate. "Arishen is completely besotted with you. I noticed it the very first time you came into my workshop. How has this escaped your attention? He would listen to your advice even over my own, and that's saying something."

"But … he never listens to me," she stammered. "He always gets so angry with me. You must be mistaken."

"No, he's not." The voice came from further inside the chambers. Shuut came to the door a few moments later. "We didn't think we should tell you if he couldn't do it himself, but he's been like that since you saved them all from their Paradise."

"Ah, in that case, I beg your pardon, young Rilla," said Timothée, realising his error. "I did not mean to make you uncomfortable. I honestly thought you knew. In any case, the gift is yours, freely given in thanks for your words to Arishen in a difficult situation. I shall take my leave of you now."

He was half way down the hall when he heard the girl's footsteps behind him. He stopped and turned to face her. She reached up and gave him a swift kiss on the cheek.

"Thank you," she said with a small smile. "No lintep has ever given me such a perfect gift before. It's truly a work of art."

He stared after her as she ran back down the hall and disappeared into her chambers. Timothée hoped that he hadn't made a terrible mistake, not with the bird, but by telling her about Arishen's feelings for her. How could she not have realised?

Chapter Forty – Aislen's decision

Lukys paced in his chambers, waiting for the bell to signal the end of afternoon lessons. He had organised to meet with the Paradisians, as well as a select few others, to discuss how they might go about destroying the next Paradise without such drastic measures to avert bloodshed.

The loud knock on his door startled him. It was not yet time for them to meet. He quickly crossed to the main entrance to his chambers and opened the door. Aislen stood there, patiently waiting for him.

"Aislen, my dear, what brings you here so early? Not that I'm unhappy to see you, of course." He moved aside to let his daughter into his chambers, finally noticing her sombre expression. "Is something the matter?"

"I think I've made my decision, father," she told him uncertainly. "I know you would have been happier if I'd had a child of my own. It has certainly made this question of succession a difficult one. By all rights, after our family, the crown should pass to Lord Aaron and his family, which would make Shuut the next queen after me."

Lukys sharply drew in his breath.

"And that's exactly the reaction the rest of Illaria would have if she succeeded me," Aislen smiled grimly. "I have no doubt that she is ruthless enough to be a good ruler, but her wandering ways and her lack of original power would make things difficult for her. So I've decided not to name Shuut as my heir."

"That's ... a wise decision," Lukys admitted as he sat on a chaise beside his daughter.

"That brings me to Rilla as she is Nyssa's younger daughter, she is next in line after Shuut. However, there appears to be something you've tried to keep hidden from me. She seems to have a formidable relationship with Ambassador Eliséo."

"Aislen, I ..." Lukys tried to explain.

"No, don't say a word," she told him. "She will tell me if and when she wants to. Suffice to say that I suspect there is little anyone could do to force Rilla to live in Illaria for the rest of her life, however long that may be, and I doubt it would be good for the lintep to live under one ruler for such a long time."

Lukys stared at his daughter in wonder. How had she figured it out? She hadn't been involved any of the times that Rilla had shown her extra powers, accidentally or otherwise.

"I can't fathom choosing Daegan or Marilisa – Illaria could not cope with either of them. So then I have Braedan. He is powerful, though not as powerful as Aaron's family. He is kind and gentle. His wife, Luisella, is one of the most loved lintep in Illaria. Together, they would lead our people with a kind heart and a firm hand.

"But that would leave them with a difficult choice themselves. Umi or Ulf would inherit the crown afterwards. I have no doubt that either of them, given training, would grow to be a good monarch, but I've seen too many siblings torn apart by their rivalry for the crown. Being twins, the line between who should rule would be even thinner than usual. I cannot bring myself to be the one who comes between them."

Lukys stared at her in confused silence. He was certain she had settled on Braedan.

"Kora would be the next choice. It's true, she has been away from Illaria these past many years, but did you notice how easily the people welcomed her back? I know you missed Pér's performance in the square the other night, so you may not realise how much your people love him as well."

Lukys could not abide by this. "She may not have told you that she intends to train lintep from these broken Paradises. There will not be time for her to rule Illaria."

Aislen gave him a withering look. "I'm certain she will find a way to do both. Kora is a very resourceful young lintep. Or did you forget that she travelled the Outworld for years, searching for the reason Ophélie's creation needed to be destroyed?"

"I'm certain she will not want the crown," Lukys insisted. "And what about after Kora? You can't seriously think our people will accept a child who was raised in a Paradise as their king."

"Actually, I do," Aislen answered calmly. "I think Plyke would make an excellent king, when his time comes. In fact, he would be the best placed to continue mine and Kora's work to bring lintep into a peaceful relationship with humans, considering he has a human Partner."

Lukys couldn't hide his anger. "I know it's your choice Aislen, however ..."

"It is my choice, father," Aislen told him firmly. "Unless you decide to name another as your own heir, but I think your people might have a word or two to say about that, then this decision is mine and mine alone.

"You told me to choose and I have done so. I know you think Kora is not the best choice, but your judgement is clouded by Pér. That man did everything he could to make you dislike and distrust him, simply so that he could live his life without being manipulated by you. This seems to have had the unintended side effect of not allowing you to see that *everyone else* in Illaria loves him. They will be overjoyed to have Pér sitting by Kora's side when she is queen."

"Aislen, I ..."

Lukys was startled by a knock at the door. He angrily left his daughter to answer the call. Isis stood in the hall, twisting her fingers together. She immediately stopped and backed away when she saw him.

"Isis, you're early," he snapped. Lukys noticed her flinch at his tone and took a moment to calm himself. "Forgive me, Isis. Come in, let me her all about your first meeting."

He motioned her inside but Isis stopped short when she saw Aislen. With a hand on her back, Lukys gently pushed her forward once more.

"I ... didn't mean to interrupt you," the young mistress stammered.

"Nonsense," Aislen smiled at her. "Father and I were done talking. Besides, I've heard about your committee and I confess, I'm just as anxious as my father to know how it went."

The young lintep's brown eyes sparkled at the enthusiasm in Aislen's voice. She sat across from them and explained which students they had spoken about and which skills it had been agreed they would be taught.

"A surprising outcome," Lukys mused, as he rubbed the brown stubble on his chin. "Do you really think it wise to arm Shuut with such a deadly skill?"

Isis flushed and spoke forcefully. "That poor girl has just as much right as anyone else to defend herself from a monster like Lishe! Without using Nyssa's power, how can she possibly defend herself in any other way? Sucking the energy out of another creature takes a surprisingly small amount of power, if it's done correctly. It isn't the same as stealing power, so it won't matter that Lishe has more power and skill than Shuut."

"Calm yourself, Isis," Lukys put out a hand to touch her skin. He was surprised, and not a little irritated, when she pulled away from his touch. "I see Rilla has gotten to you."

He'd known that girl would be trouble. Her aversion to skin contact had been one of the first signs of Rilla's rebellion to the way lintep lived their lives. He knew she would change how others used their power on one another. It cut him deeply to realise that Isis was one of the first to make that change.

"Father, you're being unreasonable," Aislen told him, as she gently placed her own hand over his. Instantly, a wave of calm flooded over him. "For whatever reason, you decided from the moment you met her that Rilla would be trouble. Has it not occurred to you that she is just like most of Aaron's family, including Princess Rilla, whom your own father loved and adored?"

"I don't simply *think* she will be trouble," Lukys retorted like a spoilt child, "I *know* she is trouble."

"My king, that is quite ungenerous of you," Isis blurted out, before covering her mouth. There was a flicker of anger on her face before her hand came away. "I hate to point this out to you, but for the most part, that poor girl only gets herself into trouble because of you. You make her furious and that makes her boil with anger. With her powers so strong on the fire side, it's no wonder the poor girl can't control herself."

"Well said, Isis," Aislen said softly. "In fact, I believe this is exactly the same point Aaron made, is it not? It's the very reason Rilla, and her family and friends, are to join us this evening to discuss the destruction of the next Paradise – so that you don't put her in a position where she has to take rash actions."

Lukys stared from one lintep to the other, barely able to believe his own ears. They were both right, of course, but that didn't make it any easier to listen to their words. He knew he was going to have to calm down before Rilla arrived, else he might force her into yet another blunder with her powers.

"We'll both stay with you, father," Aislen told him. "Together, Isis and I will make certain that Rilla stays safe and you behave yourself."

Lukys looked at his daughter curiously. *Is it possible?* "Aislen, my dear, by any chance, have you read thoughts or overheard conversations that are none of your business?"

"Truly, father, it's a wonder the entire castle hasn't heard half of these conversations and thoughts. If they had anywhere near the amount of power as Rilla and I, it would be difficult for them *not* to hear."

Lukys stared at his daughter in shock. Was it possible that she had been doing exactly what Rilla had been reprimanded for, her entire life? Was the only difference between them the fact that Aislen knew it shouldn't be possible, so she kept all that extra knowledge she had a secret from everyone?

"Yes, Father," she answered his unasked question quietly. "I'm certain, if you search for us without the threat of reprimand, there might be a number of lintep with these peculiar skills in Illaria."

The afternoon bell tolled, catching Lukys unprepared for all the time he had spent waiting for it. All he could think was how many powerful lintep he'd caused to hide from him, including Pér. He hurriedly went to pull the silver handle near his door twice. He had previously alerted the kitchen that he was to have guests dine with him that evening.

Rilla and Shuut were the first to arrive. Shuut tried to hide her laughter at something as Rilla elbowed her in the ribs. When the young red haired girl saw Aislen, she briefly closed her eyes. If Lukys hadn't known what she was doing, it would have simply appeared that she was taking a deep, calming breath. When she reopened her eyes, she looked over at him.

"There is little need for complete secrecy now," she told him. "We've decided it will only hinder our efforts at this point to hide the truth." With a strange look towards Aislen, she added. "Besides, I have a feeling Princess Aislen already knows part of what we hide. Call whoever else you need for this meeting."

Lukys saw Aislen struggle to hide a smile as she bowed her head slightly towards Rilla. Did Rilla know what Aislen could do? Shaking his head in wonder at the things he was *still* learning about his family, Lukys cleared his thoughts.

"Very well, then. Plyke will be arrive shortly with Tika, Kora and Pér. At this point, it might be prudent to summon Mistress Kayte, Master Aurelius, Guiscard and Master Graham."

"What about Arishen?" Rilla asked, a slight blush appeared on her cheeks as Shuut stifled a laugh. Lukys had little time to wonder the reason.

"I've already sent a message to Master Reuben to bring him along. Aside from that, can anyone think if we've missed someone?"

Isis cleared her throat. "Perhaps Master Bastienne?"

"Indeed, father, Master Bastienne should join us. Uncle Kynon may like to be involved as well."

"Kynon?" Lukys couldn't hide his surprise. "Why would Kynon want to be involved?"

"He has changed," Aislen replied evasively. "You might at least ask him. In fact, Rilla and I can take a walk down the hall to see if he is free."

"Why not just invite the entire family?" Lukys muttered under his breath.

Temper, father, Aislen's voice sounded in his mind. *You might actually do well to invite Braedan and Luisella given how involved they've been in this.*

* * *

Aislen walked slowly, giving Rilla the chance to work through her thoughts. Before they rounded the corner, her young cousin stopped her.

"How do you do it?" she asked, clearly frustrated. "How did you manage to keep all of that knowledge to yourself, to the point where no one ever realised you knew in the first place?"

"That's certainly an interesting question coming from you, Rilla," Aislen replied softly. "From what I hear, you did the same thing with so many people in your Paradise. The only difference was that you knew it would cause their deaths if you said anything.

"I have known for a long time that what I can do is quite unusual, even among powerful lintep such as there are in our family. Once I noticed that no one else I knew could hear things that weren't directed at them, I made the decision to keep the knowledge to myself. It could only do one of two things – make everyone suspicious around me or entice my father to try to use these skills to his own advantage. Neither of these options appealed to me, so I remained silent."

"Does ... does your power roam around by itself while you sleep?" the young girl asked hesitantly. Aislen smiled at her, suddenly overcome with emotion. She pulled Rilla into an embrace that clearly shocked the girl.

"I think we are more alike than anyone has yet realised," she whispered into Rilla's ear before pulling away from her. "Perhaps you might trust me enough to help you with your current predicament with heat and cold. I understand you've allowed Kora to share the load with Mistress Isis, however, I think it may become too arduous with just the two of them. You don't need to decide now. Let's fetch Uncle Kynon and get back to the others."

Aislen rounded the corner and knocked on Kynon's door. There was the sound of shuffling feet on the other side before the door opened. Kynon looked at her curiously.

"Have I missed an appointment?" he asked her.

"No, Uncle. I simply thought you and your guest," she said motioning to Master Bastienne who was sitting at the table behind him, "would like to join us. We're having a little discussion about the destruction of the Paradises and if there might be a better way to go about it than the first one."

Aislen felt his flattered embarrassment at being included in the discussion, but she hid away any trace of that knowledge. It was simply another one of the many times she'd had to do a similar thing with other lintep.

"Of course, Aislen," Kynon replied. "We'll follow you shortly. Master Bastienne was telling me another story from his home town. It really sounds like quite an interesting place. I'm almost inclined to leave Illaria simply to visit it."

"Take your time," she told her uncle. "We're still waiting on a few people to arrive from town, so you can meet us in father's chamber at your leisure. Come along, Rilla."

With that, she took Rilla and walked back towards the king's chambers. A sudden wave of revulsion flooded over Aislen. She turned back to find a pale faced girl behind her. Without trying to influence her feelings, Aislen took Rilla by the hand and to her own chambers. Aislen's chambers were the same size as her father's, taking up the entire length of a hall. She calmly took a key from her pocket, unlocked the door and ushered the girl in.

"Now, would you like to tell me what you just saw?" she asked Rilla in a non-assuming way.

"One of the rebels in Goraburg has just been killed," Rilla replied in a whisper of a voice. "He ... wasn't even fighting. He had been captured and interrogated and now ... now they've gone and killed him. Why would they do that?"

"Would you rather they let him go free?" Aislen asked her, not bothering to hide that she knew exactly what Rilla was talking about, even though she hadn't been present at any of the conversations that would have given her that knowledge. Rilla didn't answer, but Aislen could feel her horror.

"Think about it this way, Rilla. Any one of these rebels would have tried to kill your grandfather, would they not?"

Rilla nodded, her eyes shone bright green. Aislen saw her expression change to one of relief.

"What else do you see?"

"Lord Aaron is still safe," she told Aislen. "He and Eliséo are going to find the other rebels in the tunnels now."

Aislen pitied the girl. There were some things a child simply should not be forced to witness. Her life had been difficult and violent enough as it was. She didn't need to see these things when she wasn't even there.

"Rilla, is it possible for me to talk with your tree? I won't presume to ask to talk with your elf, as he must be quite busy at the moment."

Rilla tapped her teeth together, her eyes shining bright green. In a sudden movement, Rilla reached out her hand to hold Aislen's arm. Aislen's mind swirled as she was confronted with the image of a tree larger than she had thought possible. The smooth black bark soared up into the highest reaches of the sky, a few silver leaves rustling in the unseen wind.

Princess Aislen, an alien voice sounded in her mind, *I am Elessa. What need have you to speak with me?*

Aislen struggled not to flee. She'd never felt her own mind invaded in such a way. She could feel the tree rifling through her mind, searching for anything untoward.

Elessa, I simply wish to ask if you could shield Rilla from unpleasant visions while her grandfather is in Goraburg. I'm certain your elf would ask the same thing if he or she wasn't so preoccupied with other matters at the moment.

You word things in an interesting manner, Princess, for one who knows the exact identity of my elf, as you call him. I apologise for not shielding Rilla from these visions. I had not realised she was subconsciously watching.

With that, the alien voice withdrew from her mind, leaving her feeling thoroughly exposed. *Had Rilla seen everything her tree had?*

"Don't worry," Rilla told her with a halfhearted smirk. "I wasn't listening and I didn't watch. I know how it feels when Elessa decides she wants to check if you're trustworthy. What did you ask her?"

"I simply wondered why she or your elf…"

"You can say his name, you know," Rilla interrupted her softly. "I know you must have worked it out by now."

"Why she or *Eliséo* hadn't shielded you from. These beings who live for hundreds of years are used to it. I have a feeling they may forget that you are not yet seventeen years old and can't cope quite as well with these things as they do."

Rilla's mouth opened slightly as her eyes widened. Apparently, the girl herself hadn't thought that through either. From the confused smile on her face, Aislen assumed her gesture was appreciated.

"Let's get back to my father's chambers. I think they'll be missing us by now. But, Rilla." Aislen looked closely at the girl. "You can knock on my door any time you need me. Please don't think of me as the princess. I'm still your cousin and I'll always have time for you, no matter what the problem. Consider my offer to ease Isis and Kora's burden. I promise I'll keep you safe."

Without allowing her the chance to instantly refuse, Aislen ushered the girl out of her chambers.

Chapter Forty-One – New plans

Lukys opened the door with a look of concern. Aislen had taken much longer to return from Kynon's chambers than he had expected. In fact, both Kynon and Bastienne had already arrived. Lukys couldn't help but think Rilla must have done something. With tight lips and barely a perceptible shake of her head, Aislen instantly alerted him to hide those thoughts. If she could hear them, the likelihood was that Rilla could too if she wasn't purposely keeping her powers in check.

"Most of the others have arrived now," he said aloud. "We await only Master Reuben and the seer."

"He has a name, you know," Rilla chided him. "Don't forget what 'the seer' has done for you recently."

"We await only Master Reuben and *Arishen*," Lukys repeated himself, ashamed that such a young lintep could have cause to correct him. Trying to hide his anger with himself, Lukys closed the door behind them. "They should be here by the time the food arrives. Is there anything we can discuss without them?"

He saw the shared look between Kora and Pér and prepared himself for whatever it was they were going to say. There was rarely a time when either of them looked like that and had insignificant news.

"I would like your approval for an idea I have," Kora began. He nodded, slightly unsettled by the fact that she would actually ask for his approval on something. "I've been thinking about Abelin and any other lintep children we might encounter in the Paradises we destroy. For now, Abelin has accompanied us here with his Partner, but as you have so dutifully pointed out to me, we can't bring every lintep child we find to Illaria.

"I would like to begin a kind of school for these lintep. I realise their parents, if they know who they are, will not have the means to pay for lessons or even to send their children on a journey to us. In which case, I have decided that we shall travel around to them."

"You wish to leave Illaria again?" Lukys asked incredulously. "Not immediately, I hope."

Kora looked at Pér, who nodded encouragingly at her as he held her hand. Plyke came to sit by her side, with his head on her shoulder. Tika sat beside Pér, the musician's arm around his shoulder.

"We've discussed it at great length," she advised him. "For now, the only lintep who needs our assistance is Abelin, so I will remain here and teach him myself, if none of the other teachers agree to volunteer their time. However, once we begin to find more lintep, even if they aren't from broken Paradises, I would like to ask for volunteers from among the lintep in Illaria, whether they are teachers or not. Most lintep are quite skilled in at least one or two areas. If any of them would like to travel with us, even for a few weeks, their assistance would be gratefully accepted.

"With your permission, I would bring each of the students to Illaria myself when their power is close to peaking, so that they are in no danger of losing their power or dying. This would mean that I won't ever long be absent from home."

Lukys was shocked by her response. When he'd told her to do what she would back in the broken Paradise, he didn't expect her to actually volunteer her own time to the task. He was surprised by how thoroughly she had thought it through. Clearly, she had the support of her entire family.

"Before you decide, King Lukys," Master Bastienne interrupted, "might I suggest that some of these lintep be sent to towns other than Illaria? I fear it is not very well known within your fine stronghold that there are indeed several lintep settlements scattered throughout the Outworld. The lintep within them would be better placed, and just as able, to assist with peaking powers. It may ease the burden on Kora."

"That would mean she would be absent even longer from home," Lukys mused aloud.

"Not necessarily," the old master pointed out. "Depending on how many lintep we discover, the lintep settlements might be quite happy to take in entire families and resettle them within their community, well before their power peaks. There would be no shortage of work for them."

"Do you really think those villages would agree to help?" Kora asked excitedly.

"I don't see why not," Master Bastienne shrugged. "If they settled down in the villages, they would be treated the same as all other lintep there. If their parents can teach them well enough, then they do. However, there are very few parents who can teach their children all the different skills they need to learn. Most often, the task of teaching the children is shared amongst the villagers, each teaching the skill that they know best."

"Kora, would you agree to that?" Lukys asked hopefully. Aaron would never forgive him if he didn't at least try to keep Kora somewhat close to home. "Your main task could then be to find new homes for all the lintep who need one. I'm certain this would leave you with more time to regularly visit your own home."

There was no doubt in his mind that Kora knew exactly what he was doing, but she showed no hint of anger. Thankfully, Bastienne's suggestion had inspired too much excitement in her. She nodded and motioned the old master over to speak with her family. Lukys smiled at how she had completely embraced Tika as a second son and how quickly Pér had taken to the two boys.

Master Reuben and Arishen arrived not long after food had been brought up from the kitchen. Lukys kept the conversation light over their meal, knowing they would need their strength if the meeting went well into the evening. Once the kitchen staff had taken the empty dishes away, he called the meeting to order.

"We've destroyed one Paradise, however our work is not yet done. As far as Kora's findings show, there are at least another ten Paradises to destroy. Even though she didn't directly attack us in the Outworld, there is little doubt that Lishe witnessed the destruction and so will be desperately trying to find a way either to stop us or to somehow steal all the power in the Paradises for herself.

"Our task now is to find a better way to approach the destruction of future Paradises. We must aim to avert bloodshed at all costs, but we *must* destroy the Paradises. If anyone has a suggestion how better to deal with the problem, then I'm happy to hear it."

"How do we know you really will listen to us?" asked Plyke, skeptically. "You didn't listen to Rilla at the first Paradise and she had to save Tika because the Paradisians thought you and your guards were attacking them."

Lukys bit down a retort at that. This was exactly what Aaron had chastised him about. "I have had time to reconsider the events in that broken Paradise and have come to the realisation that perhaps I was a little harsh on Rilla. I should have listened to her. In fact, I should have asked the opinion of all of you who lived in a Paradise. You should know better than anyone else how Paradisians would react to the destruction of their barrier."

"I have a suggestion," Tika raised his hand. Lukys nodded for him to speak. "If one or two people go into the Paradise, to talk with the leader or someone like Brynt, to warn them of what was about to occur, instead of just destroying the boundary without warning, that might work."

"It may work with a handful of them at most," Kora interjected. "There were a few which were peaceful enough for them not to react badly to such news. All the others would attempt to stop you if they knew what you were planning on doing."

"What's your idea, then?" Tika asked her. "You're the only one who visited all of them."

"I don't know," Kora shook her head, "but can you imagine someone like Erton allowing you to destroy his Paradise? A man like that would lose everything if he wasn't the leader of his sheep anymore."

"It would take more time, but what if we managed to talk to more of the Paradisians, to let all of them know what was going to happen?" Rilla suggested.

"You'd have a pitched battle on your hands between the sheep and the renegades," Aislen reasoned. "And if the renegades were already the weaker party, as it seems may be the case, they will be slaughtered before we can help them."

"I have a suggestion," Arishen spoke up hesitantly. "What if we did it the same way as the first one, only with less people? If there were only a few people, and certainly no crystal dragon in sight, they would have no reason to suspect that anyone was invading. There would be fewer of us to protect, so no lintep would have to resort to extreme actions to save us."

"You say 'us' as though you expect to be one of those few people." Lukys raised an eyebrow at the seer. "However, I agree that might be a solution. Pyrid would have to be waiting a safe distance away to bring in more lintep to help the Paradisians, just like we did at the first Paradise."

"That's another problem," Kynon pointed out. "We don't have enough lintep, guards or otherwise, to keep leaving them at these Paradises until they can fend for themselves. We need another solution for that as well."

"Kynon, we have enough problems to deal with, without you adding to their number," Lukys sighed, rubbing his temples with his fingers. "Perhaps the karliki can help us with that, once their own troubles are over. Let's tackle that problem later."

Lukys saw the look from Aislen. They both knew Kynon was correct – that there weren't enough lintep in Illaria who would willingly travel to a Paradise to help humans. There were barely enough for the next one, so that problem would not wait long.

"Are we going to destroy our one next?" Plyke asked. "I doubt there are any more lintep there or one of us would have noticed, so our only problem will be dealing with Erton."

"He won't be a problem," Rilla replied quietly. Lukys could see fire in her eyes. He glanced over to Isis who was already moving to the girl's side. A quick word in her ear and the fire disappeared, leaving behind a pale face.

"Perhaps it would be best if you stayed behind for this one, Rilla," Lukys suggested. "After all, you and Plyke should not miss any more lessons than you need to."

"With all due respect, King Lukys, we're going to this one – *all* of us," Rilla replied stonily. "Erton will not be given the chance to kill any more innocent Paradisians if we can help it."

"Besides, as much as his sheep follow him, there were others there who actually liked us." Plyke glanced towards Rilla. "Well, most of us anyway. They will trust us."

Lukys looked to Aislen for her advice.

"I agree with them, father," his daughter said firmly. "There is no reason to leave that Paradise any longer than necessary, especially if we know for certain that people are being murdered there."

"Can we go tomorrow then?" Plyke asked.

"No, silly," Tika replied. "It's already too late to organise horses and food for tomorrow. Besides, we need Pyrid to fly us there and he isn't here."

"Can we get word to him sooner than he was meant to return?" Isis asked, purposely averting her gaze from Rilla. Lukys knew what she was asking, but didn't want to push the young girl any further that night.

"I don't think that would be wise," Aislen answered for him. "We can use the time to organise ourselves. Let's talk about this specific Paradise. How will it be destroyed? Who will go? How many people will need to be left behind? How many people are likely to flee or fight?"

"I don't want to go back there," Kora replied quietly. Pér put his arm around her protectively. "I fled for my life. I never want to see Erton again."

"I'm going," Rilla replied firmly. Plyke, Tika and Arishen were only a second behind in agreeing with her. Lukys was about to protest when he caught Aislen's eye.

"I would like the chance to help destroy one of these Paradises. Perhaps, this time, *you* can stay behind and I'll go," Aislen said to Lukys. "I doubt the good people of Illaria will appreciate your absence every time a Paradise is to be destroyed."

"I can't risk you out there," Lukys told her. "You're the heir to the throne. What would happen if you died?"

"Then you would have to start training *my* heir rather quickly," she replied easily.

"*Your* heir?" Kynon asked in surprise. "I didn't realise you had one."

"I suppose this is as good as time as any," Aislen looked around the room. "I know it's been difficult for some of you, knowing I don't have any children to pass the crown down to, so I've decided to name my heir in the event of my untimely death. I've thought long about this decision, and though there are many who might protest, I believe this is the best decision. Kora, I name you my heir."

Kora paled at her words. "Aislen, be serious! Everyone knows I disagree with so many things in Illaria. Why would you even suggest it?"

Aislen smiled as Lukys scowled at her. "Times are changing, Kora. You and I are just what Illaria will need to help them through this."

"Uncle Lukys, surely you don't agree with her," Kora pleaded. Lukys remained tight lipped.

"It's a wise woman who doesn't want the crown," Kynon told him, "but that will only make you a better queen."

"Believe me, I've heard Aislen's reasons behind this decision. She did not make the choice lightly," Lukys told her. It would not help matters at all for her to know he did not agree with Aislen's decision.

"Does that mean ..." Tika looked at Plyke, one eyebrow raised.

"What?" his Partner asked. Comprehension dawned on him. "Oh no, not a chance. You can't be serious!"

"Just wait until the twins hear about this," Braedan groaned.

"I can't wait to see the look on Marilisa's face when she finds out," Rilla said to a chorus of laughter.

"Enough of this," Lukys said once the laughter died down. "We have much to organise. Aislen, if you're adamant that you're going, I'll leave the final preparations with you. Pyrid won't arrive for almost a week, so take your time to figure out exactly how you want to proceed.

"As for you three," he said, looking at Rilla, Plyke and Shuut, "I believe Mistress Kayte will be teaching you some extra skills before you next depart into the Outworld."

He saw the slight look of annoyance pass over the healing teacher's face at his comment. From what he had understood, it was Isis who had pushed for the three of them to learn. Kayte seemed, as yet, undecided about the matter.

"Come to my classroom tomorrow, after your last lesson," she told them. "Don't breathe a word to anyone – not even your cousins or friends. I do not want this knowledge spread widely. It's bad enough the three of you even know it is possible. If it weren't for that, I wouldn't even consider teaching you the skill."

Chapter Forty-Two – Rebels

"What will you do with them?" Lord Aaron asked as they finalised their plans. He had interrogated the captives for half the night before collapsing onto a pallet. He assumed they had been further interrogated in a ... less savoury manner once he was done with them.

"They have been sentenced to death," Lord Ilya informed him bluntly. "All rebels have forfeited their right to live."

Aaron understood the need for the decision. If the rebels weren't killed, any one of them could continue the fight, even if Vladimir himself was killed. Understanding that did not mean he had to like the idea that captives were to be unceremoniously slaughtered.

"Will you wait until the others are found?" he asked, not wanting to see more death than necessary.

Ilya shook his head. "You took as much information from them as you could, as did we. There is no reason to keep them alive any longer. It will only give them an opportunity to escape. If you do not wish to remain here, Eliséo and Anya can take you for a short tour of the tunnels."

Aaron shook his head. There was too much to be done for him to waste their time in that manner. "Do what you will," he told them. "I came here to help, not to hinder. What are your plans for the rest of the rebels?"

Ilya looked over to Eliséo. The elf nodded. "I shall accompany you, Anya, Ermolai, Rufina and Demyan to the surface. Grigori will stay here to protect Ilya in case any rebels manage to evade us. Kazimir will join them before we leave or we will never have peace again.

"Once the six of us are aboveground, you can describe where the rebels are hiding. I know the Outworld better than most, so with any luck we should be able to find them without too much difficulty. All rebels are to be put to death, however, it would be prudent if you could interrogate at least one of them to discern if there are any other hiding places for them. Are we agreed?"

The karliki nodded. Eliséo looked closely at Aaron. Much as he'd volunteered to help them, Aaron found himself drawn into this situation further than he had intended to go. There would be no way out now until the rebels were all dead and Lord Ilya was free to rule the karliki in peace. Aaron nodded along with the others.

"Very well, then, Anya, find Kazik as quickly as you can and bring him back to me," Ilya told the master stonemason.

"Let me help you," Lord Aaron offered. He thought of Kazimir Sergeyevich and took a brief look in Ilya's mind for him. Sending out a tendril, he found the old karlik asleep on a slab of stone. "He appears to be sleeping," he told Anya, as he projected the image into her mind. She stepped back in surprise at the sudden intrusion to her mind.

"I will find him," she said, cautiously backing away from Aaron. The look in her eyes reminded him of his grandchildren. Rilla and Plyke had fought against this as they arrived in Illaria. They didn't want anyone in their minds, manipulating their feelings.

Growing up in Illaria, being constantly surrounded by lintep who did such things in the normal course of the day, Aaron had found it difficult to understand their reticence about it. Shuut had lived like a lintep, but then again, she had spent almost ten years with Nyssa. His daughter had taught her how to do that from her earliest days and Shuut admitted she freely used that skill to keep herself safe in the Outworld.

It seemed only those who had never lived amongst powerful people, such as lintep or elves, were averse to this particular use of their powers. This thought struck him as quite interesting. He thought back to Kora's youth – she too had mentioned she didn't think it was right to use those powers on humans. Had she known any karliki at the time, Aaron assumed she would have extended those sentiments to cover that race as well.

"I'm sorry, Anya," he said as she backed out of the room. Uncomfortably, he turned back to see the captives huddled against the wall of the cavern, staring at the lifeless body of rebel who had ambushed him the day before.

"Lord Aaron, why don't we step into another cavern while these rebels are taken care of?" Eliséo suggested. "We may as well save time while Anya is finding Kazimir. You can show me images of where the other rebels are hiding so we can attempt to locate them. Ilya, do you happen to have a map of the Lesa Mountains?"

Ilya nodded and pulled a roll of parchment from a locked cabinet. "You can use Misha's old chambers, just down the tunnel. We'll call you when we're ready."

Aaron followed Eliséo out of Lord Ilya's chambers, thankful that he would not be forced to watch yet another person die. There had been too much death in his lifetime. He wished he could see an end to it, but it seemed as though that was not to be for quite some time. At the very least, he would need to help with these rebels. Then there was still the question of the remaining Paradises that were to be destroyed. There, they were in danger both from the Paradisians and Lishe. He found himself surprised that she hadn't made a fuss over this first Paradise they had destroyed. Was it possible that she simply hadn't noticed yet?

He doubted that was the case. As Plyke had pointed out, how else could the people of Hedgefall have known about the broken Paradise so soon if they hadn't been told by someone who had watched it happen. The only person it could possibly have been was Lishe. So then why hadn't she reacted? What was she doing that they couldn't see? Surely she would not be content to simply wait for them to destroy more Paradises. What was her plan?

"Lord Aaron?" Eliséo called out hesitantly. Aaron snapped out of his thoughts and looked up at the wary elf. "If we step in here, we shall not be disturbed."

Aaron nodded and followed the elf in. Together, they unrolled the parchment map which Ilya had given them. Aaron was amazed at the amount of detail on the map. It appeared to show every inch of the Lesa Mountains, from the foothills at the edge of the Brambles River to the high teeth of the Drakos Mountains.

"They're deceptively artistic for people who spend almost their entire lives around cold stone, are they not?" Eliséo asked with a smile. "Of all the creatures in the Outworld, the karliki are the ones who never fail to remind me how little I truly know them. Now, what can you tell me of where the rebels are hiding?"

"Would you ... do you mind if I project the images to you?" the lintep asked, suddenly hesitant to use his mind powers without first asking permission. He waited for Eliséo to agree before sending out a tendril to the elf's mind.

Many of the images he'd seen were of small groups of karliki gathered in a dimly lit room, as though they had tried to recreate the darkness of the tunnels. There were very few sunlit images. Those that there were, were unusually bright in his mind, as though the sun shone brighter than ever before. He interpreted that as the karlik's eyes not adjusting well to the sunlight.

"Can you make out anything?" he asked, once he'd shown all the images. "From what I can tell, they are not out in the open. They must have found a cave or a hut somewhere nearby. It does not appear to be too far away as they can travel back and forth to Goraburg with distressing ease."

"It will not be distressing to us for much longer," the elf stated coldly. "Once we've narrowed down their location, it will make it much faster for us to reach them."

"That is true," Aaron admitted. "I don't know which direction they went. Can you tell?"

Eliséo's eyes shone bright silver. Aaron wondered whether he was talking with his tree or Rilla.

"Elessa has confirmed my thoughts," Eliséo announced. "They travel downhill to flee, uphill to attack. It's a surprisingly poor choice, however, in light of the circumstances which made them flee, perhaps going downhill was their fastest, and therefore, best option.

"I do not think they have gone as far as Thistlehall. It would take them too long to travel back and forth. Did you hear any sounds in their minds? Were they near the river?"

Aaron closed his eyes and sifted through the memories he'd seen in each karlik's mind. He tried to block out everything but the sounds. He heard water, slightly muffled when they were inside the hut, but it was certainly running water. He focused on just a few of the memories, trying to see as much detail as possible. One of the rebels opened the makeshift door of the crude hut. It was dusk. The sun was setting on his right side as he walked out of the hut. Also to his right was a stream. It was deep and fast flowing enough that he couldn't easily wade in it without being swept downstream.

Behind the hut was a steep, but short cliff. To the left, there were trees – the same trees that dotted the entire Lesa Mountains. In front was the sort of scrub that could be found at the foothills of the mountains.

Aaron projected all of this to Eliséo. The elf was better travelled than any other person he had ever met, even more so than his oldest granddaughter, who had travelled quite a bit of the Outworld in her days as a banwep.

"Does any of this look familiar to you?" he asked the elf, not daring to hope for a definite location.

"I have an idea of where they are hiding," the elf said as he pointed to the map. "Look. Here is the Yoswen Stream, which runs through the Lesa Mountains to meet up with the Bramble River. It is the only body of water in these mountains."

"Do I want to know why it's called that?" Aaron asked skeptically. Eliséo raised his eyebrow. "I thought as much. So, we'll be attacking karliki and possibly defending ourselves against Yoswen."

"It could be worse," Eliséo shrugged, "Yoswen are cowards against large groups. With six of us, we should be safe enough from them.

"The rebels are still on the west side of the stream. From the looks of their hut, it was hastily put up by the rebels themselves. They appear to have built it up against a rock to protect their backs. So close to the stream, they must expect no one could possibly attack from that direction. They will likely be guarding the west and south fronts only."

Aaron looked at the map as the elf pointed out each feature they had seen in the memories. "That stands to reason. They are the only ways we could possibly approach them."

Eliséo shook his head. "Not so. I think we should approach along the stream. That will certainly give us the advantage over them. With six of us, we should find their hut without much difficulty. Then we attack from the water. They'll be dead before they have time to draw their weapons."

"Don't be so eager to kill them," Aaron chided. "Remember that I need at least one of them alive so that we can discover if there are any other hideouts or rebels who have already infiltrated the tunnels again."

Footsteps outside Mikhail's chamber caused them both to turn. Despite Aaron's words, Eliséo drew his sword and stood at the ready.

"Put that thing away," said Anya as she entered the room. "I've brought Kazik to Grisha and Lord Ilya. It is time to go."

* * *

With a few final words to Ilya, Eliséo steeled himself against the task that now rested on him. He would once again be testing his powers in a dangerous situation. The best plan he could devise at such short notice was to ask the elements for their aid, yet again. It was something he had rarely done in the past, and most certainly not to the extremes that he had pushed himself to in the last few days.

If word of this got out, every elf in Silvaren would know he was a royal elf. He wondered if they would assume he was Eléna's son. Were there any other royal elves he didn't know of? Ensil was his father. Perhaps that was the difference between himself and Liessa. He'd never asked Eléna who her father was. It had never seemed important before. But if Eliséo's power came from the union of Eléna and Ensil, without Ensil being a royal elf, perhaps it was possible for more elves to have greater power than the few who did.

Concentrate Eliséo, a voice sounded calmly in his mind. *These thoughts are indeed important and you should ask your mother when you are next here, but put them away for now. They will only distract you.*

"Eliséo, are you ready?" Rufina asked him hesitantly. "We should hurry if we are to find them before they become suspicious that none of the karliki returned from their ambush mission."

Eliséo blinked away his thoughts. Elessa was right, as was so often the case. He needed to focus now. Unless they found anything to use as a makeshift raft, he would need to use his powers to transport them safely and unseen down the Yoswen Stream.

"We should be back within two days," he told Ilya. "If not..."

"You'll be back," his old friend replied firmly. "You'll be back."

Eliséo smiled grimly and quickly embraced his old friend. With a whispered word, he created the mist bubble around the four karliki, the lintep and himself. They would at least leave the tunnels unobserved. It was the best chance he could give them. As Anya took the lead, Eliséo found her looking back at him every few steps.

"What is it Anushka?" he asked.

"My apologies, Eliséo. I realise you must have some reason not to want to constantly use your powers, however, we would travel much faster with your air platform."

At her words, the others turned to him, half expectantly, half hoping. He sighed inwardly. She had a point. There was no use in making them walk now when they all knew what was possible. With another few whispered words, the six of them were gently lifted off the floor and swept along the tunnel under Anya's direction.

Using his powers, it did not take them long to reach the stairs leading up and out of Goraburg. Eliséo hesitated and looked up the height of the stairs. Travelling with the air platform along a smooth surface, whether steep or flat was one thing. Going up a steep flight of stairs in that manner was completely different.

"It think it would be best if we walk up here," he told them as he dissipated the air platform. "I do not want to risk our lives before our mission is over."

At that statement, all possible protests were silenced. The six of them began the long climb up and out of Goraburg. For many of them, it would be the first time they had ever been out in the open air.

They walked swiftly and silently up the stone stairs. Eliséo noticed how Aaron stumbled a number of times on the way up. He doubted it would have happened so often had the lintep not been so tired. He wondered if it would have been wiser to allow him to rest before taking him out on this mission. Speed was important, but it would be useless if it meant mistakes would be made.

It took longer than he had expected to reach the entrance to Goraburg. He had to remind himself that only Anya, Aaron and he had ever made the journey to or from the surface before. As hardy as the karliki were, there were no other passages as steep as this one in the tunnels.

Eliséo felt his way around the entrance and found the matching lever that he was accustomed to turning on the solitary snow gum. He turned it firmly and the mouth of the tunnel opened to reveal a dark forest. Few stars penetrated through the canopy above them.

"What now?" Anya asked as she closed the opening behind them. "Do we wait for daylight?"

"No," he shook his head. "We have no time to waste. We head for the Yoswen Stream. If we find anything akin to a raft, that will help us on our travels. If not, we have other means."

As they headed towards the Yoswen Stream, still enshrouded by the mist bubble, Aaron moved closer to Eliséo. "Do actually you have a plan?" he asked.

"If we want to make this as safe for us as possible, and still leave one rebel alive for questioning, I can think of only one way. Once we find their hideout, you will need to use your powers to surround them all. It will be more like an execution that way, but it will be our best option."

"I see," Aaron's voice was quiet in the night air. "What you say makes sense. Only..."

"You didn't really want to be part of this," Eliséo finished for him. He sighed and put a hand on the old lintep's shoulder. "Aaron, I want you to know that I would not have asked this favour from Plyke, but you have more experience and more control over your powers. You are, without a doubt, the most amazing lintep I have ever known. I do not ask this favour of you lightly. Know that I will be in your debt for helping me save Ilya."

"I believe that makes us even then," Aaron smiled sadly at him. "Were it not for you, I would have lost two, possibly even all three, of my grandchildren. My Kora would never have returned, and though she died on her way home, I would never have known what had happened to my Nyssa.

"I know you still watch over Rilla, though I confess I shall never entirely understand how, but knowing that she has you and your tree to protect her eases my mind. You think I am amazing, but I think Rilla and Plyke may live to become even greater lintep than myself. To know that you care deeply for both of them is a great comfort. You'll still be there to watch over them when I am cold in the crypt."

At his words, Eliséo's heart grew cold. He knew Aaron meant for him to be pleased by this, however he couldn't help but feel a chill at the thought that there would be a day when Aaron would not be there to look after his grandchildren. He could only hope that day was many years away.

"There's nothing here," Rufina said as they reached the bank of the Yoswen Stream. "No raft, no boat, nothing."

Five pairs of eyes looked up at Eliséo expectantly. He took a steadying breath. He had never tried anything like this before. It wouldn't be like going under the river with Rilla. This time they would be floating above it, travelling as swiftly as the water itself, in search of the rebel hideout.

Chapter Forty-Three – Extra skills

Kayte looked up from her book as the sun began to set. She shook her head at the stupidity of what she was about to do. Teaching Shuut had been one thing. Teaching Rilla and Plyke, whose powers were still peaking and uncontrolled, *that* was a completely different matter. She was still angry with Isis for suggesting it, even if the cousins knew such a skill was possible.

With a weary sigh, Kayte left her book and walked down from her bedchamber, on the third level of the castle, to the classrooms. As she passed Isis' door, she bumped into Rilla who exited the room with a worried backward glance.

"Sorry, Mistress Kayte," Rilla mumbled, looking up at her. Kayte quickly looked into Isis' room before the door closed on them. Miette was still inside.

"So I see Miette is learning her extra skill this afternoon as well." Kayte fought the urge to laugh. "I think you begin to see why I'm not so keen to be teaching *you* extra skills."

"That's not fair!" Rilla cried out as she followed Kayte down the hall and into her room. "I didn't ask for this extra skill, whatever it is and I tried to convince Miette *not* to learn to shoot fire from her fingers."

"And yet, you didn't complain when Isis tried to refine that particular skill with you." Kayte glared down at the girl, arms crossed tightly across her chest. "Don't think I don't know about that."

Rilla shook her head as Shuut and Plyke entered the room. "I didn't ask for that. I didn't even want it. Mistress Isis was the one who insisted I would be safer knowing how to do it properly before going into the Outworld again."

"We're not here to argue," Shuut interfered. "We're here to learn how to defend ourselves against Lishe, should she come within arm's reach."

"What?" Rilla and Plyke asked together, looking at Kayte.

Kayte motioned the three of them to a seat. "After her first lesson, Shuut requested that I teach her how to take energy from another person. Yesterday, it was decided that all three of you should learn this skill. I don't agree, but must bow to Isis on this matter."

Kayte watched their reactions carefully. Shuut and Plyke were clearly pleased, but if she didn't know any better, she'd have thought Rilla was actually upset, or annoyed, to be learning this extra skill. Perhaps Isis was right about her.

"Rilla, I understand you've already done this with Plyke, so would you like to begin? Take Plyke's energy."

Red curls swayed as the girl shook her head. "I ... don't want to do that again."

"I don't mind, Rilla," Plyke said as her placed a hand on her sleeved arm. "It will be good to learn how to do it properly."

"No." Rilla shook her arm free. "I *don't* want to learn how to do that. This is exactly how Lishe would have started. Even if we're only learning to steal energy, rather than power, the skill will be similar. I don't want to learn anything like that."

"If Lishe gets anywhere near you ..." Shuut began.

"Then there will be plenty of lintep around to stop her," Rilla finished. "If anyone else hurts her, or kills her, no one will think twice about it. But if *I* kill her, everyone will call me a murderer. I don't want to become my father. You can practise this skill on me, but I don't want to learn it myself."

Kayte contemplated sending a tendril down the hall to Isis' classroom, but decided against it. She didn't want to disturb Miette's lesson.

"Fine." Kayte turned to Plyke. "You've a little more skill than Shuut. Take Rilla's energy and pass it to me. I will give it back to her and then it's Shuut's turn. When you can both do that part adequately, you can give it back to Rilla yourselves."

Plyke stared at her blankly. Kayte rolled her eyes.

"Rilla, do you remember how you took Plyke's energy?" The girl nodded, tightlipped. "Please explain it to him."

Tapping her teeth together, Rilla glared at Kayte. The mistress only raised her eyebrows.

"Remember we were holding hands? I could feel your strength and imagined myself tying a knot around it." Rilla shrugged. "Then I pulled."

Kayte sat perfectly still, not daring herself to say or do anything. She'd forgotten how simplistic Rilla's view of the situation was.

"You mean, you used a tendril of your power and tied it to my power and took that?" Plyke asked with a shake of his head.

"I ... don't know. I don't know if I took your power or your strength."

Rilla looked over to Kayte. The healing mistress shook her head.

"You took his strength," she replied firmly. "It isn't possible to borrow someone's power."

"How can you tell the difference?" Shuut asked. "It's all just energy, really."

"The difference is, Plyke had the same reaction as you did in our first class and I know I took your energy, *not* your power," Kayte replied, flustered. "Do you remember how it felt when Lishe tried to steal Nyssa's power from you, before she placed the mind snare on you?"

Shuut paled.

"Now you know the difference. It's a much more brutal process to steal power from someone." Kayte sighed and placed a hand over Shuut's. "*This* is how you take energy. You feel that person's strength, like Rilla said, and you draw it out of them, slowly and carefully."

As she saw the banwep weaken, she gave her energy back. Shuut pursed her lips.

"That doesn't explain it," Shuut told her coldly. "All I felt was my strength draining, not how you did it."

Kayte shook her head. "This is why I would not normally suggest teaching a novice such skills. An advanced student would have been able to feel exactly what I'd done."

Plyke held out his hand. "Do it to me."

Left with little choice, Kayte held the boy's hand and took his strength until his arm went limp, then gave it back again. The confused expression he gave her made Kayte uncomfortable.

"What is it?" she asked him, as Plyke looked over at Rilla. Slowly, he turned back to face Kayte.

"That's ... not how I felt when Rilla did it."

Kayte felt her heartbeat quicken.

"No." Rilla crossed her arms.

"Rilla, I need to know what you did." Kayte tried to reason with the girl. "Explain it to me again."

Shuut laughed. "You're scared!"

"I beg your pardon," Kayte replied in a low voice. Shuut stared at her defiantly.

"Asking her to explain it again won't help. You clearly didn't understand it the first time. Rilla needs to *show* you and you're scared." The banwep sat back, hands behind her head and smiled cruelly.

"I don't think Rilla was using my energy, not entirely," Plyke ventured. "I mean, she may have taken some of my energy at the same time, but I think ... I think she may have borrowed my power."

Kayte shook her head. "I told you, Plyke, that isn't possible. You *can't* borrow power. It doesn't work like that."

"But it made her own magic stronger," he insisted.

Kayte closed her eyes and took a deep breath, thinking back to the day she'd first spoken with Rilla and found out all the things she'd done. She hadn't asked what had happened – why she'd had to ask Plyke for his help.

"Will one of you show me your memory from that day?" she asked them.

Shuut shook her head. "I can't help you there. I had the mind snare on me. I have no idea what these two were up to."

Plyke looked over at Rilla who refused to look up. "You can look at my memory."

Kayte sent out a tendril to the boy's mind. She stopped as she saw his magnificent wall. It was unlike any she had ever seen before. There was no way she could get in there, without severely damaging his mind. She waited patiently for him to recall the day and show her the memory himself.

Plyke stood looking at the raging river. Beside him, Rilla and Eliséo argued. Quite suddenly, a floating leaf exploded into flames. Rilla looked terrified. Plyke knew he had no real reason to hide his power anymore, but was still fearful of it. Rilla was so much braver than he was. Not knowing how much it would help, he offered his strength to her. She held his hand and moments later he fell to his knees, weak and breathless. The memory blurred until Rilla helped him to his feet.

They walked under the river. Plyke continued to lend Rilla everything he could. He felt himself getting weaker, but refused to let her carry the burden alone. It was only when Rilla asked him to get another leaf for her that they realised how weak he was. She released her hold on him, and as though he had never helped her before, Plyke felt revitalised.

"Why did Eliséo need Rilla's help?" Kayte asked. "Why didn't he ask both of you for help?"

The three students exchanged glances, none of them spoke.

"I see." Kayte spared little effort masking her annoyance. "Well, without seeing Rilla's memory, I can only assume that she borrowed your energy."

"Or you could just let her do the same thing to you," Shuut smirked. Kayte shot her an icy look. The banwep shrugged. "No better way for you to know exactly what she did than for her to show you."

"Has it occurred to you that I might not *want* to show her?" Rilla asked.

"Your feelings don't particularly matter," Kayte pointed out to her. "I need to know what happened and you'll have to show me. Isis is down the hall if you run into trouble."

Kayte tried desperately to hide her fear before holding out her hand to the untrained, undisciplined girl. She knew how it felt when someone took her energy, after all, she'd been a student once as well.

What Rilla did was completely different. Kayte felt everything draining out of her – power, energy and strength. Whatever she had inside, it was all being drawn out through her hand and into Rilla. She squeezed Rilla's hand with whatever strength she had left and attempted to pull it all back into herself to no avail – she was already too weak.

"Rilla, stop!" Kayte called out in a strangled whisper.

Suddenly, she was her complete self again. She shook herself free of the girl's hand and stared at her in shock.

"What did you do?"

"I don't know," Rilla said quietly. "I sent a tendril through my hand, into yours. I tied it to what I thought was your strength and pulled."

Kayte bit her lip. "Much as you don't want to learn this skill, I think you should change your mind. What you just did is a lot more dangerous than what I intended to teach you. You can't accidentally kill anyone with my skill, but I'm certain you could with yours."

Rilla paled, tears glazing her eyes. Kayte smiled kindly at her. "It isn't so bad, Rilla. At least you're learning your limits."

"Great," Rilla replied halfheartedly.

"Is there any way to defend against this type of attack?" the banwep.

"Not really," Kayte replied cautiously. "If you do it quickly enough, there simply isn't time for anyone to defend themselves against it. They can only prevent you from doing it by maintaining their distance from you in the first place."

Kayte spent the next few hours showing each of her students how to steal and replace energy, and only energy, from each other. It was a difficult lesson for all of them, but she was pleased to see Shuut master the skill just as quickly as the others.

Chapter Forty-Four – Surprise attack

They swiftly floated downstream on the surface of Yoswen Stream, towards the Bramble River. Much to his disbelief, Eliséo had managed to keep them all safely contained within his mist bubble, on an air platform. In all his long life, he had never used his powers as freely as had in the past few days. It felt surprisingly liberating. He began to understand how Rilla was so intoxicated with her power. How had he never realised it could be like this before?

You were made to live in the shadow of your sister, Elessa told him grumpily. *I've always known how powerful you were, Eliséo. You should not have to hide who you are.*

Elessa, we've been through this before, he inwardly sighed. *If I show who I am, they will force me to take the crown or try to kill me.*

I'd rather you took the crown than continue living a half-life, especially now that you've tasted true freedom.

You don't mean that, he replied gently. *Imagine having to share me with Silva. She has ever been the tree of the royal elves. For over seven hundred years, I've been so careful not to touch her with my bare skin for fear she would instantly realise who I was and bind me to her.*

He could feel the discomfort within his tree. It was not something either of them wished to dwell on. It was possible for elves to be bound to multiple trees – many elves did that throughout their long lives. What neither Eliséo nor Elessa had understood or asked was whether the first bond was discarded with the beginning of the new bond. They both hoped their bond could never be broken.

"Can you see anything?" Aaron asked beside him, jolting him out of his conversation with Elessa. "It's too dark for my old eyes."

"I haven't seen anything yet," he replied, scanning the eastern bank of the stream. "There haven't been any rock faces similar to the one in the memories. We have a while yet to go before we reach the foothills of the mountains."

"Is everyone clear on what we do when we find them?" Anya asked. Without giving them a chance to reply, she reiterated the plan. "Eliséo will bring us safely and quietly onto the bank. Aaron will use his power to surround the karliki within and around the hideout. The five of us will go in and kill the rebels, leaving one alive for questioning."

Everyone nodded. The plan was a good one, as far as these things went. Eliséo was glad Aaron had agreed to use his power to subdue the rebels first.

The sky was tinted orange by the rising sun. Ermolai pointed to a rocky outcrop. Eliséo looked over to see a crudely built hut up against a small stone cliff. With a single thought, he guided the mist bubble towards the eastern bank of the Yoswen Stream and gently dissipated the air platform, leaving them slightly unsteady on solid ground.

They looked around for scouts, but saw none. Aaron nodded for him to dissipate the mist bubble. His power would not be able to penetrate through it. With a sudden lurch in his stomach, Eliséo wondered if there was a safer way. He pursed his lips and whispered the word to end his spell.

Everyone waited in silence, muscles stiffened in anticipation. They heard startled cries suddenly die away inside the hut and looked warily at Aaron.

"I didn't think to cover their mouths," he muttered. "Go and do what you must."

Anya had taken it upon herself to lead the karliki. Eliséo followed after them sword at the ready. He was almost inside the hut when he heard the sounds of struggle and shouting from within. In confusion, he turned to see Aaron splayed across the leafy bank. From the corner of his eye, he spied a movement in the trees. Somehow they had missed a karlik lookout.

Without a second thought, he ran after the karlik. He knew this forest better than most, and with longer legs than the karlik, he easily gained on the rebel. Not knowing if the struggle within the hut would leave any rebel survivors, Eliséo determined to keep this one alive if he could.

The karlik climbed a small group of rocks for higher footing. She pulled her daggers out and turned to face him. Eliséo used all his training to calm his racing heart. In a fight as deadly as this, one wrong move could be disastrous. He feinted once, twice, seeing how the karlik would react. She parried with jerking movements, losing her footing a little each time. He waited until she had slid down within his reach. Quick as lightning, he beat down on her daggers, disarming her. The stunned karlik stood still just long enough for Eliséo to ram the hilt of his sword into her forehead. He caught her as she fell, unconscious, off the rocks.

Dragging her along behind him, Eliséo hurried back to the bank of the Yoswen Stream. As he neared the hut, he heard a loud, angry voice.

"Kill me then, cowards!"

With a shock, he recognised the voice as Vladimir's. As he emerged from the trees, he saw Anya, Ermolai and Rufina surrounding the unarmed traitor, daggers all pointed towards him. Each time he lunged at one of them, they would cut him, but draw further away. Eliséo could see he was trying to force their hands into either allowing him to escape or killing him there and then. Not wanting to waste any more time on games with the traitor when he knew Aaron was lying unconscious on the ground, Eliséo used a power he'd never attempted to before.

Within seconds, Vladimir's legs were encased in thickly packed dirt, effectively rooting him to the spot. Anya looked up at him questioningly as he deposited his unconscious rebel next to her.

"Demyan?" he asked. She shook her head silently. It was a small price to pay for the capture and death of the rebels, but it still felt like a pointless death. He turned away from her to find Aaron.

The old lintep was where he had left him. Eliséo looked closely and noticed a gash on the back of his head. His head swam as he knelt down beside the motionless body. He took the lintep's arm in his hand, feeling for a pulse – any sign of life. It was slow and weak, but it was there.

Elessa, I need Rilla. To his surprise, she hesitated. *Elessa, now!*

I promised to keep her from seeing any more of this, she told him.

I don't care what you promised, he told her angrily. *Her grandfather could be dying. I need to know if there is anything I can do to help him.*

She relented and Rilla was in his mind. Before she had a chance to panic, Eliséo spoke to her.

Do you know of any way to increase a lintep's natural healing ability? He asked her, careful to avert his eyes from her grandfather's body.

I ... don't know, she replied warily. *I remember healing Arishen with your help, but that left you wounded and I don't actually know how I did it.*

Rilla, this is important, he told her. *Get Mistress Kayte immediately!*

* * *

Rilla opened her eyes to find Aislen staring at her in shock. The princess had agreed to spend the night watching over her. They had still been holding hands from when they fell asleep when Eliséo spoke to Rilla. Without wasting time explaining things to her, Rilla sent out a tendril of her power down to Mistress Kayte's chamber. She woke the healer and urged her to come quickly.

Within minutes, Kayte was at the door. "What is it?" she asked as Rilla pulled her into the room.

Shuut awoke at the commotion. Rilla didn't know what else to do, so she held Kayte's hand and placed both Shuut and Aislen's hands on her bare arm and opened her mind to Eliséo once more.

* * *

She's here, Rilla told him. *Aislen and Shuut are with us.*

Kayte, is there any way you know of to increase a lintep's natural healing ability? He asked, hoping against hope that they would find a way. Aaron's breathing now more laboured.

280

Eliséo? Kayte asked in confusion How ... *What are you talking about?*

Taking a deep breath, Eliséo turned to look at Lord Aaron, knowing they would see everything he did through his bond with Rilla.

No! Aislen's mind reeled from the image of her favourite uncle, unconscious and bleeding on the ground. Rilla could feel her agony as though it were hers. It only served to amplify her own feelings. She couldn't lose him as well.

Kayte, think carefully. Eliséo drew the attention away from Aislen. *Rilla once used me somehow to help heal Arishen. We don't know how she did it, but it might be the only way to save Aaron. Do you know what she did?*

I would have to look at that memory, Kayte replied cautiously. *This is not something I'd want to guess at.*

Without giving her a chance to deny the healing mistress access to her mind, Elessa rifled through Rilla's memories until she found the one she was looking for and projected it into Kayte's mind.

It's a dangerous strategy, Eliséo, Kayte finally spoke. *It requires Aaron to be at least partially conscious for him to use you. You already know that it will open a similar wound on your head. Are you certain you want to try that?*

I don't think I have a choice, Kayte, he replied.

Without wasting any more time, Eliséo tried to rouse the injured lintep. With his double vision making him nauseous, he motioned Anya over to him.

"Help me turn him over," he instructed. Together, they managed to turn the lintep enough so that his face was visible. The pale skin chilled Eliséo to the bone.

Gently, he tap Aaron's cheek, trying to rouse him. A low groan escaped his lips. His eyes flickered, but remained shut. Eliséo didn't notice Anya leave until she returned with a handful of cold water from the Yoswen Stream. She threw it in Lord Aaron's face, trying once more to rouse him. He barely stirred. Eliséo sank into despair as he realised there was no way to wake him.

I have an idea, Aislen found her voice. *If we can all see and feel each other's minds because of our skin contact with Rilla, would the same be true if you hold Aaron's hand?*

It should be, Eliséo replied, taking the old lintep's hands in his own. He felt Aislen instantly reach for Aaron's mind.

After what felt like hours, Lord Aaron's mind flickered into consciousness. Eliséo felt a flood of pain wash over him before everything went black.

* * *

Rilla reeled back in shock as Eliséo disappeared from her mind. *Elessa, what happened?*

I don't know, the old tree replied. *I can't see anything.*

Where is Eliséo? Rilla screamed, ice coursing through her veins. *Where is he?*

I can't get through to him. It feels the same as when you shut yourself off in your tower or when you had the mind snare on you, Elessa tried to explain. *He's still alive, for now, but the amount of pain that flooded through him ...*

Rilla felt herself fall to the floor, her arms wrenched free from the people that surrounded her. There was a terrible emptiness inside her. Had they just bought Aaron's life with Eliséo's?

www.ingramcontent.com/pod-product-compliance
Lightning Source LLC
Chambersburg PA
CBHW061019120726
47910CB00006B/2009